THIS
WEATHER
OF
HANGMEN

by
SYLVIA ADAMS

Published by

GENERAL STORE
PUBLISHING HOUSE

1 Main Street Burnstown, Ontario, Canada K0J 1G0
Telephone 1-800-465-6072 Fax (613) 432-7184

ISBN 1-896182-64-X
Printed and bound in Canada

Layout and Design by Derek McEwen
Cover Illustration and Design by Honz Petersen

General Store Publishing House gratefully acknowledges the assistance of the Ontario Arts Council and the Canada Council.

Canadian Cataloguing in Publication Data

Adams, Sylvia,
    This weather of hangmen

ISBN 1-896182-64-X

    1. Lucky, Charles–Trials, litigation, etc.–
Fiction. 2. Trials (Murder) – Ontario – Kitley –
Fiction. I. Title.

PS8551.D3225T44 1996   C813'.54   C96-990060-0
PR9199.3.A32T44 1996

First Printing October 1996

Dedicated to my mother, Olive F. Adams
David and Anne
Jane, Michael and Susana, Danny and Meredith

Acknowledgements

The author gratefully acknowledges financial assistance in the form of a grant from the Canada Council.

The author wishes to thank the following people: Bryan Moon, Frances Itani and members of their advanced fiction workshop; Juryroom Workshop; founding members of the Leeds and Grenville Genealogical Society; members of the Lavell, Vaux and Clute families; Assistant Crown Attorney Douglas Mackintosh (retired); W.E. Hunter; D.A. Grant; the Honourable John R. Matheson, Q.C. (retired); Wayne Clifford; my editor, Susan Code; illustrator Honz Petersen; and many other supportive fellow writers.

The author also acknowledges the assistance of the late Duncan McClure; the late Wilfred Bruce; the late Dr. W.J. Wyatt, Brockville pathologist; and the late Bill Sleeth, Deputy Sheriff, who discovered some of the Luckey papers in the Brockville Court House, twenty-five years ago.

Introduction

On October 8, 1892, just two months and four days after the Borden murders occurred in Fall River, Massachusetts, the bodies of John James Luckey, Sr, his wife Martha and daughter Mary Ann ("Minnie") were found burned in a fire which destroyed their farmhouse at Newbliss, Ontario. Charles Sandford Luckey, son of John and step-son of Martha, had just been released from the Central Prison in Toronto after serving a year for larceny. Charley, not on good terms with his father, had been seen in the vicinity of the fire.

The Borden and Luckey cases had many similarities, yet Lizzie Borden, accused of murdering her father and step-mother, lived on in folklore while Charley Luckey did not. A legend might be defined as equal parts mystery, skepticism and exaggeration, with a grain of truth and perhaps a dollop of wishful thinking. Charley probably had the same prerequisites for notoriety as Lizzie, yet, thanks to the press, Lizzie captured the public's sympathy. Her image was transformed from that of a homely, thirty-two-year-old woman with bulging eyes to a distressed young maiden, frail and attractive, victimized by the dispassionate forces of the law.

Notwithstanding the fact that the Borden case was front page news at the time of the Luckey tragedy, the Canadian press turned to local material for comparisons, its headlines proclaiming Charley's alleged deed "Worse than Birchall's Crime!" Preceding the Luckey murders by two and a half years, the Birchall case was regarded as Canada's most sensational scandal. The cold-blooded killing of young Freddie Benwell by Reginald Birchall had shocked both sides of the Atlantic, since both murderer and victim were Englishmen who had landed in Canada only a few days before the murder.

Birchall, talented, witty and urbane, showed a cool nerve in the face of the scaffold that made him a Victorian anti-hero. His execution established the reputation of a mystery man who called himself J.R. Radclive and who might one day be summoned to meet Charley under similar circumstances.

Detective William David Greer of the Attorney General's department, assigned to the Luckey case, conferred frequently with his mentor, the self-made legend John Wilson Murray. Both were veterans of the Birchall case, but it was Greer who swore to bring Charley to the gallows.

The foregoing are but marginal notes to help put the Luckey case in perspective. Charley's family has continued to live and prosper in Kitley Township, largely unencumbered by the shadow of the family black sheep. An air of protectiveness which can be detected to this day arose in the people about them. And although a few whispers went around the countryside for decades, they have never been echoed on a national scale.

What happened that October day, and Charley's part in it, will never be known for certain. His emergence as a victim of the times in which he lived does not necessarily make him a sympathetic figure. The need to know can sometimes be satisfied only by instinct and educated guesses, by armchair sleuthing and flights of fantasy tempered with our own experiential view of history. Fiction, in lifting us from dismal uncertainties, may protect us from unwelcome truths or unveil the century-old mystery of what the trees saw, the walls heard and the ashes whispered on the wind.

Contents

Title of the manuscript and
quotations are from the poem,
"A Lament in Winter"
from
Man In A Window
by Wayne Clifford
and are used with
permission of the poet

Part I

THE FIRE

This conspiracy is brought against me by the times,
The command for hesitant silence of the wind,
a transparent snow, invisible on edge

Chapter One

November 8th, 1891

The guard felt sorry for him, Charley could see that. The detective, Montgomery, kept glaring at both of them. Between running to the lavatory for nips from his flask, and darting out onto the platform to see if he could spot the Toronto morning train, Montgomery kept needling. "Lucky Mr. Luckey!" He doffed his hat and gave an exaggerated bow. "Ain't you the centre of attention, now. Star of the Ottawa railway station!"

Charley held his breath, determined not to flinch as the detective breathed in his face. Gin, at this hour!

"Not quite what you expected, eh?" Montgomery's lip drew back in a sneer. "Handcuffed to a guard, heading for the Central Prison. Signed up for a whole year, too. They're rolling out the red carpet, you know. A fancy meal of bread and water, a fitting for a posh new suit, and one verminous blanket to sleep under." He slapped Charley's jaws with brisk, mocking strokes. "A badly needed shave and a haircut. Then it's the broom shop for you, my lad!"

Charley's wrists felt raw where the handcuffs rubbed, but he stared straight ahead. The station was crowded: whiskered businessmen with black bags, bustled matrons with squalling children, boys pushing handcarts with grip piled precariously high. The aroma of fresh, unwrapped loaves tumbling from a bakery wagon battled more pungent odours of tethered livestock, rotting fruit, sweat from the armpits of deliverymen.

"Think you had it tough on Holland's farm, Luckey? Wait'll you see what Massie has in store for you. You'll think you've been dropped in the Black Hole of Calcutta. One lad –" Montgomery paused to

2

make sure his audience was listening – "one lad, a foolish young slob like yourself, pulled a hair from the warden's horse's tail. Slam! Into the dark cell!" He swept his hand out in an extravagant gesture, almost knocking the cane from a passing gentleman's hand. "And poor old O'Neill, three months in the dark cell, sad case. Crazier'n an outhouse rat when they let him out." Montgomery tapped his forehead. "And the menu. Bad beef, mostly. Served it all one summer. Didja hear about it? Not a man in the prison didn't have the runs. Sundays – no slop pails. Had to use their dinner plates."

The look that passed between Charley and the constable was not lost on Montgomery. Ignore him, the guard's eyes said. Crazy as a hoot-owl himself.

"Don't waste your pity on this scum, Dicks," Montgomery said. "Know what he did?"

"Of course, sir."

"Larceny. Stole Mr. Holland's coat."

"Yes, sir. It was all over the court house."

Montgomery snorted. "Damn right it was. Holland hasn't stopped talking about it yet. The judge could hardly get him to shut up and take notes the other day."

"Damn good court reporter, sir."

"Maybe so. But d'you know, after all the bellowing he did about the thieving, Holland wasn't even going to lay charges. All he cared about was getting his precious Persian lamb coat and hat back from the pawnbroker. And I'd spent weeks on the case, tracking down this young bastard here. Weeks! Harry Montgomery, Ottawa's answer to John Wilson Murray!" He felt the flask's outline in his pocket and began edging toward the lavatory.

"You ain't no Murray, stake my life on it," Dicks muttered.

"What's that?" Montgomery spat toward a spittoon, missing by inches. "Murray's all talk, anyway, I'll wager. By the time I've finished with Luckey here I'll have a list of charges long as your arm. Hear that?" He leaned toward Charley. "I've already got a warrant for harness stealing, and the minute you're out of the Central, I'm slapping it on you!"

"I never stole a harness, Montgomery, and you know it," Charley said through clenched teeth. "So I took Holland's coat. I was going to return it. Just needed quick money, is all."

Montgomery rolled his eyes. "Maybe somebody peached on you."

"Come on, Montgomery. Prove it, then." Charley glowered at a small girl who stood pointing at his chains, at the mother whose gloved hand hauled her away. Damn Montgomery for getting under his skin! Miserable cur!

Miserable cur. That's what his father had called him, last he'd heard. He'd wired home, borrowing the money to send the message, hoping the old man would bail him out. There'd been no answer, of course. But then Montgomery announced he'd had word through the grapevine. "Your pa wouldn't spend money on a wire, but he passed a message on. Let the miserable cur take his medicine. A year in gaol'd be good for him." Of course, you couldn't believe half what Montgomery said, but it sounded like his father. Montgomery had punched him on the arm then, a blow too hard to be called friendly. "Your pa said you used to be his favourite son, but not any more, he's had enough of your shenanigans." And a funny look had come over Montgomery's face, grim, almost tearful.

Charley fought back the urge to bolt, dragging the constable along with him. He was going to be run on everywhere, same as home. The youngest, and motherless, he had had some advantages as long as his sisters were there to mother and fuss over him and calm his father's ruffled feathers. But three girls married and moved out. That left only Minnie. His favourite sister, but no match for his father, no buffer between him and the old man's wrath.

His memories of his mother were just impressions of warmth and softness, of being tucked into the bed he shared with Hugh, his closest brother. Then a lot of whispering and tiptoeing around, the Christmas before she died. Women with foul tonics and smelly ointments, pushing him aside to get into her bedroom. A man they called a bleeder, with sharp instruments in a little case, calling for clean cloths, coming out of his mother's room with the cloths in a bucket stained red. Months earlier, there'd been the squalls of his new baby brother, always sick, always crying. He'd died back in the summer, not quite five months old, and that winter, just after the new year, his mother had died.

Two years later his father had married again, that sour old pickle Martha Lyle. She and Charley were enemies from the moment they set eyes on each other. He remembered going into the parlour, seven years old, seeing her close up for the first time, beady little eyes in the doughy face, dull brown hair scraped back into a bun. All the family had assembled to wish her and his father well on their marriage. The older children shook her hand. Sarah, the eldest, living a stone's throw down the road, had come in with her four-year-old. Little Christina, chubby and shy, curtsying and handing a bouquet of wildflowers to Charley's new stepmother. Charley had waited his turn to shake hands, wriggling in his stiffly starched shirt, scuffing Hugh's hand-me-down lace-ups, already too tight.

Suddenly his father was shaking him by the shoulders. "Charley!" Everyone turned to look. "Your hands are filthy. Minnie! Where's Minnie?" And Minnie, pale, frightened, she couldn't have been more than sixteen, hurried up to them. "Aren't you responsible for seeing that this child is presentable?" Minnie nodded hesitantly. "Take him out to the well and don't bring him back until he's cleaned up!"

And Martha Lyle had clucked her tongue. "I can't abide dirty hands," she said.

From then on, Old Marthy, as he called her behind her back, was always looking over his shoulder. She never went off the property except to Sunday church or across the road to gossip with Andrew Parker's wife. She had moved right in the day of the wedding, with her sober bonnet and her pious, mole face and her battered steamer trunk reeking of mothballs. She had scrubbed and scoured until she damn near took the finish off everything, all the time clucking disapprovingly. Her way of hinting that his sisters hadn't kept house right. She showed them all kinds of ways to make beef go further and turn clothes inside out and restitch them to get another turn out of them. She boasted that there wasn't a woman in Kitley Township could get more mileage out of a pair of britches than she could.

Somehow, Charley's life had never had direction after Martha came. He'd been banged about from pillar to post, living partly at home, partly at his brother Johnny's after Johnny married Liza Ann, going to school when he had to, working by times for other farmers. He'd never called Martha mother. He took a perverse pleasure out of turning up at mealtimes with grubby hands and of running his fingers through his hair just after Martha had made him stand still so she could slick it down. And when she remade his brother Sam's old britches for him, and proudly displayed her handiwork so his sisters could see, he'd gone out that same afternoon and torn them, all up the backside, climbing the fence at Daley's. He smiled, remembering how furious she'd been. "You'll come to a bad end!" she'd screeched.

She had run on his sister Minnie, making a regular workhorse out of her, especially after the others left home. And Minnie never said a word, just did everything she was told. She was nine years older than he, but just about as big as a minute. One of his first memories was of being carried outside by her all around the farm, while she carefully sounded out, "Cow. This is a cow, Charley. Say cow. This is a hen. Say it, Charley. Say hen." How little Minnie had ever lugged him around he'd never know.

Charley stepped back to avoid a beggar, noting the shock on the man's face as he spied the manacles. The man shuffled away quickly, glancing back once with an expression both sorrowful and smug. Even beggars pity me, Charley thought. Even beggars feel they're my betters. He tried to pull his sleeve down over the chain. How would Minnie feel, seeing him? She'd escaped her prison, gone to help the two sisters homesteading out west. Between them the sisters had ten children, mostly boys, and there was enough women's work to keep Minnie busy for years to come.

"Train's late," the constable said amiably. He glanced at his watch. "Shouldn't be much longer." Montgomery had disappeared.

Charley nodded. Dicks wasn't a bad sort, quiet spoken, unruffled. "Don't mind Montgomery, he's mostly bluster," Dicks said. "He's got a lot of years in with the force. You've heard of that detective up in Toronto who's making a name for himself – Murray? Old Never-Let-Go, they call him. Well, Harry likes to think he's like him. Instead, he's been passed over for promotion and now there's talk of firing him."

"No wonder."

"Well, he's got four little mouths to feed. Just found out there's another on the way." Dicks shifted his weight, leaning toward Charley. "Don't pay no mind to what he says about the prison. That was years ago. All been cleaned up now." He smiled, and the corners of his eyes crinkled. "Think ahead, lad. What're you going to do when you get out?"

"I've got a brother runs a cheese factory up by Pembroke. I'll go up there, give him a hand." An exaggeration. Sam didn't run the factory, just worked there summers. "You remind me a bit of him." Dicks was taller and older perhaps, but with that same slow smile. The last he'd seen of Sam was over two years ago, at their brother Johnny's new house. Sam spent his winters at Johnny's just as Charley used to. After the property dispute with their father in '84, neither Sam nor he had ever lived at home again.

People were always remarking how much alike he and Sam looked, despite six years between them. But how different they were in temperament! Johnny pushed Sam around just as Father did Minnie, something Charley wouldn't stand for. Sam didn't seem to mind. He'd chop wood and mend harnesses and boil flax to a gel to make a special treat for the horses. Mealtimes he'd be scraping carrots for Liza Ann or putting mutton chunks through the grinder. The children loved him. He'd make kites for Esley and tease Victoria until she blushed beet red. "Got a beau yet, Victoria?" he'd say, grinning. "I heard down by the school that you was chasing the boys." And Victoria would pretend to be angry and flounce out of the room, dark curls bobbing. But Saturdays, when she rolled pastry for her mother's pies, she'd make a special one just for Sam, blueberry or apple, carefully pricking the top crust with a plump, winding S. At night, even Johnny seemed to think Sam had earned the right to relax in a kitchen corner with his books, though Johnny himself seldom joined the family, making an excuse to go off in the buggy.

Sam would be thirty-two now, still shy with girls probably, not sought after as a beau because he kept in the background. He'd blush worse than Victoria if a girl spoke to him. The last Charley knew, Sam was fixing to go to dairy school. "I'm going to learn everything there is to know about the business," he had said. "Make lots of money, just like Johnny."

Montgomery emerged from the lavatory, stuffing the flask into his pocket. "Something else about Luckey, Dicks," he started, his face flushed.

"Leave off, sir, that's my advice," the constable said politely.

"That's right, you bastard, you're like a dog with a bone, won't let go!" Charley broke in.

Montgomery threw back his head and roared. "Old Never-Let-Go! Didn't I tell you, Dicks?"

A group of elderly women, hair coiffed and blued, clutched their handbags tightly as they paused, gaping.

"Seriously, Dicks, this young whelp was charged with attempted suicide a few years back. Lovesick, he was. Can you imagine? Should have made a quick, clean job of it, Luckey." Montgomery jerked his collar upward with one hand, rolled his eyes and stuck his tongue out sideways. "Shoulda hung yourself. That's what I'd do, I were you. Save everyone a lot of trouble, putting you away."

Charley said nothing, watching the ladies step gingerly around a puddle of mucous. "Getting so you can't go out-of-doors!" one muttered as they hurried on, rustling bengaline.

"If Vizard finds you've been drinking again, sir, you may wish you had hung yourself," Dicks said softly.

Montgomery's face reddened. "I have a couple of nips and it's all over town! I stop by the saddlery yesterday to see my old man and he's on my back. `You're gonna get fired, pull up your socks!' Throws my brothers up at me, threatens to cut me out of his will. Me, his favourite son, called my own firstborn after him!"

The train roared into the station, belching blue smoke, and they fought their way to the platform through the crush. "He's all yours, Dicks," Montgomery said as Charley and Dicks mounted the steps to the coach. The detective stepped aside. "I'll be waiting when you get out, you no-good wastrel!" he shouted. "Remember the warrant!" People pushed past, ignoring him as they boarded.

But Charley, on the top step, swung around, eyes black with hatred. His voice was barely audible above the trains' heavy snuffing. But Dicks heard him. Montgomery, chilled suddenly, saw his lips form the words.

"When I get out of this," he said, "I'll make it hot for them all! Wait and see!"

Chapter Two

Friday, October 7th, 1892

They came out together, he and a man called Balloon. He had been straining to get outside into warmth and sunshine, but the sky was overcast and a light drizzle was falling. He could see their breaths, faintly. They stood outside the high walls, their eagerness to taste freedom suddenly tempered with a reluctance to let go of familiar things.

Charley drew a line in the mud with his heel. "Where you off to?"

"Got relatives in town. Think I'll look them up before I move on. Gotta start looking for work once I hit Montreal."

"Work." Charley scuffed his boots, erasing the line. "A little holiday'd be nice. All we done for the past year is work."

Balloon wheezed agreement. "Never a day off. The only ex-cape was the dark cell."

Charley straightened up. "Never saw the inside of one."

"Me neither." Balloon chuckled. " 'Course, there was another way out. Do yourself in! Like stupid old Scratch, opening his wrists with that piece of hoopiron. Saw him sharpen it."

Charley shivered. "I'd never do that, either."

Balloon drew his coat over his corpulent figure in an effort to connect pegs with loops. "Cold! They don't bother about whether or not the clothes they gives you fits right."

"True. Boots hurt like hell." Charley tried to wriggle his toes. "Look at the tops. One don't even close."

"Let's find a store. Get ourselves some hootch." Balloon turned and crossed the road, jumping from one muddy ridge to another to avoid the rivulets between. "I promised the boys I'd get some tobacco in to them."

"You got money?" In his haste to follow, Charley slipped into a puddle and felt water seeping through his open boot.

Balloon, on the curb, took his money from an inside pocket and counted. "Eighteen sixty-five. Twelve dollars overtime plus rail fare. What about you?"

Charley dug into his pockets and displayed a handful of bills. "Not much. Didn't get as much overtime as you."

They found a shop where Charley bought a small flat bottle of rye. Balloon asked for a dozen plugs of Old Chum and, after long deliberation, picked out a large gin and something amber in a tall, thin bottle. "For my relatives." He shoved a bottle in each coat pocket, grinning. "Lots of thirsty cousins."

They sauntered back to the Central, where Balloon slipped some tobacco to a guard at the gate, whispering instructions. Back on the road he said, "You never know whether you can trust these buggers to pass it on." He pressed a plug on Charley and they found a park bench, chewing and spitting in companionable silence.

At two they parted, shaking hands. "Good luck, Balloon. I don't guess we'll meet again," Charley said. "Don't know about you, but I'm never going back there." He watched Balloon's broad back retreating before turning toward Union Station.

He was surprised at his sense of loss. Balloon, with his ready humour, had made the past year bearable. They had met on his first morning at the prison, been stripped, bathed and searched together, shared a breakfast of boiled beef and stale bread before being escorted to the warden's office. Balloon had winked. "Customary introductory lecture from His Highness." Handcuffed together, they had stood in the large, high-ceilinged room, armed guards between them and the door.

Charley had looked around in wonder. Plain, heavy wood everywhere, polished until it hurt your eyes. Inmate's work. The man before them looked dwarfed behind the enormous oak desk. He had a pinched, rod-up-his-ass look. Charley'd met that type before. Never had a day's fun in their lives, didn't know how to laugh. Presbyterian, no doubt. Like his father.

"Gentlemen," the man said, like Charley and Balloon were two businessmen who had dropped in for a chat, "it behooves me to instruct you on the purpose of the Central Prison and the role of the inmate here."

Get that, Charley thought, behooves. He caught Balloon's eye, trying not to laugh, behooves made him think of shoeing horses.

"I'm James Massie, warden," their host continued. "You will address me as sir at all times. It's only fair to explain why you have had the good fortune to be brought to the Central instead of some other penal institution." He gave a bleak smile, like he had just found a fly in his soup and wanted to draw his host's attention to it in a nice way. "We're relatively new, in our nineteenth year, and pride ourselves on providing an answer to the problems besetting the province's gaol system." He gave a dry little cough, putting a fist up to his mouth briefly. Next he'll be offering us sherry from the sideboard, Charley thought.

"Am I making myself understood?"

Charley nodded, trying to look interested.

"You men are intermediates. That means you fall into a class between the vagrants and inebriates of local gaols and the violent repeaters in penitentiaries. To give you a fair chance at rehabilitation, the law has sentenced you to a place built for offenders serving one to two years." He paused. "I might add that the Prison has been my own home for the past ten years."

From the corner of his eye, Charley could see that Balloon was studying the ceiling, the corners of his mouth twitching.

"Now, gentlemen, I keep no record of the conduct of the prisoners, only of the misconduct. Remember that, and we should get along well. Every man must work hard. In addition to little daily tasks, such as blackening the guards' boots, you'll be assigned to a workshop. As an incentive for good behaviour, you can earn small gratuities for piece work. A model prisoner may even –" He sat back with another frosty smile – "may even earn a minimally shortened term for exemplary behaviour. *Minimally.* After all, you *must* pay your debt to society." He consulted a gold pocket watch and appeared satisfied that his briefing was on schedule. "Either of you know the tailoring trade?"

Charley looked down at his toes. He had a sudden image of Old Marthy stitching britches by the light of the coal lamp, her nose so close to the cloth he sometimes thought she would thread the needle through it.

"We'll start you in the broom shop then, cutting and labelling. And one more – you're not dismissed yet, Mr. Luckey!"

Charley, half turned, snapped back to his position.

"I've heard it said prisoners would rather spend three years in the penitentiary than two years here. Why? I make this place a factor in deterring crime! Discipline is strict. You'll be heavily guarded at all times. No talking to your neighbour. And tell your friends not to bring delicacies to supplement your diet. They'll be turned back at the door. Tobacco, in particular, is a luxury we don't allow. In the past, when it was permitted, prisoners expectorated all over the floors." He wrinkled his nose, as if detecting a bad smell. "I've even seen men use a slice of bread as a spittoon." He rose, turned his back to them and gazed out on dead leaves raked into piles. "That'll be all, gentlemen."

Alone on a park bench, anxious for the hours to pass until train time, Charley took the plug of Balloon's Old Chum from his pocket and bit off a chunk. All in all, the Central hadn't been as bad as Montgomery had predicted. Getting along with the warden and keeping your record clean was a matter of not getting caught committing what they called infractions. Talking to other prisoners. Snitching a carrot from the garden. Dealing tobacco brought in by outside bricklayers hired on to help fill a government rush order. You had to work like hell but you got paid for it. He'd cleared twenty cents over the stint some days, and here he was, walking out with six dollars in overtime. And the broomshop was preferable to sticking yourself with one of those big leather-needles in the shoemaking room or cutting your hand off in the machine shop. A soft touch, the broomshop, and being messenger was even softer, with chances to chew the rag if you were careful. He could tell the warden liked him, too, as much as he ever liked anyone. Charley would bow, "G'day, sir," whenever he saw him in the halls, and the warden would bob his head briskly, like a hen pecking for feed.

The food was awful, everything boiled, but you could have a second half order of bread if you wanted to. I was right not to complain about the food, Charley thought, nor about the cold or the stench or that old fool howling at night after lights out. I never even complained about that jackass groping me in the broomshop every time the guards weren't looking. Funny how they've got eyes in the back of their heads when you don't want to be found out and turn blind when you'd like some help. It's a rough lot in there, surly and downright vicious, except for Balloon and maybe young Taylor and Rivet, the chief tobacco dealer.

"What's you in for?" Balloon had hissed one day soon after they arrived. He pretended to be absorbed in measuring a length of wood for a handle. "I bet you was a bank clerk caught embezzling, just as you was about to board a steamer for South America."

Charley pushed aside a pile of wood shavings. "Just call me McPherson, king of the cheesemakers." He stuck his chest out, hooking thumbs through imaginary suspenders.

Balloon's plump face creased into a smile. "What'd ya do? Bop somebody with a cheese?"

Charley stifled a laugh as a guard passed. "How'd you know? There was this foreman, see? Got in a fist fight with a friend of mine, said he wasn't putting the cheese in the press right, too much being wasted. Pushed my pal's head down into a bucket of whey. So I goes back to the curing room, see, and I gets this ninety pound cheese and roll it along the floor. Knock him clean off his pins. Before he can get up, I tie his hands and feet with a cheesecloth. Didn't hurt him, but he was mad as hell."

Balloon's eyes widened. "For that you got a year?"

Charley grunted, pleased with his story's effect. Balloon leaned closer but before he could speak a stick crashed down on his knuckles. "Back to work! Dark cell next time!"

In August of '92, Charley had been assigned messenger duties. One day, as he was passing the broomshop with a sheaf of orders for stores, Herman Taylor, a weasel-like fellow, came through the door pushing a cart of straw bundles.

"Privileges, eh?" Taylor said as they walked together down the hall. "This is my second trip to this hellhole. How about you, McPherson?"

"Seems to me that's nothing to brag about," Charley said.

"Hear you've been selling the guys a lot of guff. You're no cheese king. Not old enough, for one thing."

Charley shrugged. "So? He's my brother."

"What're you really in for, McPherson? Beat somebody up and rob them?"

Charley rolled up the sheaf of orders. "You could say that. Beat a guy up in Smith's Falls. Threw him through a window. Want me to show you?"

"Smith's Falls. Family there?"

"Out Kitley way. All except my sisters in Manitoba."

"You going back there, d'you think, when you get out?"

Charley whipped the air with his roll of papers and whacked it against his thigh. "You bet I am. Some people there I'm going to make it hot for one day."

The day had come. Hardly aware that the drizzle had stopped, Charley spat out the tobacco and took a drag from the flask. Returning the flask to his back pocket, he rose from the bench. The rye warmed him but made him hungry. Four o'clock. He sauntered along to the Queen's Hotel on Front Street and stood outside, trying to muster nerve to swagger up to the entrance. Damn the lumpy parcel. Too big for his pocket, and he felt foolish going about with it tucked under his arm like some old biddy's reticule. Look like I'm off to market, he thought. How could he look important with a foot-long parcel in white paper?

"Not thinking of having tea in there?"

Charley wheeled around. The young man facing him in the fading light was dressed poorly but neatly, the collar of his thin jacket turned up and his shoulders hunched against the wind. Something familiar about him.

"Why not? If it's fit for dukes and earls, it's fit for a cheese king, wouldn't you say?" Charley tried slipping the parcel inside his coat but it bumped against his flask. Looks like I've got one big tit, he thought, pulling it out again. "Ever hear of McPherson, the cheese king?" He waited for the look of surprise and respect to come over the stranger's face, the way it had over Balloon's.

"Can't say as I have. You from around here?"

Charley shook his head. "Just passing time 'til my train comes." He eyed the gabled brick building with its fancy awnings and cupola and the lawn like a plush carpet patterned with leaves. "You don't drink out of your saucer in there, I'll wager. More likely you sip from dainty teacups thin as eggshells and crook your pinky." He made an arch of his little finger, at the same time pushing his nose up with the index finger of his other hand.

The stranger joined in the spoofery, snapping his fingers. "A slice of lemon, my good man!"

They laughed. The newcomer thrust out his hand and shook Charley's vigorously. "John Hannah."

Charley offered his flask. "Take a swig of this, John Hannah. Warm you up. My name's – Kingsley. Charles Kingsley." A lovely ring to it. Royal. Rich. Educated.

Hannah took the flask and gulped noisily. "I'm heading home from Winnipeg. What train you taking?"

"The nine o'clock."

"To Ottawa? What luck! Same here." Hannah handed the flask back. "What d'you say we go for an ale, to kill time?"

"I know another hotel near here," Charley said. "Not so grand as this, but good enough. Pub and dining room." They walked south toward Union Station and crossed toward the St. James Hotel.

Seated in the pub, Charley studied the fellow opposite him. Familiar, somehow. Decent sort, clean shaven, not an outcast from the Central, for sure. Had he met him in Ottawa, at Holland's farm, perhaps? "I get off the train before you do," he said. "I don't go all the way to Ottawa."

"Neither do I," Hannah said, deftly rolling two cigarettes from scraps of tobacco in a little bag. He offered one to Charley. "Irish Creek. I get off at the Smith's Falls stop and walk from there. It's not far."

Irish Creek! Christ! Charley resisted an impulse to shield his face. Small world. He'd been to Hannah's home once, years ago, with a group of young people bent on having a sleighing party one frosty New Year's Eve. Hannah had a pretty young sister with big dark eyes that she kept batting in Charley's direction. Hefty girl, real corn-fed look to her, quite an armful if he'd ever had the chance to get close enough. He lit their cigarettes. "I still get off before you do," he said. "Carleton Place."

"I don't think so, Kingsley. You change at Smith's Falls for Carleton Place."

"I get off first, stake my life on it. Want to bet?"

Hannah waved his arms in a gesture of refusal. "We'll prove it when the time comes, Kingsley."

Obviously, Hannah didn't remember him. The phoney name had thrown him off. If he ever remembered who Charley was, Charley would make a joke of it, pretending he'd recognized him all along, laughing about how he'd fooled him. He'd slap Hannah on the back. "So you don't remember me? I'll wager your sister would . ."

At six they studied the menu tacked up outside the hotel dining room. "Too rich for my blood," Hannah said. "Bread and cheese'll do me." He went off in search of a restaurant.

"Meet you back in the pub in an hour," Charley called after him.

Tea at the St. James appealed to him. There was a blazing fire in the grate, a bakeshop smell, and all kinds of little cakes and pastries like he'd never seen before. All sailing by on trays borne by white-gloved waiters. Class. He ordered a plate of cold meat and another of scones, which came piping hot on a china dish, with a little tub of jam.

Here's something to tell Hannah, he thought, as his tea arrived, lemon slices in a separate dish. There was even a piano tinkling somewhere out of sight, far enough away to cheer the customers without disturbing them. "De Camptown races sing this song, Doo-dah, Doo-dah!" He tapped his foot rhythmically. It was quiet in the dining room, the hum of conversation as low as bees in buttercups. Lots of well bred ladies, sitting on their bustles, unwinding yards of fur from around their necks, and snapping their manicured fingers at the waiters. He loaded thick jam, whole raspberries, onto a scone.

A young blonde woman came in wearing a Persian lamb cape, hair wound round her head like a coronet, with a small fur trimmed hat dipping down over her forehead, its veil tied under her chin. She reminded him so much of Miss Harriet Reilly that he almost choked on a mouthful of scone. He nodded hopefully in her direction but she gave no sign. Should he go up and introduce himself, find an excuse to engage her in conversation? Excuse me, Ma'am, but you remind me of someone I used to . . . Even his imagination failed him, refusing to cross the forbidden barrier into memory, *that* memory. Someone I used to hold in the highest esteem – wasn't that the way they said it? He stuffed the rest of the scone into his mouth, aware that he reeked of ale and tobacco; she'd never give him the time of day. The old battleaxe with her, dressed in black from head to toe, a vicious, furled umbrella balanced against her chair, would be her mother. She'd give him short shrift, for sure.

He dawdled over tea, blotting up crumbs, chewing every morsel of meat down to the last shaving of fat, planning to leap to his feet as soon as the ladies showed signs of departure. Help her on with her cape, now draped over the back of her chair. He'd pause for a moment, slipping it over her shoulders, hands lingering as he breathed in the scent of her hair, her sleek white neck.

The waiter stopped by his table, laboriously writing out his bill – "Was it the ham you had, sir, or the corned beef?" – and, curse his luck, didn't the ladies adjust their gloves and pick up their things! Miss Harriet's double shrugged into her cape and they swept out without a glance in his direction. In spite of stuffing himself, Charley felt empty and hollow inside. He paid up and elbowed his way past incoming customers, bumping into Hannah at the door.

"Hold on!" Hannah said. "Was the tea that bad?"

"Great!" Charley patted his belly. "Damned if I didn't eat too much." He burped loudly for emphasis.

"Let's have one more ale before train time," Hannah said. Charley looked past him but the ladies were nowhere in sight. He shrugged and followed Hannah.

In the pub, he said, "Hannah, tell me about Manitoba. I got sisters there, one in Lyleton and one in Wawanesa. Another sister gone there to help out." He wiped foam from his lips with the back of his hand.

"Half Ontario's defecting," Hannah said. "Homesteaders everywhere. Lots of land for the taking but damn hard work." He glanced at his watch. "We better be going."

Charley rummaged in his pockets as they hurried along the street, cursed as the train chugged into the station. "Can't find the damn ticket." The conductor regarded him sourly, hand extended. "Ah, here it is."

Hannah dove for the white parcel as it slipped from under Charley's arm. "Here, give me that, I'll carry it." He caught it neatly just before it hit the platform.

"Did you say you're a cheesemaker? Must pay well," Hannah remarked, settling himself across the aisle from Charley in the almost deserted car.

"Yeah."

"At Carleton Place? Which factory?"

"Not exactly Carleton Place." Charley rubbed his right eye.

"Not Perth!" Hannah cocked his head and regarded his new companion with wonder. "The mammoth cheese!"

"The what?"

Hannah laughed. "Holding out on me, eh? You've been in Perth, working on the world's largest cheese. Eleven tons!"

Charley nodded hesitantly, avoiding Hannah's eyes.

"Tell me about it, Kingsley."

"Nothing to tell."

"Come on! I hear it took the milk of ten thousand cows."

Charley stood up and stretched. "Gotta take a piss. See you later."

When he returned several minutes later, he hoped Hannah would have forgotten the cheese. He was wrong.

"D'you think they'll be sending it to the World's Fair in Chicago next spring?"

"What?"

Hannah drew in his breath. "The cheese, man!"

"Y'know, Hannah, I been living and breathing cheese so long, I vowed to turn the next man who said the word into whey."

"But you've done well for yourself," Hannah persisted.

"Took a bet. Ten dollars."

"Yeah? What on?"

"My weight." He peeled off his coat in spite of the chill, rolled up his left sleeve and flexed his muscles. "How much would you say I weigh?"

Hannah shrugged in the semi-darkness. "Hundred-seventy?"

"Hundred-eighty. You lose. Too bad I didn't bet another ten!"

Hannah pulled his pockets inside out and turned his hands palms up. "You can't get blood from a stone. Anyways, you been living high off the hog. How much you got to show for your bet?"

Charley shivered and put his coat back on. He drew the flask from one pocket and a handful of change from the other. "Chickenfeed!"

They passed the flask back and forth, trying to keep warm. Charley slumped in his coat, resting his parcel against his right thigh to block the draft. Just when he thought his companion was asleep, Hannah said, "You ever been in love?"

Charley straightened up, all his senses alerted, like a rabbit in a thicket. How much of himself did he want to reveal to Hannah, or to anyone else for that matter?

"Once," he said finally. "Oh, I've had lots of sweet young lasses, many a quick roll in the hay, but love? Just once." He thought of Harriet Reilly again, that long blonde hair falling in waves when he loosed the tortoise shell combs, the shimmer of lace and velvet that time, the only time, she'd let her gown fall to the floor around her feet. "Harriet," she had corrected him. "Don't keep calling me Miss Harriet." She smiled that wonderful smile, the one that shattered the grand lady image, the wealthy, finishing school, unapproachable image, which told him that she was so young, only seventeen, and in love, and the object of her love, incredibly, was him, Charley.

"Tell me," Hannah said. "How'd you know it was love?"

But he couldn't tell him. For once he was at a loss for words, unable to think of a single wisecrack or joke. Could he say it was love because it looked and sounded like love, smelled and tasted like it, like nothing he'd ever known before? That it was the colour of love, blonde hair and blue velvet, and that maybe he knew it was love because mixed in with all those wonderful feelings was the feeling of fear? Fear that it would slip away from him, that he'd lose it and never get it back?

"Her father was a cheesemaker," he said. "Owned a string of factories, dozens of them, all in the Utica area. I worked for him all one summer. I first laid eyes on her when she come in the buggy one afternoon, to pick her father up."

Hannah stretched out on the seats across the aisle, folded his hands and waited expectantly.

"I proposed to her," Charley went on. "Didn't know her long, but I fixed to marry her. I knew she was the only one for me."

"What did she say?"

"She said ask her father. I knew what that meant."

"Sent you packing? Thought you weren't good enough for his daughter, I suppose."

It had been worse than that. Harriet's father had been an Irish Catholic. Charley's father, Presbyterian born and bred, had come from Ireland as a lad with his mother, after his own father had been killed in a clash with Irish Catholics in the north.

"There wasn't much her father could do, was there, if you'd decided to run off?"

"Oh, there was plenty he could do. We were both under age, see. He had me practically tarred and feathered, run out of town you could say. Then he wrote my father a letter threatening to sue. My father promised Old Man Reilly he'd see to it I never got in touch with her again."

"Seems to me your father could have considered your feelings."

"Not for an Irish Catholic, he wouldn't." Charley drew his legs up under him. "Maybe that's how you know it's love. You know it's hopeless from the start, but something makes you keep on. The whole world turns against you, but you just step off the edge and let yourself go. It's like –"

"The long drop," Hannah finished. "The hangman blinds you with the black cap, and you step off into nothing."

Charley nodded hesitantly. "'Cept that that's the end of pain," he said. "With love it's only the beginning."

"Did you ever see her again?"

"I wrote her. Never got a reply."

Hannah sat up, hugging his knees. "Maybe her mail was, you know, seized. But you got over it?"

Charley was silent in the growing darkness. He took a last swallow of rye, got up and opened the window. The rush of cold air made him gasp. He tossed the flask out, watching it bounce against the ditch in the gloom before it smashed against a rock.

"I knew a fellow near Irish Creek." Hannah was rubbing a cramped muscle in his leg. "Shot himself because of a broke-up love affair. Unrequited love, the papers called it. Big funeral, him only twenty years old."

Charley shuddered and closed the window.

"What's the matter?"

"Someone walking on my grave." The joke sounded hollow. He was shivering uncontrollably as he sat down again, pulling his coat collar up.

There was a bullet in his hip. But he didn't want to talk about that, either.

Chapter Three

Saturday, October 8th, 1892

Charley was running home. Smith's Falls to Newbliss, eight miles from whistle stop to farmhouse. Down through the township of Kitley, along the Brockville road, past farmhouses, barns, silos and pastures with the sounds of early morning pursuing him. Milk pails clattered, a horse whinnied, cartwheels rumbled on the macadamized road. The world stirred and woke to a day that promised threshing weather.

He ran with the steady ease of youth, unencumbered by footwear, for his boots, an old pair with checked tops from prison stores, had burst along the seams. After hobbling as far as the tollgate just south of Smith's Falls, he had sat down disgusted, wrenched them off and thrown them into the bush. As an afterthought, he had pulled off his threadbare woollen socks and tossed them away, too. Easier to run barefoot.

Now, a stranger in the neighbourhood of his youth, he spoke to no one, looked neither to right nor left. Spurring him on was the exhilarating thought of freedom, a gift certain as daybreak, endless as the trees and roads and hills that stretched ahead of him.

Joseph Moorhouse saw him, pacing the snake fence between field and road, carrying a small white parcel, four miles out of Smith's Falls. John Polk's hired man, going after cows, was about the breadth of a three acre field away when Charley passed, still running. At half past five, Alex Mercier, on his way into town, hailed him and got no answer. Charley slowed to a walk momentarily, then ran on. Alex Mercier, turning to watch him, was able to report later that the stranger wore a black suit, black Derby hat, a factory shirt laced up in front and a white tie of the kind that is always tied. He was running barefoot, with his pants rolled halfway to his knees. Strangers in that part of the country were bound to be noticed. A stranger thus attired was bound to be remembered.

The occasional spans of maples, hickory and basswood sheltering him from the first probes of daylight, almost bridging the road in places, just beginning to turn from night shades to red and amber, were only part of the reason Charley went unrecognized. Years away from the neighbourhood had wrought changes in him. His face, instead of being bronzed from a spring in the sugar bush and a summer ploughing and haying, had an unhealthy pallor from his year behind bars. He was heavier and a little flabby, from inside work and prison fare, and his dark hair, clipped convict style, was hidden by his derby.

He'd shaken hands with Hannah by the Smith's Falls freight sheds and watched him disappear into the darkness before he cut through the back paths to the Brockville road.

Much of the land on either side of him was poor, uncleared, flat for the most part but falling away in little dips and hollows, rock strewn, just big enough to break a cow's leg or crack the blade on a plough. His father's land wasn't much better, prized at one time because it was home land, meant for all the Luckey sons to till and plant and build on, to marry and raise their families on. It had been coveted by Charley and his brother Sam, mostly because it was once dangled before them like a carrot in front of eager young rabbits. Their father had all but sold it to them eight years ago and then changed his mind. Charley, remembering, felt bile rising again.

Even when his father had thought he was being good to him, he had a way of making Charley angry. First of all, back in '84, he had announced he was going to hand over his property to Sam and Charley, for natural love and affection – strange words from his father – and then he said he wanted thirty-eight hundred dollars for the three small parcels of land. Everybody, even John Edgar the conveyancer, said it wasn't worth more than half that amount. Strange that his father would be so hard on his own sons, especially when they didn't work regular. They made cheese in the summers, for a pittance, and helped out at Johnny's for hardly more than room and board.

He remembered Johnny hauling him and Sam out of bed one March morning extra early. "Father's got an appointment at John

Edgar's, 8:30 sharp. Get all the chores done, and I mean *all*, and dress fancy, Sunday clothes he says." And Johnny had planted the sole of his boot firmly on the backside of Charley's nightshirt.

He and Sam had done their chores in record time and wolfed down their side pork and eggs and wriggled into their Sunday-go-to-meeting clothes, nearly strangling themselves in the boiled collars, Sam silent but looking pleased, Charley grumbling. They'd gone outside to meet their father and been sent back in to clean their fingernails proper. Hell, they'd been clearing brush out back of Johnny's the day before. It wasn't as if it was a cheese factory work day, when their nails had to be pared and scraped before they could so much as handle the pails at the weigh station. But Father said, "Damn, don't some of them soap-and-water rules rub off on you permanent?"

They had piled into the back of the buggy and set off, Father cracking the whip and Old Marthy sitting stiff beside him, a wicked pin fastening her black felt to her crown. Her looking straight ahead, with nary a 'Morning to either of them.

They had parked in the lane by the new stone wing where John Edgar conducted his business. A sign over the door said:

JOHN EDGAR

Postmaster of Newbliss, Justice of the Peace, Commissioner for

TAKING AFFIDAVITS IN THE QUEEN'S BENCH, AND

COMMON PLEAS

CONVEYANCER, LIFE INSURANCE AGENT, &C,&C.

Their father kept grouching because the lane was already filled with buggies and saying John Edgar'd better not keep him waiting, he'd gone to all the trouble of making a special appointment, not like these glumphers that come in off the road expecting the red carpet. Sure enough, the big parlour was full.

"You lads know better'n to keep me late." His father removed his hat and dragged one foot, then the other, over the bootscraper, motioning them to do the same.

Charley let Sam go ahead of him. "Why do we have to be all prettied up when everyone else here stinks of the barn? Clomping around in muddy boots, jostling to get a warm spot near the woodstove."

"Cold still, ain't it," Edgar called from the other side of the room.

Charley's father grunted agreement, raising an eyebrow and pursing his lips, meaning to remind John Edgar that he should be first in line.

The conveyancer beckoned them to a corner where a desk and a couple of wooden chairs were set out. "About as private as a railway station," his father muttered, planting himself firmly in the nearest chair and motioning Martha to the other.

Edgar seated himself behind the desk and leaned forward, ruffling the papers before him with a swish of his long, white beard. "About half these people just come to chew the fat, John. Now, which hat am I wearing for you today?"

Charley and Sam stood side by side, like sentries guarding royal thrones. "I'm deeding my properties over to my two boys here, and taking back the mortgage," their father said. "Young Charley here's not of age, but I guess I can trust him. Won't be eighteen until the last of this month. My youngest."

Edgar uncovered his inkwell and took up a long, black sliver of a pen. "Last shake of the bag, eh."

"Could say that. Andrew died a babe, you recall, and Martha's only, Maggie, the same." His father eyed the white beard, now perilously close to the inkwell, and rubbed his own grizzled whiskers. "It's time I handed over the reins and retired. Will, my eldest, been dead a year and a half."

"Grave blow, grave indeed." Edgar shook his beard sadly. "Him only what – thirty-three? And I hear his young widow's sickly now."

"Not long for this world."

"Died without issue, did he?"

Charley's father nodded. "Johnny's the only son with a family, and he's well fixed. Seems right that I settle the property on my other two lads here."

Edgar paused, pen poised above a long form with *This Indenture* scrolled in fancy letters at the top. "What about the other boy? The one between Sam and Charley. Hugh, wasn't it?"

Charley stole a glance at Sam, who was staring straight ahead. What was that expression of Old Marthy's, something about rushing in where angels fear to –

Marthy came alive suddenly. "Dead, for all we know!"

His father looked like a thundercloud. "Dead." Lips a thin, white line.

Charley shifted, hot in the tight black suit, Hugh's hand-me-down. He'd been roped into wearing it two Sundays ago, to get accepted into the church. Sighing, he stole a look at Sam; being grown up meant waiting around in heavy weeds, looking mournful and itching in places you didn't dare scratch. Sam looked unperturbed.

The crowd was thickening, everybody waving papers, trying to attract Edgar's attention. "Over here, John! Just your signature." "Need an affidavit sworn here!" "John, could you read me this letter? Forgot my glasses." The last request from a seedy-looking fellow. Charley caught Sam's eye and winked. "The old bugger never learned to read, more like it," he muttered.

He watched as the conveyancer scratched out page after page of boring documents describing his father's properties, copying from other old papers. Edgar paused. "How much you asking, John?"

"Thirty-eight hundred."

Edgar shot him a look of disbelief. "For your three properties? The one on lot fourteen, where the house is, and the others –" he squinted at the old paper – "part of lots fifteen and sixteen, in the fifth concession? That's all, you say?"

"It's enough, ain't it?" His father crossed his arms, his beard jutting forward. Edgar wrote "Three Thousand Eight Hundred," and underlined carefully.

All the men signed their names and Martha made a strange, inverted V. Edgar wrote "Martha her mark Luckey" around it.

"Stupid old bat," Charley hissed to Sam.

Sam reddened and looked down at his shoes. "Not her fault. You know how Father feels about women's book learning."

It was clear now and warmer, with shafts of light between the trees. Charley paused to catch his breath and hook a stone from between his toes. It had been eight-and-a-half years since that visit to John Edgar. The deed had been registered two days later, on March 29, but not the mortgage. The mortgage that had been registered had been a different paper, one for twenty-five hundred dollars, with Johnny as mortgagee. The family quarrel it sparked had never been resolved.

Charley had gone back to his father's only once after that, for a Thanksgiving dinner Johnny had dragged him to. "Father wants to make it up to you. He wants to be friends." Johnny's wheedling had surprised him. "You were always his favourite, you know." Johnny thought he'd given in to his flattery, but it wasn't that at all. He'd gone with them to please Liza Ann, so she wouldn't feel she had to fuss and leave a special feed behind just for him, because it was Thanksgiving.

He was hardly more than a mile north of Newbliss and already he could smell the cheese factory owned by Liza Ann's uncle Will Jones. Smells of home, of wood, barnyard, curdling milk. Hardly more than an intersection in the macadamized Brockville road and the dirt line road called Coad's Road, Newbliss was comprised of a handful of houses, a couple of small hotels, the stone schoolhouse, Orange Lodge and John Edgar's post office. A rowdy bar, an equally rowdy Temperance Society, a brass band known round the countryside. Only the cheese factory held any attraction for Charley. He'd heard the place was dying anyway, young folk moving north to Smith's Falls or south to Brockville. The pride that his father took in the place, musing on the days when old schoolmaster Mackay had named it for his native Irish village, was lost on the younger generation.

A mile north of the crossroads, Charley turned west toward a shortcut to the farm. The Brockville road took a westward swing just below Newbliss, passing his brother Johnny's farm. Avoiding early market-goers, he sought the shelter of the trees.

He paused and consulted his pocket-watch. Six a.m. His father had been letting the farm out on shares the last he'd heard, so it was hard to say if he'd be about yet, doing whatever chores he still did. It was Saturday, market day in Smith's Falls, much warmer than yesterday; his stepmother would be doing her cooking in the summer kitchen. He pictured her pouring fresh, foaming milk from pail to pitcher, stirring oatmeal, frying eggs in the big black spider. They were probably alone in the house, his father and stepmother, unless Gran was still alive. She'd be up in her eighties. Poorly the last time he'd seen her: rocking mechanically, shrivelled and slack-mouthed. He'd taken her hand, dry as paper, in his, and she'd peered at him, bunching her eyebrows together, like a child trying to figure out an arithmetic sum. "Willie." "It's Charley, Gran." "Charley." Her face broke into a smile. "Charley." But he couldn't be sure she knew.

The cool, soft grass caressed his feet as he ran beside the fence bordering Will Daley's farm on his right. Across the road, a little to the west and set well back, was his father's house, not yet in view. Montgomery, that miserable cur, would be waiting in Ottawa with a warrant. He could see Montgomery's lip curling, smell his gin breath.

Stupid bastard, did he really think Charley would go straight to Ottawa, begging to be arrested?

He pulled his hat down over his eyes and strode swiftly and silently, swinging his parcel. He couldn't be seen from the road here. It was the same place he and Hugh had hid, one day years ago, and peered through the trees at Johnny's cart rattling along the road, the kiddies in the back, Johnny bellowing, "Where are you, you young whelps? You're in for a horse-whipping!" Cracking his whip viciously. Hell, it had only been a prank, and Johnny had cooled off long before they got back to his place.

It had started out innocently, with him and Hugh at the Smith's Falls market on a November day, snow starting. The kids, Victoria and a little friend, had been shivering with the cold, so he and Hugh had swiped a horse blanket from a neighbour's cart and put it over the kiddies' legs. The neighbour'd been mad as hell, looking all over for his mangey bearskin and Johnny'd been red-faced when one of the old biddies peddling turnips had spotted it in his buggy. Charley and Hugh had taken off on foot, their feet already chilblained, breath coming in white spurts as they ran laughing along the road. They'd made it all the way to Daley's, to this very spot, while Johnny had searched all over Smith's Falls and down the highway for them.

Johnny had sounded so much like Father that day, yelling about a horse-whipping. God help him, Johnny was the last person he wanted to run into today. He'd always had a special spot in his heart for Liza Ann and the kiddies, but Johnny, thirteen years his senior, was just like Father, seldom supporting, often hard-fisted without call, always demanding more than he meant to pay for.

People were always reminding him how good Johnny was to him, what a great example. Even Sam. Sam would say, "He just wants us to be more like him, Charley – work hard and have something to show for it." The "something to show," in Johnny's case, was a two-storey, sand-coloured brick home, four years old, pointed out as one of the finest modern farmhouses in the eastern end of the country. Sam didn't believe the rumours that the house was financed by a politician who had given Johnny money on the sly to buy votes with. Johnny had been instructed to buy hay for the farmers, to secure their votes. Fat chance of that! Built himself a house and stocked his own barn with hay. "It's true, Sam," Charley had said. "Exactly the kind of thing Johnny would do." But Sam wouldn't hear of it, any more than Liza

Ann would, not that they'd dare to raise the subject with her.

There were a lot of things about Johnny that Sam turned a blind eye to. "He'd sell old Gran if he thought he could make a buck," Charley had told him, the last summer they had cleared brush together. "It's his own pockets he's looking to line first." But Sam had just gone on sawing the log in front of him, and Charley had thought, `Keep my mouth shut'. Sure, up front Johnny was a pillar of church and society, but behind the scenes he was a flirt and a womanizer. Charley'd seen him in Smith's Falls with women while Liza Ann was home, boiling his shirts and baking his favourite dumplings and making sure his children looked like they'd stepped out of little bandboxes. Please God they turn out like her, not him. He'd seen Johnny's buggy parked by that widow's house, Clara somebody, and once he saw him out driving with a painted up young tart, her up front beside him, arm linked through his.

He hadn't told, of course. Liza Ann would be upset something terrible, though it was hard to believe she knew nothing about it. She'd have to be deaf and blind. "Where's Johnny off to?" he remembered asking her one night, just after Johnny had rushed out with his hair trimmed and slicked and his face freshly shaven. "Cattlemen's Association or something," Liza Ann had muttered vaguely. Charley had looked at her closely, not having the heart to tell her the cattlemen had met the night before.

Whenever Sam defended Johnny he brought up the matter of the land deal. "He told us it was a risk, him setting himself up against Father. He was thinking of us, you know, wanting to give his own brothers a better deal." Of course, it had been Johnny's way of cutting himself in, and he had been asking four per cent interest, but there was truth in what Sam said.

"You'd be better off doing it my way," Johnny had said the night after their trip to John Edgar's. He and Sam had been sitting at the kitchen table, hunched in the coal oil lamp's light, when Charley came in from the stable. "You've already signed the mortgage with Father, and you've got thirteen hundred to put down in cash – mostly yours, Sam – but my advice is to pay the mortgage off as soon as possible. Father wants to hold the mortgage until 1896, which means he's going to keep control. I'd think twice about that, if I were you. Come here, Charley, sit down. This concerns you, too." He sat back so Charley could see the paper spread out before them. "This is the deed

to Father's properties, see. I'm to register them tomorrow. These" –
he held up another paper – "are my calculations for a mortgage to be
held by me."

Charley squinted in the dim light. "I can't make head nor tail of
squiggles and blots."

Johnny had ignored him. "By my calculations, Father's getting a
real good deal here. He's offering three per cent on the mortgage, very
low, but with interest compounded have you figured out just how
much you'll have paid him in principal and interest by 1896?" He
slapped the paper in front of him. "Now, if I take the mortgage, I'll
give you interest at four per cent but you'll be paid off by the end of
'88. That's with a mortgage of twenty-five hundred, of course. You
pay me your thirteen hundred, pay off nine hundred in the first year.
The remaining sixteen hundred would be divided evenly among the
next four years."

"You mean, by '89 we'd be in the clear? Own it lock, stock and
barrel?" Sam's eyes were shining.

"Right. Even with the higher interest rate, you're further ahead.
I'll show you." Johnny scribbled more figures. "You pay up sooner, so
your total costs aren't so high. Understand? Only about half!"

Sam straightened up. "Father won't go for it."

"Father doesn't own the property any more. You do." Johnny's
voice took on a note of irritation. "You two are the owners. You want
to take out another mortgage, it's up to you." He threw down his pen.
"Let me handle Father."

Sam leaned forward, elbows on the table, fingers ruffling his dark
hair. "If Father won't go for it, it'll be on my shoulders. I'm the one
put a bug in his ear in the first place."

Charley smiled, remembering how slick Johnny had been, that
oily quality in his voice, a politician. "Sam, Sam. Let me handle it.
You're pretty smart, Sam. Want to learn business. You got to learn all
you can about property deals, how to make money. Right?" Sam had
nodded. "And Charley, you're under age, but I'd take a chance on
you, same as Father. Give you the opportunity to make some money
and own property at the same time. Just think, in a few years you boys
could become tycoons. Your poor old brother Johnny could be
coming to you for a handout!" Laughing, he'd slapped them each on
the back.

Johnny'd had the new mortgage drawn up in Smith's Falls. Sam and Charley had signed it and left Johnny to register it. Charley had thought no more about it until the big blow-up two weeks later.

His father had come round to Johnny's, waving his fists and shouting that he hadn't known about the second mortgage until he discovered his own hadn't been registered. He called them everything he could think of and threatened to lay charges of fraud. He'd sworn out a paper in the Court of Chancery, something about title or interest being called into question. They'd had no choice, wanting to avoid a full-scale war, signed his property back to him. That had been the end of it.

Johnny had acted as if nothing had happened; a cool one for sure. But Sam and Charley never called Father's place home after that. They stayed with Johnny off and on, worked his farm, and he'd paid them, peanuts, but better than a kick in the snout.

By the spring of 1890, Charley had had enough. He waited his chance and approached Johnny in the yard one day, just as he was carrying logs for the fireplaces. "You owe me six months' wages," he said. "When am I going to see some of it?"

Johnny paused, shifting his armload of logs. "Soon, Charley, have patience. I've had to hire more carpenters for the building I'm contracting for in Smith's Falls. And the cost of seed's gone 'way up. Just a little longer, all right?"

"You've got money to spend on them fancy ladies."

Johnny'd thrown down the logs and gone after him, fists cocked. "Damn you, don't you ever let me hear you say that again!"

Charley ducked the first punch and brought his right fist up into Johnny's stomach. It had taken Sam and a hired man to pry them apart. Later, when they'd both cooled down, Charley said, "Look, Johnny, I'll sell you my sap buckets, dirt cheap."

Johnny's eyes narrowed. "Seems you want money bad, Charley. Got your own fancy lady?"

Charley'd gone beet-red. It was true he'd been seeing a girl near Toledo. Hardly a fancy lady, Bessie. Hung about her place after chores, and sometimes she would come out to the gate and talk. He was embarrassed because he never had any decent shoes and he'd been really stung when he overheard her say to a friend, "Oh, I always know when it's Charley out by the gate, even from my bedroom window. Same old shirt." Their laughter had followed him down the road.

"How much'll you give me for the buckets?"

Johnny had roared with laughter. "What good are your buckets without my maples, anyway? I'm the one with the trees!"

"Piss on you," He grabbed an axe and broke up all the buckets. "Now tap your trees!" He packed his clothes and left.

Charley felt safe for the moment, striding along in the bush. Johnny would never spot him here, and if Montgomery came looking for him, he'd always be one step ahead of him. He was alone and free, and no one was watching.

*   *   *

Sarah Jane Daley was watching. She was milking in front of her brother Will's barn when he came down along the fence on the bush side, walking swiftly, looking neither to right nor to left. When he came out to the line road he veered west and crossed the stone road to the Lockwood property on the corner, climbing the fence with a small white parcel in his right hand. He put his left hand on the fence, then his feet, and hoisted himself over. Sarah Jane stopped to watch him because he was a stranger. In the half light of morning, she noticed that his feet looked white, as if perhaps he was wearing light canvas shoes. He disappeared over a rise in the ground in the direction of Elgin Lockwood's farmhouse, beyond which lay the Luckey property. A pedlar, perhaps, Sarah Jane thought, turning back to her milking.

Home. Sheltered by the maples lining Coad's Road, Charley surveyed the farm. It lacked the noise and activity of earlier years when all the family was there, and had a rundown, almost deserted appearance. He was surprised, a little dismayed even, to see how his father had let things go.

Directly to the south of him was the barn, quieter than he remembered, and sadly in need of repair. The house, set at an angle, faced neither the line road nor the Lockwood property, which abutted on the macadamized road. What could be seen of it was actually the back of the house; the front, or parlour, door opened to the south-west on bush and swamp. A one-storey house with a sleeping loft, its main body built of logs on a stone foundation. On Charley's side, the milkhouse and log woodshed. The frame summer kitchen, newer than the rest of the house, protruded on the south east corner, its closed-in stoop facing him.

He sat for a moment under the maples with his coat folded under him. The ground was still damp from Friday's rain. His stomach rumbled. He hadn't slept on the train, hadn't eaten since the St. James. He could almost smell pork back and eggs, imagined mopping up the grease with a thick, ragged slab of bread. And, God! – some of yesterday's rye would go down well, shame it was gone. He ran his tongue over parched lips.

He wasn't sure how long he sat but it was completely light now. Carefully he skirted his father's property, edging down along Lockwood's fence until he was close to the front of the house. He crossed a small field and entered his favourite haunt, the sugar bush. Sap bubbling in the shanty, he could almost hear it! He rubbed his fingers together, remembering what it was like to butter them, to pull taffy in the shrinking March snow. He and his brothers, making taffy and rolling about in the snow, shouting with laughter. All their best times had been here. He sat down on a stump, looking toward the house. The sun was higher now, bathing it in full light. It was going to be a clear, warm day, Indian summer. A threshing day.

A man, stocky and gnarled, older than Charley remembered him, his work clothes hanging loosely, appeared on the stoop and crossed to the barn. A horse whinnied. The grass and the trees were silent, the slight breeze that stirred them not uttering a whisper. An elderly woman followed the man outside, dashed a pailful of water on the ground and paused to appraise the day. The way she stood, one hand on her hip, he could tell she was arguing.

Charley was still, waiting in the sugar bush.

Later he said he never went near the house all day. He sat in the sugar bush. He washed his feet at Bruce's spring. At noon he went into Johnny's field and ate some haws. And he slept. He heard no screams nor threshing machines. In the late afternoon he sat on a rail fence three hundred yards away. But he never went near the house.

Chapter Four

In 1892, a century of unprecedented progress was drawing to a close. Horseless carriages, steamboats, telephones, railways, photography, balloons and gliders were the vanguard of a dazzling future, vital, attainable passports to the best of all possible worlds. The ordinary folk, the salt of the earth, who tilled the land with gnarled hands and read the Bible on Sundays, grasped the edge of the dream, but could not quite admit it to reality. And along with the invasion of gadgets that clicked and roared and honked and whirred and clanged came Darwin and Huxley, fully beyond the pale of their credulity, uttering blasphemies against the God who had fashioned them in His own image. He was the same God who would have given man wings if He had meant him to fly.

Politically, Canada limped along in the shadow of her mother country. Sir John A. Macdonald's death in 1891 had left to Canadian politics a parade of transient prime ministers. In the fall of 1892, Abbott, the reluctant prime minister, who hated "politics and what are considered their appropriate methods," prepared to step down after a short, wearying tenure. Macdonald's prodigy, Sir John Thompson, still young at forty-eight, was eager to lead the country, and who could foresee that two short years hence he would drop dead while lunching with Queen Victoria?

Pestilence hung heavily in Canada's harbours that fall, and the newspapers fanned public apprehension by reciting cholera statistics, folk remedies and hastily resurrected formulae for preventives from an even more superstitious era.

A theme of righteousness, often awash in mawkish sentimentality and self-conscious posturing, ran through the eastern Ontario newspapers. A preoccupation with the macrocosmic, the lugubrious and the bizarre adapted itself easily to the florid style and didactic moralizing of the age.

Temperance, the Salvation Army and pilgrimages to St. Anne de Beaupre jostled for space with a horse trader who committed suicide by taking "Rough on Rats." Whole sermons were culled from the proposed early store closings – six p.m. – and tongue-in-cheek deliberations on women's wearing suspenders, dubbed "gallows." Ads for Burdock Blood Bitters and Dr Williams' Pink Pills – "Beware of imitations" – vied with nuggets of useless curiosities: "Silk worms are sold by the pound in China"; "The market price of a wife in Equatorial Africa is 10 bundles of hairpins."

A move to elevate Columbus to sainthood on the four hundredth anniversary of his discovery of America was vetoed because of his affair with a married woman. "The fair charmer was a Jewess," the papers twittered. And even the rural papers, generally concerned with the merits of West cheese over East cheese and diagrams for the perfect henhouse, paused to deliver protracted romanticisms on the death of Tennyson. Throughout the papers, daily and weekly, ran a thread of limp-wristed, sentimental serials.

All of this concerned John James Luckey senior very little, if at all, as he brought his buggy from the woodshed and hitched the horses to it. He had a long mental list of chores to be done. The chickens he had killed yesterday must be loaded and taken to Smith's Falls. He hoisted bulging sacks onto the cart. Market business would keep him in town until noon. When he returned, there were repairs to be done to the house and barn. He would finish sealing the doors and windows against the cold and check for loose pipes. If there was time, he would take a look at the stoop door that Johnny was supposed to have fixed. It still swung shut while you were trying to walk through it unless it was propped open. Then, if it was still light enough, he'd go down in the cellar and take stock. Winter supplies were laid by, but potatoes had shown a good deal of rot this year; chances were they'd not be getting through the winter with their store.

Martha called from inside.

"What's that, woman? Speak up!" Bother the woman, she knew he had trouble hearing.

She appeared at the door with a pail. "I said, stovepipe. The pipe in the summer kitchen. Can't you get Johnny to take a look at it?"

"I'll secure it myself, all in good time."

She tipped the pail, heaving the contents on the ground. Water splashed on the ground by the stoop. "I'll be going across to Parkers mid-morning. I found the stewed rabbit recipe Mary Ann was asking for."

"Press my meeting clothes before you go, woman. You'll not be forgetting tomorrow's Sunday." An elder in St. Andrew's church at Toledo, he took pride in perfect, meticulous attendance.

"Every Sunday for the last nineteen years," she muttered.

"What's that? Rather gossip with the neighbours, would you?" He gave her a piercing look, his heavy brows knitted together. There was less work for her to do these days, with the family all gone and the chores lightened, but he couldn't abide sloth and she knew it, by God! He'd never thought much of the Parkers anyway, C of E they were, next thing to Roman Catholic. Upstarters, too, newcomers to Coad's Road, bought up some of Will Jones's land only a dozen or so years ago. And hadn't Parker had the gall to be taking him to court back in '79 and getting four dollars damages out of him for that cursed ewe he claimed was his! The assault on his pride and his pocketbook still rankled. "You've got plenty to do, woman. I can set you to mending harnesses if you're caught up on the cleaning and pickling."

"Minnie'll be home this afternoon to lend a hand. I have it on Johnny's word." She turned, holding the door open. "Surely Liza Ann's run out of things for her to sew. Those kiddies don't have to look all the time as if the Queen's about to pay a visit. That fancy new house is going to Liza Ann's head and she could do with a word about where Minnie's place is."

Old John grimaced as Martha disappeared and the stoop door clapped shut. "Things could be worse. She could be finding herself a man."

There was a hoot from inside the house. "Fat chance! She's thirty-four now, and no beaux comes calling."

"Thirty-four, is she?" he shot back. He picked up his horsewhip, examining a crack in the handle. "And how old were you, Missy Lyle, when I was plucking you from a life of spinsterhood?" His face contorted into a grin. Thirty-five, she'd been, and no daisy of a woman. Strong-wristed and plain-spoken, a proper helpmate to raise a brood. He'd first noticed her when his daughter Christina was keeping company with one of the Lyle brothers. He grunted. It had been years since the day he had looked at her and realized that whatever spark had kindled his interest had long since died. "There's work enough for Minnie, too, when she comes." His only answer was a clatter of dishes.

"I'll be wanting my beard trimmed. She's good with the scissors!" More than any of the other girls, Minnie reminded him of her mother, Cursty. There was a softness about her, not in looks but in manner, a generosity in her love for everyone, like his Cursty had had. Pity she'd never have kiddies of her own, Minnie, although there'd be the danger she'd spoil them rotten, just as Cursty would have, if he'd let her. Minnie made the family – brothers, sisters, nieces and nephews – her whole life. The other girls were long gone, marrying young and moving out to start their own brood.

Sarah, the eldest, was forty-five, the age her own mother had been when she died. And there was only a year's difference between himself and Sarah's husband. He'd warned her against marrying a man so much older, but she hadn't listened. Then young Christina had married Martha's brother, around the time he and Martha married. And his youngest girl had found a John McKenzie to marry, her own maternal grandfather's name, no relation. Foolish girls, hauled out west homesteading, by husbands with visions of wealth.

He patted the horses and took two small lumps of sugar from his pocket. Once every Saturday one small treat, something he frowned on if anyone else tried it. It was something only Minnie had caught him doing. He had a sudden image of her, packing Martha's old steamer trunk to take out west, laden mostly with gifts she'd made herself. "Look," she'd said, "embroidered collars and violet sachets for the women, nighties for the little girls, white with blue smocking. The same for the baby. But the boys – what shall I make the boys?" She'd got him whittling then, crude soldiers and tiny whistles, he all the time grumbling. "Those girls have no business luring you away." The older one had flooded them with pleading letters: "We've mostly got sons, Father, already doing men's chores, and I've been poorly since Edgar was born. Couldn't you let Minnie come, Father? We'd all chip in for her ticket . . ."

He'd held them to their offer and not let Minnie go until the ticket arrived. In spite of his grumbling, it had done his heart good to see her all excited, eyes shining. She was so like a little woodland animal most of the time, scurrying about with a frightened, hunted look. The change would be good for her.

So Minnie had gone, pecking him and Martha on the cheek at the station, waving her hanky out the window, shouting promises of letters. And she had written home every week, begging news of everyone, giving accounts of Edgar's antics. Then along about February in '91 had come the bill for a full set of uppers. Minnie's apologetic letter. "Please, Father, everyone here is up against it, working so hard for so little. The crops weren't nearly as good last fall as expected, and the children have all been down with the croup and needing medicine. I haven't the heart to ask them to pay for dentures."

He'd sent the bill back to her with a terse note scribbled on it: "Times is hard here, too." She'd not get round him, any more than the others would. If she'd been earning her keep under his roof it might have been different. Christina had written, of course, adding her pleas to Minnie's: "She's needed that work done for a long time, Father. The dentist said the poison in her body was making her ill." In the end he'd sent a part payment, along with a letter ordering her home before she could spend more money she didn't have. A flurry of protests had come, even from the older grandchildren. And Johnny and Liza Ann had taken Minnie's side. She hadn't come home until last winter, almost a year after his orders.

The ground was soft from Friday's rain and his gaiter boots left their prints as he walked from the woodshed to the gate and opened it. He moved slowly and deliberately, feeling the rheumatism sear his legs and back. He was short and stockily built, with small feet and hands and broad, powerful shoulders.

As he returned to the house, still holding the whip, wiping the warm moisture from the horses' mouths on his pants, Martha called out, "Is Mr Devlin coming today to get his cattle?"

"Didn't say." He scraped his boots on the stoop and went in. The door swung shut behind him.

"He hasn't paid you yet, has he?"

"What business is it of yours, woman? Money matters aren't your affair." Devlin, an Ottawa alderman and cattle drover for thirty-odd years, was as good as his word. He'd put five dollars on his cattle on Thursday; the other seventy-three was promised. "He's taking the bull, too," he said. The bull was a steal at twenty dollars but he wanted to get rid of it.

"You want to be sure you get your money."

He rounded on her then, snapping the whip against the wooden table. "What d'you want to know about the money for, eh? You'd like to know where the key is, wouldn't you? Wouldn't you! Won't do you any good, it's not there!" He threw the whip on the table and grasped her by the shoulders. "Are you thinking you'll be watching when I put Devlin's money away? You'll go in the other room, same as always!"

He released her and she fled to the parlour. Let her go sulk, he thought. He'd gone in once, to find her sitting on the sack of sugar that stopped up the parlour door to outside, to keep the wind out. Dry-eyed, looking like thunder, twisting her apron in her blunt, rough hands. Good place for her, maybe the sugar'll sweeten her up if she sits there long enough. But the image had lingered, of Martha sitting, not on the chairs she kept carefully covered, waiting for company that never came, but on the old sugar sack that didn't matter, as if it was the only place she was good enough for.

He looked around the kitchen. Already a pot was filled with fresh-killed fowl, ready for boiling. Potatoes were peeled and cut up. She'd be coming out to close the gate after he left, the same as always, and have it open on his return.

Outside again, he climbed up on the buggy and cracked the whip. The horses trotted out through the gate and turned right onto Coad's Road. Across the way, the Parker farm lay quiet; a little further down on his left, sounds of activity reached him from the Daley barn. He saw no one. Looking south across his own land, he was resigned rather than satisfied. Having let it out on shares since the summer of '84, he had decided to work it himself again this year, although not like he used to. I've earned the right to take it easier, he thought. Chores won't be done at dawn. I'll not be replacing the livestock and poultry we kill. A country squire I'll not be, nor will my pockets be overflowing.

He remembered the cold, dismal day over fifty years ago, when he had landed with his mother in Quebec. His mother had rented a small place in Kitley, turning it into a rooming house, while he worked and saved to buy his first piece of land. By the time he had enough to buy his own lot and build a farm on it, he'd had a wife and four tots to feed. Forty pounds it had cost him, a king's ransom, for that first fifty acres. Worth every penny; he'd gained a reputation for being a sound, hard businessman. Hard work and Christian living are the keys to prosperity, he'd told his boys. So far, only Johnny had listened. He thrashed the horses. "Yup, there! Giddup!"

Johnny was the most prosperous of all his sons, the only one with real ambition, and he looked after himself first. Only last spring he'd come over to help out on the farm, supposedly out of Christian charity, then demanded payment for his time and services! "I'll take you to court, you old scoundrel!" he'd shouted. And he had, for the paltry sum of $6.22. The old man grimaced. He knew how to deal with Johnny, served him with a set off for old grievances, to the tune of $48.80, for eight bushels of oats, a stack of hay and a breach of agreement in not putting out manure. He had a long memory; it came in handy when they needed reminding who was head of the family.

Sam, on the other hand, wasn't a bad lad, the easiest-going of the lot. Wouldn't always be content just to make cheese. He was learning the business inside out, poring over books at night, talking of attending dairy school and setting up his own factories some day. But he was thirty-two already, not even paying court to a girl. Better get a move on. According to Johnny, Sam had invested in a small plot out on concession three last spring, but Sam never said a word, hardly ever paid a visit, in fact. All he needed now was to get sweet on some girl in Pembroke, and he'd be wanting to stay there, sell his property. If he turned a profit, and stuck to his ambitions, he might turn out the best of the lot.

Except for Sam and Johnny, there was no one left he could pin his hopes on. Will, the eldest, was dead ten years, and Hugh had struck out for Chicago the same year Will died. That left only Charley, and he never spoke of Charley any more, not since that gin-swilling detective had called around last year, more nerve than a canal horse, nosing about, full of wild stories. He cracked his whip sharply as the horses trotted toward Smith's Falls.

"Your boy's best put away for a good long time," the detective had said. "Protect society. Bad egg." He'd rambled on about how Charley'd stolen a coat.

Young wastrel, always needed an iron hand. Hard-mouthed little devil, set himself against them all from early days. Except when he wanted his father to save his bacon. The girls had all spoiled him, fussing over him one minute, neglecting him the next, so that Martha had trouble keeping him in line. A bad egg, needed a horsewhipping. But this city detective, what right had he to come around, stirring up trouble? "Goddam ye, be gone!" he'd shouted at Montgomery, raising the axe he'd been splitting logs with. "Be gone, or I'll be giving you a blow you'll not forget!"

"I've a warrant for harness stealing," Montgomery had persisted. "And I heard he sold a load of your hay that he had no business to. We could lay a charge for that, you know. Put him away a good spell."

"D'you not understand me?" He had made a hacking motion with the axe.

"Wait a minute!" The detective had jumped backwards, his face white. "I'm just doing my job, sir. I knew you were an upright citizen, refusing to bail him out of his jam. He's got to own up, pay the price. That's all I'm saying."

He'll get nothing from me, in cash or sympathy, Old John thought. But to the detective he'd said, "Be off, now, and don't come back! I'll make short work of you if I see you around here again!" He'd chased him all the way to the gate, waving the axe.

Damn Charley, he thought, clutching the whip. Johnny was the son most like himself, both the good and bad sides of him. Johnny had drive, couldn't abide them that didn't, and was hard-fisted when he was crossed. Always got his pound of flesh. The old man's eyes narrowed. He'd take care of himself first, and Martha, of course. And Minnie, for as long as she'd be helping out at home.

He cracked his whip again as the horses trotted briskly along the road. A breeze came up, rustling the gold leaves of elm and basswood flanking the road. Banks of sumac seemed to catch fire as the sun broke through a cloud. His face relaxed. It was going to be a glorious October day.

*   *   *

Below the Luckey farm, on the southeast side of the road, Minnie Luckey prepared to hem her niece's new skirt in the sitting room of her brother Johnny's house. The pungent scent of the relish put up yesterday with the last of the tomatoes hung in the air, mingling with new wood and lemon oil.

"Keep still, Victoria," she said through a mouthful of pins. "Time's short if you want to wear this outfit to Sunday School tomorrow."

Victoria snapped to attention, ramrod straight, pretending she was singing "God Save the Queen" at morning exercises. Nine-year-old Esley mimicked her, saluting briskly and collapsing in laughter on a nearby sofa where articles of clothing reposed.

Minnie slipped pins through the light wool at regular intervals. "Mind the new clothes, now. I've laid them out so's they won't need pressing again."

The kitchen door opened, releasing the aroma of apple, cloves and cinnamon. Liza Ann appeared, mopping her face with a corner of her apron. "When you're finished, Victoria can roll out some pastry, and we'll use those windfalls for apple dumplings. Pity you can't stay for supper, Minnie."

Victoria bobbed her head, keeping her body rigid. "Yes, Aunt Minnie, stay. Stay!"

Minnie sighed. "I'd love to. But you understand how it is. Martha's been complaining about having to do all the work."

Liza Ann knew how much Minnie liked to get away from the old farm. "There's not much to do now, with just the two of them."

"There's heavy work." Minnie's voice was mild. "Water to haul, loads of washing. Martha's fanatical about cleaning. She's not as quick as she once was, and Father's slowing down, too."

Liza Ann fastened a loose wisp of fair hair into place. So like Minnie, working like a beaver without complaint! The only time she stopped for a cup of tea was when she could see that Liza Ann needed one. Mornings when it was obvious Johnny hadn't come home all night, or evenings when he hadn't turned up for supper, hadn't sent word, Minnie would say to Liza Ann, "How about a cup of tea now, my throat's dry as a bone and yours must be, too." She would push Liza Ann gently toward the sofa and nudge the hassock into place with her tiny foot. She would fetch the flowered china from the sideboard and brew a great pot, strong and bitter, the way she thought Liza Ann liked it. And Liza Ann would load sugar into her cup, and lace it with fresh cream, and gulp the tea down while it was still hot enough to scald her throat and bring tears to her eyes. All the while she fought to hide a great rush of feelings – worry that Minnie would detect a lack of gratitude for the horrid tea, humiliation at Johnny's treatment, fear that one day Johnny might turn her out of this beautiful showplace she tried so hard to make into a home he would be proud to return to, fear that he would replace her with one of his scarlet women.

Running a household was medicine to Liza Ann. Bleaching and ironing the linens to spotless perfection, laying the table out for

English tea, with the daintiest cups and finest silver and monogrammed napkin rings, scouring pots until she could see her reflection in them – these activities were balm, things which sent her fears scampering away into dark corners. "You could eat off those oak floors," she had heard Minnie tell a neighbour. "And the neatness! A place for everything and everything in its place, Liza Ann always says." It was true. The children had been taught from infancy to pick up and put away and keep their clothes from getting soiled. Each had toy chests, book shelves and a large wardrobe.

She crossed the room to straighten her favourite oil painting, a gilt-framed woodland scene that hung above her velvet upholstered Queen Anne settee. Everything here bespoke her dedication to the home – the flowered draperies with matching cushion covers, antimacassars and doilies she and Minnie had made, polished vases of dried flowers arranged by her own hands. She was the envy of women for miles around, praised and respected by everyone. Everyone except Johnny.

Johnny spent less and less time at home. There were times when she would look at him across the table and remark to herself that his sleek good looks were growing coarser, his lips puffing up with a flabbiness, the corners turning down cruelly. Did I ever love him, she would ask herself and the answer would come back, yes, I loved him, but this is not the man I loved, not the same man at all. At night when they were preparing for bed she would find herself hoping he would not insist that she perform her wifely duties while he perhaps would be remembering the arms he had been in the night before, or imagining her thickset body was slim and inviting like that of some dancehall girl from one of his trips.

"Mother could hem the skirt if you haven't time, Aunt Minnie," Victoria was saying. "But I'd rather you did it. You've done all the rest."

"That I have." Minnie slipped the last pin into place. "Now, let's get it finished. Off with you, Esley." He galloped off, slapping his sides and shouting, "Giddap!" Victoria wriggled out of the skirt and stood in her lace petticoat.

On the sofa nearby lay Minnie's masterpiece, a grey wool coat belted at the waist, its rolling collar edged with rows of white braid. Beside it reposed a waistcoat in figured maroon, with wide revers and gilt buttons. Minnie had laboured long nights in dim lamplight to produce these prizes, ever since the August afternoon Victoria had torn across the fields to the old farm, waving an article from the *Rideau Record*: "The up-to-date blazer is a tight fitting long coat, a sort of modified Russian blouse . . ."

"It's just what I've always wanted, Aunt Minnie. Could we make it?" Minnie had smiled. Everything Victoria liked was just what she had always wanted. Her approach was always the same. Could we make it always turned into "I knew you could make it, Aunt Minnie!" A bubbly endorsement sealed with much dancing about and hand-clapping and a great bear hug.

Minnie straightened up, looked around for thread and scissors, and put her hand to her forehead.

"Are you all right, Minnie?" Liza Ann asked. "You're looking quite dyspeptic."

Minnie felt in the pocket of her apron. Yes, the thread and scissors had been there all the time. "No more than usual, I guess." She wished people would stop telling her she was a bad colour. Threading a needle, she took up the skirt and stitched swiftly and surely around the hem.

"We could have a cup of tea, perhaps, before you go, and some of the lemon bread we made Thursday."

Minnie shook her head. Liza Ann was a little too fond of her own baking. She'd got terribly beefy, consoling herself no doubt with Johnny away so much. "Father will be back from market in a half hour and they'll be sitting down to dinner. I'll have to make a show of being hungry." She smiled apologetically.

Poor little mouse, Liza Ann thought. Always so eager to please, hiding her own feelings. Did she ever cry herself to sleep, wishing she had a man to warm her bed and kiddies of her own to bake and sew for? Everyone takes advantage of Minnie and so do I, she thought guiltily. But Minnie'd do anything for the children, and Victoria's silly chatter is preferable to Martha's nagging and Father's outbursts.

"Done." Minnie held the skirt against Victoria's waist; then, satisfied, spread it on the sofa beside the other clothes.

"You've got a few minutes, Aunt Minnie." Victoria grasped her aunt's hand and tugged her toward the front hall and up the stairs to a trunk in a recess at the end of the hall.

"Victoria, you shouldn't –"

"It's all right, Aunt Minnie. Mother said I could look through it.

See what I found," she said, throwing the lid up. She took out a small piece of ecru lace. "Wouldn't it look nice on a velvet dress?"

"It's awful small."

"I see myself in emerald green," Victoria continued, "or maybe ruby red. What do you think?" She twirled around, rhapsodizing, her long hair swinging. "I might get asked to parties this Christmas – oh, and do you know what's the latest? Cobweb parties! Everybody has a string and as they move around it gets all tangled about the furniture. And, do you know, last year's dress is up to here on me –" She tapped her knee.

"Disgraceful," Minnie said, and giggled. She was being manipulated.

"Let me show you how to dance, Aunt Minnie. I've been watching and –"

"Shush, child!"

But Victoria put her left hand on her aunt's shoulder and, facing her, grasped Minnie's left hand in her right. "Like this, see? One, two, one, two." She whirled them around until Minnie was quite dizzy.

"Aunt Minnie, you don't weigh anything, not even as much as Esley!"

Flushed and gasping, Minnie stopped, pushing Victoria's hands away. "I must go. I promised to help Martha with some preserves right after dinner."

"Stay a little longer." A clock struck the half hour.

"I can't dear, really. Suppose I get home just as Martha is sealing up the jars? That's pretty poor timing, wouldn't you say?"

"Aunt Minnie, don't be such a goose," the girl said. "No one was ever killed because of poor timing."

But Minnie fled down the stairs to the front door. "I'll be back soon," she called to Liza Ann. "Tell Johnny goodbye for me!"

Liza Ann joined Victoria on the porch. They watched as Minnie crossed the road and jumped the ditch. She turned and waved, then climbed the fence and disappeared, a little brown mouse scurrying into the fiery folds of autumn.

Chapter Five

. . . The Stealthy Approach

to the place, ever looking, always watching to see that none were observing, the entrance, the murderous attack on the lone defenceless woman, the arrival of the unsuspecting husband entering in with eager expectancy to meet and greet his own, the sight that awaited him and the fate; the homecoming of the daughter, thoughtless of danger, the awful sight she beheld, her wild rush from the place of carnage, her piercing shriek for help which came not – her end; these and much more than these of the incidents of that shocking crime, none may know except him who holds the guilty knowledge close locked within his breast and Him from whom no secrets are held . . .

Rideau Record
October 13, 1892

Chapter Six

The scream was shrill and agonizing, with an edge of terror to it. A breeze from the southwest carried it across Daley's farm where men were threshing in the early afternoon. Some heard it plainly; Michael Loman and Silas Hitchcock junior, up in the haymow, heard nothing. It was followed closely by a second scream, low at first, rising in a crescendo of panic, dying away slowly. Will Daley, propping his barn door open with a log, felt his hackles rise. "Sounds like it's coming from the Luckeys'."

Jack Phillips paused in his inspection of the straw deck on his thresher and looked across the road. "Can't see anything. Too many cedar bushes." He glanced at the others: should they go over?

"Sounds as if John's children are playing." Ansley Stewart winced as he straightened up from scraping muck off the wooden wheels.

The men laughed. "Old John's startin' over, is he?"

"Life in the old dog yet!"

"Get off with you. I meant – young John's kiddies," Ansley stammered, settling his derby on his white head.

It was ominously quiet, the world crowded with earth colours and organic smells – fresh cut wheat, horse dung, damp armpits. They grouped together, bronzed hands still for a moment, faces solemn and expectant, like a congregation waiting for the announcement of the next hymn.

"Better get a move on." Will Daley was already weary from a morning of drawing in corn. "The days are short."

"Right, boys, the horsepower's set." Jack Phillips turned on the thresher. Other farmers' fields were waiting; how much longer would the weather hold?

They worked for half an hour, until the thresher coughed and sputtered. "Boxings could be worn out," Silas junior said, turning it off. "Might have to babbit them."

Jock Brunton, spreading hay in the mow, threw down his fork. "Look there! Smoke!" Heavy and black, the cloud was drifting from the southwest toward them. "Fire! Fire at the Luckeys'!" He dropped out of sight, reappearing a moment later at the barn door.

Paced by Silas junior, he tore across the field, fair hair flying, with Daley and Loman close behind. "Parker's up ahead. Andrew! Chrissake, what's up? What's happened?" Andrew Parker and his daughter ran on, ignoring the calls, not slackening their speed. Ansley Stewart and Silas senior lingered behind, putting the horses away.

No time to spare, Jack Phillips said to himself. He leaped on the Daley mare, his legs slapping her sleek sides sharply, and whacked her flank with uncharacteristic vehemence. "Giddap, Bess, come on!" The Luckeys were kin, Old John his uncle by marriage. If they were in trouble, he had to reach them. There'd be just the old folks and Cousin Minnie, none of the Luckey sons there to help.

He had never felt close to his cousins. Accompanied by his older brother Willie he used to catch bullhead and build snow forts with Sam and Hugh and Charley. Hugh had been Jack's age, Sam his brother's. Little Charley had tagged along, not always welcome but determined not to miss anything. Hugh had been the odd one, discontented, getting in scrapes at school, threatening to pack and leave home. And he had, when he turned nineteen – threw a few clothes in a sack one night and hopped a freight, bound for Chicago. Never heard from since. The family didn't talk about him.

Once they were grown up, Jack Phillips hadn't seen much of his cousins. He'd spent his winters in bush work for his uncle near Ompah. Sam went to Pembroke in the summers, Charley knocked about loose-footed, turning up now and then like a bad penny. Did a stint or two for Jonas Bruce, making syrup and trying his hand at carpentry. Jonas had thought the world of him, said he'd never seen a harder worker.

But there was something about Charley. He didn't have a chip on his shoulder like Hugh, but he seemed lost somehow. He went about trying to get attention in ways that showed a lack of common sense. He took to carrying a gun when he reached manhood – no harm in that, really, a lot of young lads packed a revolver, but Jack Phillips could never see what the attraction was. He suspected that Charley thought him a little soft, working and saving to buy his own thresher, teaching Sunday School. Getting himself engaged to Eliza Moran, wanting to settle down. Charley didn't seem to have a grip on life. He was full of boyish pranks which might have been hilarious when they were all sugaring in the bush or bathing without their knickers in the quarry.

Jack used to see him strutting about Saturday evenings in Smith's Falls with a bunch of swells, all chewing tobacco and twirling their revolvers, vying for attention from the young ladies. He'd pointed them out to his betrothed, who had lowered her eyes demurely and avowed no decent girl would be attracted, a declaration which relieved him immensely.

But Jack's mother would say in her soft Scottish burr that they mustn't judge the Luckey boys harshly. "Lost their mother – my dear sister Cursty, rest her soul – when they weren't but bairns. Their father's hard on them. It's like he doesn't want to care for anyone again. It's some people's way of bearing their loss easier."

"Did he love Auntie Cursty?" he'd asked one day, struggling to move a bushel basket of potatoes from the kitchen door to the table.

His mother was thoughtful. "In his way, I guess."

"But he married again. Too bad she's such a sourface."

"Who says she's a sourface?" His mother had gathered an apronful of potatoes, dunked them into a partly filled pail of water and reached for a scrub brush.

"Hugh and Charley always said so."

"That poor woman works her fingers to the bone, same as the rest of us." His mother's normally quiet voice had been raised ever so slightly. "All those children not hers and her only bairn taken from her by the Lord."

The bond of family threatened to overwhelm him now, as he galloped past Loman and Daley, urging the mare on. "Are the Luckeys there?" His heart went out to them. Good people they were, not glowing with love and goodwill like his mother, but hard-working and God-fearing, not deserving of misfortune.

"Bound to be. John's back from town."

"Is it the house that's burning?" They would be struggling to get their belongings out. It was broad daylight, a clear, bright afternoon. There was no chance they would be napping.

The gate to the farm was open. A black cloud billowed from the east side of the house. But how peaceful, how innocent it all seemed. It could have been stumps being burned for potash, or a bonfire in the bush, the lads huddled around it, frying fresh-caught bullheads from Irish Lake. How deceptively comforting and inviting! The horror inside Jack Phillips grew. The Luckeys had to be inside!

Ahead of him he saw Andrew Parker running into the smoke. His daughter Isabella, an ungainly girl in her twenties, clutching her heavy skirts, hurried after him. From the corner of his eye, he saw the Parker farmhouse across the road, young Leonard leaping off the porch and sprinting across the front yard. Uncle John would be glad of all the help.

He dismounted just inside the gate – no need to frighten the mare by forcing her closer to the fire – and ran after Parker into the swelling shroud of smoke.

* * *

Andrew Parker was struck by the awful stillness. He wondered where Old John was. There were no shouts answering his, not even the dog's barking. "I'll look a fool, barging in," he had said when Mary Ann called him. "Martha's probably let the taters boil dry." He had been in the kitchen, lengthening his suspenders a notch, hoping to ease the discomfort brought on by heaping seconds of rabbit stew.

"Come see for yourself," his wife had yelled from the porch.

"Yeah, Pa," Lenny had piped up. "Smoke. Looks like its from the other side of the woodshed."

As soon as he'd looked he'd known it was no laughing matter. Without stopping to pull on a jacket, he had raced across the road. All that wood – log house, frame attachments – a tinderbox if ever there was one!

While he felt a dawning horror, one small corner of his mind acknowledged relief that he was not playing the jackass by going over. Old John was a cantankerous one, squabbling in court with his own flesh and blood; Andrew had had to take him to court once himself, back in '79, in a dispute over that damned ewe that had disappeared on Christmas Eve. He'd marched right over and confronted Old John, who wouldn't budge, denied everything. Dared to be taken to court. Well, Andrew had shown him! Four dollars he'd asked and four dollars he'd gotten, and court costs as well. And a lot of bitter feelings for months after. Outsiders, Old John still called him and his Mary Ann, full fifteen years after they'd taken over the Jones property. And Andrew born and raised in this very township, back on the second concession, while Luckey himself came out from Ireland! No matter, they were friends now and the wives certainly liked to get together and gossip. About the only chance Martha ever got to be social.

His heart thumping, he ran past the woodshed to the east side of the house. "John! Miz Luckey! Anyone here?" The closed-in porch was ablaze, the yard deserted. There was none of the frantic activity he expected, removing furniture, drawing water, calling out. Had they gone somewhere seeking help? Surely they'd come to him first!

He heard the sound of hooves followed by Jack Phillips's voice. "Uncle John! Where is he? Still in town?"

Young Lenny appeared through the smoke. "You stay back!" Andrew snapped. "Get on home. Your ma said you weren't to come!"

"I saw him come back, remember? I told you," Lenny said.

"You saw –"

"Mr Luckey. About two."

Andrew seized a pail of water standing nearby and dashed it at the stoop door. Potato peelings and marble-sized potatoes flew into the fire, spitting and crackling. "Is the buggy in the woodshed?" He kicked mightily at the door. Through the glass he tried to see into the main kitchen, wondering if the vague shape he glimpsed on the floor might be a body. Before he could get a better look, the heat singed his hair and eyebrows, forcing him back. "Try the parlour door!" He ran past the blazing summer kitchen to the front of the house.

Isabella, coming from the west side, found him there, kicking frantically. "Goddam that door! What's holding it?" It burst open just as he heard Daley's threshing gang arrive. When he opened his mouth to call, heat seared his lungs. Choking, he tried to enter the parlour. Dense smoke stung his eyes; beneath his feet a mass of something lay smouldering. A body? He tried to move it with his foot. Oh, God, not a body! He forced himself to look.

"Pa!" Isabella clutched at him. "The roof! It'll cave in!" He wanted to tell her the summer kitchen would collapse first, the fire must have started there, but it was impossible to speak.

"What –?" She gasped, following his gaze.

He pulled her back. "Carpeting. Only – roll of carpet."

Will Daley appeared beside them. "Can't get in the kitchen." He doubled up in a fit of coughing. "Where are they?"

Andrew shook his head numbly as Will pushed past him into the parlour, backing out with a seared hand. "Nothing except carpet. Was it blocking the door?" Andrew tugged at Will and Isabella as the flames roared closer. "Back! Never saw the Luckeys – use – this door."

They retreated, sidestepping men with buckets forming a chain to the well.

Will pointed to a window on the south side of the summer kitchen, from which smoke was rolling. "Only window open in the whole house!"

Andrew brushed sparks from his sleeve. "Try the bedrooms. West side."

But Will had already disappeared. "Mr Luckey! Anyone here?" His shout was drowned out by sounds of a window crashing to the ground.

A thump, followed by a loud crack came from the east side. "Stoop door's in!" Andrew stumbled after Will toward Jock Brunton's voice.

A group of men crowded the stoop. "Lord, an inferno! Never get in this way." Phillips was holding a kerchief to his reddened cheeks.

"Where are they, for Chrissake?"

"John's still in town."

"He's not," young Hitchcock said. "Passed me in the buggy as I was going down to Will's."

"The buggy!"

"Check the woodshed." Andrew almost collided with Daley, struggling through the smoke with a huge barrel of soap. "First thing I laid my hands to," Daley gasped.

Andrew and young Silas, cloths pressed to their mouths, groped their way into the woodshed, scraping past piles of hoarded wood to push out the buggy. There was no longer any doubt: the Luckeys were in the house, Old John as well as Martha, God help them. And where was Minnie? Smoke and rabbit stew warred in Andrew's stomach; he bent in pain.

The wind whipped up in sudden gusts, blowing the smoke toward the village, where Coad's Road crossed the Brockville highway. Running out of the woodshed, eyes streaming, Brunton held up two axes. "Right at the back – leaning against the wall. Look at this one! Blood on the handle!"

"Your finger's bleeding." Andrew pointed to a large sliver.

Brunton looked at his hand in surprise and dropped the axes as the woodshed roof collapsed behind him.

The crowd of rescuers swelled. "Pull the walls down!"

"Can't save the house. Stop the fire from spreading!"

Phillips drove forward a team of horses, pulling a rope to which was attached a long, heavy chain. "Fasten the pull-down hook. Quick, now!" Fumbling hands secured an anchor to the end of the chain. "Come now, you've got to run right into the smoke!" The horses reared and whinnied; men retched and coughed, patting and pulling at the horses, trying again and again to throw the hook over the top of the milkhouse wall, until finally it caught and dug in. Phillips cracked the whip, driving the horses away from the milkhouse until, with a resounding crash, the wall fell.

"Again!" Whinnying, pulling, cracking the whip, until the north wall of the main kitchen teetered and crumbled.

A muffled explosion, followed by a shower of sparks sent young Parker reeling. "The milkhouse! Dad – hear that?" He ran for safety as a tongue of flame shot up to lick the sky.

"See that?" Phillips leaped from the wagon. "Not a hope of getting them out now. Look out!" The roof of the summer kitchen caved in and half a dozen men scrambled up on the remains of the porch to peer into the main kitchen.

"A body! There's a body in there!"

Brunton and young Silas elbowed their way forward with buckets, smashing glass and dashing water wildly into the kitchen. Andrew thrust a shoulder between them and found himself at the front of the group, the stench of roasting flesh assailing his nostrils. Ansley Stewart, beside him, vomited into the embers.

The body was lying on a sleeper, near the door, horribly burned.

"Holy Mary, Mother of Jesus!"

"No face. It has no face!"

"Miz Luckey." Andrew's voice was barely above a whisper. "Can't get her out. Too hot."

"Water. More water!"

"Get a pole. Wire!"

Brunton ran toward the stable.

"A pole, Jock. Make a hook on the end."

"Anyone else in there?"

"Can't tell. Kitchen floor's fallen into the cellar."

"Look – in the cellar – a man's body and – and what else?"

"Could be the dog. Poor devil!"

"Ansley! Give a hand, someone! Ansley's collapsed –" Will and Parker dragged Ansley Stewart away from the fire out onto the grass, fanning him. "Lie still, old man." Parker took his pulse. "We'll get someone to take you home."

"Where's Johnny? He's been sent for, hasn't he?"

"Irish Creek, dealing cattle." The voice, low and tearful, was a woman's. In the gathering dusk, Jack Phillips turned and stumbled toward her, his hand extended, realizing how grimy and dishevelled he must look. She grasped his hand in both of hers. "Liza Ann," he said. "Don't come any closer."

"Jack – Minnie's in there." Liza Ann, her blue shawl about her shoulders, swayed back and forth, sobbing. Behind her, a knot of neighbouring women hovered, pale and frightened.

Jack Phillips wanted to weep with them. God, Minnie too! He made to signal Brunton and Daley, but they were already spreading the news. "Come over here." Phillips gripped Liza Ann's arm and led her to Ansley, who was leaning on Parker. Embracing her, the old man wept. "Liza Ann, oh God, what could have happened?"

"They must have had time to get out!"

"Why didn't they escape?"

The baritone of a grocer named Richards rose above the chorus, ominous and measured. "Someone could've set the fire."

"They weren't murdered!"

"Murdered and the house set fire to?"

"Look at the bodies. Arms and legs missing. Heads gone. Old John's had his skull smashed in."

Liza Ann cried out and turned away, to be swallowed up in the folds and embraces of the women.

"What went on in there?"

It was six o'clock before, with the heat and smoke and debris and collapsing timbers and clumsy wires, they got all the bodies out. Darkness pressed; above them the sky glowed orange. There was little left of the summer kitchen as Parker trod warily, peered into a pot containing charred chicken bones, nudged with his foot a black, crumbling mound. The odour of burnt sugar mingled with that of the chickens, wood and bodies.

Phillips picked his way through smoking embers behind him, mopping his brow with a sooty kerchief. "Is it murder? People are saying the doors were barricaded."

"Fire's almost burned itself out." Andrew edged past the hole in the kitchen floor. "That stoop door always shut unless they propped it open. And they never used the parlour door at all."

"Didn't Johnny fix the stoop door last year?"

"Might've." Andrew scuffed some embers, sending sparks flying. "I was in the kitchen not two weeks ago. I pointed out to Martha about the pipes being too near the timber. The pipe leading into the tin attached to the board was not fastened very secure."

"Was she worried?"

Andrew shrugged. "Said they'd been running things that way a long time."

Jack Phillips, his eyes stinging and the horrific stink of charred flesh in his gut, wanted nothing more than a chance to slip away to his Eliza. He felt suffocated, from the oppressive crowd, the morbid curiosity of the newcomers, the utter uselessness of all their efforts. The Luckey buggy stood by the gate, the barrel of soap and the axes beside it, all that remained of the family possessions. What was the good of plucking a tiny heap of bones from the ashes, just to bury in the ground?

Whispers of questions followed him as he pushed past throngs of people and crossed the yard to the lone apple tree behind the barn, seeking fresh air. Ahead of him, he caught sight of something white. Bending down, he snatched the object from the grass and held it in his palm. "Teeth!" His stomach lurched.

"Teeth! Whose teeth?" A crowd surged behind him. "Where'd they come from?"

"Look, they're clean and dry –"

"Just fell out of someone's mouth?"

"Anyone here lose his false teeth?" Nervous laughter.

He held the teeth out to the crowd. They were dry and yet cloying somehow, and made his skin crawl. He felt suddenly as if he had violated someone's private parts. "Might be evidence." In the crush he wasn't sure who took them from him.

Evidence. The word echoed through the group. He hardly dared to think of what.

The mob swept him along toward the gate, where Johnny

Luckey's pair was charging through, nostrils streaming, his cart rattling wildly behind them. Johnny leaped down before they had come to a full stop.

"Easy, boy!" Men grasped the reins.

"Done our best, Johnny."

"Weren't no use!"

"Take it easy, Johnny. Over here!"

There was silence while he walked over and stood looking down at the three soaking masses lined up on the grass, shrugging off comforting hands. "Minnie, too," he breathed.

"We've – we've a box here, Johnny. For – them."

"Christ! It can't be more than four feet long!"

A box four feet long. Hands strong and gentle helped load the bodies. Someone retched. Others closed their eyes, gritted their teeth and lifted. Women turned their heads away, all except Liza Ann, who watched her husband from the shadows. Plenty of time to go to him yet.

Jack Phillips was watching. "Liza Ann. If there's anything we can do –"

She turned and looked full into his eyes. "Thank you, Jack. All of you. I know you're exhausted."

"Exhausted," Andrew Parker agreed. "But who's going to sleep tonight?" He echoed the question that would keep them all awake. "What went on in there?"

* * *

It was almost dark when John Polk left Smith's Falls for his home on the third concession of Kitley Township. In his late thirties, he sported a trim brown moustache which gave him the air of a man much older. The cart horses he had bought the previous summer from Johnny Luckey set off at a brisk trot, as anxious as he for home. A day in Smith's Falls, haggling, loading feed, struggling to free cartwheels mired in the market yard's soft earth, had left him yearning for fresh country air. Tonight, however, the air was heavy with an acrid smell and the sky was haunted by a pale glow to the southwest as he headed down the Brockville road. Something was burning. Not just a grass fire.

Between Shane's schoolhouse and Lee's gate, going over a rise in the ground, he saw a man coming toward him, walking swiftly by the roadside hedge. He seemed to be wearing gaiter boots. Suddenly – so quickly Polk was not sure how it happened – the man was in the middle of the road, right beside his horses. "Evening," Polk said, startled. The stranger said nothing, staring hard at the horses and then at Polk as the cart passed. Locked in some strange, unnerving communion, they looked over their shoulders at each other. The stranger's eyes seemed to burn through the dusk. Like a mountain cat, Polk thought. The experience so disturbed him that he reigned in, turned around in his seat and watched as the stranger jumped a ditch, a light coloured parcel in his hand, and turned at a bend in the road.

John Polk saw himself as a civic-minded man, God fearing and plain spoken, given neither to bragging nor fabrication. Something's amiss, he said to himself, and I'm going to get to the bottom of it. Still shaken, he cracked his whip again and continued toward home. He had hardly pulled into his driveway when Ida called out that there was a fire at Luckeys'.

"Keep my supper warm," he ordered her. Without pausing, he turned his rig around. He'd seen Old Man Luckey at market just a few hours ago, holding up a couple of chickens by their feet. What could have happened?

By the time he arrived, the farmhouse was gutted. Hordes of onlookers were leaving, white-faced, but latecomers like himself were still arriving, full of questions. A box rested on Johnny Luckey's cart, horses hitched, ready to bear the load away. He recognized Parker and Daley and Phillips, their faces streaked with soot, and Johnny, head bowed, hunched in silent grief near his horses. Johnny's wife hovered close by.

He tied up his horses and ran over to a cluster of men standing at a polite distance from the mourners. "Strange thing," he heard one say. "Broad daylight and they none of them got out alive."

"If we'd come when we heard the screams," Phillips was saying, "we might've saved them. Must've been Minnie."

Everyone talked at once. "Don't blame yourself, boy."

"Don't blame us. No one's fault."

"You heard what Richards said. Someone did them in."

"Have to be a stranger."

"No strangers around here –"

"That traveller with red stockings –"

"Just a tinsmith."

"Stranger all the same. Anyone know his name?"

"Hold on." Polk broke through to the centre of the group. "I saw a stranger, heading toward Smith's Falls."

"Carrying a parcel?" A fellow he recognized as one of the Ronans sauntered toward the group. "I passed a man with a parcel. Bolton must've seen him, too. He was right ahead of me, coming down to Luckeys'"

"I saw that fellow this morning." A man named Moorhouse scraped his boot in the dirt as if looking for clues. "Wore dark clothes."

"And a white shirt," said Ronan. "I bade him goodnight and asked if he'd come far. He didn't even answer."

"I asked him if he knew where the fire was," a farmhand called out from the gate. "He said it was hay burning."

"Looked like a man who'd been up to some mischief. Didn't he strike you as strange?" Polk asked.

"Not an amiable man," Moorhouse said drily, stepping back to let Polk climb up on the cart and look in the box.

There was silence except for Polk's groan. Then Jack Phillips said, "That's all that's left of them."

Polk drew in his breath. "I'll get him."

"Who?"

"I don't know his name, but I'll find him. Who'll come with me?"

"Where?"

But Polk was already running to his cart. No one followed.

"Where are you going?"

"Smith's Falls." Polk leaped into his cart. Snatching his whip, he brought it down savagely on his horses. "To get Chief McGowan."

Chapter Seven

The sun burns through the autumn chill. A horse whinnies. A wind rears suddenly and yellow leaves scuttle across the brown mane of grasses. There is a whisper of smoke, a faint acridness, not of woodstoves lit for dinner or heating bathwater or easing chills in arthritic joints. Smoke from a different fire, something ominous, something –

Don't go in there don't go in there! Oh God OH GOD!

"Are you all right, man? You're pale as death!" Someone was shaking him, gently at first, then harder.

Faces swam in and out of crackling dry gloom. "Wh – where?"

"Doncha remember coming in?"

It seemed years ago. He'd come to the Palace Hotel in Smith's Falls because he was cold, his feet throbbed and he knew the slippers he'd bought at Gile's weren't made to last. Besides, he was hungry. And thirsty. Give his last nickel for a glass of whisky. He just didn't know where in hell to go. Didn't feel like hobbling out to the station, just to be told there wasn't another Ottawa train until morning.

He could still smell the fire. It rode on the fringes of the night air, like a name on the tip of the tongue or a dream teasing the memory at daybreak. A haystack burning, he *knew* it, he'd seen it with his own eyes, hadn't he, a haystack big as a house, and people running, running in all directions.

There was something about the hotel that reached out and took hold of him the way the Central Prison had. He felt stifled. His brain balked, like someone had clamped irons on his thoughts. The hotel was relatively new, but the walls were sooty behind the flickering sconces, the moosehead over the fireplace had a moth-eaten look, and a nearby sofa had a ridge of horsehairs spilling out below the arm rest, like a lopsided beard. A path was worn in the rug across the vestibule to the counter. He stopped inside the door. The man behind the counter turned from stuffing papers in a pigeonhole. Christ! Willis, the proprietor. "Evening, sir. Can I help you?"

He wiped his feet, shifting the parcel and boots he was carrying, and looked down at the oversize slippers, his blistered feet disappearing into them. The store clerk at Gile's hadn't glanced at him once, just went on entering figures in a ledger, pursing his lips when Charley asked for slippers like the ones in the window.

"Size?"

"Nine."

"Brown or black?"

"Don't matter."

He'd pointed to a rack of slippers that Charley inspected. "No nines here."

Bleating annoyance, the clerk had gone into a back room. "Just a ten in brown. Try them on?"

"Uh – no. No. I'll take 'em."

"Ninety cents, sir. Box?"

"Nope."

The clerk had plunked a dime in Charley's palm, tossed the dollar bill in a drawer, and picked up his pen.

Charley had limped out, still wearing the gaiter boots. Damn near pinch my toes off, he said to himself. Hell of a lot more painful than the boots he'd thrown away going down to Newbliss – when was it? Only hours ago? Sitting on a curb, he started to pull them off when he heard footsteps and whistling. They stopped alongside him.

"Don't take your boots off there, you'll stink up the whole town!" The fellow said it real familiar, like he knew Charley. Then he'd bent way over and even had the nerve to tip Charley's hat brim up and peer at him nose to nose. "Oh, sorry, mac, thought you was someone else." Charley heard him whistling as he went off down a side street.

How long ago was that? He'd walked the short distance toward the hotel across from the train station with no sense of time having passed. When he'd seen the proprietor he'd hovered just inside the door, afraid to step into the light. Willis knew him! Before he could decide what to do, Willis came around the counter and made straight for him.

Charley pulled down his hat brim and studied the rug where the pattern wore away into grey fibres flaked with mud. The smell of something burning was in his nostrils, in his bones.

"Got to make sure the door's shut," Willis said, passing him. "The fire's not drawing too well and we don't want to waste heat, do we." He satisfied himself that the door was snug and returned to the counter. "Come in, come in. Is it a room you're after?"

He doesn't recognize me! But it was dark by the door. He hesitated, shivering, watching flames lick feebly at stout logs. The moosehead cast a baleful eye on him. *Be careful!* Then flames leaped up with a roar and Willis grunted satisfaction. "No need to stand there, sir. Warm yourself at the fire, if you like. Sign in later."

"I – just came in to – I just wondered – could you direct me to the barber shop?"

"To the right. Behind the partition."

"Still open?"

"Of course."

Still he waited. If he crossed the room and passed Willis, would the man recognize him? *Don't do it*, the moose said. *Don't take any chances.*

"Where'd you say?"

Willis shot him a perplexed look over his spectacles. "There. Right behind me, man, to the right!" He turned with a sigh and began sorting mail.

The barbershop was larger than he expected, well lit and smelling of soap and bay rum. "Evening, sir." The barber raised his eyes briefly, then pressed a clump of grey hairs flat between index and second fingers and cut crisply. "Cut?"

"Shave." Charley removed his hat.

"Ah. Right, sir. Looks like the last fellow sheared your crown real good." He nodded toward a row of wooden chairs where a couple of oldtimers sat smoking. "S'all right," one of them assured Charley, drawing on a corn pipe. "We're just here for a chinwag."

They were all looking at him, he was certain of it, out of the corners of their eyes, sizing him up. He tucked the boots and parcel under his chair and tried to look unconcerned.

The barber whisked his customer's neck and snatched off his towel. Pocketing coins, he motioned to Charley.

An array of scissors and cutthroat razors winked from a tray on the counter. Charley could see the armbands holding sleeves rolled just above the elbow, dark hairs standing out on the barber's forearm, the shirt, spotless except for one tiny red drop just above the heart. Eyes closed, he heard the razor whip back and forth on leather, felt the foamy bristles dabbing his face with urgent wet kisses. Cold, they seemed, kisses from the grave. There was a pause while the barber called for hot water, and the sound of it splashing into a basin. Then the razor scraped downward with swift, sure strokes, slicing through the two-day stubble, along his jaw and down his throat over veins taut as a razor strop. He could imagine it cutting into his flesh, dripping blood, his blood, all over the towel that bound him, shroud-like, in his chair.

"Hear about the fire?" a rough voice said from the doorway.

"Been hearing about it all night." The barber paused, and Charley heard him dipping the razor into the basin, swishing it around. Waves of voices crashed against him as the men all started talking at once. The hot razor touched his left jaw and he jerked.

"Keep still, sir! Damn! D'you know how long it is since I nicked a customer?"

He felt styptic sting his cheek like a mosquito bite.

"You all right, sir? You're a trifle pale."

"Just – get on with it."

"A lot of the boys was puking their guts up out there. They say you couldn't recognize any one of them, skin all peeled off."

"I'll go over you again, sir. Quite a lot of stubble. Closer shave this time."

"And the girl. All that was left of her –"

"Hold on, sir! Sit back down! You ill?"

"He's looking peaked."

"Watch where you're going, fella!"

"See that? Walked right into the doorway!"

Oh God what is it what is it what is it –

"Get you a doctor?"

"Willis! Quick, get the doc!"

"Got to get back to my customers. Just let him rest a bit. Here, sir. Sit down."

"No. No doctor. Let me rest a – a bit." He was sitting on the sofa beneath the moosehead, surrounded by curious faces. In the mirror on the opposite wall, the moose's eyes shone in the light from the fire. *I done nothin'*, the moose said. *Strung me up anyways.*

"Sorry. Can't think what ails me."

"You're white as a sheet, man. Something you et?"

"Didn't eat nothing." He doubled over, hugging himself. "Oh, God, I'm dying. I know it. Dying for sure."

Willis's watch chain dangled from his vest as he bent to pat Charley's shoulder. "Been drinking, lad?"

Charley shook his head.

"Come on, own up, lad."

"Uh – just a glass of beer in the afternoon. Wouldn't account for the way I feel." He dabbed at his forehead with a handkerchief, wincing as he touched the bruise. "A train. I got to catch the Ottawa train."

"Nothing till morning, I'm afraid. Two then."

"The earliest."

"Four-thirty-five." Willis straightened up and regarded him thoughtfully. "Why not take a room, now. Only a dollar."

The onlookers drifted away as Charley rose and stumbled to the counter.

"I got to be on the first train."

The proprietor's pen was poised over the register. "I'll see that you're called. Name?"

"Is there – could I get a drink here? A whisky, maybe?"

"Sorry, lad. Saturday night, you know. Shall I enter your name for you? You're in no condition." The pen hovered. "Didn't catch that. Charley –?"

Another murmur from Charley. Frowning, Willis cupped his hand about his ear, then shrugged and wrote "Charles Kingston" in a hasty scrawl. He took a key from a hook behind him. "Number four. Upstairs on your right."

* * *

"Your name is Kingston?" In the dim light of number four, Police Chief Robert Alexander McGowan towered over him, flanked by William Willis and Corbett the marblecutter. Charley sat on the side of his bed in his underwear.

"Kingsley. I said – Kingsley."

McGowan's booming Irish brogue filled the room. "These men are my witnesses, young fella. I've another in the hall, someone who can identify you as a suspicious character he saw this evening. They've come and dragged me away from band practice with my nighthawk friends and that's serious business!" His witnesses stood in wooden silence, Corbett holding the chief's concertina.

"Now. Would you be telling us where you spent Saturday?"

"Saturday?"

"Yesterday, man. We're into Sunday now. Almost two a.m.!" He waited. "Speak up, lad. Were you out in the country?"

"No."

"Were you out on the road running to Fairfield?"

"No!"

McGowan sighed. "Were you out on the Brockville road?"

Charley stared at his feet. "Out – visiting. An uncle."

"Name of?"

"Turner. John Turner."

McGowan snorted. "I been chief here for four years. I guess I'd know if there was a John Turner in Kitley." He seized Charley's pants from the bedpost and began searching the pockets.

"He – he lives in Bastard Township."

Willis moved closer. "What part?"

Charley stole a glance at him and gestured vaguely. "I – I'm not acquainted with the place."

"Doesn't make sense," McGowan muttered, crossing to the door. "You know a family name of Luckey? Polk! Come in here!"

"Sir! I try to run a quiet, respectable establishment here!"

"Relax, Willis. Polk, this the fellow you saw?"

John Polk stood stiffly in the doorway, hat in hand while Charley gaped at him. The fellow with Johnny's horses! Christ, what was he doing here?

"Would you be knowing any Turners in Bastard, Polk?"

"Never."

"You know Bastard?"

"Like the back of my hand. Crawling with Polks, no Turners, I'd stake my life on it."

"This the man you saw?"

"It is. Out by the schoolhouse."

"Young man, tell me God's truth, now. Is it a fire you were watching?" McGowan spread the contents of Charley's pockets on a small night table. "Watch chain, train ticket to Carleton Place, bills and silver." He looked up. "Can't hear you!"

"I said – yes."

"You saw the fire. Didn't go to help?"

"It was a haystack burning. I – thought."

In silence they watched McGowan count. "Twenty-four dollars in bills and one-seventy-five in change. Quite a lot to be carrying around. Are you certain, sir, you don't know the Luckeys?" He opened a small white parcel propped against the bedpost and poked at its contents. "Underwear. Well, sir?"

Charley raised his hand in resignation. "All right, boys. I'll tell you why I gave the wrong name." He nodded at Willis. "I didn't want you to recognize me."

Willis stared at him blankly.

"I'm Charley. *You* know. Charley Luckey."

McGowan slowly lowered the parcel to the bed. "Charley L – Jesus-Mary-and-Joseph! Charley Luckey!" He looked from Polk to Willis, saw the shock on their faces. "And – you didn't go to see your folks?"

"I – was ashamed. I stayed in the bush all day."

Willis pressed his fingertips to his temples. "But, man, they were burning to death. D'you mean to say –"

"I'd – just got out of the Central."

"I'll do the asking, Willis. Police matter. All right, let's get some answers. Where'd you get this money?"

"Prison. I had thirty dollars when I left."

"And the footwear standing in the corner there?"

"I bought the slippers tonight. Here in Smith's Falls. And the socks. My feet were hurting."

But it was the pair of buff gaiter boots that McGowan picked up. "These. Where'd they come from?"

"Toronto. I got them in Toronto."

"All right. Now, once again, where did you spend Saturday?"

"In the bush." He saw Polk retreat to the hall as McGowan began pacing. "I did."

"I been a policeman from me eighteenth birthday. Five years with the Royal Irish Constabulary. A good stint as detective with the A.G.'s department. Me only thirty-four and a lifetime already of upholding the law. And I swear –" He looked around to gauge his audience's reaction. "I swear, boys, I never, never did see nor hear the likes of this.

You're telling me, Charley Luckey, that you saw your father's house burning and never went near it?"

Charley pulled in his shoulders, pressed a fist to his forehead, his nose. *Something's burning –*

"Was there not love enough in your heart, man, for you to go and help your father when you saw the fire?" He seized Charley by the shoulders, shook him hard and stepped back, wiping his hands on a handkerchief he took from a pocket. "Why go all the way out there to spend the day in the bush?"

Charley sat silent, staring into space.

Oh God –

When he spoke his voice was the faintest of whispers. "To kill time."

McGowan took a pair of handcuffs from his pocket. "Charley Luckey, I'm arresting you for murder."

ENTR'ACTE

Cornwall, November 1892

"Just jerk 'em in the air, do you?" Sheriff McIntyre held the lantern over the odd-looking contraption, shining it on the gentleman's hands.

"Quick, clean and painless. He stands on the ground – no steps to climb, all wobbly-kneed." The man who called himself Thomas Ratley or J.R. Radclive, depending on his sphere of activity and the company he was keeping, puffed out his chest. "My invention!" He descended the ladder where he had been checking the iron pin which secured the chain holding the 350-pound weight in place. He shook the two uprights vigorously, grunting satisfaction. "Want a demonstration?" Squinting, he jabbed a cold finger at the side of the sheriff's neck. "That's about where I place the knot."

"No offence." The man's just doing his job, the sheriff reminded himself. Don't antagonize him. But the memory of the trouble the hangman had put him to, to say nothing of the expense, rankled. The sheriff went by the book. The Attorney General's department had decreed last January that Radclive be appointed to carry out "due and proper execution of capital sentences" for the Dominion of Canada. Even if he had not carefully filed away his copy of the order-in-council, the sheriff could hardly have been unaware of the appointment, with the newspapers trumpeting it about that $700 a year would be paid to the "high salaried life destroyer."

As soon as he'd known Slavin was to swing, McIntyre had attempted to contact the executioner. After fruitless inquiries, he'd sent his deputy to Toronto, where he'd gone straight to the Sunnyside Boat Club, only to learn that Radclive had been fired from his job there. Two of the trustees had got up a petition. Put them off their feed, they claimed, the hangman

66

bringing in their trays. The deputy then embarked on a still hunt, which he managed to spin out for several days before finding his quarry and settling arrangements. That had been six weeks ago. The hangman had arrived last Tuesday, three days early, and put up at the best hotel in Cornwall, at public expense. "I've just despatched a gentleman in New Brunswick," he'd explained. "No point in going home to Toronto only to turn around and come back." He'd charged a whopping bill at the taverns, entertaining local roisterers with gruesome details of his exploits.

"Sad business, sending Slavin to Kingdom Come," the sheriff said. "But how else is justice to be served? Let him out, he'd do the same thing again."

"Killed a bobby, didn't he?"

"What? Oh – yes. And the other day he hit gaoler McDonnell a terrible blow on the head, trying to escape."

Radclive blew on his hands. "I expect I'd act the same way, with the end near." He tightened the rope to the pulley and gave it a short tug. "Just a lad, hardly into long pants. He's thinking of all the things he hasn't done. Foreign lands to conquer, spirits to quaff, wenches –"

"He pounded his cell door with his boots until two a.m., yelling nonsense like, 'What's the good of being tough unless you're good and tough?' His last hours would have been better spent in prayers and confession –"

"Or a good slug of whisky."

The sheriff resisted the temptation to expound on intemperance, at the same time marvelling at the steadiness of the executioner's hands. The man had spent the night lurching from one tavern to the next and McIntyre had had to request overtime police patrols to control the curious crowds that followed him down the street. "Should've brought me a wire cage," Radclive had joked to the constables. "I could sell tickets. Make a hell of a lot more brass that way than I will for despatching Slavin!" Doffing his hat to the onlookers, he clicked his heels together and gestured extravagantly. "Step right up, ladies and gentlemen! More fun than a Punch and Judy show!"

"You've a fine town here, many a good watering house."

The sheriff murmured assent, wondering if Radclive had seen the papers. The Ottawa Journal *had sneered at his promenading the streets with a chip on his shoulder just waiting for someone to knock it off. The* Cornwall Freeholder *had accused him of glorying in his business, citing the revolver he brandished publicly. The* Ottawa Citizen *had sniffed that* it was to be hoped he would keep himself more secluded in future when about to engage in a judicial killing.

"No chance for a reprieve for this one?"

"None. A reprieve would mean he'd be back on the streets in no time, up to his old tricks. At best a common thief."

"At worst?"

"A murderer twice over, probably."

Radclive was kneeling by his equipment box, honing the knife that would cut the rope. "Or a hangman. We're all hangmen, given the right circumstances."

"Circumstances?"

"Bellies to fill. A fire to be stoked, to thaw the chilblains."

"But, surely, man, there are other jobs –"

"Right you are, sir. Right indeed."

"Why then –"

"Someone has to do this job. You won't do it." The hangman glanced up, his gaze as steady as his hands. "The judge won't do it. Not a man on the jury would, either."

The light was spreading behind the rooftops. "It's almost time to bring him out," the sheriff said. "Do you have everything you need? What about your mask?"

"Mask?" Radclive snorted. "Does a judge wear a mask to pronounce sentence? Does a jury when they bring in the verdict?" In the half light his grin was diabolical as he jerked the short rope, dislodging the pin anchoring the chain. The weight dropped with a shuddering crash, denting the frozen ground. "All in working order, sir. We're ready."

Alone, he drew the weight up into place again, secured it, adjusted the rope and waited, hunched in his Prince Albert coat. A light burned in the gaolhouse, but all was quiet. He'd met Slavin on his arrival, a scrappy blighter who looked as if no amount of scrubbing would get him clean. Grime clogged every pore, dust greyed his greasy hair. Perspiration rotted the fibres of his clothes. The prisoner had been tossing a bible after a frocked gentleman, screaming, "You might as well take a chance at turning an iron bar into a ham sandwich as try to convert me!" The clergyman had scuttled past as the guard swung the cell door open. Radclive had bobbed inside, extending a hand. "Good-day, sir! I'm the man who's come to relieve you of the troubles of this world."

"I know who you are! Birchall's murderer!" Slavin had kicked at his *slop pail, sending its contents spattering up the wall. Then he stood, fists cocked, snarling like a dog at bay.*

Radclive had pulled a cigar from his waistcoat pocket and appraised his adversary. Before him stood a younger self. He could have belonged, as Radclive had, to the vast hordes of weavers, fellmongers, smockfrock makers and rag and bone men that had perched on the edge of starvation in the English midlands a generation ago. Radclive bit the end off his cigar and gestured to the guard, keeping his eyes on the prisoner. "Got a lucifer, mate?" He remembered the row of thatched ironstone tenements in Horsepool Lane, the single outdoor privy serving a dozen families, spreading diseases that carried off half the nippers before they were school age. They had shared their meagre quarters with a quill winder and a scrofulous old maltster. When it rained, effluvia from the pigsties by the back door lapped about their feet while they ate, seeped under their beds while they slept. "I was taken from school at the age of ten and sent out to carry a basket," his father had told him. He'd been a harsh, hard-drinking man, quick with the birch. "None of this hanging about, book learning, like a rich man's son. Just learn your sums. I'll put you to work." His father had worked his way up: porter, fruiterer, grocer, a man of some standing in the wretched community. And he himself, official executioner, stand-in for the Minister of Justice, had lingered in school, more out of defiance than ambition, like the rich man's son his father despised. Fourteen he'd been when he finally left, able to speak and write like a gentleman.

The little band approached across the gaol yard: sheriff in full regalia, gaoler, handcuffed prisoner, coroner. A moment or two and Slavin stood before him, hair slicked down, spotless shirt, pants with knifelike crease. "Dyin's a good way to get a new suit of clothes," he said, his mouth twisting into a lopsided smile. He watched as the hangman took a short rope from his box and began to pinion his knees. "I'm ready. More nerve than Birchall, that's me." Squaring his shoulders, betraying no sign of chill, he nodded to each official in turn. "Goodbye, gentlemen. Let 'er go."

Radclive paused, fingers spreading the black cap from within. One twist of the rope of fate and they would have changed places, he the condemned killer, Slavin the man paid to murder him. "I'm sorry to have to do this," he said.

Slavin looked him boldly in the eye. "I'm sorry, too," he said. "But I'd still rather be in my shoes than yours."

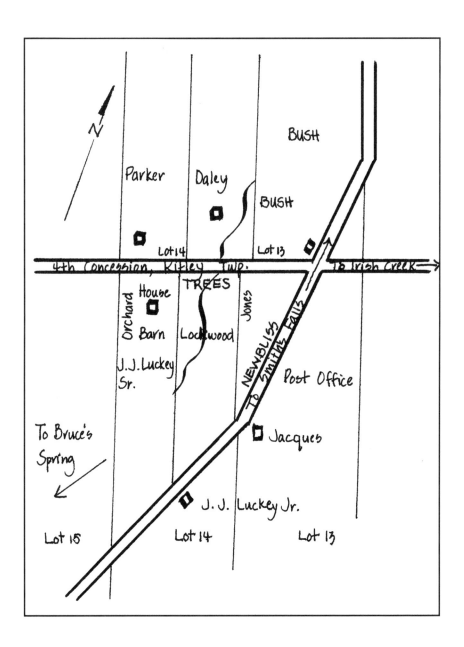

Part II
THE INQUEST

Again I listen, afraid, and bear arms to defend this victim,
since a small discovery of whispers

Chapter One

"I had no idea who he was, of course." John Polk fastened the top button of his woollen jacket, watching his words puff forth and vanish. Ahead of him there was no answer but the cracking of twigs and crunching of dead undergrowth as Chief McGowan forged through the thicket. An acre of swamp lay between them and the sugar bush behind the Luckey farm. Here the smell of the fire lingered like an afterthought, mingling with rotting leaves that shored up bleached stumps and scabbed over lacerated patches of ground, and the mud that had hardened into amorphous masses as the temperature dropped overnight.

"I guess I wouldn't have had any choice if I had recognized him. I did my duty, you understand, same as anyone would." He was aware of the heavy, frosted block of moustache on his upper lip compressing his words, making them distant and sanctimonious.

A light tendril of mist curled about McGowan's boots as he half turned without slackening his pace. "Don't forget to watch where you're stepping, Mr Polk, sir. Footprints, y'know. Mustn't step in them. Got to match the boots to 'em." He waved a large jute sack and trudged onward, face reddened beneath his peaked navy cap, ulster billowing out behind him.

"I feel sorry for young John and his family," Polk continued. "But what could I do?" A lock of wavy hair fell over his forehead as he stumbled and grasped a branch laden with shrivelled berries.

McGowan ignored him, gesturing with his free hand. "That tree.

Isn't that about where he would've stood?" He crashed through the brush, a bear on the scent of prey, muttering expletives as his spotless Irish frieze caught on thorns. Polk, wiry and fit, dodged the offending bushes and arrived at the tree a step behind him.

"Careful, Polk! Someone's stood here a while, leaned against the tree, perhaps."

"He'd have a clear view of the house from here."

"Trouble with these prints, he's walked over and over them. Hard to get a solitary one."

"What about the fence? Isn't that where he said he sat watching the fire?" Polk set off toward a low rail fence. "About forty paces, wouldn't you say?"

"You'll have to veer more to the left, if you want to find a spot where he'd have a view of the fire, no trees in the way."

Polk nodded. Did the man think he was an idiot? He respected the chief's uniform, and his energy and dedication, but it wasn't easy to forget that he could be an idler when he chose, giving the illusion of authority by stating the obvious and issuing hollow orders. A cross between a peacock and a buffoon at times, carrying a duster so he could wipe off a bench before lowering his newly-uniformed haunches to it, wrapping himself in that great trailing coat in early fall. Polk fought down his annoyance. "That would make it about here."

"Right you are. There's a beaut." Here the soil was softer, a fine, dark sand. Here ragweed and dandelion grew among the sugar maples, along with remnants of milkweed and the occasional mauve wild aster. McGowan squatted, pulling a buff gaiter boot from the sack and setting it carefully into the indentation. "As God's my witness, this is it. Here's the boot. That's the footprint. When he made it, the ground was still damp from Friday's rain. Now the print is nicely set by last night's chill and undisturbed by the fools who swarmed over the farmyard."

Polk knelt on one knee. "Same number of impressions from the screw nails. Five on the outside and four on the inside."

McGowan thrust the boot at his companion, fishing in the sack with his free hand until he located a tape measure. "Facing toward the house. We've got him, Polk. We've got our man. We know he stood here and watched the house burn."

"That doesn't make him a murderer."

McGowan stared at Polk in disbelief. "Who was all for having him arrested? Who combed Smith's Falls for me last night, breaking up band practice, me in the middle of my solo –" He broke off at Polk's expression. The fellow's receding chin positively quivered! "With good cause, of course. You did the right thing."

"If he was guilty, why wouldn't he run away? Keep running?"

"Where to? You can't outrun the law. Suppose he fled outside my jurisdiction? Murray's boys would run him down. Months, years, but they'd do it." The men stared at each other over the footprint; Polk could see that, for all his bluff and frippery, McGowan had a gaze that was clear and cold. "Not going soft on me, are you, Polk?"

"I – don't know what to think. Young Charley's saying he was afraid to come home after being in gaol. It is possible – just possible, Chief – that he did spend the day here in the bush, as he says."

"And didn't go to help when he saw the fire?"

Polk sighed, like a pedlar bent under an unbearable load. "You're right. I can't account for it, nor for his behaviour when I saw him on the road. Of all the strange things that happened, that bothers me most. There was something about that moment that made my hackles rise. But the family –"

"Hold the bloody boot still, man. Sole up." McGowan stretched the tape from toe to heel, groped for a notebook in the folds of his coat and made a notation with a stubby pencil. He measured the foot and wrote again. "Ten and a half inches. Perfect match. There's the proof!" He returned the boot to the sack and clapped Polk on the shoulder as they stood up. "Only you and God are my witnesses, Polk, and since God isn't likely to testify, you'll have to." He offered his pencil. "D'you want to write down the measurements so you'll remember?"

Not given to blasphemy, Polk bit back the suggestion that God be subpoenaed. "I'll remember." He smiled faintly as the chief licked the tip of his pencil and carefully printed "Oct. 8, 1892 – 200 yds. from house" above the figures. He knew exactly when the chief had been presented with his first little black notebook. November '90, after his scandalous dismissal and rehiring that divided the municipal council – the whole town, in fact – into two camps, one for the chief and one against.

First there'd been whispers about his frequenting local hotels for purposes other than upholding the law; then there'd been rumblings about his negligence in submitting written reports and accounts.

Lastly, there'd been widespread consternation over the amount of property he'd acquired in the short time he'd been in town.

Town council fired McGowan and, like schoolboys pooling allowances for a treat, had raided reservoirs set aside for granolithic sidewalks and incandescent lighting to hire an inventor-turned-policeman from Hamilton. That had been in May 1890. The corporational romance lasted all of four months, until Chief Vernon ran afoul of the mayor, packed and departed, muttering, "Doughheads!" Laughter still echoed around the countryside.

Polk, seeing no humour in the episode, resisted taking sides. The hoteliers, who carried on a running battle with the councillors, had been quick to start a draft-McGowan movement, resulting in McGowan's triumph over seventy-eight job applicants and the resignation of two bitterly opposing councillors. Three hotelkeepers had escorted McGowan from his new detective agency to the Smith's Falls town hall. There a disorderly meeting, replete with catcalls and spitballs, had culminated at midnight in a rousing cheer as McGowan was hoisted to his supporters' shoulders and paraded down Beckwith Street to the watering house of his choice. Laughter, singing and the strains of "Oh, Susannah!" rendered on a concertina wafted across Smith's Falls until daybreak.

Polk, temperance himself, had to admire the Chief's zest for life, his capacity for round-the-clock activities and hail-fellow-well-met air. Shortly after his rehiring, McGowan had been formally presented by the mayor with a special case-record book. To the council's delight, he began religiously entering details of all observations, expenses and skirmishes and could be counted on to pore over his notes whenever consulted, in or out of court. He had cleaned up Smith's Falls to the general satisfaction of the local paper, which no longer published dire predictions that the town would soon be run by railroaders. He put the run on Roumanian gypsies who swooped down on the community each July, kept doorsills and window ledges along Beckwith Street free of loafers, monitored the market's weigh scales and was duly reported to have surrounded (single-handed) a Montague farmer who was driving his horses on the sidewalk one November night.

If he occasionally used colourful language or tortured the Queen's English or socialized after hours, officials were willing to look the other way. After all, he'd to taken his old job back without a pay raise, giving the lie to rumours that his short-lived stint as a private investigator had been a resounding success.

"Damn!" Reaching down, McGowan pulled a handful of tiny, flat red burrs from the cuff of his pantleg. "Watch it, Polk! They're all up your backside!" The Chief took a clean, pressed handkerchief from a pocket, dropped a handful of burrs into it and folded it carefully. "I noticed some burrs on the prisoner's clothes. Sim-yew-lar, I'm sure. This could clinch it, Polk, the burrs along with the footprint."

The sun was now bright and he shielded his eyes as he looked toward the south. "Can't see Johnny's house from here. I haven't approached the family. Thought it best to give them a few hours' peace. But I understand the daughter, Miss Minnie, came across the fields from her brother's farm yesterday afternoon. Could she have passed through here, d'you think?"

"She'd have gone further east a little, through Lockwood's property. There's a better path there."

"Then she'd have crossed her father's yard –" McGowan wheeled around – "See that apple tree, not far from the barn? She'd have crossed over to her father's property there, passing the tree."

"Ah. Where Phillips found the teeth."

"Exactly."

They retraced their steps through the bracken toward the smoking ruins where a crowd had gathered. McGowan paused to give orders to a constable at the edge of the clearing. "Don't let anybody wander back there by the tree and fence, see? I want it kept unmolested, if you know what I mean, until the government detective shows up."

"Yes, sir. When will that be, sir?"

"Some time Tuesday. I'll wager it'll be Billy Greer. He knows the territory. Spent three months in Smith's Falls in '88, trapping two firebrands during the Scott Act trouble."

Polk hovered behind the officers, giving a backward glance at the swamp, where the last vestiges of mist were disappearing. "I remember the barn burnings," he said. "Undercover man, Greer. Worked in a carpenter's shop for three months in town. Not a soul knew he was a policeman before the trial."

McGowan grunted. "None better, except perhaps Murray himself. You must have followed the Birchall case, back in '90. Greer and Murray hacked their way through a bog far bigger and worse than the one out back here. Brought the body out."

Polk shuddered, watching ghostly fingers of mist clutch a nearby log. "It was front page news for weeks. I recall walking down Yonge Street in Toronto just after they found the body. Some of the stores had pretty gruesome window displays. Like pieces of the tree stump the victim's arm had rested on."

"They'll not be making a circus out of this case," McGowan said. "At least, not as long as I'm in charge."

"You have to hand it over?"

"The murders took place in Leeds County. Brockville's jurisdiction. If Charley'd been arrested at the scene of the crime, we'd have nothing to do with it. As things stand, the inquest testimony will be given here on Wednesday, in McCrum's blacksmith shop at Irish Creek. But any trial will have to be held in Brockville."

"But all the witnesses are in Kitley and Smith's Falls."

"Makes no difference. They'll be paid to travel to court – a pittance, probably."

"Is Greer the kind of man to get a confession out of Charley?"

"I started as Chief in Smith's Falls in the fall of '88. Just missed the firebrands' trial. But I knew him before, when we were both on special assignments for the A.G. They moved him to Toronto and took him on full time, as Murray's assistant. McGowan brushed his arm, shedding invisible burrs. "You can be sure of one thing. He'll get a confession out of Luckey, even if he has to do it by deceit. He'll want to talk to both of us as soon as he gets here."

"I'll certainly testify at the inquest."

"We've got him cold, but unless he confesses, there'll be a long trial, too."

The sun was strong now and Polk could feel beads of dampness on his moustache. "You can count on me to do my duty as a witness."

"Juror, too."

"What? Come now, Chief, I can't be both!"

"I need a strong inquest jury. I've been up all night, man! Down on my knees, going over the grounds. Knocking on doors, getting statements. I knew no one was sleeping, man! I've talked to scores of people." He bent suddenly, picked up a fresh wood chip and tossed it away in disgust. "You see? Evidence! I'll be searching for it in my sleep, if I ever get any! I'm doing my part, and do you know how many men have volunteered to serve on the jury?" He held his hand up, thumb and forefinger joined in a circle. "Everyone has something to say until

I mention jury. It's like they think I've dropped in on them to indulge in a bit of idle gossip. They say, 'Yes, I was acquainted with the victims – shame, isn't it?' Or, 'Oh, of course I saw the fire.' They'll admit they saw Charley on the road, or the tinsmith with red socks, like it makes them members of an ex-clew-sive club. Mention jury, though, and they clam up. They're threshing, or there's a barn-raising in Bastard or a church-fixing bee in Toledo. One fellow even went so far as to say he couldn't serve because his wife was having a baby! How's that for an excuse!" McGowan threw back his head and laughed.

Polk remained unsmiling. "The Luckeys are well-known. When people see what happened to a family much like their own, living in the same circumstances, worshipping at the same church, it's almost as if they're being asked to reveal family secrets, or betray a relative's trust. It's a brotherhood of sorts."

McGowan shifted the sack, brushing stray threads of jute from the sleeve of his ulster. "Maybe so. But I advise them to view the bodies if they haven't already. Smell the scorched, rotting flesh, put their hands on it, lift up all that's left of what used to be the body of a grown man or woman. Many of them won't keep their breakfasts down! Then I put all the facts before them – Charley's nice little vacation at the Central and how, the minute he gets out, he comes straight home, looking for trouble. I explain about the boots, how they've got to be his father's, since Charley left his own on the road. Last of all, I point out how he watched the fire and never went to help. That alone is an admission of guilt, if you ask me."

Polk resisted the impulse to comment that no one needed to ask the Chief's opinion. "I guess Johnny'd be afraid it would ruin his children's lives, to say nothing of the effect on his business."

"Don't fuss so much, man! You act guiltier than young Luckey. You're a hero! We've got this case all sewn up, you and I, so that all that detective from Toronto has to do is bring the rope to hang him."

Polk brightened, marvelling at how easy it was to fall under the Chief's spell. "Is an inquest really necessary, then?"

McGowan stared at his companion. "It's the law, sir! Any death not from natural causes, no apparent reason." He squinted in mock incredulity.

"But when we already know charges should be laid?"

McGowan snapped a dry hollow stem beside him and rubbed the powdery residue between his fingers. "But we don't know how they died, do we. Were they killed by the fire, or did he strike them down first? We may never know, unless he tells us."

"Does it matter how he killed them, as long as we know he did?"

"Probably not. We feel it in our hearts –" He thumped his chest. "In our hearts, Polk, don't we, that he's guilty of some misdeed, and that misdeed caused the deaths of three people. But that's not good enough for the law. The law's going to poke and worry at the case, like you or I at a wood fire that won't quite catch, until every piece is in its place and bursting forth with all the answers. That way they assure everyone that they won't be hanging an innocent man. So you see, the post mortem, the inquest, the trial – just so much fancy window dressing designed to confirm what we already know."

As they started across the barnyard, Polk was amused to see McGowan assume his public image of authority. A consummate showman, towering over every other man, hailing friends and waving away reporters with extravagant swirls of his ulster. "Morning, Parker, Daley. Get any sleep last night? Nor did I. You! Young man, you're from the *Toronto Mail*? Didn't take you long to get here. Did ye sprout wings and fly?"

Women, gloved and bonneted, talked in hushed tones. Men, some still in yesterday's blackened workclothes, shifted planks and combed through the rubble. A handful of older men, Sunday-garbed, drew on their pipes and offered casual advice. Children played tag about the barn. Reporters hovered, listening on the fringes of conversations, pencils poised.

McGowan rushed to grasp the edge of a table being hauled from the cellar's mangled heap of chairs, bottles, jars, kitchen utensils and bins of burnt potatoes. "Look at this, Polk. An entire winter's supply, enough to feed Agnes and the kiddies from now till April! Maybe those who won't offer themselves for jury duty out of respect for the victims might be persuaded by the sobering thought of all that waste. Attention, everyone!" He set down his cargo. "I'm looking for jurors for tomorrow's inquest. Don't all volunteer at once!"

Polk shrank into the background, awed by McGowan's sudden patience as the crowd tried to deflect him from his demands. The Chief agreed with Jonas Bruce that yes, he believed Charley was the best worker Jonas ever had, and no, perhaps they didn't have absolute proof of murder; he assured two boys that the flimsy stick they had found was not the murder weapon; and he listened intently while

Martin Mercier related how Charley smashed up sap buckets at Johnny's two years ago.

"He is telling that his brother does not use him square," the sallow, hollow-eyed Mercier said. "He say he pay them back if he ever returns."

McGowan pulled out his notebook. "Pay them back, the whole family?"

Mercier shrugged, holding his hands out, palms up. "*Je ne sais pas*, Chief. But I remember – I am trying to – what do you say? – pacify him, but he say his family they do not own him any more, even as a friend."

"He could hardly blame the old man for a quarrel about sap buckets."

"*Mon Dieu*, he is not quarrelling with his father. His father he see him later that day and they talk very friendly."

Polk was edging toward his cart when a caravan of rigs arrived in a cloud of dust, horses' flanks steaming. Mayor Frost of Smith's Falls, the eye of the storm, leaped from the lead wagon. "I just want to see for myself, before church," he boomed, adjusting a small white flower in his buttonhole. "Continue, gentlemen. I'll just poke about on my own." Setting off with his entourage in the direction of the apple tree near the barn, he gave a running commentary in his basso profundo. "Ahead, to our right, is the tree where young Phillips found the teeth. Look, now!" He bent slightly, mindful of his expensive suit. "There's a slight discolouration here, in the grass. Could be blood. Upon my word, it is blood, or I'm a Dutchman! McGowan, make sure you write this down."

McGowan gritted his teeth. "Done, sir."

"Looks like I'll have to forego church. First time in years." The mayor drew himself up to his full six feet three inches. "I'll be at the lockup, McGowan, if anyone's asking. I'll get young Luckey to confess if anyone can."

"What makes you think he'll talk to you, sir?"

"You'll see. I'll trick him if I have to." He stumped toward his buggy, waving a cigar and followed by his supporters.

McGowan was quiet, writing in his notebook. "How many men would you say were here right now, Polk?"

Polk counted. "Eighteen."

"Did you count yourself?"

Polk shook his head.

"Nineteen, Polk. Nineteen good men and true." The Chief stepped forward and raised his hand. "All right. Parker, Daley. Ferguson, Coad, Murphy. And the rest of you. You're my jury. I've got all your names here, in my book. If any one of you forgets to show up tomorrow, ten a.m., at Johnny's, I'll clap you in the lockup so fast you won't know what happened to you!" He turned to Polk. "Dr Reeve won't be back for a few hours yet. I'm going to the Palace Hotel to talk to Willis again. What say we meet there for a wee libation?"

Polk frowned. "It's Sunday, Chief."

"What? Oh, so it is. So it is!" The Chief threw back his head and roared.

Who else, Polk thought, could get away with such irreverence on such a grave occasion? As he climbed into his buggy, he could hear McGowan driving off down the road, his laughter echoing on the crisp morning air.

Chapter Two

Victoria was in the haymow, hair lank and unribboned, knees drawn up to her chin, the piece of ecru lace clutched in her hand. She'd risen early, heard her father go out to water the horses. She'd dressed quickly, putting a starched white pinafore over her blue housedress, then watched from her bedroom window as Dr Reeve's phaeton rattled up the lane to pick her father up. They were going to the station at Irish Creek to meet Coroner Vaux and the Brockville police chief. Breakfast smells had risen from the kitchen as she tried on the blazer Aunt Minnie had made, waltzing in front of her mirror. Then she'd had another fit of weeping and put it away in the wardrobe, smoothing it carefully. She'd taken her treasure box, the one with the seashells glued to the top, from a drawer and removed a handful of newspaper clippings showing slender ladies of fashion with captions like, "an enormous bouf fancy on the upper arms, a clinging smallness to the hips, and a train." Underneath lay the little piece of lace, transferred from her mother's trunk the day before. There'd be no velvet dress for the holiday season. No celebrations. No parties. No Christmas. She couldn't see herself ever dancing, ever laughing again. The deaths hadn't just broken her heart, they'd set her apart from the rest of the world, forever.

Saturday evening she'd wondered where her parents were as dusk gathered, surprised that there was no supper on the table, no clatter of pans, no fire in any of the grates. Surprised especially because she thought she could smell something burning faintly, somewhere. Kindling for the woodstove, perhaps, or a hickory log in the back parlour fireplace.

It wasn't like her mother to leave her and Esley alone. Victoria went through the house, the woodshed, the barn with a mounting sense of alarm. Then she'd challenged her brother to a game of checkers, spinning it out as long as she could. She put out bread and jam, filled tumblers with milk, cut squares of her mother's johnny cake and poured maple syrup from a large tin can into bowls. The sticky sweetness comforted her at first, filled her with so much energy she challenged Esley to a game of hide-and-seek. Then, quite suddenly, she felt sick, and threw herself on the parlour sofa clutching her stomach. Much later, half asleep, she heard noises outside. Rising, she called Esley and peered through the window. Lanterns in the gloom, shadows alighting from buggies. Her mother came inside, followed by a horde of people. Neighbours whisked Esley off upstairs, offering to take her too. "I'm not going!" She had that prickly feeling in her scalp – was that what people meant when they said your hair stood on end?

"She's thirteen," her mother said. "She has to know."

So they told her. About the fire. The deaths. Not about Charley, she found out about him later. Charley, the one she never thought of as an uncle, more as a big brother, a tease. "See that girl walking by the gate?" he'd say. "I sat behind her in second book. Used to dip her pigtails in the inkwell." Or, "You know that farmer your father's meeting with? I tied his horses' tails together one day, out in pasture." She'd laughed along with him.

Her mother held her and they sobbed together. She resented the neighbours hovering, registering the grief that belonged to her family, memorizing it to pass on to others. "They mean to be kind," her mother whispered. Someone washed the dishes; someone else put the kettle on and got out teacups; a cousin asked where Esley's nightclothes were, he could stay with them.

After that no one made her go to bed. She thought at first she had suddenly become an adult, privy to their secrets and unquestioned wisdom. But no one listened when she spoke. No one made her wash or dress or eat throughout the next day. In fact, no one noticed her at all. Time had been suspended, the way it was in holiday season; but what was stranger – almost unheard of – routine was forgotten. All the orderliness and manners she had been raised to observe didn't seem important any more. Visitors arrived at odd hours and stayed long past the usual limits of politeness. Her mother didn't yawn or glance at the clock. They brought meatloaf and great steaming casseroles of scalloped potatoes and baked beans.

And all day Sunday, a steady parade of carts rolled by the house, sometimes stopping while a driver would get down to adjust a bridle or inspect a horseshoe, all the time eyeing the house. Faces would appear at windows of closed coaches, gloved hands wiping clean circles; children would pop up in wagons, shaking bits of hay from hair and clothes, like dogs shedding water after a swim.

This morning, when she'd gone downstairs, there'd been a semblance of order again. Her mother and Esley were sitting at the dining room table, a Sunday ritual although it was Monday; a white linen cloth was spread, one Aunt Minnie had embroidered with daisies; silver was laid for four, carved wooden rings held starched serviettes. Esley was stirring his oatmeal round and round, looking as if he was bursting with questions he didn't dare ask. Her mother sat over her oatmeal, undisturbed in its bowl. Her hand was resting on the table, extended toward a cream jug, as if she'd forgotten what she was reaching for. Across from her, at her father's place, a boiled egg, topped and untouched, sat in its glass cup, a dribble of yolk congealed on the side. Her father wasn't there.

"I'm not hungry," she said. "I'm going back to my room." Her mother nodded absently. She seemed to have aged overnight. She hadn't slept well, nobody had, because Victoria had had a nightmare and awakened the whole house. All she remembered now was that someone was coming after her with an axe. When she tried to run, her feet became mired in something heavy and sticky and she couldn't move them. She looked down and saw that the mirey, sticky stuff was blood.

Back in her room, she'd brushed her hair and studied her swollen, lumpy face in the mirror. Wrapping herself in the big, knitted shawl that had been Great-Grandmother Luckey's, she picked up the piece of lace and went out to the barn. Her father hadn't put the padlock on – he never did, and there would be no thieves sneaking into the barn today.

She had thought she'd be afraid to go in. It was light out, about eight o'clock, but from the doorway she was staring into gaping blackness. The spring wagon, just inside the door, gradually took shape as her eyes adjusted. She pulled the door to without closing it. Even though the box on the wagon was closed, the smell from it invaded the barn. She was reminded of the cured meat that hung from the rafters in their smokehouse. Even that wasn't as frightening as she had thought it would be. It blended with the odours of cattle and chickens and the rich, golden smell that hay has in autumn after it has absorbed all the summer sun it could possibly hold. There was a soft cluck in the darkness, a swish of a tail, a scratching of feeble claws. The two luminous eyes of the barn cat shone from a corner. A great sense of comfort washed over her: she knew suddenly that the barn was the right place for them. For one crazy moment she thought they should rest there forever, instead of in some chill, airless plot in the cemetery, amid unfamiliar bones.

She felt they knew she was here, knew what she was thinking; that, whatever it was that had happened on Saturday, they were peaceful now. She could never see them again as they had been in life, they would not be laid out in their coffins for everyone to see, as Great-Grandmother Luckey had been. No one would exclaim how natural they looked, lying with folded hands and waxen smiles. She would have to hold them in her memory.

Even their home was gone. She thought of the summer kitchen, where the windows were almost always open from spring thaw to Thanksgiving, with the scent of lilacs, summer rains and compost drifting in as the months changed; and the winter kitchen where cheese and raisins and apples crowded the smells of rust and ageing wood.

Her Grandmother Martha was part of those kitchens, with her stubby, blunt-nailed fingers, steely hair anchored into a pot-scrubber bun. "Let me curl your hair, Grandmother," she'd begged as a child. Once, just once, her grandmother had drawn two chairs up to the table side by side and sat down in one while Victoria clambered up onto the other with a comb and brush. She'd stayed there long enough for Victoria to remove the long hairpins and wind the coarse, straight strands around her fingers. "Let me use the tongs, Grandmother."

"Tongs? I don't have such a thing."

"Mother does. She heats them on the stove and makes ringlets in her hair. Then she does mine."

"Tongs is much too dangerous for children to play with."

"I know where Aunt Minnie keeps hers."

"Curls is sinful. A vanity. If the Lord wanted us to have ringlets, we'd have been born with them." She'd pushed her chair back and got up, pinning her hair as she went to the larder, turning at a sob from

Victoria. "Shush, now. Would you like some cheese?" She'd brought a dish to the table, lifted the lid and cut the usual paper-thin sliver. "Curls don't look right on me. I learned that a long time ago, when I was a young girl."

When she thought of her grandfather, it was the yard Victoria remembered. She could see him at the pump in summer, sloshing water on his grizzled head, thwacking his felt hat against his thigh until the barn dust puffed out in clouds. He was a clean, neat man, yet always he smelled of age and earth and things that grew in darkness. It wasn't an unpleasant smell; it was part of her grandfather. She had murky memories of him lifting her onto his cart and placing the reins in her hands. "Now, Victoria, you're the coachman. Giddap, Ben!" The old carthorse had clopped slowly through her grandfather's yard, barn to gate and back again, her grandfather walking alongside holding firmly to the bridle.

The wagon's shafts were facing the barn door. She moved around them and ran her fingers along the wagon's side. No dust. Her father was as meticulous as her grandfather. She could picture him on Saturday evening, waiting until the men who had helped him had left the barn, then wiping all around the wagon, lantern in one hand, cloth in the other, carefully picking up every last speck of dust, then lovingly running the duster over the box itself.

Victoria reached up, touched the box and felt her heart start to race. She could imagine them in there, not as they were now, but as they used to be. They pressed close, their thoughts pulsing through the wood, telling her it was all right. They were smiling – "gone to their reward," the neighbours would say – as they had said of Great-Grandmother Luckey. A beautiful phrase, a beautiful idea; she could see them in shining white robes, haloes blooming around their heads, Grandfather rewarded for his perfect attendance at church, Grandmother Martha for never giving in to the temptations of vanity, both of them praised by the angels for always saving everything and never wasting time. St. Peter would welcome them. She felt proud and humble, all at once.

She missed Aunt Minnie most of all, of course. The tears she shed were selfish, a mourning for herself, for the hole in her life that would always be there. There would be no Aunt Minnie to dress her with mustard plaster when she had the croup; help stitch her bridal gown, when the time came; or rock Victoria's babies as she had rocked little Edgar in Manitoba.

She climbed into the haymow, clutching the lace, tears falling hot on her hands as she hoisted herself from rung to rung. She sat for a long time in the gloom, looking down at the box, the hay rustling beneath her and catching in the loose yarn of her trailing shawl. The lace felt soft and cool against her face, as gentle as Aunt Minnie's fingertips stroking her cheek when she had a fever.

Resting her head on her knees, she inhaled the starchiness of her pinafore. "I'm never going to school again," she had told her mother last night. It was the first time she had spoken to anyone except Esley since the morning. She had been demoted to childhood again, shooed upstairs to look after her brother, not too young for responsibility but excluded from discussion. "Victoria, please. We'll talk about this another time." Her mother was sitting before the fireplace in the back parlour, easing back and forth rhythmically in her rocker. Her eyes were red-rimmed, the linen handkerchief in her lap damp.

"Did he do it, Mother?" The grownups knew so much they hadn't explained. "Tell me!"

Her mother stared into the ashes. "I don't know," she said finally. "We – just don't know. Oh, God."

She didn't ask where Victoria had heard the rumour. Victoria didn't tell her that she and Esley had been hiding on the stairs, peeking through the wooden posts at the grownups gathered in the front parlour that same Sunday afternoon.

Chief McGowan and Mayor Frost had arrived together by accident, stamping their feet on the mat, dwarfing her slim, tall father between them. She felt a rush of sympathy for her father, bowed and shrunken. She loved the way his hair swept up in wings at the sides. He would shake his head, run his fingers through his hair as if angry or bewildered, and his hair would slip right back into that same neat, glossy pattern.

Mayor Frost's voice rumbled over the other voices like cartwheels on gravel, something about earning the prisoner's trust.

The Chief's voice rose. "He confessed to you?"

"Admitted he sat on the fence watching the fire."

"We know that." A note of sarcasm.

"Look, McGowan, I'm just trying to help things along. I sat down with him on his bench for a talk, man to man, asked him how he could sit and watch his father's property destroyed."

"And?"

"No reply, I'm afraid. Just a great heaving of the chest." The mayor gave a rasping demonstration; Victoria imagined his broad chest rising and falling. "I said, 'Your father and step-mother and sister were burning up.' He said, no, that his sister was out west. His grandmother would be in the house. Has no one told –"

"Charley's pulling your leg, man. How could he help but know?"

Charley! A huge knot grew in Victoria's stomach. It pulled tighter and tighter until her knees felt weak and tears stung her eyes. She glanced at Esley. He seemed frozen, knuckles white as he clutched the post. How much did he understand?

The mayor rumbled on, about having to see for himself, getting the guard to fetch the gaiters. "Then I asked Charley to put them on and stand in them. They were much too short for him. He admitted they were too tight."

"And what does that prove, sir?"

"Well, now, they can't have been his boots, can they. John – I understand your father had a much smaller foot than Charley. Would you recognize his boots, d'you think?"

Victoria craned her neck. The chief was wearing the expression her father had the day Charley left. "Sir, I'm in charge of this investigation and I'll thank you to let me run it as I see fit!"

"Calm down, Chief. I'm not trying to tell you how to do your job. I just thought I'd better get to the lad before he gets confused by all the attention. When I left, the lockup was like a zoo. A whole lineup of nosey-parkers waiting to interrogate him."

"I'll put a stop to that!" McGowan touched his cap to her father and turned the doorknob.

"You'd be well advised to. I'll go along and help, if you like. My word carries weight, I daresay. Good day, John. Remember, if there's anything –" The mayor pumped her father's hand again and his footsteps echoed McGowan's across the porch. Their voices carried through the open door as her father watched them. "By the way, McGowan, have you examined the clothes yet?"

"Nothing for him to change into, sir."

"Could be blood on them. Surely –"

"He's not going anywhere, sir. Lots of time."

The rest of the afternoon had been like a dream, the crowd thinning, the pile of coats diminishing, someone lighting lamps. Her father looked tall again, ready to take command. "I've arranged for three coffins and a separate hearse for each. The service is set for Tuesday at St Andrews, with the Reverend Flemming assisted by pastors from Frankville and Merrickville. Sam will arrive tomorrow. He and I will lead the mourners." Murmurs of agreement.

Cramped and chilled, Victoria didn't dare move. She saw her father cross to the window and gesture to the flickering lanterns bobbing along the road. "We're part of the grand tour," he said. "Next they'll go to Father's, to pick over the rubble. Civic duty or Christian charity, apparently. A good many will come away disappointed, so they'll drive past here again, hoping for a glimpse of one of us. Some will wait until I go out to the barn and start calling through the fence. 'Mr Luckey, is it true your brother committed the murders?' 'How does it feel, Johnny, a brother for a murderer, especially when . . .'" His voice broke.

On the stairs, Victoria cringed; she wanted to cover her ears but was afraid she would miss something. Esley tore upstairs and slammed his bedroom door. She heard the singing of his bedsprings and pictured him hurling himself face down, burying his sobs in his pillow. She ought to go after him but she was paralysed.

"How can they be so cruel?" Her Aunt Sarah moved from the window into shadows. "Isn't there something that can be done to make the funeral private?"

Her father crossed the carpet in measured steps, back and forth, back and forth. "No. I've inquired."

"Grief should be a private thing. We should at least be allowed that dignity, for the sake of Father."

"It's no use, Sarah. We have Charley to thank for this. Our lives will never be the same. The whole world owns us now. We're tainted, as good as criminals ourselves."

"Nonsense, John!" Victoria was surprised at the sharpness in Ansley Stewart's voice. "You'll go on living your lives here, and be judged for your own actions. The Lord will see to that. Trust in the Lord, John."

Her father's face twisted into a wry smile. "You think so, Ansley? We'll never be anonymous again, anywhere."

Her mother's fingers were picking at her black skirt. "Will they be bringing him to the funeral?"

"No! I told McGowan that, no matter what instructions he got from Brockville, he was not to let Charley attend the funeral. He's not to release him or to bring him under guard. He swore he wouldn't."

"Thank God!" The exclamation echoed around the room. Only Ansley sat silent, white head bowed.

"Ansley. You don't agree?" Her father's feet clicked on hardwood, whispered across the carpet, clicked on wood again.

"John – we haven't talked to Charley. I know what you're thinking, but what if there's been some mistake? An accident, maybe. Perhaps he stayed in the bush, like he said. Charley was a prankster, not a murderer. If we abandon him, we'll divide the family. We'll have the whole countryside taking sides."

"No matter what we do that will happen."

"We have to hear what he has to say."

"Ansley, three people we all loved are dead." Her father gripped the mantelpiece, his face turned away from the others. "I won't talk to Charley. Whatever went on at Father's yesterday happened because of him. I know it. It just doesn't make sense for Charley to have come all the way out here to sit in the sugar bush."

"Life doesn't always make sense. Look, John – I know you don't want to be pressed on this, and I understand how you feel. But the fact is, Charley's being made sport of. It reflects on the whole family, don't you see? Half of Kitley has trooped to the lockup, poking and prodding at him as if he's some sort of rare animal on exhibit. Charley should be telling his story to us, or to a lawyer."

"I should hire a lawyer to protect him?" Her father's voice was bitter.

"Legal counsel could protect all of you."

"I can't see that. I'm sorry, but I can't contemplate helping Charley. Maybe he didn't intend to, but he murdered them!" Her father came abruptly into the hall and Victoria tripped up the stairs, wheeling out of sight on the landing just in time.

Now, in the haymow, she heard voices outside. The barn door swung wide and a rectangle of sunlight flashed on the floor. "I could have sworn I shut and padlocked the door after you and Vaux left yesterday, Henry." It was her father, with Dr Reeve and Chief McGowan.

"I scoured the countryside around Irish Creek for Hannah yesterday evening," McGowan was saying. "The fellow on the train. I thought he was a product of Charley's imagination until I came across his family finally. They claim he came home and left immediately and they had no idea where he was. So they said."

"Taken off again, has he?"

"Don't worry, we'll track him down."

"Everything's in order here, Johnny," Dr Reeve said. "Dr Vaux and Chief Rose from Brockville have gone ahead to your upstairs sitting room, to swear the inquest jurors in. You did a fine job, McGowan, rounding up enough men on short notice."

"Thank you, sir. Always happy to oblige. I understand Vaux announced there'll be no post mortem."

Dr Reeve pulled a handkerchief from a back pocket and blew his nose loudly. "Absolutely. If I thought it would tell us anything, I'd press for a post mortem. But it would be of no use whatever."

"What's this Vaux like?"

"Brit. Citified. Competent, but doesn't like to get his hands dirty, I suspect." He folded his handkerchief and replaced it in his pocket. "Social reformer. Campaigned to bar citizens from raising pigs within the town limits. Now he's got another bee in his bonnet. Thinks schoolchildren should receive smallpox vaccinations."

"Has he considered there could be other reasons for a post mortem, even if the results are inconclusive?"

"He thinks it's a waste of time. But you're right. If nothing else, it would protect the medical profession against future criticism. The trouble is, not enough is known about the condition of a body's organs after a fire. Congestion of the lungs could tell us something in the usual circumstances, but not when the organs have been exposed during the fire. I'm sorry, John, I know how distressing this must be for you, having to listen to all this." He clasped her father's arm awkwardly.

Father's got to stay strong, Victoria thought, so the rest of us can.

When the men left, she got down from the haymow to slip away, but it was too late. A stream of men was already pouring out of the house and across the yard, Andrew Parker in the lead. A scolding sea of hens parted before them. She recognized most of the men and could guess who the others were. The uniformed stranger matching strides with Chief McGowan would be the Chief from Brockville. The handsome, middle-aged man with the white buttonhole would be Dr Vaux. "We'll get the viewing over with as soon as possible," he was saying in pear-shaped tones. She saw the front door of the house bang shut behind the last man, the heavy black and purple wreath, newly hung, wobbling from the impact.

Trapped, Victoria slipped back up into the haymow. Post mortem. Jury. Inquest. What did these words mean? Inquest made her think of the Spanish Inquisition from history class. Torture – fingernails ripped off, eyes gouged out. She shuddered.

"Leave the door open! Hang a lantern. We need lots of light here!"

A ruminative lowing rose from the shadows. A sleepy tabby stretched, rolled over and pawed lazily at loose straw.

"Only jurors, police and coroners! The rest of you – out, or I'll clap you in gaol!"

She looked down on bowed heads, hunched shoulders and impatient elbows. Two uniformed arms extended, two hands pried open the box. "They're all in here, doctor? All three?" Victoria put her face down on her knees, covering her head with the skirt of her pinafore.

Grunts and scuffling told her the doctors were being helped up onto the wagon. "Anyone can't see, get in the haymow!" Oh, no! She retreated into the shadows as the ladder shook and bodies spilled over the top and into the hay.

"Quiet! And put out that pipe, sir. We don't want another conflag-yew-ration!"

Someone tittered and the crowd at last settled into uneasy silence.

Dr Vaux's schoolmaster tones made Victoria imagine him, pointer in hand, before a class. "I ask you to note carefully, gentlemen, the condition of the bodies before you. The skull and limbs of all three are gone, but the frontal bones remain."

"That's Mary Ann, the daughter. Minnie."

"Burnt to a crisp! A child?"

"In her thirties."

Dr Reeve coughed. "The middle one is Old John, Vaux. The only one I knew. See, you can still distinguish his features, although the skull's been shattered."

"Shattered! What do you doctors make of that? Hit from behind?"

"The axe!"

"Now, this body – the least burned – is Mrs. Luckey. That's right, Andrew, turn her over."

Victoria, her head covered, trying not to listen, heard the heave of alarm. "Christ, look at that, will you! Bright red blood on her chest!" Her nightmare flashed before her, her feet mired in sticky pools of blood.

"Look how bright it is, as if it could have happened a moment ago. That's proof of murder!"

"Stabbed in the heart? What d'you think, McGowan?"

In spite of herself, Victoria crept forward, peering between two onlookers perched on the edge of the mow. When a youth turned, looked her full in the face and turned back, growling, "Murder!" she realized no one cared that she was there, no one would even remember. Her eyes were drawn to the blackened lump that was her Grandmother Martha, to the heart's blood, bright as one of the wild poppies that grew in the black soil by Bruce's spring.

"This is something I've never seen before," Dr Reeve was saying. "Not in all my years as coroner. What do you make of it, Vaux?"

Dr Vaux fingered his buttonhole with pale, ringed fingers. "In this modern world, you'd expect us to have all the answers," he said. "Yet we don't really know exactly when or how she died, and the blood on her chest won't tell us. If you're wondering if it could confirm murder – that's impossible."

"It could have been done with the wire we pulled her out with." No one seemed to hear Andrew Parker, struggling to maintain his footing on the wagon.

"We've no way of knowing what it means," McGowan breathed. "Even if we did, would Charley's fate be any different?"

"That boy will swing."

Victoria stopped up her ears. It was Charley, her uncle, they were talking about. She hadn't seen him in years. She didn't want to see him now. But she'd never believe it, no matter what they said. She tucked the lace into a pocket and waited for the men to leave. I'll never tell anyone what I saw and heard, she said to herself. Not if I live to be ninety.

Chapter Three

Tuesday, October 11th, 1892

Chief Robert McGowan stood on the platform at the Smith's Falls station as the early morning train from Toronto rolled in. Uniform pressed and free of burrs, mud spatterings from his recent trips sponged away. If there was one thing he insisted on, it was looking the part. He was used to working odd hours, driving himself to the limit on little sleep. At thirty-four, he was just beginning to feel drained by the rigours of a job that often took him from his bed in the early hours to break up a drunken brawl or answer some frivolous complaint about treed cats or strayed chickens. The last time he had had a good night's sleep had been Friday, before the Luckey murders. The crime had renewed his longing for his government detective days. He realized how much he missed the thrill of chasing down clues, the headiness of being the centre of attention, directing investigatory traffic, with reporters hanging on his every word like it was gospel. Now the events of the past few days were telling on him.

Yesterday noon, after viewing the bodies at Johnny's barn, he had rushed home to try and catch an hour's sleep before setting out for Ottawa. The children had been tearing up and down the hall outside his bedroom, whooping like savages. Even though he'd freed his wife from heavy work by bringing out a servant girl from Ireland, Agnes had proved an indulgent, ineffectual mother. She would alternately scold and offer treats while the young blighters engaged in water fights or careered past her in a game of tag, screeches drowning out her soft voice. "Agnes-me-love," he'd bellowed yesterday from beneath the quilt, "muzzle the young divils before I break their precious little necks!"

She had appeared in the doorway, dewey-eyed with apology, looking so fetching that he'd grabbed her apron. Before she could utter a word of protest, he'd reeled her in like a prize catch, his hands fighting through layers of petticoats and pantalets to soft, warm skin. "This'll teach you to misbehave, milady!" By the time she'd gone back to nattering at the kiddies, he'd given up all thoughts of sleep and dressed for the tedious trip which he knew would keep him from home until the early hours of Tuesday.

Not partial to rail travel, he'd taken his own rig, with the blind faith that the urgency of his mission would persuade the town council to reimburse him for expenses. He seldom won council's blessing where money was concerned, but there was no denying they wanted the Luckey matter cleared up. The papers were calling the case the most atrocious in the history of Canadian crime, careful to point out that it took place "in a community where all strive to live at peace and goodwill with each other". The council, sensitive in their newfound notoriety, detected notes sarcastic and castigating in such pronouncements. Their impulse was to sweep everything under the rug post haste.

The Chief had driven his rig straight to Montgomery's Besserer Street residence. It seemed the ex-detective seldom strayed from home nowadays, so it was a safe bet that he would be there or in a nearby tavern. "He was fired from the force several months ago. Drinking," a chatty officer had told him when he telephoned the Ottawa Police Department. McGowan had the greatest contempt for men who couldn't hold their liquor. A certain amount of merry-making was good in the right place and time, but to lose your job through drink and indulge in self-pity and sloth – unthinkable! There wasn't pressure on Montgomery to provide, either. "His father's worth forty-fifty thousand," the Ottawa source had confided. "Owns a saddlery on Rideau Street. Set his son up in one of his properties." All Harry had to do, it seemed, was make the rounds of the pubs. Eat, drink and procreate. This last was what he did best. He had a raft of kids, the oldest about eleven, and a wife who hardly emerged from one confinement before she was preparing for the next one. With two kiddies of his own, McGowan knew he would have handled the situation differently. He had lost his own job once, but only because of those arrogant humbugs on town council. When he'd returned to Smith's Falls, borne in triumph through the streets, there wasn't a man there could touch him. Harry Montgomery was a man to be pitied, if one had pity to waste.

Outside 77 Besserer, he had tethered his horses and appraised the modest, two-and-a-half storey brown brick. It was exactly the kind of investment he was scouring Smith's Falls for: good, solid construction, close to stores, offices and hotels. It rose, straight and narrow, devoid of the gingerbread and gothic embellishments of its sisters, with a tin-roofed harness shop attached on its east side. With his hotel and court connections, McGowan was often among the first to hear when debts were forcing a man to sell his property or when a family was emigrating to Manitoba, seduced by rumours of wealth and early retirement. He would jump in with a low cash offer on places where upkeep was minimal, then rent them out dirt cheap so there was little tenant turnover. Roofing and carpentry maintenance he bartered for, consulting his mental list of those owing him favours. He pictured himself buying up hotels and business properties next, a real estate mogul by age forty. Obviously Montgomery's father had bought this house as an investment; whether or not he still regarded it as a profitable deal, when it housed a penniless, ne'er-do-well son, was moot.

As McGowan watched, a young woman, smudges of fatigue beneath her eyes, appeared on the cluttered porch, a squalling infant in her arms and a straggly-haired tot clinging to her skirts. A bit lardy, McGowan thought; a freshening cow. She descended the steps, nudging aside a tiny wooden caboose with her foot. He saw a flash of bare ankle, cotton stocking rolled down over the sides of low slippers. God forbid that his Agnes should ever sink so low! "I'm looking for Harry Montgomery. Is he here?"

She jerked her head toward the house. "Sleeping."

Holy Mother, it was early evening!

"He takes private cases. A lot of night work." Her face brightened as she dabbed at the drooling infant with a corner of her apron. "You got work for him?"

A shudder went through McGowan. The woman had so little pride she was almost begging him! "I just want to ask him some questions about a case he worked on."

She directed him to the wretched little front parlour. Some effort had been made to add homey touches: a crocheted afghan on the worn sofa, chintz curtains on the doorway to the hall, to stop drafts. He declined to share the sofa with a mangey tomcat, horrified at the thought of its hairs patterning his uniform. He heard the woman's slippers flopping on the stairs, her shouts of "Harry! Get up! Someone to see you," joined by a chorus of babbles and lisps. He looked at the heavily draped window, wishing he had the nerve to pry it open and admit fresh air.

When Montgomery appeared, McGowan was shocked. The fellow was younger than he was, yet he looked ten years older, bulbous nose mapped with broken veins, neck dry and scrawny as a hen's comb. He squinted at the badge on McGowan's cap. "Not local, are you."

"Bob McGowan, Chief, Smith's Falls." McGowan extended his hand. "I've come about Charles Luckey, a fellow you sent to the Central in '91. If you've seen the papers, you'll guess why I'm here."

Montgomery yawned and scratched his armpit. "Don't get the papers. Shall we go somewhere, sit down and talk over a pint?" A hopeful glint shone in his eyes.

McGowan fought down a mounting thirst, letting revulsion overtake him as he looked into the red-rimmed, watery eyes. "Sorry, sir, but I regard myself as being on duty, having come on a matter of utmost importance." His Smith's Falls acquaintances might have snorted at this noble declaration, but McGowan had his rules: drinking with a known drunk was taboo.

Montgomery shrugged. "Call me Harry. Sit down. Emily, brew us up some of that Colombian coffee."

"Ain't much left." She poured water into a pot and slapped it on the woodstove.

They sat at the kitchen table. The coffee appeared, unaccompanied by so much as a biscuit. Counting the hours that had elapsed since breakfast, McGowan was embarrassed to hear his stomach rumble. He gave his attention to the chipped mug before him, pondering the smoothest spot to place his lips and resisting the urge to put his elbows on the splotched oil cloth.

Montgomery waved his wife away, poured a little coffee from cup to saucer and blew on it. "Charley Luckey. Ah, yes, I remember. Worked on Andrew Holland's farm, the court reporter. Stole and pawned his Persian lamb coat and hat. Sent up for a year. Dicks – have you spoken to Constable Dicks? – he accompanied Luckey by train to the Central Prison." He slurped deeply from his saucer. "Surly bastard. Uttered threats."

"Threats? What sort of threats?" McGowan took out his notebook.

"Said he'd make it hot for them. Just that. Nothing more that I recall."

"Who'd he mean? You? The prison authorities?"

Montgomery's saucer wobbled. "He don't scare me."

"Yes, man, I daresay. But who did he mean?"

The ex-detective put down his saucer and tested the cup's contents. "Whole bloody world for all I know. What's he up to?"

"Murder. Father, step-mother, sister."

"Holy Christ!" Montgomery's saucer chattered against his cup as he lowered it, sloshing coffee on the cloth. He sat, pale and shaken, letting the rest of his drink grow cold as McGowan told his story. At last he said, "I remember remarking he'd come to a bad end." His fingers traced vague circles in the puddle of coffee. "Yes, I'm sure now. It was his family he was making threats against. He had it in for his father because the old man wouldn't bail him out of his scrape."

"Would you testify to that in court?"

"Nothing would give me greater pleasure, unless it was to watch him swing." Montgomery made motions of tying a noose around his own neck and pulling on a rope.

Repulsed, McGowan looked away. "There's something else. We found money on him. Twenty-five seventy-five, to be exact. He says he brought it from the Central. They say they gave him train fare to Ottawa and six dollars in overtime pay – I've confirmed that with them. The rest of the money Luckey says he took into prison with him. Do you recall whether or not he had any money on him when he left Ottawa?"

His host didn't hesitate. "Not a penny."

"He says he took it in in his mouth. A common method. But was he checked – do you remember?"

"Of course he was checked, man! Are you suggesting I didn't do my job?"

"Calm down, Mr – Ah, Harry. This is just for the record. So he was checked – clothes, bodily orifices, before he left Ottawa, and found not to be in possession of anything, money or otherwise. And he had no opportunity to get his hands on any money between Ottawa and the Central?"

"Absolutely. He was handcuffed to the guard. Never left alone. I myself saw to that. I never left his side from the time we took him from gaol until he got on the train. I stood beside him and talked, friendly-like. He was a disagreeable sort, would have been violent if he hadn't been restrained. Had a chip on his shoulder the size of a barn."

McGowan unwrapped a package from an inner pocket and spread its contents on the table. "Twenty-four dollars in bills and one-seventy-five in coin. Now, this is the money I took from Luckey early Sunday morning, when I arrested him. Most of it can't be accounted for. The five"– he picked up a bill – "we're pretty certain came from a cattle dealer named Devlin."

"Yes, I know him. An alderman here, travels a lot. I hear he's gone west on a buying trip, might not be back for weeks."

"He did some business with old Mr Luckey on Friday and gave him a five dollar down payment on some cattle. I caught him as he was boarding the train in Irish Creek early Sunday morning and described the fiver. Didn't have it with me. He said the bill he gave Luckey was old, dark and greasy. Could be it, would you say?"

The sight of the money seemed to make Harry restless. He rubbed his thumb and forefinger together. "Well, if that's all, Chief, I'll be taking my leave. I've got a case to work on this evening, see." He put his hand in his pocket and McGowan heard coins jangling. Not enough, he was sure, to slake a thirst the size of his host's. He was tempted to toss a few coins of his own on the table – for good will, the coffee, the slattern and her bawling children. But the money would find its way into Harry's pocket for the case – no doubt a case of ale or cheap wine.

As he stepped into the front hall, McGowan noticed the woman regarding him sourly from the shadows. Without a hint of guile or sensuality she pulled a breast from her unbuttoned housedress and shoved the nipple into her infant's mouth.

That was the picture he carried with him on the long journey home as his stomach growled like cartwheels on gravel, and the rig's hubs squealed like a restless infant. Oil, he thought, they need oil. He tried to concentrate on squeezing the oil can, caressing oil from it to daub on raw places. Home, he barely had enough energy to put the horses away, hang up his uniform and stumble into bed. Running his cold hands under Agnes's nightgown, squeezing plump, firm flesh, he shocked her into wakefulness. "Just checking," he murmured. He was asleep before she stopped giggling.

That had been three hours ago. He forced his eyes to focus on the tall, well-proportioned passenger alighting from the Toronto train. Billy Greer wore a sack coat of Scotch tweed and a derby shoved back to reveal a prematurely receding hairline. His face was long, his nose straight and his light moustache trimmed and shaped. He looked shrewd, intelligent, patrician. His eyes were the coldest blue McGowan had ever seen.

They shook hands. "Bob McGowan," the Chief said. "Just missed you in '88 when you worked on the firebrand case."

Greer laughed. "I'm probably remembered here as a carpenter, and a bad one at that. The perfect cover. It took three months, but Ringer and James grew to trust me like a brother. They warmed to anybody who knew how to ply them with liquor."

"A good job, putting them away. Fourteen years, wasn't it?" He waited as Greer picked his grip from a baggage cart. "I've booked you a room at the Palace Hotel. D'you want to freshen up –"

"We'll go straight to the crime scene. Pity I couldn't get here sooner. Murray would have come himself, you understand, but he's involved in an embezzlement case in Chatham. I understand the Supreme Court Assize opens in Brockville October eighteenth. Young Luckey has put us in a tight spot, committing murder so close to trial time. It's my guess the case will have to be put over. Has he got a lawyer?"

"No. No money. His family isn't about to treat him to a defence under the circumstances."

"Then it's sure to be put over. The Crown can't proceed unless he's represented. At least it'll give us more time to work the case up."

They climbed into McGowan's rig. "I've marked the area around the bootprint and sent out word that it's not to be disturbed."

"Did you take an impression?"

"No, but I have the measurements. And I took a witness with me." McGowan cracked the whip over his pair.

"How is our prisoner, by the way? Has he confessed?"

"Not yet. Many's the man has tried to shame him into it."

Greer pulled a Pocahontas cigar from his pocket and bit off the end. "Perhaps he should be encouraged instead of shamed. When a man thinks he's committed the perfect crime he has the urge to tell all and bask in the admiration of the fellows he's outwitted. I've known men who couldn't keep the smirk off their faces when they saw they had baffled authorities. Few of them are smart enough to keep their mouths shut at that point. They're warped, of course, but they'll do anything to go down in history."

"Somehow I can't see Luckey bragging to us. We're the enemy."

"You'll see how it's done. A little companionship and the understanding of a like-minded soul. Worked for Murray dozens of times." Greer struck a match on the sole of his boot and lit his cigar. "Didn't work with Birchall, I admit. Guilty as hell, but he never confessed to killing Benwell. I guess he felt his place in criminal history was assured, anyway." He puffed on his cigar. "Such a fuss. Women wrote to him, thousands of people signed petitions seeking a pardon. He may have felt a confession would have hurt his wife, though it's hard to believe he had feelings for any other human being. Is Luckey protecting anyone?"

"He's a country lad, hasn't the sophistication of a Birchall. It's my guess if he won't confess it's because he's convinced himself he didn't commit the crime."

"Is he remorseful? Suicidal?"

McGowan shrugged. "Doesn't communicate, just sits huddled in a blanket in a corner of his cell. As for possible suicide, we've taken the usual precautions. No suspenders, no cutlery."

"Any crime in the family?"

"What?"

"Does he come from criminal stock? Murray subscribes to a theory that crime is hereditary. If a man's forefathers were criminals it's born into him."

"Not a blot on his family that I know of. Oh, it's rumoured about that his brother's house was built with money funnelled from a reserve to buy votes for a local M.P. Seems Johnny siphoned it off and there wasn't a thing the member could do. Shows a dishonest streak, but hardly in the same league as murder."

"What sort of company did Luckey keep?"

"Not good, I daresay. But the larceny was his first serious brush with the law. Not much chance to socialize with criminals there. He did take a shine to a fellow called Balloon, keeps saying Balloon would swear to what a straight fellow he'd become."

Greer snorted. "That's like asking a counterfeiter to be sure to pay you in bills. What about the fellow on the train?"

"Hannah? Decent sort, from what I can learn. I'm trying to track him down. Our main strengths, though, are the bootprint and the witnesses who can testify that Charley made threats against his own family. I've lined up interviews with them for you. The funeral will take up most of the afternoon and be attended by the whole countryside. It's in Toledo, a village just south of Newbliss. We'll be there."

"Good. We can learn a lot, watching and listening." Greer tapped his cigar with his forefinger and watched the ashes drift away. "I asked at the Central about the money you said they gave Luckey. They were all stunned by the news. Massie kept saying, 'Not young Luckey. Why, he's just a big, soft, innocent boy.'"

McGowan transferred the reins to his left hand and began fumbling in an inner pocket. "He's probably feeling a fool, after releasing Luckey a day early. That's a sign of trust, a reward for good behaviour that isn't given lightly. The fact that one of his inmates went straight from prison and committed murder reflects on Massie's judgment."

"Massie's had administrative troubles the past few years, but they gave him a sound endorsement at the last commission hearings. This won't help his reputation at all."

"They'll be saying he's gone the other extreme, too soft."

Greer grunted assent. "While I was at the prison I got statements from the bursar and storeskeeper. The bursar says Luckey was given twelve dollars and no more."

"Ah, here it is." McGowan brought forth a small packet, handing it to Greer as they turned off the Brockville road at Newbliss. "When you get the chance, note the fiver. It's probably the one the cattle dealer gave Old Man Luckey. And take a look at the ten. I have my suspicions that's blood smeared on it."

"So you brought the bills. What about the teeth? Do you have them in your other pocket?"

A faintly superior note, not lost on McGowan, had crept into Greer's voice. City mouse talking down to country mouse, the Chief thought, reminding himself that he had once been a city mouse himself. He laughed loudly to cover his annoyance.

"We'll have the bill analyzed," Greer continued, "along with his clothes. Any blood on them?"

McGowan pulled on the reins. "Whoa, there! Hard to tell. Some reddish brown stains, which may be old. The gaoler's getting him some clothes today, so we can take everything he's wearing."

"About time. We'll send it all to Toronto for the guiacum test."
He paused, gratified by McGowan's look of bewilderment.
"Suspicious scrapings, saline water, tincture of resin guiacum. Add a
dash of hydrogen dioxide; if there's blood present the mixture turns
bright blue."

"The accused can always say the blood is an animal's, or his own."

"As long as the material hasn't been washed, the shape of the
corpuscles in the stain tells whether or not the blood is human. But
you're right – as to whose it is, I doubt if there'll ever be a foolproof
test for that. But you know, Bob, the beauty of the test is –" He
gripped McGowan's arm – "often it's all that's needed to pry a
confession out of a man. Tell him you've found human bloodstains
and he knows you've got him."

Alighting at the Luckey property, they started across the field to
the fire site. The place was deserted except for a constable, a couple of
reporters and a gentleman taking measurements and sketching. Greer
wandered about, pausing periodically to pick up objects. Some he
smelled, some he held up toward the sun, others he pondered
wordlessly and cast aside. He paced the distance between apple tree
and house, house and barn, barn and well; asked questions about the
teeth, the screams, the direction of the wind the day of the fire, the
time lapse between scream and smoke. He looked on in dismay as
McGowan drew out his notebook. "Use your eyes and ears, Bob.
Develop your memory. You miss a lot, with your nose on the paper.
You see words forming instead of theories; you're chasing grammar
points instead of clues, smelling ink when you should be smelling
guilt." He snapped a low branch from a nearby tree and began
prodding with it, parting the grass neatly and bending it back, like a
barber sectioning hair for a trim.

In this fashion, reporters dogging his footsteps, Greer followed
McGowan through the swamp trail. A moment later he stopped and
bent over. "What's this? Back here, McGowan! Here we are, not ten
feet from the maple tree – the one you think he stood under? – and
what have we?" With his stick he scooped up a weathered black change
purse, lying open. "The old man's purse? Lying here all this time,
unnoticed by all the amateur sleuths?" He plucked it from the stick,
inverted and shook it. "Empty."

McGowan walked on ahead, his pride in playing tour guide
evaporating. "This way to the bootprint," he said. Amateur, indeed!

Was he being lumped in with the noisy rabble that had hampered his investigation Sunday? Was there a hint that he hadn't trained his men properly, given clear enough orders? Even if he'd found the purse himself, who was to say it hadn't been there for months? Let's see what other rabbits you can pull out of your hat, Mr Prestidigitator, he thought.

* * *

Billy Greer, in tattered shirt, pants held up by a greasy cord twisted through belt loops, lurched the short distance to the town hall. Reeking of the whisky he had carefully poured down one sleeve, he looped thumbs through imaginary suspenders and staggered up the walk.

McGowan, grinning broadly by the steps, grasped him by the collar and shoved. Billy bounced against the railing and sat down hard on the bottom step.

"Holler to wake the banshees and all you'll get is the bum's rush!" Roaring with laughter, McGowan herded his charge past gathering bystanders, touching his cap to the ladies.

All in the space of a minute and a half, Greer was propelled into the town hall, along a corridor and down some steps where he was thrust into a brick-lined cage eight feet square. The door clanged shut as he stumbled forward, stopping just short of a figure crouched in a corner.

"Company, Luckey!" McGowan shouted. "Sorry our guests have to share, but accommodation's limited here. The royal suite's being renovated, y'see, and all the rooms with private bath are occupied." His boots echoed on concrete. "If you need anything, just ring. We're here to serve you."

Billy could hear the rumble of McGowan's laughter as he collected himself, making a show of smoothing his rumpled clothes and scratching himself. "Damn, I didn't do nothin'!" In the light from the crude opening near the ceiling, his hands looked pale and refined. He shoved them in his pockets. "Leastways, not when the Chief was around." He gave a sly wink. "I'm just a poor man, trying to keep body and soul together. Like yourself, eh? Maybe I did take something now and then, but we've all got to live, haven't we?" He felt in his pocket, sidled up to Charley and whispered loudly, "Share a cigar? No? Here, take it. It's yours." No response. "Not now, mate? Maybe later."

Feeling in all his pockets, he sighed. "Could've sworn I had a match." He put the cigar away and observed the figure who sat motionless before him. He waited. One hour. Two.

He tried again. Young Luckey was hardly the garrulous type. The comradely approach didn't work. "Bet you're in for something simple." He hoped his voice struck a balance between curiosity and childish pride. My-father-can-lick-your-father. "Now, I'll own up to you if you promise not to peach on me." He looked around as if to make sure the guard was out of earshot. "I killed a man once." He waited for some response, some sign that he was heard. "Didn't mean to, you know, but we had a set-to on a freight and I pushed him off. Never got caught."

The prisoner rose, brushed past him without looking at him and shuffled over to the bars.

"My name's Billy and I'd like to shake your hand if I may. I think we should be buddies 'cause we may be in here together for a long time. What's your name, fella? Mac? All right, I'll call you Mac. What did you do, Mac? Rob a bank? Whyncha tell me about it?"

Charley wheeled around at last, looked at him briefly and turned away. "Stay away from me," he said softly. "I never have any truck with tramps."

* * *

The bum banged on the cell door and yelled something to the guard. Sounded as if he was mad as hell about something. The funniest thing, though, was the way the guard came straight away, unlocked the cell and let the fellow walk out under his own steam. Charley retreated to his corner and pulled his coat around his shoulders more closely. Still freezing here, damp and mouldy, not even the warmth that a lighted candle could give.

It wasn't until he heard voices and laughter from the Chief's office that he understood. They'd tried to outwit him, crafty bastards! It sounded as if they were enjoying a huge joke at someone's expense. "Call me a jackass, it's worked before," the drunk's voice said, sober now. There seemed to be a gang of men hooting and guffawing. He could smell their cigars mingling with the aroma of steaming mutton and potatoes on the tin plate shoved inside his door moments ago. Every few hours a tray appeared, marking off the different periods of the day, periods the rest of the world lived by. Time to water the horses, milk the cows, gather eggs. Time for his Harriet to change from morning dress to afternoon finery, mutton sleeves, lace at the throat. For him time passed almost unnoticed, punctuated only by the call to empty his slops, the trays delivered and retrieved mostly untouched, the occasional exchange of words with McGillivray, the day constable. It seemed years since he'd parted from Balloon, met Hannah, watched his beloved's double pick daintily at her tea cakes in the St James Hotel. It seemed a lifetime since he'd run along the Brockville road, filling his lungs with the first fresh air he'd breathed in a year, filling his head with plans for freedom.

His gaolers weren't unkind. They brought blankets and tucked them around him as he sat, knees to chin, in his corner. They lit fires to warm the place up and expressed surprise hours later to find him in the same position, huddled beneath the blankets, teeth chattering. McGillivray would remark on the weather, ask how he felt. "Always damn cold in here," he'd say.

In his first full day here, a parade of busybodies had kept pounding him with questions until his head was numb. He said little, but they hung on his every word, some taking notes, like he was a celebrity. He couldn't remember what he had said. At some point a gentleman in a grey suit had come to the door and told him he wasn't to talk to anyone, he must do what was in his own best interests and for the time being that meant keeping quiet. After that, no one bothered him. He liked the peace and quiet but he wondered: why would anyone bother about what happened to him?

This morning he had been overcome with thirst, gulping down several cups of scalding tea before the food was passed in. "Still not hungry, lad?" McGillivray had asked, collecting the tray an hour later, the grease hardened around the pork hocks. He couldn't explain his lack of interest in food. He felt full, somehow, bursting with an acrid smokiness, like a side of beef hung on rafters in the smokehouse. The food would arrive looking undercooked, the meat oozing blood sometimes, but it offended his nostrils and his tongue with a black, unearthly bitterness. It was more than a smell or a taste; it was something that seeped through muscle and tissue and bone, through the dark, smouldering caverns of his mind. Oh, God, why? He couldn't remember why.

A scraping of chairs and shuffling of feet. "Kidney pie at home tonight, Billy," he heard McGowan say. "Praties in their jackets. My Agnes is putting on a spread in your honour."

A door opened. Chill air swept down the steps and through the cell; voices ceased as the door banged.

"Now, McGillivray, perhaps we can proceed with that interview," a strange voice said.

"The Chief knows more than I do." Charley thought he detected a note of reluctance in McGillivray's voice.

"I want to hear it from someone who's been right here with him. Personal touch, y'know. If I can get an exclusive slant – you know, about his interests and habits, how he's reacting to all the publicity, does he froth at the mouth and bay at the moon, or is he just like you and me?" A self-conscious laugh. "Keep the reader entertained. Help me keep my job. Beat our competitors."

"*The Globe*, you say?"

"Right. Now, you say you don't know what to make of him?"

McGillivray coughed. "To be sure I don't. If someone looks in on him during the day, he's crouched in his corner. Once in a while he comes to life and stares back at them, looks them up and down. Showing bravado, maybe, to make us think he's innocent."

"Does he talk at all?"

"He don't talk to everybody. Mayor Frost came Sunday bragging that he'd get a confession and after about an hour went away muttering to himself." McGillivray coughed again and blew his nose. "Damn, I've had a cold for as long as I've worked here. Chill gets in your bones. Now, as for young Luckey, he's downright odd if you ask me. One of the hardest characters I ever had dealings with. Shows no signs of fear, yet when he thinks he's alone he looks lost and troubled."

"I meant, does he talk to you?"

"Oh – yes. Yes, indeed. Every subject but the murders. Not a word about them since he came here."

"Think he'll get off?"

"Not a chance. Why, only today the gaoler noticed something strange about one of his trousers pockets. Soaked in blood, I'd say, a brown stain, dried and caked. And when he examined Luckey's vest it looked like blood specks on it, too. You could see where he'd tried to scratch the spots off with something sharp."

"You don't mind if I take this down, do you? Tell me, did he offer any explanation?"

"He seemed pretty anxious and said he could prove how the stains got there. Before his arrest in Ottawa last year he got in a row, got struck on the head and lost a lot of blood. That's what he said. At the Central Prison some spots were erased in the laundry and he says the cloth was scraped with a sharp instrument."

There was a pause. "I've got to light the lamps now, sir. Should've done it an hour ago. Poor fellow's got to fumble about in the dark for his supper." Keys rattled and a chair rasped.

"I appreciate this, McGillivray. You don't mind being quoted, do you? Oh, by the way, did anyone tell him the funeral was this afternoon?"

"Not that I know of. I guess no one wanted to raise the subject, any more than he does."

"One last question, off the record. Just between you and me, do you think he did it?"

Silence. In the darkness Charley held his breath. Finally, McGillivray said, "I'll tell you this much. When I think of Charley Luckey, I see him swinging from a rope. That's the only end for him. Look at it this way. If they can't prove he did it and he gets off, the taint will follow him the rest of his days. There'll be no place on God's earth where he's welcome, where he's able to lead a life untouched by the scandal. Would you accept him? Could I accept him, make a friend of him? Believe me, that boy's days are numbered. Life, if it's granted to him, would only be a living death. The rope isn't just fitting, it's the best he can hope for."

Charley sat on the floor, letting the cold paralyse his buttocks and work its way upward through his body. His hand traced the rim of his tin plate and brushed a moist, wobbly softness. Fatty chunks of mutton swimming in the muddied water the cook passed off as gravy; potatoes, cold and slimy; a leaden heel of bread which, in daylight, he knew, would show a rind of mould. He grasped food in both hands and crammed it in his mouth: a whole potato, a great shard of stringy meat, a sodden lump of fat. His teeth ground against gristle and tissue and sinew, gravy dribbled from his chin onto his shirt, and still he kept shovelling food in until his cheeks bulged and his jaws ached and his eyes began to water. Blindly he sought the bread, tore off a wedge, felt the sharp crust gouge his lower lip as he pushed it in.

He chewed for a long time, forcing cold tea down to help him swallow, feeling blasts of chill air as the constable and his visitor took their lengthy leave. He could no longer hear what they were saying, didn't care to. Fumbling for the last crust, he wiped it round and round the plate in frenzied circles until he imagined the tin gleaming coin]like in the darkness. He held it before him as he would a mirror but no reflection met him, nothing assured him that he was here, alive, able to be seen. He thought for a moment he was going to laugh, so absurd did it all seem, but when he put his hand up he discovered his cheek was wet. He dashed the tin against the wall, seven years bad luck if it shattered, but no, it didn't shatter, it bounced on the floor and rolled away. "McGillivray!"

The wind ceased as the front door closed. The bulk of the constable loomed behind a swaying lantern. "Yes, lad, like a light, would you?"

"Were you talking to someone?"

"No one important." The constable lit a wall sconce in the corridor and came to the cell door. "Finished with your tray?" He stiffened as the prisoner's hand grasped his sleeve. Inmates were not allowed to put their hands through the bars and this one, this one in particular, never touched anyone. Shied away, in fact, shrank into a corner when they insisted on examining him for lice or inspecting his clothes. He unfastened the fingers from his arm and watched as they curled around the bars.

In the lantern's feeble light, the constable saw what could have been a mirror image, a figure his height, weight and breadth. The man who faced him behind the barrier could have been a younger self, but his shoulders were stooped like an old man's; he smelled of fear, the fear of an animal trapped and waiting, hackles up, taking on the colour of its surroundings in an effort to be invisible. Only the eyes gleamed pale and bleak. He had a sense of hungers unsatisfied, old wounds unhealed, a spirit fragile as a shell. He was surprised when the shadow spoke.

"McGillivray. Oh, God, McGillivray, what's to become of me?"

Chapter Four

Wednesday, October 12th, 1892

"You can't put it off any longer." Disturbed at the querulous note in her voice, Liza Ann piled pine kindlings on the paper in front of the firebox, criss-crossing methodically. There was nothing to be gained from handling Johnny this way. He'd snap at her or walk away without answering. This morning he simply stood beside the stove, hands gripping the back of a kitchen chair, knuckles white, gazing beyond her at the pail of ashes in the corner. She knew he heard her, for his jaw had twitched as she spoke. The right words eluded her, as always.

She'd been raised Methodist, over in Wolford Township. Johnny had appeared one Saturday in the spring of '77, promoting a line of farm machinery. She'd met him by the front gate, such a handsome, dashing figure she'd been quite overwhelmed, blushing and lowering her eyes when he greeted her. It was unseasonably warm, too warm even for the muslin fichu she had thrown over her green cotton dress, which whipped about her thighs in the breeze. "Excuse me, ma'm, you wouldn't be the lady of the house?" She'd shaken her head, speechless. "Would Mr Baldwin be about?" Liza Ann had gestured toward the field where her father was sowing wheat.

Thereafter Johnny had found frequent excuses to visit and Liza Ann had been the envy of her friends. He wrote notes and brought little gifts he picked up in his travels about the countryside: a scrimshaw brooch, a pomander, a scent bottle with a belt hook. Flattered by his unabashed admiration, she'd accused him of kissing the Blarney Stone. "You've got the loveliest eyes, Liza Ann. The longest lashes I've ever seen!"

Swept off her feet, she ached to marry him, although he was a year younger. "You'll never want for anything, dear," her mother had said, giving her blessing. Johnny was ambitious, sure of himself, polished and courteous, a cut above her other suitors. Her father had puffed calmly on his pipe. "That young man'll go a long way." High praise, coming from her father.

They were married in the spring of '78, she in the finest satin with a lace Bertha collar, all stitched by herself on the Singer machine Johnny had brought from Boston. To this day she tried to pretend with her parents and brothers and sisters that Johnny had fulfilled her dreams and their expectations. She would cry into her pillow nights he didn't come home, bitterly regretting her youthful infatuation. She gave her family expensive gifts at Christmastime and proudly described their new home. But she didn't encourage them to visit.

Would it have been better to become an old maid, rotting on a farm out back of nowhere? She would look at Esley and Victoria. They made everything worthwhile. Truly, God was good. His ways mysterious, but His goodness everlasting.

She added another layer of kindlings to the firebox and waited for Johnny to answer, surprised to see new lines around his eyes and the faintest frosting at his temples, where the wings of hair began their upward sweep. *He's exhausted by all this. As I am.*

Yesterday's funeral had been a nightmare, their private grief turned into public scandal. A three-ringed circus. Things had changed irrevocably. She didn't know who her friends were any more. People who only the day before had brought food hampers and offered to do chores stopped talking when she approached. A gloved hand would cover a gasp, eyes would fail to meet hers. Pursed lips held back the words she knew were spoken once she was out of earshot: *this would never happen in our family!*

Ansley had scarcely left her side. She had a sudden vision of how they must have looked yesterday, trailing the three hearses on foot, down Toledo's rutted main street to St. Andrew's Church. Johnny beside her, then Sam, Sarah and her husband, and last the grandchildren. Only three of John J. Luckey's eleven children there to mourn him. Two out west, Charley in gaol. Will, baby Andrew, baby Maggie and Minnie dead. And Hugh – dead, too? God only knew.

It had hurt her to see how Victoria's friends, Jenny and Effie and Mabel, had stood gaping as they passed, how one of Esley's schoolmates had snickered and another had scooped up dirt to throw before being chastised by his mother. After the service, Jenny had come over with a new shyness and had taken Victoria's hand and just stood there, saying nothing, until her mother called sharply. Even then Jenny had gone on holding Victoria's hand and Victoria had bitten her lip and turned away. "Awfully sorry, Miz Luckey." Jenny's mother had unfastened her daughter's fingers from Victoria's and tugged her away. "Dinner's been in the oven all day. Come now, Jenny, or the roast'll be burnt to a cinder!" As the words sank in, the woman's face reddened. She fled, almost pulling Jenny off her feet, leaving Victoria gazing down at two wobbly exclamation marks left by Jenny's oxfords.

Yes, we mustn't talk about burning roasts ever again. Next we won't be able to talk about lighting woodfires! Liza Ann bent to pick up pieces of hardwood from the bundle beside the stove, heavy bombazine tugging her downwards, anchoring her to the floor in a black circle. It took all her strength to straighten up again. If it hadn't been for the children she couldn't have kept going. She had to set an example, pretend that adults always knew how to act. It didn't always work, of course. "Oh, why didn't we make Aunt Minnie stay to dinner?" Victoria kept repeating. She had no answer. Right in front of the children, she'd broken down when the police questioned her about the teeth and again later, when Sam had burst into the kitchen, dropped his grip and rushed over, enveloping her in strong arms while Johnny watched from the doorway. She could still feel Sam's hand patting her hair awkwardly, the bristles of his cold chin digging into her neck. Sam, sharing his grief. More than Johnny had done, but she hadn't expected him to. His grief was locked within, shared with no one.

She spaced the larger pieces of wood, careful to bring them even with the end of the firebox, then replaced the covers. The coal would go in after the polishing ritual. Pulverized stove polish, already dampened, waited in its metal holder on the back of the stove, brush and cloths arraigned beside it. Dipping her brush into the polish, she swept it across the black iron exterior, matching her voice to the casualness of the brush strokes. "Johnny. You really must decide this morning, you know."

"Must you do that every morning, woman?" He hadn't moved, hadn't looked at her.

"What?"

"Every goddam morning! You're a fanatic!" He tore the brush

from her hand and flung it, watching it bounce off a cold burner and land with a spattering on the linoleum.

"But – you always –"

"How many wives clean and polish the stove before the fire is laid, while the family waits and shivers, stomachs rumbling?"

Liza Ann stared at him, not daring to give in to the urge to clean up the mess on the floor. "It's my chore, Johnny, done while you do your chores for breakfast. Only you're not doing yours today. You've got help." It was true. Friends and neighbours, conscripted to serve as inquest jurors or simply determined to have an excuse to attend the proceedings, had sent sons and nephews and hired hands to do Johnny's work.

"So could you have. You sent the women away."

"So I did. I wanted the house to be mine – ours – again." How could she explain the awkwardness she felt? Yesterday after the funeral the house had been overrun, people wolfing down heaping plates of salads and beans, drinking jugs of tea, breaking open corn liquor in the woodshed, while children tore about colliding with their less nimble elders, snatching cakes from passing trays. There had been so many unfortunate questions, awkward attempts to pry, all disguised as concern. People had even spelled out words in front of Esley, as if a nine-year-old was too slow-witted to catch on. And Esley kept tugging at her sleeve, sounding out the words, whispering, "Mummy, what's a torso? What do they mean, post mortem?" And, pointing at a portly gentleman holding forth to a circle of ladies, "Why's he keep spelling everything?"

She'd packed the children off to the kitchen finally and set them to rolling paper for spills, even though the jar on the mantle was crammed with a week's supply. Victoria's eyes had been full of reproach. "I'm a grownup now, Mother."

"Then mind your brother for me. Please, Victoria."

Victoria had been troublesome all day, and who could blame her? She'd thrown a tantrum in the morning, insisting on wearing black for the funeral, although Liza Ann had laid out the grey worsted cut down from her own last year. "Grey is for under twelve, Mother. It says so in the etiquette column. Don't you know anything?" The explosions of rudeness were new and increasingly frequent. "I'm going on fourteen!"

Liza Ann choked back tears. Was Victoria going to take after the darker side of Johnny's family?

They had argued until Johnny had roared at them and Victoria, suddenly meek, had given in. Then there'd been the business of the veil. Victoria had pounced on one in an attic chest that hadn't been opened since summer '91 when Grandmother had died. Folded among the crepe and bombazine, forlorn armbands and great purple bows for wreaths, it begged attention. Liza Ann had given in this time, lacking the strength to talk sense into Victoria. Too young for a veil, she thought, but we all want to hide behind masks. There'd barely been time to air the clothes and she swore she could still smell the ox-gall she'd cleaned them with before packing them away. She sprinkled everything liberally with toilet water.

Groping for a soft cloth, she bent down and started wiping the spattered linoleum without taking her eyes off Johnny. "I'm sorry. I'll start the fire." Picking up the scuttle, she began dropping coals into the firebox on top of the wood. "There's salt pork."

"I'm not hungry."

"But you said –"

"I don't want any!"

"You didn't eat yesterday."

"How could anyone eat? Did you eat?" He buried his face in his hands, digging his nails into his temples. "I've been harassed without mercy since Saturday night. Even my own family won't give me any peace! Fighting over what to wear to a funeral as if it's nothing more than a Sunday band concert, complaining about housework you didn't need to do in the first place, and now – 'Make up your mind, Johnny.'" He minced about the room. "'You have to decide today, Johnny.' Go back to your polishing, woman. All you're good for."

Liza Ann bit her lip. He got more like his father every day. And she – at times she felt herself becoming Martha. She tried again.

"It's only that the inquest starts at nine. Ansley says –"

"Spare me Ansley's words of wisdom. I know, I know. We'll be seeing Charley. We can't avoid it. I wouldn't attend at all if that detective hadn't had me subpoenaed."

Liza Ann began buffing the stove mechanically. "Victoria and I have to testify, too. It's only because of the children that I'm asking, Johnny. We have to think of what's best, or perhaps least harmful, for them."

"Is finding legal counsel for a murderer going to help the children?"

"Johnny – suppose he's innocent. Without counsel he'll be convicted for certain. The taint will be on the family."

"Suppose he's guilty. Suppose counsel gets him off. How do you know we won't all be murdered in our beds – the children too?"

The cloth became a ball in her fist, her fingers kneading it. "Look, Johnny. I don't know what happened, but I can't believe Charley's a murderer. Not – that kind of murderer –"

"What kind, then? A nice, polite murderer? One who apologizes to his victims?" He bowed from the waist, pretended to pluck a handkerchief from the air and hold it between thumb and forefinger. "So sorry, my dears, I'll chop off your heads as gently as possible!"

She hugged her elbows against her ribs to keep from shuddering. A show of weakness was like a red flag to Johnny. In the ensuing quiet, the words she whispered scarcely reached her own ears. "Charley should be represented."

"You're asking me to pay for his defence?"

"It's just that – someone should listen. Speak for him."

"And someone – meaning me – should pay for someone to speak for him."

"You're the only one who can."

Johnny moved to the window and looked out, his back to her. "You never liked Father." It was a juvenile ploy, to make her feel guilty, somehow responsible for the whole thing. Johnny's way of deflecting the issues at hand. No, she hadn't liked the old man. Harsh and mean, unfeeling and unforgiving. Lived a Christian life, though. *More than I can say for you, Johnny. Women weren't afraid to come within arm's length. Kept his hands to himself and Martha always knew where he was nights.*

"I – respected him. And Martha. Their ways weren't mine, perhaps, but I got along with them." *Better than you did.* "And you know how fond I was of Minnie. I can't tell you how much I miss her."

There was no stopping Johnny once he was obsessed with the urge to hurt. "I'll bet. You'll have to do all your own sewing now."

She put the cloth down gently. *I won't let him upset me, I won't.* But guilt flooded her as she remembered her secret relief that the house was in order with all the company that had passed through. All because Minnie spent her last days selflessly as always, slaving to put someone else's house in order.

While Minnie relieved her of the sewing, Liza Ann had scoured the meat safe, white-washed the fruit cellar and lined up all the preserves on fresh oilcloth with military precision. She'd fished the whisky flask from the back of the medicine cupboard – a cache unknown to Johnny – mixed a little of its contents with water and lovingly wiped her precious oil paintings. With Minnie's help – was it only a week ago? – she'd taken the winter flannels and woollens from their chests and hung them outside.

On the Friday, while the children were in school, they'd chopped up a pailful of potatoes, spread them on the carpet and swept like fury. "Wasteful, Father calls it, using potatoes," Minnie had said with a short laugh. "But then, he doesn't hold with carpets, either." Liza Ann had shuddered, recalling the hideous yellow oil cloth Martha and Minnie had made for their floors from the cheapest tow cloth the old man could buy. Before a month had passed, it had curled up around the edges. How unnecessary it had all been, when the broadloom Johnny had brought the old couple from one of his Winnipeg sallies lay rolled up against the unused parlour door to keep out drafts.

Liza Ann rubbed the stove's smooth belly until she could see her face in it, the anxious pursing of her lips, the deepening lines spreading out from the corners of her eyes, lines Sam had once teasingly called laugh lines. *Rub! Rub away the guilt!* But the sheen that emerged only increased her guilt. She swallowed, determined not to shed more tears in front of Johnny. Minnie's legacy, a clean house to mourn in. Poor, poor Minnie. They could look in any corner, under any chair, inside any chest, cupboard, drawer.

"How will we ever know what happened unless Charley talks?"

"I know all I want to know." Johnny disappeared into the front hall and returned, shrugging into his good black coat. "Do you realize when it came time to place them in their coffins, there were pieces of bone and – tissue – that they didn't know where –?" He broke off, squared his shoulders and tucked the ends of his white silk scarf inside the V of his coat. "Which side are you on, Liza Ann?"

It was six a.m., barely light. "The inquest doesn't start until nine."

Ignoring her, he peered into the mirror above the kitchen sink, slicking his hair back. Liza Ann shivered. What was it he had said, about the children being murdered in their beds? "Where are you going?"

"I have business to attend to."

"Johnny." Her hands twisted the cloth. "You're right. About

Charley. I'm sorry. You must handle things as you see fit." She followed him to the door. "Will you be back to pick us up?"

There was no answer as he slammed the door and pounded across the verandah and down the steps.

* * *

Johnny bypassed the buggy standing in the yard and strode straight to the stable. He saddled and mounted the chestnut, smiling grimly as he thought of Liza Ann peering from behind lace curtains. Let her, he thought, let the damned woman wonder. He urged the horse north on the Brockville road, passing the Newbliss intersection. Five minutes later, he turned east onto an overgrown dirt road. His mood lifted, his pulse quickened as he contemplated what lay ahead. Old Red's stance was jaunty, his mood light, almost conspiratorial. He knew the road. No other living soul had accompanied his master here. Pebbles flew out from under his hoofs as he skirted potholes, veering to follow the road's erratic line. Up a sharp grade, down a leaf-strewn slope, on between clumps of birch where the road almost petered out, grass and boulders taking over the pathway.

"Whoa!" Draping his coat and scarf over a rotting snake fence, he tied Old Red loosely to a weathered post and climbed over. He felt young and reckless as he half-slid, half stumbled down an incline, picturing himself speeding among the trees with the swiftness and silence of an Ojibway. Above him Old Red snorted; from somewhere a bluejay called, and all around him golden leaves broke from branches and floated feather-like into the air. Soon his heavy boots were sinking in mud.

He edged out onto a line of sun-bleached rocks and picked his way across a stream. A tousled dark head bobbed among the reeds near the opposite bank. A boy of six or seven, naked from the waist up, shook himself like a wet puppy. "Johnny! You gone long time. Not come see us since the day Rafe bled the stallion."

"Surprised to see me, Dui?"

The boy tossed his head. "I could hear the chestnut soon as you turned onto the road. Besides – no one else crashes through the trees like a bear." He put his hands on his hips in mock consternation. "How you expect me catch fish when you shake the air like that?"

"Fish? Where's the pole I gave you?"

"I catch with my hands – like Rafe." The boy pointed to the bank where two small mudpout lay gasping.

Johnny threw his hat down beside the fish and scooped some water up and over his face. "So. You're still here."

Dui nodded.

"Your sister, too?" Sister or mother, he wasn't sure which, but he went along with what he'd been told.

The boy nodded again. "Violette, everybody. Rafe, too. He broke out of gaol."

They climbed a hill where the grass was waist high, crossed a field of clover and entered a grove. Johnny took out his watch. No more than twenty minutes had passed since he had slammed the door on Liza Ann, yet he was in another world. Campfires crackled, lean dogs yapped. In a clearing ahead he saw a circle of wagons, garishly painted wooden huts perched atop platforms on high wheels. Men carrying buckets and axes hailed him, women passed silently with kettles and bundles of firewood. They were a swarthy, mottled people, with moles and freckles the colour of charcoal and hair straight and black and thick as horses' tails. A hardy people, lean-muscled, large-boned, the adults graceful, the children the most beautiful he had ever seen, up until the age of eight or ten when their huge lustrous eyes lost their innocence and their faces took on a crafty look. Johnny glanced at a group of women oiling their hair, running long fingers through cascading tresses. "Where is she, Dui?"

"Yonder, getting eggs."

Johnny felt the tension leaving his body. He had been drawn to these people, in spite of a disastrous first encounter. He had been returning home one evening last June from a brief and highly unsatisfactory assignation in Smith's Falls when his horse had reared without warning, bringing his wagon to a halt so sharply he pitched forward, dropping his whip and striking his head against the shaft. In a flash he was surrounded by a swarm of hard-faced, black-eyed people: men, women and children, most of them barefoot, all with gold hoops in their ears.

Brown hands grasped the cord that had been stretched across the road, tied to trees on either side. "Gimmee, mister, gimmee," the children shouted, pressing forward with outstretched palms. Long, sweeping skirts, wide-sleeved waists and all manner of scarves, kerchiefs and shawls swirled about him: scarlet, vermilion, purple, saffron. Dizzy with colour, ravished by it, he put a hand out to hoist himself back onto the wagon seat.

It was then that he saw her, standing back by the side of the road, her expression a mixture of disdain and amusement. A girl – how old? Eighteen? Twenty-five? Fairer than the others, a nut brown girl, tanned skin, enormous liquid eyes, hair tumbling to her hips. She was less angular than the other women, full-breasted, softer, in colours of the wild rose and field buttercup.

He had parted with the contents of his purse that night, and the following Saturday, his bruise like a battle scar upon his forehead, had sought them out, unable to talk himself out of what he knew was madness. He had been a long time getting to know them, and wouldn't have gone to the trouble had it not been for her.

On long summer afternoons, when he was supposed to be at Irish Creek on business, he sat on a stump a little apart from their camp and watched them. He told such a tangle of lies to Liza Ann and his other women it was a miracle he wasn't found out. The objects of his attention ignored him, even when he offered hootch to the men and trinkets and taffy for the women and children. They'd trotted out their treasures finally, when they realized he wasn't going to go away, to show him they needed nothing: whole bolts of silk, animal pelts, necklets of twenty-dollar gold coins. He understood then that they begged and hoodwinked the locals for the sport of it.

They were nomads, not true Romany but rather what his Gran from the old country called Didikai, mixed blood gypsies. A strange, heterogeneous blend they were, of courtly manners and fox-like cunning, disarming generosity and unpredictable rapacity, abysmal poverty and unaccountable riches.

They smelled of woodsmoke and animal skins, of bear grease and rot gut brandy. While Violette – ah, Violette! – smelled of spring rains and summer hazes, of green shoots coming up out of the earth. They spoke a language he couldn't identify and had names like Etelka and Peregrine and Rosealma. They knew everything there was to know about horses, including how to rejuvenate an old half-dead mare long enough to sell her as good stock and how to bleed a horse so the animal felt nothing. They read the palms of his people but never their own, and cured grippe and ague and thorn festers and snakebite with secret blends of herbs.

When they knew him better, they shared the liquor they made in great stone crocks and dumped stolen booty at his feet, urging him to choose a gift. They showed him pears grown in bottles, the glass having been slipped over the blossom on the branch and left until the fruit matured, when the bottle was taken down and filled with brandy. They roasted squirrels on spits and passed the meat around in steaming enamel bowls, puzzled when he declined his portion. Rafe flashed a gold-toothed smile. "We share our food before we share our other possessions." He winked and let his glance travel across the campfire, to where Violette sat wiping empty bowls with a broad, flat leaf.

Johnny, spurred on by the hint of reward, choked down the proffered delicacy. Following Rafe's example, he wiped his greasy hands on his hair, hoping he would not have to explain to Liza Ann. The women hooted with laughter watching him wash down the strange chicken-rabbit taste with brandy-laced coffee. Like Rafe, he drank holding a lump of sugar between his teeth, feeling the liquid sear his throat, not stopping until the cup was empty. They sang then, while some blew on reeds and others strummed odd, makeshift instruments. Rafe leaned toward him. "You want to see her dance?"

Johnny nodded. He ached for her, and the ache grew as he watched her hips thrust and sway in hypnotic rhythm, her nipples press against thin silk. Faster and faster she danced, closer and closer to him, until he was weak with desire for her. It was after, long after, when the crock was empty and the singing had become a low, boozy slur as his hosts rocked and leaned toward each other about the dying fire, that she led him quietly, surreptitiously, to a little wagon behind the others. "Mine," she said, and climbed inside, motioning him to follow. And he had one night of the wildest, most blissful lovemaking he had ever experienced, not a fibre of his body untouched, untasted.

No one had moved him the way this strange, exotic creature had; he tried to count them all, mentally, and they paled, every one, by comparison: Maggie, Ellen, Hazel, Fanny, Clara, and others, some nameless, some faceless, all unmemorable. He knew now none had ever pleased him, least of all Liza Ann, who undressed in another room and came to bed swathed in voluminous high-necked nightgowns.

He'd returned to the camp whenever he could, which wasn't nearly often enough. The gypsies had stayed in the area, sometimes moving camp a mile or two, when locals had tried to put the run on them, their ranks swelling and shrinking as wagons arrived and departed without any warning or pattern that Johnny could discern. They kept their own counsel and seemed to communicate much as birds or woodland animals would. He had only one thing to go on when they moved camp. Violette had shown him and sworn him to secrecy. "Little pieces of cloth." She held up a strip of crimson silk. "You will find these caught on branches as if by accident. Look high, look low, for there will not be a clear cut path."

It had been so long since his last visit that he was surprised to find them still in their August camp. He followed Dui past youths sitting under a pine, two whittling small fingers of wood while a third cut thin strips of tin for clothes pegs.

They found her in a clearing. Pullets plump as butter clucked softly among the scrawny leghorns at her feet. He didn't ask where they came from. She had been gathering eggs and, unlike his other women, had no apron in which to hold them. Instead, she bunched up her skirt. She stood before him, bare-armed, barefooted, legs planted apart, skirt high on her hips. No petticoat, no pantalets; all he saw was thigh, not the smooth, plump, milky thigh of Kitley women, but hard, brown flesh. She looked wanton, noble. "I've got a prince's blood in me," she had told him once. He had shrugged indulgently. These people always claimed royal or noble antecedents, from mysterious liaisons. She wore the same rose silk waist he had first seen her in last June.

He couldn't understand why they were never surprised to see him. Here it was, not yet six-thirty and Violette's eyes betrayed no curiosity. The camp was in a state of upheaval as darkness turned to daylight. Eiderdowns splashed colour on low branches as their owners spread them out to air; other covers still lay on the ground, lumpy and misshapen as they rose and fell with the breath of the sleepers beneath.

Dui spread a scarf on the ground and watched Violette transfer the eggs to it, one by one. She picked up the corners, tied them in a knot and handed the bundle to the boy. "Careful."

Before Dui was out of sight, Johnny had taken her in his arms. "I haven't much time."

"Only a fool is a slave to time."

Tension rushed from him all at once and he laughed from deep inside. These people were as simple and primitive as the redskins. Here there would be no talk of the fire. Here, where no newspapers ever appeared, where no one could read or wanted to, he could stretch out for a little while in the haven that was Violette's wagon. A half hour there would renew him in body and spirit, fortify him for the ordeal that lay ahead. And Irish Creek and the inquest lay a little to the southeast, not a quarter hour away.

Violette drew away and caught his hands. "I saw the wreath on your door."

Christ! His hands, enfolded in her warm ones, grew cold. "What the hell –?" Usually her people went north, to the Smith's Falls market, or even to the outskirts of Ottawa, horse-trading.

She looked at him for a long moment and he realized he had made a mistake. One didn't ask questions of a gypsy. It showed distrust, and an inordinate curiosity. "Me and Dui had pegs to sell," she said finally.

Desire vanished; his muscles tightened, his temples throbbed. There was no place he could go that death and scandal wouldn't follow. "Yesterday?"

She nodded.

"You saw the funeral procession in Toledo?"

She lowered her eyes.

Angry, he felt naked, all his flaws, his secrets, exposed. "And the fire? I suppose you saw the fire Saturday?"

"We saw smoke. I do not know what day, what does it matter? The day Rafe found a stray hog in the meadow." She shrugged.

Found. He ignored the euphemism. "You came to the fire." He grasped her shoulders. "Did you see anything?"

Pulling away, she shot him a scornful glance. "We do not go to gajé's fire. Gajé make their own trouble." The word for his people was snarled. "We made ready to break camp, in case the whole world was burning. The fire died and we slept."

He was sure there was more to tell than that. "But – when did you come to my house? How did you know –"

"Your wagon was in the yard. You live in a house made of bricks the colour of a sickness of the liver." Yellow-grey. Again a scornful note.

"You must never come to my house. Never! You understand?"

"We were telling fortunes. We walked a long way, Dui and I. We were tired."

"Fortunes! Don't lie to me!"

"All right!" Her eyes flashed and her skirt swished a small gust of wind as she turned away. "I came to see your fine lady. I wanted to see what she looked like, how she lived."

"My God. I should kill you for that."

"Why? Am I not fit to knock on your door?"

"Violette." Contrite, he cupped her chin and turned her face toward him. "She must never know, never suspect anything."

"I just knocked on the door. It was after the midday meal, as you gajé say. The sun was high." Her face relaxed and she smiled, unafraid of his anger. "A lady answered, but she did not look as I expected your lady to. Her hair was tied back in a scarf like our women wear, but the scarf was ugly, the colour of dust. She wore a work dress and no rings and she was not all lard and bustle but a skinny woman, with skin the colour of your house." *Minnie.*

When? "A week or more ago?"

"It was the day we found the pullets wandering in the road, seven of them. Near the creek." She jerked her head to the right.

"What day? The day of the fire?"

She shook her head. "One moon, maybe two, before that. We went to the door and I said, 'Missy, read your fortune, good fortune, guaranteed happy future' the way I always do. She did not look like a woman with a happy future, but I did not smell death on her and I was ready to tell her happy life, good husband, many babies. A kind lady. She opened the door wider and I saw another lady at a table, drinking from a cup –" Violette crooked her little finger mockingly. "Her eyes looked watery. This is a woman who eats too much butter and salt and fries her meat in much grease. 'Close the door,' she said, 'send them away, whoever they are.' The little woman looked sorry, but she closed the door and we went away. That is all."

His knees were about to give out. "Don't ever do that again! Violette, promise me!"

She looked away and studied the trees, as if looking for answers to unasked questions. "The one who came to the door – she died in the fire, didn't she."

A python twisted in his bowels. He hadn't eaten, yet he wanted to retch. God, oh, God, what was he doing here? The whole world knew his trouble, refused to let him escape it, even for a moment. "Violette – there was a tinsmith in the area the day of the fire. Travelling alone on foot."

"Not one of us. We do not go alone among your people." He knew she was telling the truth.

He took out his watch. "I have to go soon."

"We know more," Violette said. "We heard the talk from the town. They say your brother did this thing."

He crumpled then, and she urged him toward her wagon, half supporting his sagging body. "Lie back and let me look after you." She pushed him gently back onto her straw mattress. "Say nothing. Think of nothing for a while. Later we will talk." He closed his eyes and let her comfort him in her soft, sensual ways, marvelling only briefly at his selfishness in stealing those moments. Shouldn't he feel guilty, deserting the others? It was as if he stood at a distance and watched himself, not caring. Nothing mattered except Violette, her flesh, her hair, her tongue, the warm exotic sweetness of her body.

Afterward, they shared a corncob pipe of acrid tobacco. He could see through a crack in the wagon that the sun had climbed in a cloudless sky. She took short, terse puffs like a man. "Do you love your brother?"

"I – suppose so. I did once."

"As I love Dui?"

"Perhaps."

She passed him the pipe. "No one knows the secrets in another's heart. If you put yourself inside his skin, inside his soul, what do you feel?"

He drew on the pipe, reluctant to answer. When he spoke finally, he let the words roll into the smoke, as if he was not sure he wanted them to be heard. "Suffering, I suppose. Yes. Great suffering. Confusion and sorrow. Remorse. No place to go, no one to turn to." He watched, in a trance as she took the pipe from him. "I see someone accused, perhaps unjustly. No one will listen. Someone made sport of by gossipmongers."

Violette lifted the canvas flap and dumped the contents of the pipe. "Then should you not act accordingly, as if all sorrows, all sins are yours?"

"Violette –" Whatever it was he wanted to say was lost. "I must go." He clambered out of the wagon and held his hands out, pulling her after him.

"You must not come here again."

"Why?" He blinked in the sunlight, feeling desolate as they made their way toward the stream.

"One day soon we will be gone."

"Where?" What was the use of asking?

"South." She laughed. "Like the birds. It will be a bad winter here. Death. Starvation. My people must go where it is warmer."

"Will you come back?" He knew he shouldn't ask.

Violette bent to pluck a clover. "Ask the wind. Ask the trees when their leaves are blowing away. Will the leaves come back?"

"It'll depend which way the wind is blowing." He quoted the answer she had given him before. He made a move toward her and she leaned against him, fixing the clover in his lapel and kissing him quickly. "Go!"

He left her gathering her skirt to fill with clover for the horses. At the bank of the stream he turned, needing one last picture of her to hold in his memory. A breeze whipped up and he felt a chill. He thought of Charley in the sugar bush, gathering haws. A big, soft, innocent boy, someone had said. "Violette."

Looking up, she smiled.

"I – wish my conscience was as clear as my brother's." He regretted the words as soon as he uttered them. They should have been lost in smoke, like the words that had come from deep inside his soul – or was it Charley's soul? But they hung there, between them, crystal-clear in the sunlight.

"Never say that to another living soul."

She was right. He had too many secrets. Who would understand?

Galloping away, he took the clover from his lapel and tried to fasten it on the bridle but it blew away. Old Red sped on with the fury of a young racehorse, as if anxious to return him to the real world before he changed his mind.

He dug his spurs in only once, forcing the animal to take a sharp left toward Irish Creek. As the village came into view, he wept for all the people he would never see again: his father, Martha, Minnie.

Violette.

Chapter Five

"I don't see Old Red but it's no wonder." Ansley Stewart scanned the jumble of wagons and horses choking Irish Creek's main street. "Every man and his beast for fifty miles around is here. Women and children, too." He pursed his lips and Liza Ann knew he was thinking of his own Margaret, safe at home.

Boys on the dirt road had pointed him in the direction of McCrum's blacksmith shop. "The room over the forge. It's the only place big enough." An older youth guided Ansley's rig through the wall of wagons to space marked off for the family at Nevins' Hotel, directly across from McCrum's.

Ansley edged in between a dog cart and a landau and helped Liza Ann and Victoria down. "I'll go find Johnny."

Blushing, Liza Ann murmured her thanks. Ansley couldn't have failed to notice something was wrong from the moment he had come to the house, but he'd never let on. It had been half an hour ago, when she'd already fed the children and warmed the tongs, styling Victoria's hair in long, tight ringlets like her own. While Victoria had taken Esley to a neighbour's, she had washed the dishes. Later they had sat, waiting for Johnny, Victoria pretending to practise sums on her slate until Liza Ann rose and snatched it away. "I just cleaned and pressed that outfit and now you're getting chalk all over it! Victoria, will you never learn?"

She was sorry immediately after. The child had started to cry, and Liza Ann had gone to her, and cuddled and rocked her as if she was still a baby. Where was Johnny? Was he coming back for them or should she take the buggy and go ahead? Her own tears fell on Victoria's curls. After a long time, she straightened up and went to the bureau in the hall to get her Sunday gloves and reticule. It was eight-thirty.

She was fastening her bonnet with a beaded hat pin when Victoria shouted, "Daddy's here!" But the noise they heard was the rumbling of wagon wheels, not the clopping of Old Red. Ansley stood at the door a moment later, hat in hand.

It was better to answer his questions before he asked them. "Johnny's gone on ahead." She lowered her eyes and picked imaginary lint from her sleeve. "He – had business. Something to do with the estate. I was just about to hitch up the buggy."

Ansley didn't bat an eye. He knows, Liza Ann thought. The old man knows everything. But he's kind. He shepherded them to his own wagon, helped them up with a gallantry peculiar to his generation, the generation of her father-in-law who despite his gruffness had also remembered his manners. Old men, courtly and considerate, and always – of this she was certain – faithful to their wives. None of those virtues had rubbed off on Johnny. What did such men as Ansley think of Johnny?

They rattled the four swift miles to Irish Creek, Ansley cracking his whip high, careful not to let it touch the old carthorse. He talked of the weather and harvesting and asked Victoria did they still have spelling bees at school like when he was a boy. "I could outspell anyone, even the teacher." His eyes twinkled. "Why, I remember the school inspector coming one morning while I was in second book and asking if anyone could spell Egg-wiped! Can you imagine? I was the only pupil who guessed what he meant. Egypt! E-g-y-p-t!" He laughed. "Try that one on Esley, Victoria!"

Bless him, Liza Ann thought. We could be on a pleasure jaunt, with nothing more serious on our minds than gathering milkweed.

She watched him circulating among the wagons, hailing neighbours as he headed toward McCrum's. A couple of boys were opening the blacksmith's shop, dragging the weathered doors outward, scraping baked dirt and stunted grass. Sunlight shone on the front windows, each small pane opaque with dirt. An ugly building, depressing, hardly fit for the event about to take place. There was no dignity anywhere for the dead; would there be any justice? The entrance, wide enough for a wagon to pass through into the forge, was flooded with people before the doors could be fastened back.

Victoria was peevish: her ringlets were coming loose; she was thirsty; she had a pebble in her shoe. She kept her head down as they moved through the crowd. "I should have left you with Esley," Liza Ann said.

Victoria glowered. "I'm a witness – remember?"

Before she could think of a suitable reprimand, Liza Ann heard a shout and saw Old Red in the distance, steaming and snorting, dust flying up from his hooves.

Alighting, Johnny muttered an apology, avoiding Liza Ann's gaze. Glancing around, he caught sight of a grey-suited man alighting from a buggy. "Sorry, I had business with Lavell."

Liar! Liza Ann flushed at the obscenity of her thoughts. *You saw Lavell yesterday, after the funeral.* She plucked a fragment of leaf from his lapel and dropped it into the dust, grinding it under her heel. Forcing her face to assume its mask of serenity, she crooked her arm, feeling the familiar, perfunctory touch of his hand on her elbow. She fancied she could detect the scent of another woman on him. How ridiculous, in this crush of powdered, cologned matrons! Who could it be this time? Most of the women she knew were here today. Somebody's servant girl, probably. Two or three times she had hired a girl to wash and iron, but the help never stayed long. They left on some feeble excuse, giving the impression they were afraid to say what the real reason was. When the last girl left – August, was it? – a bright Irish girl with a cheerful manner and a willing pair of hands, Liza Ann had confronted Johnny, asking him outright if he knew why young Bridget had left. "Did you do anything to send her off like that?" The girl had fled one afternoon, leaving carrots on the chopping board and sheets in the bluing tub, dashing down the driveway with her bundle under one arm, her other hand clamped to her flimsy bonnet.

Johnny had flushed darkly. "You'd better speak your mind, woman!"

"Were you – making advances?"

He had raised a hand as if to strike her, then turned away, snarling something about people not being able to take a joke. She'd remembered then, whispers at quilting bees, knowing glances in the church choir. And there was nothing – nothing! – she could do.

Hemmed in, Liza Ann set her face in what she hoped was an

appropriate smile, one that bespoke family unity without ignoring the gravity of the occasion. In her head, as always, her mother's voice parroted platitudes straight out of the ladies' section of the Farmer's Advocate. "A wife is born to please her husband. There is no greater reward on earth than that of making your husband happy." Oh, the guilt, and the resentment at the need to feel guilty! Smile firmly pasted, she moved forward. *The worst of it is, he's so smug. He thinks I don't know. And I don't really. Who. Or where. Even why.* Sometimes she caught a look on the face of a woman passing on a street in Smith's Falls or Toledo, triumphant, predatory, as if she were saying, foolish wife, you turned your back on him, took your eyes off him for an instant, now he's mine. Was she imagining things? She could never be vigilant enough. With the will to cheat came the deviousness needed to succeed at it.

Even in not knowing, I know.

She watched as Victoria danced in front of her father and brushed a straw from his shoulder. "Dad! You look like you've been sleeping in the barn. Where's your coat?"

The apoplectic darkening of his skin would have alarmed her in different circumstances. *He's left it behind, at her place! Damn him!* Her smile quivered, disappeared as she searched for a harmless topic. "Did you ask Mr. Lavell about acting for Charley?" *Harmless? Oh, Lord!*

"Don't be silly, woman." His breath rasped against her ear. "Haven't I already said I won't be roped into paying for Charley's defence? I told Lavell that yesterday."

"Then why see him again this morning?" The desire to see him squirm overwhelmed her.

"Estate matters. Got to determine who died first."

"Excuse me, sir. *The Globe*, Toronto." A young man with hair parted in the middle grasped Johnny's hand and shook it. "I know this isn't the time to intrude –"

"That's right. It isn't." Before Johnny could push past, a band of reporters crowded around him. "How do you feel about your brother's arrest, sir? Are you standing by him?"

"You mean, do I think he's guilty? That is what you mean, isn't it." Johnny held up a hand. "All right. One statement. Take it all down. Then leave us alone."

They waited, flashing each other glances that said how surprised, how moved they were, at this gift about to be bestowed.

"The chain of circumstantial evidence against my brother is very damaging." Johnny put his hands in his pockets and looked beyond them at the weather-beaten sign over the blacksmith's door. "My wife and I are anxious to see the perpetrator brought to justice, even if it turns out to be my own brother. These are hard words to say, but I mean them all the same. I myself am going to unravel the mystery, if it takes me the rest of my life." He raised his hand again, signalling the end of the interview and, clutching Liza Ann's elbow, steered her through the doors.

A shout arose and bodies reversed direction, rushing toward the street. "He's here! The murderer's here!"

"Cool one, ain't he. Don't give a tinker's dam."

How cold it is all of a sudden, even in the sunlight, Liza Ann thought. I won't look, I won't think about it, it's not real. In spite of herself, she turned and, as she clung to the door frame trying to keep her balance, she remembered yesterday's newspaper: *No talk of lynching speaks volumes for the good sense and orderly nature of the community*. What nonsense!

McGowan and the city detective were jumping from a buggy and reaching up for a third person whose legs were manacled. *Charley*! He looked straight at her in the second before Johnny pulled her inside the blacksmith's shop.

* * *

Billy Greer watched everybody, heard everything. He saw Johnny Luckey pulling his wife into McCrum's. The woman's expression was one of fierce, galled serenity, if such a thing were possible. He'd seen the expression on people too well bred to commit murder, even when it was justified. He wondered if she had practised in front of a mirror, turning the corners of her mouth up while her teeth gnashed and her eyes betrayed loathing. The child, Victoria, gloved and bonneted like his own daughters would be for church, turned to follow. Mother and daughter, same height, hair like long, charred sausages, the girl the slenderer but full-bosomed already, unlikely to escape her mother's lardiness.

He'd caught Johnny's expression before he vanished, proud of his chattels, grave and irritated and proprietorial all at once. "Seat the family in the front row," he ordered the constable who was clearing the way. Leaving McGowan and two part-time deputies to handle the prisoner, he followed on the constable's heels.

It was Billy who first noticed the foundation sleepers groaning when he reached the top of the stairs. "Clear the room! Christ, we'll all go crashing through to the forge!" Why hadn't someone told him?

Dr. Vaux, too polite even in crisis to shout the oafs down, raised his hand. "Gentlemen! An orderly exit, please!"

"Jesus! The floor won't hold! Everybody out!" Greer pushed his way to a side door and threw it open. He flattened himself against a wall as half the crowd tumbled out onto a makeshift fire escape of steep, wooden steps, some overshooting the platform and landing on a shed beside the forge. Others escaped down the inside stairs, through the forge and out onto the road. Vaux and McGowan hugged the inside stair wall, the prisoner between them. "McCrum!" the Chief boomed. "How many'll the room hold?"

Below, the blacksmith's anvil rang out with a steady, unhurried beat. "I'd say forty, maybe fifty," he called out.

Billy groaned. "All right. Jury, witnesses, lawmen. Call them by name, McGowan, and send them up single file. Count them." A laborious business, delaying proceedings. "Let's get on with it. Chief Rose expects to take the prisoner to Brockville tonight."

An hour passed in reorganization. The chosen, subdued and enumerated, settled on wooden chairs. A dozen reporters pushed into the forge and up the stairs, McGowan bellowing after them. "It's all right, Chief." McCrum picked up his anvil again. "She'll hold this many, easy."

"Bar the door." The outsiders were like flies around a honey pot. Billy had seen this kind of thing before. They'd mill about all day, the men with excuses that a horse needed shoeing or an axle repairing. McCrum would do a land-office business. So would Nevins' Hotel. The ring of the anvil and the odour of horse dung pursued him as he re-entered the upstairs room and closed the door.

Edging to a window, he rubbed a circle of dirt away and peered at the crowd below. Women, mostly! No pride, starved for excitement. Mostly matrons built like railway carriages, solid blocks chuffing along. The last time he'd seen such bloodthirsty curiosity had been at a hanging in L'Orignal in '90.

Dr. Vaux was planting a chair at the front beside the exhibit table, facing the crowd. "Witnesses when called will come forward and give evidence here! Jury on the right, the press at the back."

Charley was pushed to the front by two constables, to be installed on a chair a little apart from the others. Vaux frowned. "Should he be seated so near the witnesses?"

Greer gestured to Charley's leg chains. "He's not going anywhere."

McGowan leaned toward him. "The fellow in the grey suit at the back. Johnny told the constable to admit him. Lavell. Local lawyer."

Greer nodded recognition. "When I was here for the firebrand trial he was in court on some matter. He angling to defend Luckey?"

"Not likely. Specializes in property deals, partnerships and the like. Owns Perrin Plow Company on the side. Johnny does business with him."

"What are those?" He watched as Lavell unfolded some legal-size papers, pointed out something to Johnny, then refolded them before handing them over.

McGowan shrugged.

Simple soul, McGowan. Too much trust and too little curiosity to make a first-rate detective. His greatest pride this morning had been in counting his jurors and announcing that not one had reneged on his promise to appear. "Threat of gaol helped!"

Billy had stared at him, aghast. "D'you realize that three of your jurors are also prime witnesses?"

"Great idea, don't you think?" McGowan had beamed like a child with a good report card. "Who better to weigh the evidence? Besides, shows solidarity."

"Only if they agree."

"They'll agree."

Greer had raised an eyebrow. The Chief's naivete was reaching legendary proportions. He seemed to order his world the way schoolboys did, with a system of threats and rewards. If it worked, it was probably because he didn't probe too deeply into the results. Last night, in their final hasty conference in McGowan's office, McGowan had bemoaned the fact that they hadn't gotten a confession. "The inquest should change all that. Now we'll get at the truth."

Greer had snorted. "You never get the truth. Just shysters and charlatans and warped minds and bad actors all swearing on the Bible and smiling innocently. You get demure little virgins and holier-than-thou pillars of society and pious men of the cloth doing the same, and sleeping at night, secure in the knowledge that they've told the truth, the whole truth and nothing but the truth. But how do they define truth? Eh? Birchall swore he told the truth, and perhaps believed his words himself. But Birchall wouldn't have known the truth if it leaped up and bit him."

McGowan had polished a button absently with his thumb. "Birchall was a liar and a blackguard. Maybe they should have sweated the truth out of him. I can't believe there aren't ways to get a criminal to tell the truth."

"Oh, he'll tell you the truth." Greer had regarded McGowan with amusement. "The truth as he saw it. He may tell us what he did and why he did it, but the reasons make sense only to him; to listen to him may be to distort the truth. Therein lies a great danger. A man confesses to a crime, tells what he perceives as truth as to motive, contaminates the account of the deed and confuses the issues with blubberings and simperings and perhaps some fist-shaking oratory. Provocation. Mitigating cause. Extenuating circumstances. In the end, the only question left to answer is, what is truth?" It's what the law is all about, he might have added. But would McGowan understand that sometimes the law had to be protected from itself? "There's a theory now that a criminal is always innocent, his parents or society are to blame. It all goes back to his childhood: he didn't get enough to eat, or always wore hand-me-downs, or got a flogging every night when his Pa rolled home drunk." Greer warmed to his subject, echoing Murray. "There's a doctor in Vienna –"

McGowan had wiped his brow. "Too complicated for me."

"I'm simply saying that reality depends upon the perceiver. One man's truth is another man's pipe dream." Murray would be proud of him, couldn't have done better himself! "Think how different a case looks to a prosecutor than to defence counsel."

McGowan, satisfied with the pristine condition of his uniform, squinted at Greer's lapels. "So both men work with the same truth, they just present it differently."

"I'm saying both men work with what they perceive as truth. Neither knows the truth."

McGowan nodded glumly. "Even if Charley confesses we may never get the truth."

"If he confesses, the truth as he sees it may get him off."

"Whoa, Billy! We haven't even got him arraigned yet."

Greer, oppressed by the close air in the cramped little office, rose to leave. "I say, does truth matter? He's guilty. Let's not cloud the issue with ifs, ands and buts. Three people are dead. We know who killed them. We feel it here." He pounded his gut. "How or why doesn't matter."

"Should we bother to keep looking for the red-stockinged tinsmith?"

"Of course. If we can show he's not our man, it strengthens our case. The tinsmith left the area before the fire started." He watched as McGowan seized his lamp and accompanied him to the door. "Our job at the inquest is to convince the right people that our evidence ensures that they're not making a mistake when they bring in a finding of murder. Then, at Luckey's trial, we convince the right people to send him to the gallows. When he swings, they have to feel righteous, vindicated, satisfied. We have to make them believe they know enough truth to justify the outcome."

"And it may not be true at all."

"Just hold onto one idea. He's guilty. How we tighten the noose matters only in the way it appears to the authorities." Greer chuckled. "At the Ringer-James trial, the judge said the evidence of men like me should always be viewed with suspicion. So be it. My evidence sent those scoundrels up for fourteen years."

As he spoke, Billy watched the shadows etch lines of guilt on McGowan's face. "You take it hard because you know these people, Bob. Maybe in some corner of your mind there exists a hope that the prisoner is innocent."

"Not a chance, Billy. He had guilt written all over him when I arrested him."

"Good. Just remember, a good detective knows everyone and has no friends. No one knows him." His eyes narrowed at the Chief's penetrating look. "How well do you know me? You don't know if I have a wife, children, a rich mistress, whether I drink to excess, gamble or amuse myself in my off hours by dressing up in ladies' bloomers." He punched McGowan's shoulder.

Dr. Vaux, breaking in on his reverie as the last spaces filled for the inquest, saw the detective's features soften as Victoria Luckey switched seats with her mother. "You have daughters, Mr. Greer? One of mine is that young lady's age. Horrible for her, this happening in the family."

But Billy's mind was far from daughters. "You question the witnesses, doctor. I'll cross-examine."

Vaux clapped his hands; Sunday-suited posteriors met wood, a hush settled. The doctor's well-modulated, antiseptic voice rang out. "Frank Mills!"

A diffident, ruddy-faced man lumbered to the front and handed Vaux a fistful of papers. "Plans of the Luckey farmhouse and vicinity," Vaux announced. "Take your time, gentlemen. Ask yourselves if they are accurate."

Fingers fumbled for reading glasses; lips moved silently; a chair scraped. Billy kept his voice low. "Christ's sake, Vaux, I didn't come all the way from Toronto to take a late morning nap!" Farmers were on a schedule dictated by nature: seasons, weather, animal cycles. The nineteen good men and true, their crops in, appeared to have nothing else to do until spring. "The plans can wait. It's the brother you should take your time with. We want family history, disputes, old grievances, threats. Give the prisoner a motive and place him at the scene, if you can."

"He's not on trial, Mr. Greer. The purpose of the inquest –"

"I know, doctor. But we have a man in custody." He patted the expensive shoulder, inhaled the minty breath. "Trust me, sir. It's to our advantage –"

"John James Luckey, junior!" If annoyed, Vaux gave no sign.

Breakfast had been tepid coffee and burnt toast at the Palace. Billy's stomach rumbled as he watched Johnny approach. A man his own age, once good-looking but fast going to seed. *All right, mister, prepare to air your family's dirty linen. There but for the grace of God go you in your brother's footsteps.*

Billy Greer saw everything: the jury shifting and resettling like a restless tide; Johnny, seating himself like some arthritic old retiree. And Charley – who had the steadiest gaze of anyone in the room, except possibly Billy himself – following his brother's movements. Cool, Charley looked. Nonchalant. Innocent. *Little bastard, you can't fool me. And I'll see to it that you don't fool anyone else!*

Chapter Six

We're the knowingest men here, me and the old bloodhound. We're watching, him to see if he can catch me at something and me because staring at my hands would just make him think I can't look him in the eye. I won't give him the satisfaction of seeing me rub my ankles, either, no matter how raw they get from that too-short chain. Hurts like hell. If there was a fire in here, how the hell would I get out in time? Greer'd think I had it coming.

His skin itched, dry patches like his father's sheepdog got in the winter. Poor old Dixie died in the fire, they said. *Come off it, don't think about it. Count the people. Looks like hundreds, all here to speak against me. Do I have any friends?*

Not on the jury, mooing in their corner like a bunch of cattle. Half of them can't read or write, yet they'll sign my life away. Is that fair? What's fair in this world? I know most all of them, and the witnesses, too. Dozens came to the lockup to gawk and pry and try to disarm me by passing on gossip about everyone else. Caught me up on local news, for what it's worth.

There's the threshers, Brunton the Scottie who works for Jonas Bruce and who found an axe with blood on it, and cousin Jack Phillips who found some teeth and is wed to one of the Moran girls. Ronan and Loman, and the Hitchcocks senior and junior, and Will Daley whose mother puts gasoline on her knees for her arthritis and Ansley Stewart who all the family calls Uncle I'm not sure why. There's Hannah from the train, looking sheepish because they slipped him into the lockup last night to make sure he could identify me. Whisked him out before we could exchange a word.

136

And all the people who say they seen me on the road coming and going, Alex Mercier and Moorhouse and Polk's hired man and one of the Stewarts and even old Willy Lyle, Marthy's brother who says he asked me what was burning and I don't even remember.

There's Jonas Bruce who has two thousand maple trees in his sugar bush and tells everybody I was the best hand who ever worked for him. And his old maid sister Alvira, curious as a cat, who I can't ever see without remembering her berry picking expeditions with us kids, stained fingers and mosquito bites and stomach aches. And Andrew Parker's brought his brood but not his wife and looks annoyed because he has to sit with the jurors and squeeze Isabella and the boys in beside Sarah Jane Daley. And she, pretty Sarah Jane, sits with her eyes down, but some time today she's going to look right at me, I'm going to will her to.

There's the Smith's Falls contingent, not one can look me in the eye, Corbett the barber and Corbett the marblecutter and Gile the shoeman and that wag who declared I'd stink the whole town up when I was sitting on the curb with my socks off. And Willis, who's got the Palace Hotel up for sale and is asking a thousand more today than it was worth last week because I, Charley Luckey, slept there. There's Frost the mayor who arrives last and expects the best seat in the house and Polk, the bandy-legged hero following McGowan around like teacher's pet. There's Liza Ann's Uncle Will Jones the cheesemaker and Jacques the postmaster and John Edgar the J.P. with wife number four or five, I've lost count.

There's Liza Ann looking teary, bless her, and Victoria sitting tall beside her, and Johnny who won't look at me, even when he has to pass my chair. Look at me, Johnny.

But Johnny, in the witness chair, was speaking to the far wall. "I am a farmer and speculator, residing on lot fifteen, concession five. My father owned 150 acres, fifty of which he lived on and a hundred in two pieces down the road. My place is three-quarters of a mile below my father's."

They were his own, folks he had known all his life. They wouldn't keep him in gaol. They'd say, Charley, Charley, you didn't do anything, whatever happened you didn't do it.

But there was a smell, sensed rather than inhaled, clinging to him like an itch, an afterthought, coming up from under all the other smells. You could smell mothballs and pomanders here, and barnyard, tannery and forge. But this was different, a mood – could you smell a mood? More an animal scent, perhaps, as if a strange dog had gotten into the pack.

People didn't speak or acknowledge him directly. But they never forgot he was there. It was as if he had marked out his territory, pissed along the boundaries, and no one would step inside his circle. Only Greer watched him and Greer, like himself, was outside the pack. But Greer was a trapper, setting snares for Johnny and everyone here who had once been close to him, Charley, feeding them words meant to take away his freedom forever.

"Father never gave me nor any of my brothers property by way of a portion." Johnny's tone was flat, as if he was repeating a recitation for which he had no ear or enthusiasm. "In a few instances, Father gave small sums of money. He wasn't wealthy, just what I'd call a well-to-do farmer."

Dr Vaux ignored Greer's signalling. "Did you ever have any legal difficulties with your father, Mr Luckey?"

Johnny hesitated, then continued his monotone. "Just a little trouble this spring. I put in crops and promised to do the reaping, but when I didn't do it during one week of bad weather, he got others to do it. Then, when we were both out of temper, I demanded pay. There were hot words. I finally had to threaten suit when he paid it."

Good, Johnny, you didn't fall into their trap. They don't want to hear about your crop dispute. Look at Greer, mad as a wet hen, steering the doctor over to the corner for a little set-to.

Vaux tried again. "Mr Luckey. Could you tell us – specifically – about a land transaction in '84?"

Again the flatness, verses by rote. "Father sold all his land to Charley and Sam and asked me to go security for them as the boys could not pay much down. I told him he had as much right to trust them as I did and I gave no bonds. This was the fall before and the next spring, in '84, there was more trouble. All I know is that Father made application to court to get his land back and got it."

That's as much as they need to know!

A flush crept up Johnny's face. "What's the point of bringing all this up? What does it have to do with the fire?"

"I'm sorry, sir. Did you ever discuss wills with your father?"

"Once. He consulted me. Said he would not cut any of his sons out." He paused as Greer nudged Vaux aside and stood before him, waiting. "I remember hearing Charley say he was well provided for by Father. Sam, Father and I were present and it may be that Father said

Charley was well provided for. Or else Sam did and Father heard him."
He stared at his feet. "I – had another conversation with Father about
wills in which I asked him to cut me out altogether and take some from
Sam and the others as we were doing well, in order to fix Charley and
Minnie up. This he said he would do, but I think he's made two wills
since then."

"Did you know of any serious charge, such as forgery, made
against Charley by your father?"

Johnny shook his head. "Never. I heard Father say he thought
more of him than any of us." He half turned toward Charley but
avoided his eyes. "I know until lately he was my favourite brother."

Bullshit! Come on, Johnny, look at me, I won't burn your barns –

Suddenly Johnny wheeled and looked directly at him and then
everything was a blur, Johnny pausing mid-sentence, mouth open,
the doctor, buttonhole wilting, Greer bending toward him
whispering. They swam out of focus, blended flesh, fabric; Greer,
closest to Charley, almost close enough to touch him, seemed to swim
away from the others and hover. *Oh, yes, he sees everything!*

Vaux was gentle. "Now, about your sister – Minnie? – yes. I'm
sorry, sir, could you tell us when you last saw her?" He studied his nails
while Johnny struggled with his composure, muttered that he had last
seen her at breakfast Saturday. "I saw – what was supposed to be her
remains –" He dragged a handkerchief from his back pocket.

"I do apologize, sir, but we must continue. Do you know what
kind and size of boots your stepmother wore?"

Johnny blew noisily. "I couldn't swear to what kind but I never
knew her to wear lace ones. Her size was probably five. My father got
her a pair of shoes last year in Smith's Falls. I didn't see them, but I
heard her grumbling as to their being hard."

"And your father's boots?"

"About a six. But he frequently wore gaiters."

The crowd bent forward, reeds in a strong wind, as McGowan
held up a pair of boots. "Taken from the prisoner the night of his
arrest!" John Lavell, at the back, rose to get a better look. Johnny
took his time. "They're of the style he often wore. Perhaps a little
heavier. I'm afraid I can't identify them as his."

Vaux took them from him. "Was your father in the habit of
carrying money on his person?"

"Yes."

Greer strained to hear Johnny's lowered voice. Whispers of blood-stained bills! It didn't take long for word to get around!

"I drove to my father's with Alderman Devlin of Ottawa. Devlin purchased three head of cattle. On my advice, he went back and purchased the bull. The total sale was $78, but as he didn't take the cattle he only paid something down to bind the bargain."

Greer waved the doctor aside. "Did your brother ever make threats to any family members? Think carefully, Mr Luckey."

Charley thought carefully, too. He was still, imagining himself in the sugar bush. Not daring to move, to look to right or left, to pop one of the haws, warm and wilting, in his mouth. He had an empty feeling, a gnawing hunger, but he couldn't move, couldn't will his hand from lap to mouth. Everything was still, leaves had stopped rustling, no birds sang from branches.

He sat there for hours, the sun warm on his head, the silence a blanket, the long, warm silence a place to go looking for dreams at night when he couldn't sleep and the dark pressed in and he smelled fear. He would sit there beyond hunger and weariness, beyond remembrance, and if he could not remember, surely no one could, not Father not Martha not Minnie. Not Johnny.

* * *

Billy Greer saw that Charley had stopped listening. "He made direct threats to me," Johnny was saying, "the construction of which I took to be that I should not be surprised if my barns burned."

"Those were his words?"

"No, but I inferred it."

No reaction from Charley. "Sir, could you tell us about your brother's suicide attempt?"

Johnny squinted. "That was five, six years ago. I visited Charley in Toronto just after he shot himself. He blamed Father for his troubles. Afterwards he came down to my place, but would not go near Father's. Father asked me to induce him to go over, but he wouldn't." He glanced hesitantly at his brother. "When I insisted, he broke down crying and said, 'There's a bullet in my body that would not be there except for Father.' I replied, 'Charley, I'm of the opinion you had a hand in shooting yourself.'"

"And did you understand from your father that the last will he made was not favourable to Charley?"

"I never saw the third will until this morning." Johnny's glance flickered to Lavell, then to Liza Ann. "It has an equal division among us."

"Thank you, sir. Prisoner! Do you wish to ask questions of the witness?" *Still day-dreaming.* "Constable! Give the prisoner a tap with your stick."

Charley's voice came from far off, but his eyes were clear, his gaze steady. "No. No questions."

"That's all, Mr Luckey. Andrew Parker, you're next."

It never ceased to amaze Billy how most of the human race developed uncontrollable coughs when there was nothing to listen to, and how quickly they muffled or swallowed them when there was. No one coughed while Parker told how he had raced the eight hundred yards from his home to the Luckey farmhouse; how he discovered the fire, the bodies. He spoke in a loud, clear voice and was plainly disappointed when waved back to his seat among the jurors.

Billy consulted his list. "Miss Isabella Parker!"

The Parker and Daley girls were sitting together, stealing glances at the prisoner. Older than Billy's own girls, but some similarity, one plain, one pretty. Showing the disadvantages of rural isolation, weathered skin and out-of-fashion clothes. His girls were coddled by their mother, wearing veils to protect their milk-white complexions, making regular trips to their dressmaker and milliner, keeping indoors at the least sign of a sniffle. But this pair before him – would they ever marry? A portly widower, perhaps, with a brood of runny-nosed children? Young Martha Luckeys! One too shy, blushing and dimpled, the other too homely, hair scraped back in a bun like a spinster school marm, glasses sliding down her nose – determined, it seemed, to repel any advances by the opposite sex. What was it about this breed of woman, he wondered, that made her keep herself to herself, almost from the cradle, turning invisible when an eligible man appeared? He'd seen it in his own family. Fear of childbirth, perhaps? An overdeveloped sense of prudery? Or some unspoken family mandate, consigning her to the role of nursemaid for aging parents and orphaned nieces and nephews? Such a woman Minnie Luckey had been, and what had it got her? An early, violent death, at the hand of someone she loved and trusted, a victim of her own ill-timed good will.

Isabella Parker lumbered to the front, a little lopsided, a carthorse pulling a heavy load. Not batting an eye when McGowan flourished the teeth. "I'm afraid I can't identify them, sir, as I never saw them out of her mouth." Not a trace of sarcasm.

"But they could be hers?"

"I doubt it, sir. They don't look to me like the kind of false teeth a young woman would wear." She wrinkled her nose but looked steadfastly at the exhibit.

"Do you recognize the prisoner?"

"I can't say as I do, sir. It's a good many years since I last saw him."

"Thank you, that's all." Billy glanced at his watch and began calling the threshers, one by one, to the stand.

* * *

Outside at lunch, accepting a sandwich and slapping a dime in the outstretched palm of a shivering hotel messenger, Billy knew his stomach would protest later. The beef was thick and moist with a great crust of fat on it. He chewed and talked simultaneously. "We're spending too long on witnesses we don't need until the trial. Right now we need witnesses who can identify Charley and place him in the vicinity of the crime; witnesses who remember he held a grudge and tried to conceal his identity."

McGowan slurped noisily from his mug. "We need a witness who saw him at the farm, at the time of the fire, axe in hand, going after the victims. Then no jury in the country –"

Billy shoved the last of his sandwich in his mouth. "Don't be too sure. There was a case last year in Ancaster, an old fellow shot to death in front of his wife and daughter. Two witnesses, four men arrested. The killers were masked. But the witnesses heard their voices, saw their height and build and walk. Wasn't good enough. They got off scot free, the lot." He handed his empty cup to an urchin. "So don't ask for miracles."

McGowan gulped the last of his coffee. "You realize the assizes start Monday?"

"I was the one who pointed that out, Bob, remember? Look, get subpoenas out for everyone who appears today. Get someone working on it now, so we can hand them out." He saw Vaux frown. "We know what the finding will be today, doctor. We have to be prepared. I'll take Luckey's clothes to Toronto to the analyst. You get the exhibits together, Bob. And don't run around clacking the teeth at everyone."

They went back inside where Billy, without preamble, called John Hannah, who averred that the parcel of underwear produced bore a striking resemblance to the parcel on the train. McGowan held up the bills found on Charley; Hannah shook his head. "The money I saw was chiefly in ten cent pieces. Oh – and he wore a watch."

"Can you describe his boots?"

"Can't say."

"Socks, then?"

"I – think they were red."

Billy waved him away and the parade continued, witnesses who saw the prisoner heading toward Newbliss in the morning, Smith's Falls at night. Polk's farmhand, anxious to make an impression, pointed a trembling finger at Charley. "I remarked to my companion the man on the road was either a robber or a murderer."

Billy thanked him. Such enthusiasm often hindered rather than helped a case simply by virtue of its sensationalism.

Polk, uneasy hero, ignored the crowd's shuffling as he related his encounter with Charley in a clipped monotone. Billy had only one question. "Are you sure the prisoner is the man you saw on the road?"

Polk's small chin set. "I have not the slightest doubt."

Corbett the marblecutter, testifying that the prisoner said he knew nothing about the Luckeys, brought Charley to his feet, manacles clanking. "Liar! I never said that! You're distorting it all!"

"You did too, Charley." Corbett scratched his belly unconcernedly. "I heard you, in the hotel."

He paused as a constable opened the side door to let fresh air in; a dozen women, teetering on the top platform and the steps below, slipped inside, whispering apologies. Several men vacated seats and went to lean against the wall.

McGowan was on his feet. "I'll question these witnesses, Greer. I was there."

"Sure you were!" Charley shouted. "You'll put words in their mouths." Willis the hotelier, propelled to the front, was pondering the witness chair with distaste. "Don't worry, Willis, I can't reach you!"

"Tell us, Willis, how the prisoner acted at the hotel."

"Very peculiar, I'd say, was of the opinion he might die at any moment. He never voluntarily gave his name, then or later."

Charley stamped a shackled boot. "Did I ask if you knew me, Willis? Did I? Me, Charley Luckey. Did I?"

"Ah, yes," Willis stared at the chains. "You did."

McGowan roared his disgust. "Shut up, you! Willis – are you positive about that answer?"

"I'm certain of it, Chief."

"When do I get to tell my side, McGowan? Me, Charley! I was there too, you know. There's lies being spread around here just to make me look bad."

The grey-suited man pushed his way forward. "Gentlemen, my name is John Lavell. I appear for the family of the victims and I must ask you kindly to keep the proceedings within the bounds of the law. This is no way to carry on an inquest." He caught Vaux's eye. "It is neither morally nor legally acceptable to discuss evidence which may be used against the prisoner in this manner. Doctor Vaux, you've conducted many inquests. You know its purpose and the manner in which it should be handled. I suggest you take charge here."

Charley struggled to his feet again. "They're telling it around that I said I was not more than three hundred yards from the fire. Where'd you get that, McGowan?"

Ignoring him, McGowan held up the vest taken from Charley, pointing out its pinpoints of brown stains.

The hem of Vaux's suitcoat shot up to his waist as he raised both arms. "Order! Hold on, Chief. It would appear from the evidence of other witnesses that the Chief is right. After reviewing the notes on today's testimony, I think we'll agree that the prisoner volunteered originally that he sat on a rail fence about three hundred yards away, watching the fire."

"But that's not – Christ, he makes it sound –" Charley bowed his head, covering his face with his hands.

It was over. They all trooped out for supper, made orderly by weariness.

Face to face with Lavell at the door, Billy noted the mixture of loathing and distrust in the lawyer's expression. He went across to Nevins' hotel and sat with Vaux and McGowan, declining supper but assaulting his stomach with cup after cup of appalling coffee. The jury, pushing two long tables together, was already deliberating between forkfuls of corned beef and cabbage. Everyone was here except the Luckeys who, Billy decided, had the good sense to stay away. "You have the form, Doctor?"

"An old one, but still appropriate."

"It won't hurt to have it ready. I don't think they'll be too long bringing in a verdict."

He was right. Scarcely had they resumed at McCrum's when the jury announced their findings:

"That one Charles Luckey, not having the fear of God before his eyes but being moved and seduced by the instigation of the devil on the eighth day of October in this year aforesaid, the said John James Luckey Sr, Martha Luckey and Mary Ann Luckey, feloniously, wilfully and of his malice aforethought did kill and murder . . . against the peace of our said Lady the Queen, her Crown and dignity."

Billy, missing nothing, saw Charley struggle to remain impassive, saw Chief Rose from Brockville hovering in the doorway, saw Johnny's wife and daughter weeping in each other's arms. Only the reporters raced out; the others stood about, as if expecting more, not willing to believe it was over. Billy's eyes hurt, as if he hadn't dared to blink them all day. His stomach quietened. "Come on, McGowan. As soon as Rose leaves with the prisoner, I'll buy you an ale."

Chapter Seven

Saturday, October 15th, 1892

"When I said they don't trust me, John, I meant the whole countryside. It's in the atmosphere." Billy Greer was pacing the carpet in his mentor's study, the restful earth tones of this favourite refuge failing to steady his nerves.

"For God's sake, Billy, sit down." Lounging on a sofa spread with animal hides, John Wilson Murray reached for a tin of Myrtle Navy and began tamping tobacco in a stout black pipe. Two retrievers sprawled at his feet. "You've arrested killers before, seen them convicted amid public moralizing and howls for retribution, and then had to fend off do-gooders demanding mercy for the poor, misguided miscreant. Look at Birchall, guilty as hell. New to this country, no family here. Yet d'you know how many people signed the petitions for clemency?" He paused. "Thousands."

"Birchall was young and wealthy. Passed himself off as a blueblood, Lord Something-or-other. Clergyman's son, wasn't he?"

Murray lit a match and held it to the bowl of his pipe. "He lent a tone and style to Supreme Court that none have equalled. Everyone admires daring, and sometimes admiration gets in the way of common sense." He pointed to a yellowed clipping taped to the wall above a table loaded with memorabilia from twenty-eight years of detective work. "From the *Peterborough Examiner.* Always meant to frame it."

Dissolving in quiet paroxysms of mirth, cheeks creased with long dimples, eyes screwed up almost as if he was in pain, Billy read:

The astonishing "nerve" shown by Birchall during his recent trying experiences was the wonder of all. A Woodstock gentleman, writing to a

146

friend in town, says the secret of Birchall's nerve is the fact that he drinks the same brand of tea kept for sale by Hawley Bros., soothing to the nerves, pure, strong and fragrant.

"A nip of whisky, Billy? You're off duty." Murray gestured toward an amber-coloured decanter wedged between a stuffed partridge and a stack of well-thumbed, leather-bound classics.

Regarding the decanter longingly, Billy shook his head. "I can't greet the wife with liquor on my breath." Arriving by train an hour ago, he'd gone straight to the School of Practical Science and thence to Murray's.

Murray rose, lit a lamp and took two glasses from a shelf. He poured from the decanter and held out a glass. "Doctor's orders. Tell Catharine I said so." He drank swiftly, slapped his glass down and picked up a copy of the *Rideau Record* from a table. "Did she strip to strike?"

"What?"

"'Did She Strip to Strike?' Didn't you read the papers you brought? Seems there's a theory about how Lizzie Borden committed the murders without getting blood on her clothes. You're familiar with her case, the similarities between it and the Luckey case?"

Billy started guiltily. Murray had a way of keeping one off balance. "I'm afraid –"

His host leaned forward, hunching his broad shoulders. "The Borden murders took place August fourth, in broad daylight. Two months and four days before your murders. Andrew Borden and his second wife, Abby, lived in a modest house in Fall River with his two daughters from his first marriage, Emma and Lizzie." The consummate raconteur, he sat back suddenly, hands behind his head. "Living with them was an Irish servant girl, Bridget Sullivan. She and Lizzie were the only other occupants of the house the morning of the murders; in other words, the only suspects. About noon, the body of Andrew Borden was discovered on a sofa in his parlour. Upstairs, on the floor of a guestroom, his wife lay with her head bashed in. The similarities with the Luckey case are striking. In each case, a stern father, a businessman, tight-fisted, fully imbued with the biblical notion that hard work and thrift would secure him a place in Heaven. A solemn, tight-lipped step-mother, childless herself and little mourned. Both apparently murdered by an offspring. Lizzie is going before the Grand Jury in November and they're sure to return a true bill. She practically hanged herself at the inquest."

Billy sipped his whisky guiltily, trying not to think of Catharine. "The same fate awaits Charley. Open and shut case."

"Maybe. But first, take a look at their backgrounds. Both Lizzie and Charley were left motherless early in life. Each acquired as step-mother, after a couple of years, a spinster in early middle age. If sketches and photographs can be trusted, a lumbering, overweight cow, the type about whom people say, if she smiled her face would crack." He flourished the *Rideau Record*, indicating the grim line drawing of Martha Luckey. "The relationship between child and step-mother was unhappy and loveless from the start."

"So the parents set up situations that invited trouble."

Murray raised his eyebrows. "Not necessarily. There's a theory in Europe, that not only the parents but all of society can be blamed for a killer's deeds. We've talked of this before. Don't you believe it. The murderers in both these cases were unbalanced. Crime, as I've said before, is a disease. Hereditary. Contagious. Look to their origins. You'll find criminals somewhere. Not necessarily murderers, criminal minds."

Billy downed the last of his whisky and bent to set the glass between a sleeping dog's paws. "There's a long-standing property dispute at the core of the Luckey case."

"Same with the Bordens. A father who was considered, at least by his children, to have dealt unfairly with them in the matter of his property." Murray gestured toward the decanter, smiling when Billy shook his head. "The similarities don't stop there. The personalities of this pair could be interchangeable. From witnesses' accounts, both are given to ungovernable rages; both made threats against family members, and – what's more – both were accused of theft. Charley served time for larceny. Lizzie, perhaps more intelligent, more cunning, seems to have gotten away with a couple of petty robberies in her father's house. Spite rather than need, apparently."

Billy resumed pacing, trying to shake himself free from the mesmerizing effects of Murray's discourse. Fatigue and whisky were muddling his brain. "How can these comparisons help my case?"

"The Borden case is two months ahead of you. If it goes sour, you may learn from the mistakes of others. There's no doubt about how the Bordens died, but they're still looking for the axe. You've got an axe but can't tie it to murder. The question that intrigues me is, did Charley set out to improve on Lizzie's modus operandi by burning the house down to destroy the evidence?"

"The fellow who found Luckey's axe is wavering about the blood on the handle. Seems when he picked it up he caught his hand on a sliver and it bled. I'll talk to him but I can't rely on his evidence alone."

"Of course. Witnesses change their minds, disappear, die even. And don't rely on the axe. What about Charley's clothes? Did you deliver them to the School of Practical Science?"

"Yes, but Ellis has a backlog. But if the trial's not until spring we'll have the lab results in plenty of time."

"At least give the appearance of being ready for trial Monday. If the defence is forced to ask for an adjournment, you come off looking sharper."

"Defence is as anxious as we are for the lab results. They think it'll prove the substance on Luckey's clothes isn't blood, or can't be shown to be human blood."

"I'll call Ellis. Did you order the guiacum test?"

Billy nodded. "There were some pin pricks of something like blood on the vest – they'd been scraped – and a dried brown stain at a pants pocket entrance. As if a bloody hand was thrust in, or a small weapon."

"Work up the axe theory."

"D'you think he stripped to strike?"

"Anyone see him prancing about naked as a jaybird?"

"He could have heard about the Borden case while in prison."

"There's more," Murray said, leafing through the newspaper. "Here we are. Subtitled, 'A Possible Solution to the Borden Murder.'" Running a finger down a column, he read aloud. "'That Mr Borden deserved some such summary removal may be no excuse for the deed, but it furnishes a reason. His grinding parsimony and brutal selfishness had ruined the life of his two daughters, had deprived them of all opportunities for pleasure and had interfered forever with their chances for marriage.' What d'you think of that? They could have been describing Old Man Luckey."

"Possibly, John. I'm checking that story about Charley's infatuation, and his father forbidding the wedding, and Charley's shooting himself. Happened here in Toronto, December of '87, at the Union House on Simcoe Street."

"Would he wait five years for revenge?" Murray scanned the next paragraphs. "Listen. Mrs. Borden goes to tidy up the guest room. Lizzie follows her upstairs and goes to her own apartment. See? '. . . where she already had the axe selected for the deed. Reaching here she removed her clothing, even to her shoes and stockings . . . Thus prepared she stepped noiselessly into the guest room and struck Mrs. Borden on the head with the axe, felling her to the floor . . . Before the blood had coursed along the carpet sufficiently to stain her feet and thus leave footprints as she left the room she had concluded her work and withdrew.' It goes on to say she dressed, then undressed again to repeat the crime when her father returned home."

A wall clock struck five. Murray checked his pocket watch and closed it, satisfied. "Other suspects will turn up. There's always some seedy character lurking about. In the Borden –"

"We've got one, a tinsmith wearing red stockings. Seen walking south on the Brockville road the morning of the fire. Dubbed Redsox."

"Red Herring, more like it." Murray fell silent for a moment, stroking the head of a waking retriever. "The most important thing you may learn from the Borden case has nothing to do with the murders or the way they were committed. Aside from all the other points of similarity, these are both cases of parricide. Cases that cause friends and families to take sides. Distrust their instincts, cloud their brains with emotions. They read circumstantial evidence as innuendo. Even confession is rationalized, thought to be forced with threats of starvation and the rubber hose." The lamp flickered, footsteps creaked in the hall; from somewhere came the aroma of bread baking. Greer's stomach rumbled.

Murray rose to signal the discussion was ending; it was time to walk the dogs. "The worst thing that can happen, Billy, is for Charley to become a folk hero. Ballads sung, petitions circulated, lasses sending bouquets and locks of hair." He took two leashes from a peg. "Come Pepper, Ginger, good boys. Perhaps your sense of mistrust, this thing you can't put your finger on, is a foreboding of just such a phenomenon."

A housekeeper appeared from the shadows and opened the front door. Murray secured the leashes and patted each dog in turn. "We'll walk as far as the tobacco shop with you." The dogs padded along easily, one on either side of their master, as Murray strode down the avenue. They halted outside a small shop. "I'm due in Hamilton tomorrow. Forgery case."

Billy dug his hands in his pockets. "I wish we were ready for trial now. Armour's presiding, a good hanging judge if ever there was one."

Murray laughed. "He's got all the crooks terrorized. Ever since that rumour that he put one of his own sons away in the pen for seven years." He opened the shop's door. "I'll be back next weekend. We'll make arrangements then to go down to Smith's Falls together."

Oh, no, you don't, Billy thought, remembering all the cases he'd worked on where the papers had given the credit solely to the Great Detective. *This one's mine!* He smiled, but his eyes were cold.

Murray's expression was shrewd and expectant, a retriever poised for the chase. He saw the resolve in Billy's eyes with satisfaction. "One thing more. He must be charged with only one murder. That way, if he's acquitted, he can be charged with a second murder. Then a third, if necessary." He disappeared into the shop, Pepper and Ginger following, tails wagging.

ENTR'ACTE

January, 1893

Harry Montgomery had a death wish. It had been with him for a long time, long before he had lost his job with the Ottawa police force, before Emily had started sleeping in the baby's room nights, before his mind had been warped with drink.

As a boy of nine, he had gone with his father and brothers to see Whelan hanged for the murder of D'Arcy McGee. They went early, before the crowd had swelled to thousands, and saw the hangman, in his blue overalls, crawl out of the gaol window onto the scaffold to test the weights. He and Frank and Bob packed snow into hard balls and threw them at the masked figure. The hangman swept the snow away and went inside without a backward glance. He remembered little else of the preliminary fanfare, being absorbed in dodging between pantlegs and bustled skirts as he played hide-and-seek with his brothers.

Suddenly a tremendous shout erupted and the crowd surged forward. Cloaks and skirts beat all about him, threatening to smother him. An elbow knocked his cap from his head and he watched helplessly as it was trampled in the slush, out of reach. A boot came down hard on his left foot, bringing tears to his eyes. Blindly, he fought his gargantuan, shifting enemy. Slammed against a wooden partition, he found its edge and, like a sailor gripping a mast during a gale, hung on for dear life. A final, spine-jarring push and he found himself on the other side. He crouched in semi-darkness, smelling a dampness and staleness that reminded him of a root cellar. Safe at last.

There was silence then, and a strange, high keening from above. The sound of a bolt being drawn. A rush of wind and a pair of scuffed boots dropped down beside him, scraping his cheek. His belly felt full of ice as he looked up and saw a head covered with a white hood. But it was the jerking of the legs he remembered afterward, and the long, ragged invocation, somewhere between a snarl and a bleat, that had emanated from the ghost-like figure. Everything had been still then, and peaceful, just for a moment, the body swaying slightly, before the partition was swept aside and men rushed in. They chased him out with threats of a caning. He lost his breakfast then, and cried all the way home, and his mother berated his father for exposing her babies to such barbarism.

It was only later, when she had tucked him in for the night, that Harry remembered the moment of peacefulness; he'd tried then to imagine what death was like, keeping very still, holding his breath for as long as he could. He pictured the mourners, his mother cradling his lifeless body, his father at the funeral throwing himself on the casket, begging forgiveness from his favourite son for his neglect and unjust punishments.

In the years that followed, he had suffered from a lack of a sense of permanence, a realization that all things came to the same ignominious end, no matter how one struggled. The preoccupation with dying had been a logical manifestation of his earlier experiences. His turtle's shell had grown soft, the crayfish he had caught in the back pond had shrivelled and stunk up his bedroom, his spaniel had dragged himself on paralyzed hind legs across the floor to heave a final spasm at Harry's feet. His preoccupation became, in time, a fascination with all things dead: butterflies petrified in jars, flies withered on window sills, worms flattened beneath carriage wheels, fish bloated and belly-up in ponds, turkeys – raw necks, glazed eyes, errant feathers – on a bloodied tree stump the day before Thanksgiving.

If someone had pointed out to him that he found these creatures more compelling in death than in life, he would have demurred. He was horrified, desolate, sickened; the ultimate sense he had was of standing on the threshold of something inexorable and apocalyptic. And the unnameable thing pulled him, a toy on a string, toward a terrible black abyss. The urge to take the plunge was at times almost irresistible.

It would come upon him in the early hours of the morning when he awoke in a cold sweat, a weight on his chest and his breath a strangled gasp. Or when he heard household sounds, the language of the home he had created, Emily shrill and punitive, slaps, wails and pounding footsteps; or when Emily brushed past him in the hall, and he realized that the girl who had captivated him fourteen years ago had become a hard-faced, broad-hipped matron whose smock reeked of urine and sour milk and whose auburn hair hadn't been washed in a month. The only time she primped was when she knew his brother Frank was coming over.

It came on him now as he stumbled along Besserer Street, his nose sharp with the pain of the cold, his boots crunching ice crystals, the echoes of his cronies' goodbyes ringing in his ears. After scrutineering at the election poll all day, he'd worked up an enormous thirst and the pull of the Captain's Inn had been overwhelming. His friends had taken turns buying drinks; Harry alone could not afford a round, but they were used to that.

A cooper, a farrier, a wheelwright, a greengrocer. Their shop-talk depressed him, but what upset him more was when they broke off and regarded him pityingly. They tried to be helpful in the most obvious ways. "Harry! The sawmill's hiring on. Poor wages but better than nothing, eh?" "Have you tried the hotels again? They're always looking for night watchmen."

He had good reason for desperation. A week ago, right after Christmas, he had found out from Frank that his father had made a new will. "He's dying, Harry, and he's decided to cut you out. Said he'd warned you often enough." And he had, of course, raving about the consequences of demon rum. God damn the old fool! He stormed over to the saddlery and confronted his father.

"You've been coddled and pampered too long, Harry. Your mother gave you the house; all you had to do was provide a living for your family. You can't even do that. What do you do? Drink up every dime that comes your way. Why should my hard-earned money go for that? Your brothers are more deserving." His father looked old and drawn, emaciated from the disease that was slowly killing him. "You'll soon follow me to the grave, Harry – if you don't go first."

He'd been beside himself with rage, mostly at himself, he realized later. "What will Emily and the children do? Suppose they're left without me. Robert's only eleven, too young to –"

"They'll be looked after. Frank has instructions, Harry. They might be better off without you." His father turned away sadly and began cutting strips of leather.

He'd gone straight from his father's to the tavern that day and hadn't come home until the next night – Wednesday, it had been. He tried to hang himself from the front hall bannister with his suspenders. All he could remember of the incident was Emily, the baby on her hip and little Mary clinging to her skirt, screaming from the top of the stairs, and somewhere behind her high-pitched voices crying, "Dad! Dad!" He'd had to promise Emily never to do it again.

It had occurred to him briefly when he saw her white face, her clear eyes reflecting the pain he was feeling, that perhaps she still loved him after all. Perhaps if there'd been more time, but the bawling and entreaties upstairs had lured her away and it had been left to Frank, summoned from his bed over the harness shop, to put ice packs on his forehead and apply balm to his grazed neck.

The town clock tolled three. The night was clear and bitter, too cold to snow, the moon a sickle of ice hanging above his head. He hunched his shoulders inside the worn mantle. The chicken feed he'd been paid for scrutineering hadn't lasted the evening and he hadn't had a detective job in weeks. His brothers turned deaf ears to his pleas for a loan. There wouldn't even be a chance to collect witness fees until spring, when the Brockville case would come up. Perhaps he could get a ride to court there with a pedlar and still hoodwink the authorities into paying his train fare. Get a false receipt. He deserved it, didn't he? After all, they needed him. He could help put that bastard Luckey away. Who else could say with certainty that the money found on the young thug wasn't on him when he was despatched to the Central Prison the year before? Harry knew. Hadn't he searched Luckey himself? Dammit, hadn't he? He stumbled on a jagged chunk of ice and was on his knees before he could save himself. With the throbbing pain came the soul-numbing desolation that had haunted him for almost a lifetime. It stayed with him as he pulled himself up and lurched the few remaining yards home.

Softly he unlatched the door. Thick air, fetid with odours of boiled cabbage, cellar mould and humans too long unbathed, seared his nostrils. His hands and ears stung as he slipped the mantle from his shoulders and heard it plop on the floor. He took his time, stumbling in the darkness of the hall, groping his way to the kitchen sideboard where the lantern was kept. Lighting it shakily, he entered the woodshed. A length of clothesline hung on a nail. A hook jutted out over the doorway. He hesitated only a moment before pushing a chair into place, climbing onto it, looping the cord over the hook and fashioning a clumsy noose. He slipped the rope around his neck and tightened it.

It seemed to take a long time, a lifetime perhaps, in the flickering shadows, while he stood a long way off, watching himself in a dream, picturing young Robert in the morning, coming to the woodshed for kindling, racing across the yard to fetch Frank. Would the boy ever forgive him? Would his own father ask his forgiveness? He felt a flash of regret – perhaps it was cowardice – but the chair wobbled, tipped forward.

It was Emily he saw at last, Emily plump and pretty as she had been fourteen years ago, her clear eyes full of understanding, her long bright hair caught up in ivory co-

Part III

THE FIRST TRIAL

October – November, 1892

Discontented movements of the trees
accuse me. One must keep company
with some one, if only to, but, or

Chapter One

In the cooling period between the alleged crime and the trial, rescheduled for April, the world as it touched on the Luckey tragedy settled once more into comfortable routine. The case had all but disappeared from the papers, the occasional tidbit being sandwiched in between the war in Dahomey and ads for miracle cures.

Shock and self-righteousness diminished, horror turned to ambivalence, ambivalence to empathy. Empathy evoked the instinctive need for insularity. People still spoke in superlatives: it was the most heinous, the foulest of foul, the dastardliest crime of the century. But the intonations were less shrill, the attitude slightly blasé, the air of a maiden aunt becoming accustomed to a brothel in the neighbourhood.

The tide was turning in Charley's favour, for reasons which had little to do with his guilt or innocence. Charley's arrest was regarded as an indictment of his entire family, causing a confusion of loyalties in Kitley Township. Who could judge the innocent bereaved harshly? Those who were undecided or easily influenced swayed like blossoms in a breeze, waiting to take their cue from the Luckeys themselves. The remaining Luckeys had conducted themselves in public consistently with decorum; what Johnny did in the dark hours when he went off in his buggy without disclosing his destination could only be guessed at and was considered beneath comment. For every utterance against Charley there would be demurring rejoinders: a comment on the business acumen Sam was developing, or the bravery of the sisters homesteading out west, or the impossibility of baking a rhubarb pie that would top Liza Ann's in taste and texture.

The lines between black and white blurred and in the resulting grey, while no one equated murder with rhubarb pie, a subtle defusing process invaded the countryside. The meddlers that the *Rideau Record* dubbed "embryo detectives" continued sleuthing on the quiet. It was a game, played over backyard clotheslines and around the woodstove in Landon's general store. A diminishing but vocal faction ridiculed Lavell for inviting certain ignominy by taking on the defence of an unregenerate killer. Those who defended the Luckeys *en masse* acknowledged a sense of duty in throwing doubt on the smug, well-oiled machinery of the law. They pulled for the Luckeys on general principles. They pulled for themselves, to salvage pride in whatever historic moments were passing before them. And they pulled for Lavell who, although not a native, had chosen to live among them for ten years, rather than for Clute the Crown prosecutor, who was a stranger and city-bred.

Greer, with Murray out of the country tracking down a forger, had been riding an exhausting merry-go-round of investigations including the Wonch case in Collingwood and a mysterious poisoning in Kemptville. Most recently, in March, investigators in a shooting at Darling's Landing had been pleading for help from the Attorney General's department, to no avail. In all Ontario, ten murder cases had the potential of coming to trial at the spring assizes; of these, the United Counties of Leeds and Grenville, with the county seat at Brockville, had three. The newspapers, in attempting to wring some significance out of the statistics, succeeded only in putting the citizens on the defensive. As it happened, the Kemptville case petered out without an arrest and charges in the shooting were put over to the fall, leaving Charley's the lone Supreme Court trial to be dealt with in Brockville.

Over the winter, Chief McGowan, locked into more mundane matters by the Smith's Falls town council, took on the added duties of truant officer and sanitary inspector. Vaux, the Brockville coroner, licensed on both sides of the border, drove his cutter weekly across the frozen St Lawrence to treat his Ogdensburg patients. Radclive the hangman travelled the breadth of Canada, from Fredericton to Victoria, in the line of duty. As for Lizzie Borden, like Charley she awaited her trial behind bars, but in very difference circumstances, being allowed to order her meals from the best hotel in Fall River.

The Luckey property had been sold in February and Martha's

family, the Lyles, had launched a full scale legal battle with the Luckeys over the inheritance. The suit revolved around the question of who had died first, Martha or the old man. Was Martha a beneficiary? Her husband had left her eleven hundred dollars and a cow. There was as yet no ruling on what would be done with Charley's portion of the inheritance, pending the outcome of the trial.

With mid-April, green shoots, rejuvenating rain and soil that would soon yield to spade and hoe sent out a heartening message. Expectations that had lain fallow for a season reached out toward the tenets of salvation and renewal, raising the spirits of those dauntless champions of the underdog, defenders of the blind faith who saw in Charley Luckey their brother, son or father.

But John Reeve Lavell, still smarting from barbs of Charley's detractors, felt neither gratified nor uplifted as he checked into Brockville's St Lawrence Hall and paid the porter to take his bags to his room. Picking up his briefcase, he went outside and walked the short block east up the hill to the court house. His feet echoed hollowly on the plank walk as he passed the new office wing of the fifty-year-old building. The court house stood in the centre of town, on a hill overlooking a semi-circular green girdled by a bridle path and a post-and-chain fence. Two children, looking uncannily like his own Franky and Marion, straddled the huge Balaclava cannon while a third stuffed its barrel with new grass. The broad expanse of Court House Avenue, banks and businesses lining it, swept away from the green to the south. Telephone poles, installed three days earlier, flanked the avenue, thrusting ugly wired fingers upward, offending his aesthetic sense. Ridges of caked mud rippled down to the Main Street intersection, beyond which the road narrowed as it approached the two mile wide ribbon of St Lawrence River. The ice was out, the waves changing from gunmetal grey to cerulean in the sunlight. Lavell, muffling a persistent cough, imagined his feet wearing their own path in the broad planks, so often had he walked this route in the past six months.

His first visit to the gaol the previous October had left him shaken, he remembered. The roof was badly in need of repair, water stains streaking the walls and ceilings. Plaster crumbled, paint peeled, offices were dim and unventilated, woodstoves unlit against the autumn chill. Charley cowered, pallid and unshaven, on the wooden bench in his cell. Lavell felt a wave of claustrophobia. "Turnkey, bring him out into the light."

Hushed consternation. "Can't do that, sir. 'E's in for –"

"I know what he's in for. I won't interview him in there. Bring him into the day room and clear it of the other prisoners. You can tell the Sheriff I'll take full responsibility."

The turnkey's scarred face twisted into a grin at this absolution of blame. He disappeared, returning moments later with Charley, hands manacled, feet shuffling as his chains clunked across the floor.

The fellow reminded him of a cellar-grown mushroom. Looking old beyond his years, yet at the same time raw-boned and unfinished, he evoked paternal feelings in Lavell, although there was less than a decade between them. He seated himself at the end of a long table. "Sit down, Charley."

The turnkey pulled out a chair and Charley stumbled into it, blinking.

"Unchain him."

"What?"

"I refuse to interview a client who is chained. Where d'you think he's going to go?"

The turnkey removed the fetters, shaking his head. "All right, boys, back to your cells!" In thirty seconds, he had cleared the day room of a half-dozen prisoners, the usual drunks and vagrants, leaving behind an old derelict moaning in a corner.

Lavell introduced himself and extended a hand which Charley shook hesitantly. "Your brother engaged me to represent you. I understand this was on your instructions?"

An almost imperceptible nod.

Lavell opened his briefcase and took out a sheaf of papers, surveying his client. He was well aware of Johnny Luckey's reasons for asking him to represent his brother. Johnny was under pressure to make some gesture to help Charley. He thought Lavell would come cheap and not fuss if his bill wasn't paid promptly. A young man in the first decade of his law practice, competent, tenacious, politically ambitious. But untried in the Supreme Court criminal arena. Optimist with a soft heart.

"You get prestige and experience. I get representation for Charley. Family's satisfied." Johnny had clapped him on the shoulder. "Remember, J.R., I'm in a position to throw a lot of business your way." The gesture still hurt, not because of its physical force, but because Johnny had made it plain that he wanted token representation for his brother, that he wasn't willing to pay for the best and didn't expect to get it.

But that's exactly what he's getting, Lavell had decided, meeting Charley for the first time. The best. What does he know of the Lavells! Doctors and lawyers for generations.

Two brothers, both dead now, had been doctors. Another had followed J.R. into law; a younger brother, only twenty-two, showed a keen interest in penology. If that wasn't enough, their father, Dr Michael Lavell, physician and surgeon, had been warden of Kingston Penitentiary since 1885. Whenever J.R. visited his family, there was endless table talk about new developments: Mesmerism from Austria, Bertillonage from France, phrenology and alienism from Germany.

He had another connection which he hoped to use to advantage. Henry Reeve, the Toledo coroner who first examined the bodies, was his mother's brother. Orphaned in infancy, Henry had been put through medical school along with J.R.'s brother Will, by Michael and Betsy Lavell. Although fifteen years older than Will, Henry had graduated the same year. Uncle Henry would be subpoenaed by the prosecution. What did he really think about the omission of a post mortem? Was it possible to drive a wedge between the medical witnesses?

From his first visit to the gaol on the day after the inquest, Lavell had been firm with Charley. "As long as I'm your defence counsel, you talk to no one – no one, understand? – about the case except me." He had sat back and smiled, hoping he exuded confidence. "No one's proved yet that a crime was committed. That's the first thing. The second thing is, you must be completely honest with me. Tell me the truth, all of it, if you want me to help you."

He tried to concentrate on defence strategies, but it was impossible to ignore the human tragedy. The burned and crumbling bodies hovered in the shadows. "Now, Charley, you're charged with one count of murder. The murder of your father. Did you do it?"

"Do it?"

"Look at me. Did you murder your father?"

Charley stared at his hands, flexing and opening them slowly. "No. No, I – don't think so." He sounded faintly surprised.

"You don't think so?"

"I didn't. I'm sure."

J.R. swallowed a rising panic. Instinct told him his client was a victim of society, incapable of violent crime. What if his instinct was wrong? Lavell felt dangerously close to the edge of something dark and frightening, something he wasn't sure he wanted to know. "Look at me, Charley. Look me in the eye. Tell me the truth."

But Charley continued to mumble at his hands. "It's just that there's – so much to remember."

"Are there things you don't remember? Think, Charley –" He leaned forward and gripped Charley's wrist – "you'd remember a thing like that."

"I didn't do it, sir. I know I didn't. It's just that I can't –" He ran his fingers through his hair, combing it backwards in quick, urgent strokes. "Can't prove it."

"Did you go to your father's house that day?"

"Just to the bush. Where I could see the house. Ask McGowan. I told him. Told everyone."

Lavell was silent for a moment, scratching notes. "We have a good chance of getting you off, Charley. But you have to help me all you can. I'll be honest with you. This is my first murder case. I know I can handle it, but I admit I'm scared. Help me."

Charley looked up, gazing directly at Lavell for the first time. He smiled, a smile as open and engaging as a child's. "You're the one who got them to stop hounding me at the inquest. J.R., Johnny calls you. D'you mind if I – ?"

"Not at all. My friends and business acquaintances call me that." A slight breeze swept in through a window; the derelict in the corner had stopped moaning and fallen asleep. "They treating you all right here?"

"I only been here since yesterday. We got running water."

"I noticed," Lavell said, eyeing the streaked wall behind Charley. They laughed, and Lavell felt encouraged. They were going to get along just fine. "Your brother's very concerned about you. He believes you."

"That's not what he's been telling everybody. Read the papers."

"He's telling it around that he went to the Palace Hotel himself and checked the story about your behaviour in the barber shop. Says it's a complete fabrication." Lavell wasn't sure himself that Johnny was right, but he decided to let well enough alone for now. "He's changed his mind, you know. Believes you are innocent."

Charley shrugged. "He believes whatever looks good. It don't look good to have a murderer for a brother."

"He's willing to help you. Gave me a retainer."

A wry smile. "Chicken feed, I bet."

"Small, yes."

"And a promise to throw some business your way." Charley laid a hand on his heart in a mock gesture of avowal.

Lavell laughed in spite of himself. "You know your brother well."

"What are you going to do when the money runs out, J.R.?"

Now, in mid–April, as he turned in at the gaol entrance on the day before the Supreme Court assizes were to open, Lavell remembered how little concerned he had been about the lack of funds last October. Eager to meet the challenge head on, fascinated by the convolutions of the case, he had brushed Charley's question aside, spreading out the contents of his briefcase, talking excitedly about strategies, witnesses, forensic advances, circumstantial evidence, all the while studying his client without appearing to. "There are two possibilities. Either we prove that murder was not committed at all or we prove that someone else committed the murders. The first possibility is the more difficult one. We would have to show not only that the fire was accidental, but also that the victims were alive when it broke out."

"Is it any easier to prove someone else did it?"

"Might be. It'd be difficult to convince the jury that, in an accidental fire, the victims didn't have time to get out of the house in broad daylight. Forensic evidence can't help us much. So we go at this problem another way. We prove, if we can, that you were not in your father's house that day and that someone else was, or could have been."

"I wasn't in the house, I swear." Charley looked confident, holding Lavell's gaze with his own.

"The prosecution's going to use the boots and the money found on you to argue that you were." He searched for a fresh sheet of paper. "We'll start by making a list of possible witnesses to help us on these points."

They had worked all day. Someone set a tray of tea on the table at some point, and later coffee and bread and cold pork. It grew dusky and lamps were lit by a shadowy figure tiptoeing past them. Lavell made a list of two dozen names – people who would remember that Old Man Luckey had a foot much too small for the boots found on Charley, and people who had seen the stranger known to the press as Redsox in the vicinity of the fire. Lavell put down his pencil and leaned back in his chair. "Here's what we know about Redsox. He's about forty, a tinsmith by trade, going from town to town repairing tinware, often taking his payment in food and lodging. On Friday, October seventh, the day before the fire, after repairing a kettle for Richard Landon, a neighbour of your father's, he stayed the night at Landon's instead of setting out in the rain. On Saturday morning, a farmer named Moran gave him a ride to within a mile of Toledo where he let him down with directions to Brockville. He thought the time was about nine o'clock and said the stranger went west toward Toledo instead of south to Brockville."

"Can't we find him?"

"Better not to. The police claim to know who he is and they insist he had nothing to do with the fire. It'll look better if we find witnesses who saw a stranger in the vicinity at various times during the day."

Charley nodded. "Because there may have been more than one."

"Right. Several people saw a stranger on the road. Except for his red stockings, they can't seem to agree on other details of his appearance." He leafed through the pages of a notebook. "Here it is. Some say he had a black leather satchel slung over his shoulder. That agrees with Moran's description. But his suit –" he seized a loose clipping – "Listen to this. 'His suit has been described as black, grey, tweed and brown. Chief Rose has tried to settle all arguments by declaring that the man's clothes had been black but were worn brown, and could have been taken for grey'!" Lavell squinted in the flickering light and waited for his client to laugh. But Charley, stirring cold tea round and round in his mug, looked pensive.

"It seems that, if Johnny believes me, he should want to show he's on my side by standing up for me in court."

"The prosecution will be subpoenaing him. That doesn't mean we can't turn his testimony to our advantage."

Charley raised the mug halfway to his lips. "I suppose that means they've got Liza Ann. And all the rest of the family. The whole countryside." He slurped and made a face. "What about the fellow who came down on the train with me? Hannah."

"Greer's got him. Our best strategy is to anticipate what the Crown witnesses will say and then discredit their testimony or turn it to our advantage." Lavell raised his eyebrows. "Let the Crown pay their witness fees."

"Will you be bringing anybody from the Central Prison?"

"If there's anybody who can show you had money on you while in prison, yes."

"I had it on me when I went in. There's a fellow there named Ree-vay, used to deal in tobacco on the sly."

"An inmate." Lavell frowned.

"Yeah. Frenchie. But my best pal was Balloon. Find him."

"Balloon?"

"He'll help. Say anything you want him to."

"He'd be under oath to tell the truth. Even at that, I don't know how much weight a convict's words carry. Sorry, Charley. Did he see you with money?"

"I'm sure he did. Ree-vay too. Ree-vay had a special deal going with construction workers and delivery men. Used to get tobacco cheap and sell it to the rest of us."

Lavell added the names to his list. "The tobacco dealer sounds like an unsavoury character."

"Balloon's the best. Find him, J.R."

Over the winter, Lavell had pursued his cause with a zeal that had gratified his client, astonished his detractors, gained him a legion of admirers and exasperated his wife. He lived, ate and slept the case, working the subject into every conversation at home, in his office, and on his many trips out of town. Every discovery of some new piece of evidence, any morsel of information that shed new light on previous evidence was an adventure, a cause for celebration. He made telephone calls, sent letters and wires trying to find out what had happened to the clothing taken to the School of Practical Science. No satisfactory answer came; he suspected Greer was at the bottom of it, giving him the runaround. He cursed publicly the unethical behaviour of the investigators. "Damn them," he railed in his weekly visits to Charley, "they'll stop at nothing to get a conviction!"

In spite of all his efforts, he had only ten witnesses for the defence on the eve of the assizes, not all of them reliable. He'd tried to track down Balloon, although he was sceptical of the convict's usefulness. "No such person," his contact at the Central had reported. The man was new on staff, but he'd checked all the records.

Now, on his last visit before the trial, he would be able to tell Charley that he had news of Balloon although he hadn't located him. He banged the knocker against the heavy gaol door and heard footsteps within. Sheriff Smart, tall and stooped, white beard brushing boiled collar, opened the door and motioned Lavell into the day room. "J.R. Come in. I'll fetch him."

Lavell coughed as the warm air caught in his throat. In the mixture of smells from kitchen and lavatory, he detected a whiff of something else. Liniment and mustard plaster. How hard it was to get rid of the odour! And Turner's Balsamic Pectoral still coated his tongue.

His client looked heavier, puffy from a winter of inactivity and a diet heavy in starch and fat. From the gaol yard, Lavell heard the crack of stone breaking as the picks of prisoners bit into it. Charley's main activity was reading. Lavell watched as the sheriff brought him into the day room, a hand on the prisoner's shoulder, enjoying a private joke. Substitute son, Lavell thought, remembering that Smart had had a son die a few months ago, Charley's age. "Here's your lad, J.R. We've got a contest going, to see who can quote the most Bible verses by the end of the week." As he spoke, the sheriff pulled out a chair for Charley. "Care to pit yourself against us, J.R.? I'll warn you, this young fella's quick with the answers. Knows his Bible well." He retreated to his office, poking his head around the doorway a moment later to fire a final volley. "Third son of Adam!"

"Seth!"

Lavell raised his eyebrows. "Something new?"

Charley glanced at the empty doorway. "It's a game. Keeps the old fellow happy. He's good to me." He patted his hair with well-scrubbed hands and stroked his trimmed moustache. "How do I look, J.R.? Are we ready for tomorrow?"

This was a new Charley, calm and in command. "All set. Robinson, the Bresse man, is coming from Montreal to testify the boots weren't made by their company. He's our ace. Witnesses say your father wore Bresse boots. Then one of the Parker boys will say he heard an explosion in the milkhouse and saw sparks and twigs fly up, suggesting the fire was accidental."

"What about Ree-vay? Is he coming, too?" From his nonchalant tone Charley could have been inquiring about a list of dinner guests.

Lavell fished in his suit pocket for a package of cough drops. "Ovila Rivet. Discharged from prison three weeks after you were. I found him working in a York Street bar in Ottawa. I wired him his ticket and arranged for him to put up at an inn on the outskirts of Brockville." He popped a cough drop in his mouth. "I hear he was drinking at the Hall last night."

Charley laughed. "Sounds like old Ree-vay. Got a terrible thirst. Couldn't wait to get out of prison and get back to his favourite pastime."

Lavell shifted the cough drop to his right cheek. "I just hope we can keep him sober long enough to testify."

"What about Balloon? You never found him?"

"I kept checking. Finally spoke to Warden Massie himself by telephone. The fellow's name is Bloom, Charley. John Bloom. I've got people looking for him but so far there's no trace. He's thought to be down in the States somewhere." He crunched the remains of his cough drop and went through his list. "I've got four people who can put Redsox in the vicinity the day of the fire. We'll make the most of that."

"Who's the judge?"

"Falconbridge. Mr Justice William Glenholme Falconbridge. We're better off with him than with Armour. That's who you'd have got last fall." He rose and prepared to leave. "The prosecutor is a Belleville lawyer, Roger Clute. He's got a lot of experience in Supreme Court, both prosecuting and defending."

"You look worried, J.R. You sure we haven't got a hanging judge?"

"Nothing to worry about." Lavell fastened his mantle. "You'll be all right, Charley. Send a note to the Hall if you need me before tomorrow." Then he did something he hadn't done since their first meeting. He shook hands with his client. Forcing a cheerful expression, he turned and left.

Charley was right. He was worried. The prosecutor and the judge were old friends who once belonged to the same law firm, about twenty years ago when Falconbridge was starting out as a young lawyer and Clute was articling. Still, they were good men, and fair. He trusted that in court their friendship would not stand in the way of justice.

* * *

Charley had scarcely been led back to his cell before the turnkey announced more visitors. He gave Charley an exaggerated wink. "Two members of the fair sex."

Fair they were, but not so fair as his beloved Harriet, who was graceful and long-legged and carried herself like a princess. These young women were short and stocky, with rosy cheeks and broad smiles. He greeted them in the day room, bewildered. Ladies' guild, he supposed, friends of Sheriff Smart, come to read the Bible and sing hymns with him. He knew the kind. Sang off key and recited prayers like arithmetic tables.

They wore something light and summery, calico or gingham, he wasn't sure, the skirts billowing out below their coats. Their bonnets were summer straw, festooned with ribbons and silk flowers in Easter colours. They were done up as if they were going to church, but nothing could disguise the fact that they were farm girls, with strong wrists from milking cows and sturdy shoes for walking in pastures and country lanes. The spring sun had already brought freckles out on their noses and bleached wisps of hair around the taller one's face. They bobbed hellos and the violets on the taller one's hat quivered. "Don't you know me, Charley?" She seated herself at the table's end and motioned him to the chair on her right. "Christina Mackie."

"Sarah's daughter?"

She hid a giggle behind a gloved hand and clapped him lightly on the arm. "Fancy not knowing your own niece!"

"Didn't recognize you, all grown up." Charley felt his ears redden. "And who's your friend?"

"Eliza Pryce," the other girl said, seating herself opposite Charley. "Your neighbour, remember? I live not half a mile from the – from where you used to –"

Christina covered up her friend's awkwardness. "Charley, we know you didn't do it. We've come to help you prove it."

Charley, searching for something to say, saw that her eyes were moist, her plain face flushing slightly. She looked – what was that word he had once heard Harriet use? – tremulous. That was it. Could this be the tiresome brat who had curtsied before Martha on his father's wedding day, who had trailed after him on the way to school, sometimes throwing stones and sticking out her tongue? She must be – how old? – twenty-three? A wonder she wasn't married. His mouth felt dry. "What does Sarah say?" He was surprised that it mattered so much.

"Mother? Oh, she said we should do what we thought best. Didn't she, Eliza. And it seemed only right – you see, we were talking it over, Eliza and I, and we remembered one day a few years ago we were over at Grandfather's. How long ago, 'Lize? Four years?"

"Oh, eight or nine, I'd say." Her companion toyed with her gloves, pulling and twisting the fingers. "The same year young Esley was born."

"Grandfather tried on everyone's shoes. It was a joke, really. He said he could wear all our shoes, no matter how small. Mine were number fives and he got them on quite easily."

Eliza nodded. "He even put mine on, and they were only three-and-a-halfs. He took a few steps in them. 'Member, Chris?" The memory brought a fresh burst of giggles. "Can you imagine, Charley?"

Christina fished in her bag and produced a pair of plain brown low shoes. "He gave me these. They were his, but he didn't wear them. Put them on, Charley. They'll be 'way too small for you, I'm sure."

Charley paled. "Father's shoes?" But Christina was already unlacing his boots. "Give a hand here, 'Lize, will you?" Eliza rose and came around the table, tugging at one boot while Christina pulled the other off. Charley gingerly stuck his toe in the shoe. "Can't."

"Stand up!"

Charley obeyed and tried again. "S'no use."

Christina gave a whoop. "See, 'Lize? He can't get his foot in at all. Those boots you were wearing when they found you, I knew they weren't Grandfather's! You'd never have got them on!" She pushed hard on his heel, trying to cram it into the shoe. "Can't pull it up over your heel at all, can you, Charley!"

Eliza drew a pendant watch from the folds of her coat, glanced at it and began pulling her gloves on. "We've got to go, Chris." She rose and held out her hand to Charley. "We're here for as long as the trial lasts, staying with friends in town."

"We'll go straight to court tomorrow and demand to take the witness stand for you, Charley." Christina snatched up the shoes and stuffed them back into her bag as Charley stood up. "Take heart, Uncle! We're all pulling for you." She stood on tiptoe and pecked him on the cheek. Following Eliza to the door, she stopped and wheeled around. "Oh, and Charley – Mother sends her love."

"She does – really?"

"Of course. You're in her prayers every night." Every word was stressed, like a lesson being spelled out for a slow-witted child. He didn't know if it was because she sensed how desperately he needed to be reassured or if she was trying to disguise the falseness of her message.

He watched them leave, ignoring the turnkey's hand on his

shoulder, mesmerized by their little shoes tapping across the wooden floor, their curls bobbing beneath their bonnets.

Keys rattled on the turnkey's hip as Charley turned at last into the shadowy hall that led to his cell. "Is it time for my smoke yet, Jimmy?" He took a deep breath and let it out slowly. *I'm like an invalid whose operation has been postponed.*

The turnkey lit a cigarette and put it between Charley's lips.

"That was my niece, Jimmy, the prettier one." He inhaled and entered his cell. "My sister's girl." The door clanged, the key turned in the lock. The turnkey, shift over, gave a quick salute and retreated down the hall.

"She says my sister sends her love." He was alone, calling into gathering darkness. "She prays for me every night, Jimmy. D'you think it's true? Jimmy, I have to know."

An echo. "Is it true?"

Chapter Two

'The temple is polluted with the dead . . .'

Roger Conger Clute made a gesture as if to ward off a persistent mosquito. Odd how a line or two from one of his prize-winning poems from Albert University days would assert itself in the midst of judicial drama. Odd combination, poet and prosecutor. Eclectic echoes of Dutch and United Empire Loyalist. Paradox of devout Presbyterian and the first man in Belleville to read Darwin. Expounder of moderation, creator of The Motto: self knowledge, self reverence, self control – for himself and his son, who, God willing, would follow in his footsteps. The very timbers of the building he sat in were shaking with unprecedented traffic. Temple, court house: places to uphold the motto, virtually synonymous in symbolism and intent. Clute, partner in the Belleville firm of Clute and Williams and veteran of more than thirty special appointments in Supreme Court prosecutions, wrinkled his nose. His corner of today's 'temple', the office of the Crown Attorney of the United Counties of Leeds and Grenville, commandeered for the Luckey trial, was polluted with tobacco smoke.

"The hell you say!" Billy Greer, lounging against the west wall, tapped a freshly rolled cigarette against a blue serge cuff. His expletive referred to the prosecutor's remark of a moment earlier on the subject of general inefficiency and particular lack of communication with the School of Practical Science.

McGowan, bellowing for coffee, was already flourishing his third cigar of the day; the Kitley coroner puffed on a pipe; clerks, constables and deputies, emboldened by numbers, were lighting up. Clute was resigned to the fact that a backwoods mentality persisted in the outer reaches of his circuit. A Supreme Court trial, in those last preparatory stages before the flag was raised and the prospective jurymen summoned to face the prisoner, was an invitation to diversion, a purging of all that was petty and pedantic. Why this was so Clute could not say, but he knew from experience that the headiness would vanish, the pulses return to normal, by the time he was gowned and groomed, his feet pounding the stairs to the courtroom like the slow, measured beat of the judge's gavel.

"The hell I don't say, sir." His sarcasm was lost on the detective, who fished a smouldering stub from an ashtray and lit his cigarette. Vaux coughed sympathetically from the doorway. From the outer office the stentorian drone of the clerk behind the chest-high varnished counter rose as he directed witnesses to the upstairs hall. Clute rubbed watery eyes. In friendlier, more relaxed circumstances, he might have acknowledged Greer as a colleague. Certainly he'd run up against him before, during one of his appointments on the defence side. Eighteen-ninety. Davis, the Marmora murderer. Greer, blunt and thorough on the stand, hungered for conviction. Clute had fought for his client against overwhelming odds. Davis had hanged.

"All the other exhibits are here, sir." Greer wagged his cigarette at a smudged carbon copy of a list. "Surveyor's plans, parcel containing boots the prisoner threw away, gaiters found with prisoner, train ticket, white shirt, small parcel containing underwear, documents, bills, coins, drawing of prisoner's foot, axe, watch and chain, dentures."

"But the clothes have fallen into some bureaucratic crack. If there was blood –"

But Greer seized the axe from the pile of tagged exhibits on the floor. "There's blood here. See? On the helve."

'The conqueror has sheathed his reeking blade
And now surveys the ruin he has made . . .'

Why those lines? Watching the detective run his fingers over the brown-stained nick, it occurred to him they were more appropriate to Greer than to the snivelling dullard he expected to meet in the dock. "Mr Greer –"

"Call me Billy, sir."

"Mr Greer. It's not the axe I'm concerned about. As far as we can tell, that's chicken blood. But I want the pants and vest which I understand you took to Toronto yourself. As you know, I've had no report and nothing's been returned."

"It's my understanding, sir, the results were inconclusive."

"Your understanding, sir, won't stand up in court. We have nothing in writing from Ellis. Is there a phone in this building?"

"In the hall, sir."

"Get Ellis. Now! I want an accounting –"

"He's away, sir. I've left a message already." Greer rubbed his jaw, studying the pile of exhibits as if expecting an answer from them. "You do have all the statements, sir. Sixty-two witnesses all told, including some to rebut defence evidence on Redsox."

Quantity, but from the witnesses Clute had encountered he wasn't sure about quality. He sensed distrust and, occasionally, hostility. He checked his watch. Almost nine. Fever pitch everywhere, smoke so thick they'd have to hack their way through it. And from somewhere in the eastern bowels of this lopsided building, its symmetry destroyed by the gaol addition, the prisoner, shaved, soberly suited, and schooled to adopt a chastened, if not downright innocent mien, was being led forth to be judged by a jury of his peers. Men who believed in God, retribution and phlebotomy, literal and symbolic. Who also believed that tomatoes were poisonous and the man who imbibed Campbell's quinine wine threw away his crutches.

Lines penned more than twenty years ago throbbed above the other flotsam in his mind:

'My pleasant places are destroyed with fire
  Nothing remains of all the heart's desire'
      Jerusalem Destroyed.

He smiled. A Tennysonian eloquence echoing the unpoetic soul of a murderer.

* * *

By two o'clock, facing a carefully chosen jury, Clute knew it was going to be a long trial. His old friend, Judge Falconbridge, squatted, unblinking, like a Buddha. The prisoner sat in the dock, awkward as a parishioner in the wrong pew, black suited, white shirted, sporting an appropriately unremarkable necktie, his gaze wavering as the clerk read the charge.

The morning crawled by, the threshers and townsfolk all reciting the dismal tales he had already memorized from their written statements. Only a couple of surprises scored points for the defence. Surveyor Wiggins's plans of the Luckey premises, for instance, were shown to be unreliable, having been drawn from measurements taken April 11, six months after the fire.

"Isn't it true, sir," Lavell demanded triumphantly, "that weeds and debris had taken over the hole and there was no way of telling where one room began and another left off? How could you guess the location of the summer kitchen, the milkhouse, the woodshed, all of which had no foundation?"

The surveyor shrugged, embarrassed.

Clute took his time, determined to appear unconcerned, keeping Mrs. John J. Luckey junior, round and rosy as a well-scrubbed scarlet pippin, on the stand for an hour, extracting a rural pastiche of vaguely uneasy domesticity. He hammered away at the denture evidence.

He spent more time putting the child, pale and demure in Oxford grey, at ease, before asking if she knew her aunt had false teeth.

A blush. Lowered eyes. "I don't think I should have known she had false teeth if I – if I hadn't – known it."

Dismissed, she fled to her seat in tears.

All went smoothly until Andrew Parker, a grizzled, sun-baked man in his fifties, took the stand.

"Could you describe the Luckey house, sir."

"The kitchen where the bodies were is in the main part of the house. The door I kicked in was the one off the parlour on the south side and there is no door between it and the summer kitchen. The partition between the main kitchen and parlour was built of boards. A door in the partition connected the two rooms." He balanced his hat uneasily on the railing. "A plain house it was, built of logs on a stone foundation."

"And the fire broke out –?"

"Over the stoop door. There were doors between summer kitchen and stoop and stoop and winter kitchen."

"Thank you."

Lavell sprang to his feet to cross-examine. "Mr Parker, where were the Luckeys cooking their meals that time of year?"

"In the summer kitchen, Mr Lavell."

"And the stoop door – was it open or shut?"

"Shut. I think it would shut if you didn't prop it open."

"And what was the condition of the summer kitchen, for cooking?"

Andrew spread broad hands, deft at bleeding steers and birthing calves, clumsy with Sunday hats. "I was in the summer kitchen about two weeks before the fire. I asked Miz Luckey if she thought herself safe with the stove pipe so close to the timber." He paused while a juror sucked in his breath. "She said it had been that way for some time."

In the stillness, Clute could hear the scratch of the judge's pen, the long scrape as he underlined.

"There was quite a wind that day, even before the fire started. The smoke blew down to Newbliss. It was blowing pretty nearly from south to north and would strike the summer kitchen first."

Clute stared hard at Wiggins. The surveyor's diagram had to be wrong! The summer kitchen had to form a wing on the south east side of the house in order for the wind to strike it first.

"The summer kitchen and roof went in first. When the roof fell in we found the bodies."

"Thank you."

Judge Falconbridge took out his watch. "One more witness. We'll continue until six."

"Call Ansley Stewart!"

* * *

Liza Ann couldn't stop eating. As soon as she entered the dining hall, the aroma of food filled all the nooks and crannies of her being – nostrils, mouth, stomach, even her brain. It was balm, elixir, mother's breast, closing out the other, jarring senses for a time, shutting off the nightmares. Her stomach rumbled; a sharp, quivering, hollow feeling, that suddenly-drained faintness she remembered so well from pregnancy, washed over her.

Yesterday had been a gruelling, wasted time. Hours of waiting, pointing out public figures, making small talk, fanning themselves with gloves and folded newspapers. The children ran their hands along the gleaming wood and brass rail of the new reporters' gallery. At one point, someone circulated a postcard, a photograph of the ruins with sketches of Charley, the victims, Polk and McGowan. Hisses. "Where'd you get this?" "Pass it round!" Guilty glances. Unspeakably cruel, Liza Ann thought. Just when they had despaired of ever getting started, a disembodied voice thundered and an echo went round the courtroom: "The judge is coming on the four o'clock train!"

Above the buzz, the voice pealed again, Moses marshalling the tribes of Israel. "All witnesses in the Luckey case follow me to the Crown Attorney's office." Fully half the crowd rose and walked out, leaving every seat behind the rail separating the lawyers' quarters from the audience vacant.

Squeezed into the Crown's cramped quarters with eighty people, clinging to the children, her bonnet knocked askew, Liza Ann felt the blood draining from her head. Nine, return tomorrow at nine a.m. Couldn't they have told them that in the courtroom? She staggered a little following Johnny out, so that Victoria looked at her sharply and Esley, clutching her hand, cried out, "Ma! Are you all right?" She smiled reassuringly, regretting that she had given in to Johnny's decision to bring the boy.

She had slept badly last night, in the strange bed. Rain muttered at the windows, shadows crouched in corners, the sheets smelled damp and earthy, like a grave. She dreamed of Martha, saw the deeply etched lines of her face melting, dragging her mouth downward, past its expression of permanent disapproval to a mask of unfathomable desolation. She saw the old woman's body, solid and waistless, its secrets wrapped in coarse cottons and raw wool, ungraced by talcum or toilet water – saw it swell, crack open, hiss and sputter. In the dream she remained detached, even when she saw the body turning, as if on a spit. Until the hand reached out.

She sat up with a start then, gasping in the close air, forcing her breathing to slow. She covered her chest with her arms, relieved that the flesh she felt was her own. When at last she was breathing evenly, she lay down again. A reporter's words came back to her, floating through the darkness: "sexless anonymity of the bodies". Sexless. Embarrassing word. Why did it come to her in the dead of night, part of dreams, with Johnny lying beside her, snoring offensively, breath thick with ale and tobacco? Why did she dream of Martha – not Minnie, who was like a sister, or the old man, who had left his mark indelibly on them all?

Martha was a sharer of recipes and dress patterns, not confidences. Yet it was Martha who reached out with her charred fingers, shredded skin hanging from bone, clamping onto her sleeve, her wrist, her unpinned curls. Her hair would stand up on her head and she would awaken with a scream caught in her throat night after night and then think, no, it's Martha, only Martha.

Why does she come? Is she trying to tell me something?

She kept a taper lit by the bed at home nights now, one long enough to last until morning, ignoring Johnny's ridicule, his carping about wastefulness. *I'm not afraid of Martha, not at all, but I can't abide darkness, don't want to be caught in it at the wrong time. Die in it.*

The hotel food smelled better than it tasted, but her appetite was prodigious. *Partly relief because my testimony is finished. And we didn't have a proper lunch, and the trial went on past the supper hour. Everyone's famished. Why am I the only one eating like a pig?*

It was her own fault, really. She could have packed some bread and preserves, as Johnny suggested. Even some sausage and a pudding or two, enough for two or three days. But she couldn't bear the thought of traipsing into court with a wicker basket of soggy victuals and weak tea. Breakfast and supper were included in the room rates. With Johnny being such a tightwad, they'd gone without lunch two days now, settling for a packet of biscuits from the nearby shop. Johnny had never stopped raving about getting their expenses out of the court. "Doesn't matter whose side we're on, the Crown's or Charley's, testifying for the prosecution is the only way of getting paid. Even then, it won't cover our costs. We can say what we like on the stand. But if we're subpoenaed by the defence, expenses'll come out of our own pockets."

She had stood her ground about lunch and regretted it now. But she was still revolted by memories of the inquest, people crunching on pickles, spitting apple seeds, peeling hard-boiled eggs, the sulphurous smell offending her nostrils. More than a breach of etiquette, it was an insult to the dead. As deeply as she resented the slurs on her sex, she admitted that women all too often seemed willing to play the role of mindless fools. They brought squalling babies to public places and shamelessly and openly nursed and changed them. They made more noise hissing their toddlers into obedience than the children themselves made. Some she was sure never bathed from one month's end to the next, just slapped another layer of talcum on top of yesterday's. And the children's silly nicknames! Tillie, Hattie, Mamie, Aggie, Zeke.

And why had Johnny put up at the Central Hotel, instead of the Revere, like the judge, or St Lawrence Hall where most of the officials were staying? Even the detective and the court reporter from Toronto and cattleman Devlin were staying at the Hall, Devlin trumpeting it about that it was the best inn in Eastern Ontario. Cheap: that was Johnny.

Their hotel was on Main Street, a short walk from the court house. A block away you could smell the hops; tough characters lounged about the beverage room doorway, hawking and spitting at the brown-scabbed spittoon, leering at every passing female. She felt Victoria's hand tighten on hers every time they walked by.

The dining room was dark and airless as a closet, its maroon velvet draperies drunken and water-marked, their fringed valances and ties a grubby mustard yellow. The set meal was roast lamb. Johnny jabbed a forkful of meat into his mouth, shifting it like cow's cud while acknowledging greetings. The children picked at their food, complaining they wanted chicken and dumplings, their regular Tuesday meal.

But Liza Ann ate voraciously. The lamb was underdone, the mint sauce too sweet, the relish too tart, the potatoes roasted to boot-like leather. She shovelled it all in and chewed until her jaws ached. The bread was stale and gravelly, but she slathered butter on it and crammed her mouth. "Not hungry, Esley? At least have some bread!" She scraped his untouched vegetables onto her own plate. Stuffed, in agony, she couldn't make herself stop. Her stays dug in, the laces etching a grim ladder into her back. Why had she had Victoria help lace her into her new corset? She longed for her old undergarment, gently coached over the years to accommodate the curves of her stomach and hips with kindness.

"Ansley slunk off." Johnny's words reminded her of Charley, the sullen, jaded tone, as if he expected everyone to let him down.

She looked around. There was no escaping centre stage here as the room filled up. *We're the main attraction.* The Polks, the Halls, the Martin Merciers, the William Willises. Men hailed them openly; wives bestowed sly, casual nods. Women with no first names, simply extensions of their husbands. Hardly more than chattels. Shadows and echoes. Widow Daley, for instance, who even in bereavement had no Christian name. A relict. Dreadful sounding epithet, a leftover to be scraped onto the marital compost heap.

Beside Liza Ann, Johnny slurped his ale, wiped his nose with the back of his hand. Bleary-eyed, careless of social graces; soon he'd be ready to brawl. Should it be a woman's goal, perhaps a married woman's only goal, to outlive her husband and be propelled into the safe if repugnant anonymity reserved for relicts?

Liza Ann shuddered. I've caught the Luckey cynicism, she thought, and here I'd assumed it was exclusively male!

A waiter brushed her sleeve in passing and for an instant she felt Martha's ravaged hand clutching at her and shivered. Martha, going round and round in her head, in nightmare fragments. Miz Luckey to the rest of the world, appendage to John J. Luckey senior. Wife, chattel. Had she been, for a moment, a relict? Who could say if she had been granted that distinction, when she could not even claim all her own bones with any certitude?

Liza Ann scooped the last morsel of lamb, tempted to mop up the gravy with bread the way the farmhands did. Bad example! A social lapse to save for a day when she dined alone, with Johnny away and the children in school. She blushed – such self-indulgence! "Ansley told us what he was going to say in court."

Johnny leaned back and lit a cigar. "Another pitcher of ale, boy!" A waiter, stooped and withered, cast a baleful eye before scurrying off, to return with an overflowing pitcher. "That's more like it, boy!" He drummed fingers on the table. "It didn't do Charley any good, what Ansley said."

"He had to tell the truth as he saw it."

Sensing friction, the children pushed their plates away. "Daddy, how long will we be staying here? Could we live here?" Esley bounced in his chair.

Johnny glared at them, a vein standing out in his forehead. "Ansley's been closer than anyone to us. He was the one who wanted us to give Charley a fair hearing – remember?"

Liza Ann smouldered. What fools we are, talking of one thing, thinking of another. Red-faced, watery-eyed, he sat back in his chair, repugnant, nonchalant. As if he had no secret life! No innocent-looking jar in his bureau in the study, tucked away behind a wad of old invoices. He never touched her now, gave no excuses. Thank the Lord. She'd seen the advertisements often enough almost to memorize them. Dr Gordon's Remedy for Men, with its bland, sly promises: "cures lost power, nervous debility, night losses, diseases caused by tobacco, opium, stimulants, abuse, overwork, indiscretion . . ."

Just the fact that the jar was hidden away confirmed her fears. It could have rested openly in the medicine box, a common soother of nerves, but no, it was pushed to the back of a drawer Liza Ann seldom touched, not privy to the secrets bound in ledgers and files.

She examined herself each morning at bath, in case she had been contaminated in sharing his bed, but there was no redness, no itching or soreness. She'd even taken to washing his dishes after everyone else's, the way she did the house cat's, and soaking his clothes in lye until he complained that even his newest shirts were falling apart. No word passed between them about the reason for her behaviour. Nonsense, it was, all the needless scrubbing and scouring, but the thought of the jar and what it stood for made her skin crawl. She recalled horror stories that women whispered among themselves: women with sores and pustules, having to have all their reproductive organs cut out, some bloating up like landed fish, splitting open and dying in agony. Others went mad and were housed in the asylum in Brockville, rocking imaginary babies or drawing obscenities on the walls with their feces. All because they had caught a dread disease from their husbands.

She began to play a cat-and-mouse game. Johnny would disappear at odd times into his study, reappearing after a few moments. She would go into the study, taking a broom or duster with her, and check the jar. At least he was taking the stuff. She would breathe a sigh of relief. He was worried enough about himself to do something. Not about her.

"Mummy, Dad." Esley set down his empty glass, a moustache of milk on his lip. "What did Uncle Ansley say?"

Johnny swore under his breath. "Can't you teach these children some manners? There'll be no talk at table unless I say so!" Just like his father.

"But Dad –"

"We're finished, Dad." Victoria folded her napkin.

"All that food paid for!"

"There's dessert." Liza Ann signalled a tray-bearing waiter. Alone of the group she accepted pudding, drowning it in custard scooped from a proffered bowl. "What's that?" She drizzled something treacly from a second bowl. A small dish held spiced jelly. "Just a daub, please?" She was eating for all of them! The waiter rotated the tray with studied nonchalance, as if well-bred ladies sacrificed etiquette to gastronomical pleasures here every day.

Trembling, Liza Ann forced herself to sink her spoon into the towering dessert with exaggerated slowness. Her face felt warm as she imagined the curious gazes of their neighbours, Halls, Willises, that whited sepulchre Polk. Guilt rose as she put the spoon to her mouth: she had no business heaping resentment on John Polk! Wouldn't she have done the same thing?

Just as Johnny had no business judging Ansley who was, above all things, honest. Ansley had a blind faith that justice would prevail. "Never fear the truth. Isn't that what Ansley said, Johnny? Only if everyone tells the truth will we find out what really happened."

"Sounds like a pulpit speech. Ansley can do no wrong."

"What did he say, Dad?" Esley wriggled in his seat. "Was it about the boots?"

"Christ, Esley, shut up." Johnny pounded the table. "Yes, goddam it, the boots! Those boots'll hang Charley yet."

"Grandfather's boots?"

"He said they looked like them. No one – no one, not even I, can identify the boots. But Ansley had to go and say –"

Custard and treacle slid down Liza Ann's throat, coming to rest on the lump of pudding. "I watched him in the courtroom, Johnny. Ansley's aged ten years. When he swore that at church he sometimes sat in the same pew with Father, I thought he was going to collapse. His hands trembled when he rested them on the rail. When he told about noticing your father's boots that Sunday last July, the judge had to ask him to speak up."

"He said the gaiters Father wore in church had brass nails in the soles, like the exhibits. How could he possibly remember –"

"But he admitted he didn't notice the screws."

"He mentioned the elastic. Worn so badly as to have a fringe, he said."

"Even then, he was apologetic, saying he only noticed because your father sat with one foot over the other."

"His sincerity was damning."

"I think it broke his heart. He wants to believe Charley is innocent." Her spoon missed the dish, clattered on the table.

"The most damning moment was when they held the boots up and he pointed and said, 'Those look like the very boots'. And you tell me he still believes Charley will come up with some explanation that will clear him? Here's to Ansley, absent friend!" Johnny raised his glass, oblivious to stares.

Liza Ann flushed. What must the Polks think? And Willis, the waiters? Most of all, the children? She felt the hair bristle on the back of her neck, as it had when Martha reached out to her. Oh, God, why did she keep thinking of Martha? Was Martha watching, too?

And Charley – did Martha come to him? "Charley never took his eyes off me while I was in the witness box. I saw his eyes fill with tears."

Johnny ignored her, lost in his own thoughts. She pushed back her chair and rose. "Bedtime, children. Come, now." Victoria pouted; Esley suppressed a yawn. Cutlery jumped as Johnny banged the table. "Look at those bastards! Sly smart-asses!" His voice rose over the hum of conversation.

Liza Ann, watching the children, bit her lip. *I won't look around. I don't want to know who heard him.*

"Used to be friends. Colleagues. I sold them farm machinery and livestock. Helped build their houses and barns. D'you think they dare betray us in court, drag us through the mud? Not on your life! They'll have me to deal with if they do." He made a fist and she stepped in front of him, blocking the view. "Oh, go away, woman, go away. D'you imagine I'd start a fight here? Go to bed. Get out of my sight!" He stood up unsteadily and wove between chairs and tables toward the outside door.

Liza Ann herded the children up the stairs. Another day gone by, another nightmare waiting. Better Martha plucking at her sleeve than Johnny rolling against her, his saliva thick on her neck. Please God he would not be back tonight. She could take the children into her bed; then perhaps she would be safe from both worlds, the real one and the one of bad dreams.

Chapter Three

Dearest Silla,

Part of me wishes you could have been with me today; part of me is glad you didn't have to endure the claustrophobic courtroom atmosphere, odours and grating acoustics, to say nothing of interminable delays and excruciating punctiliousness. You would have been amused by the distinctively rural fashion parade and much entertained by the subtle intrigues, pointed glances, extravagant gestures and occasional Mephistophelian asides – in short the sweeping melodrama. But you would have been appalled by the reactions to the testimony, both the drooling avidity of the heretofore uninitiated and the ennui of those who had heard it all before. (I know I sound like a stuffy old barrister, Love, gowned and bewigged in pedantry and incredibly long in the tooth, but if I can't expound to you in all my guises, whom can I call upon to forbear and forgive – and nod in all the right places? And if I'm going to keep a journal of proceedings, Dear Diary sounds banal. Juvenile. Friendless! To Whom it may Concern is infinitely worse: faintly juridical, and possibly posthumous!)

So I sit, pen in hand, a glass of the hotel's best claret within reach, badly in need of a couple of quills to prop my eyes open. If I could go sleepless for the trial's duration, would my vigilance be enough to save Charley's neck?

Today started well enough. I admit I was nervous, defending an accused killer for the first time (already hoping it would be the last!). I was aware that pomp and circumstance held this man here, a prisoner not only of the legal system but also of the society that produced and nurtured him. Society, that great, indefatigable spider, anaesthetized him, spinning a legal web to hold him fast. One has to be aware at all times of those arachnoid bonds, silken but unbreakable, of legal terminology and statutory observances, and the formal structure and insular style of the web, which overrides all considerations of the human element.

From the first oyez to the last adjournment, you follow the rules. At times the imp on your shoulder mutters, like Dickens' character, "The law is a ass." One little life, infinitesimal in the scheme of things, is not important unless and until you get everything else right. Ah, priorities! It is somewhat like standing naked down to the ankles before a multitude and worrying about whether or not your socks match!

In this frame of mind I began weathering what may turn out to be the longest, most onerous juristic exposure of my career. Charley seemed to have fortified himself spiritually for the ordeal, thanks, I'm sure, to the old sheriff. Clute, in his opening address, came down like the wrath of God on him, and he scarcely flinched. (The jury, of course, may interpret his lack of emotion as remorselessness.) The only time he appeared close to tears was when his sister-in-law took the stand. The prosecution's labouring of the teeth, trying time and time again to get witnesses to make a positive identification, made him very uncomfortable. I couldn't help but recall Poe's story *Berenice*, and felt the familiar shiver up my spine. No similarities in the stories, of course, beyond the echoes of a woman's scream and the ominous little box housing its pathetic contents.

Clute, convinced of Charley's guilt, is formidable. An honourable opponent to the last stroke, professional down to his fingertips. No breath of scandal, ever.

A murder trial is not like any other kind of courtroom procedure. There can be no reversal, no restitution, no resurrection. There is an underlying gravity, a faint rumbling of doom. The accused, imprisoned in his box much as the dentures are in theirs, is the object of speculation and innuendo, pity and revilement, his every expression and action minutely scrutinized and interpreted.

Silla, I alone of all the people in that courtroom have contracted to "save" Charley. I cannot let him die.

Tomorrow, I thrash about in a sea of medical testimony. Between you and me, I concede that a post mortem would have added no useful information. But in court I intend to use the omission to prove apathy and negligence in the investigation. Once an arrest was made – as it was almost immediately – there was a resistance to thoroughness. The government detective didn't arrive until the third day after the fire, you recall, and then made an ass of himself in the lockup, cavorting as a drunk. If an arrest hadn't been made so soon, would more effort have been put into examining the victims? Would there have been more questions about possible accidental death?

Another point: shouldn't we record whatever observations we can make through a post mortem, even if we cannot interpret it today? For are we not living in an age which has seen more progress than any age before it? (Yesterday I heard of an Englishman who has invented a magic box which actually takes pictures of people moving about. Suppose we had recorded our inquest, our medical examination, this way!)

Suppose, long after the trial, perhaps after we're all dead, a new process evolves enabling men to interpret the post mortem findings as we record them now? (I see you smiling, Silla, wondering if it is the claret talking! I assure you my glass is half full, and the fuzziness in my head is no more than honest weariness.)

I won't get a chance to argue these points in court. The best I can do is try to drive one more nail in the prosecutorial coffin.

Which brings me to my last visit to Cedarhedge that Sunday in March – something you would have heard about first hand had I returned with a voice! You warned me to wear my wool muffler but I, smelling spring in the air, left it on the bannister. I headed for the Kingston train light-hearted, light-mantled – and light-headed. Franky and Marion waved from the window, and I could see you in shadow behind them, holding the little one, perched firmly on the aproned mound of his soon-to-be playmate. I almost turned back then: it didn't seem right to be going to Father's without all of you. Only the thought that Uncle Henry would be at Cedarhedge urged me on. You might think I went with larceny in my heart. I had no intention of purloining a Crown witness, but who could resist doing a little digging? I just wanted to determine his thoughts without Vaux's influence.

We observed the entire Sunday ritual, of course: church, a groaning table of home cooking, the customary taffy pull after Sunday School, and parlour games, round-the-piano singing, and Father's evening prayers. For me it all meant taking the late train home; that, as you remember, was my downfall. The temperature had dropped, the railway car was appallingly cold and with the engine breakdown halfway to Smith's Falls, I spent an extra three hours huddled in my seat, shivering. You paid for it too, spending the next two weeks making mustard plasters and onion poultices. To say nothing of your forays to the local apothecary, seeking a magic elixir to ward off pneumonia. While I wheezed my way through preparations for the biggest trial of my life!

All because I went to Cedarhedge. All through the day, in the midst of wasp-waisted sisters, cousins and in-laws, I pictured you, resting your swollen feet on the hassock in the library, and I missed you more than I ever had in my life. Until now!

After dinner, we men retired to the study where port and cigars stood untouched on the sideboard, not even Henry availing himself. Father never stints, as you know, but his being a steadfast abstainer somehow casts a pall.

Eventually, Henry edged toward the fireplace at the far end to light his pipe. I followed. "Post prandial post mortem?" His eyes crinkled. We went through all the pros and cons of the issue, like dancers performing a two-step, I making all the predictable arguments for a post mortem, he following along with all the perfectly executed rebuttals. Were the victims alive when the fire started? What matter, they could still have been wounded or dying. Even knowing the answer wouldn't tell us the means of death. Examination of the bodies might only have had adverse repercussions for the accused, be injurious to my case. It was too late, in any case, to set matters right.

"You have to respect Vaux," Henry said. "He's one of the best. You'd like him, in other circumstances."

Irrelevant. In vain I protested that my case didn't rest on post mortem evidence. "If you help me plant one shred of doubt in the jury's mind that the investigation was performed with care and integrity, Charley will be exonerated."

Henry looked at me from under those beetle brows. "J.R.," he said, "you know as well as I do that Charley was in the house that day. Maybe it was all a horrible accident, but it's something he's lying about. Placing him there at the time of the fire makes it harder to prove his innocence, no matter how the investigation was conducted."

Silla, the glass is empty, my eyes drooping. Only the vase of daffodils some thoughtful maid placed on the dresser burns brightly. A good omen?

Take care, Love.

J

P.S. Yes, if it's a girl we'll call her Kathleen.

* * *

Across the hall in number nineteen, Billy Greer paced the pitted hardwood from door to dresser to bed and back again. An inmate in a prison cell. If Old Never-Let-Go could see him now his eyes would crinkle in that slow, mocking smile. "Billy," he'd say, "what have you got to worry about? It's not your neck that's going to be put in the noose. Not this time, anyway."

As he walked he muttered, and as he muttered he thought he could see his breath, so cold was the room. "One thing we don't lack is witnesses. The numbers are overwhelming. What we lack are witnesses with good memories – who can speak with authority. Yes! Those are Miss Luckey's teeth. Yes! Those are the old man's boots. Hallelujah!" He gave a childish skip and punched the air.

"For heaven's sake, come to bed." A face framed by red-gold hair smiled from the pillows. Billy, who would have sworn he hadn't a poetic bone in his body, had remarked not an hour ago that the slender arms reaching toward him were like graceful swans' necks. Now, barely glancing at his inamorata, he turned back toward the door, resuming his pacing. "You don't understand. I couldn't get Murray to come down to the murder site until he returned four weeks ago. Been out of the country since early November. He's always saying a trail's never so cold that it can't be warmed up. But he was out of sorts, and on the train home to Toronto claimed I'd wasted his time bringing him down to Newbliss. Took me to task for all sorts of things."

"You're doing your best." The woman twined a strand of bright hair around a finger.

"But that's not the point, Cath –" he caught himself – "Cassie. Best's not good enough. The last thing Murray said to me was, make sure your witnesses remember their initial reactions. People forget or misinterpret what they've seen. You can smell uncertainty on a witness just as you can guilt on an accused."

Cassie rose on one elbow. "That's the second time tonight you've called me by your wife's name."

Billy strode to the bed, bent and kissed the freckled nose.

"Forgive me, Cassie dearest. It's just that tomorrow's the medical evidence. I'm a little out of my depth."

He'd met her while working undercover in '87. A sober young widow, pleading for protection, fearing her barns would be burned by firebrands. Surprised and delighted when she'd turned up in court today, he'd slipped away with her as soon as he could after adjournment, supping at an out-of-the-way roadhouse.

"You'll be no more out of your depth than the jury. Less so, I should imagine. And you don't have to examine the witnesses."

Billy sat on the bed, letting talcum and toilet water waft over him, surprised he wasn't roused by the pale shoulders and half-exposed breasts. "That's part of the problem. I wish I could be the one to interrogate them in court. Lead them in the right direction, drop them at the first hint of disaster. As it is, I try to brief the witnesses before they're called."

"But there are so many!"

"Yes, and some don't show up when they say they will, or they fail to report to the Crown's office. Then when they do arrive, they're surrounded by reporters. Some deliberately avoid me."

She pulled at his string tie. "You could be tracking some of them down tonight. Right?"

He resisted the urge to scratch his groin. True, he'd meant to look up Hannah and Brunton, and to sound out the coroners again. Instead, he had given in to a familiar weakness, departing the roadhouse in haste, meal unfinished, and smuggling Cassie past a dozing hotel clerk. Once inside, he'd found anxiety replaced desire. He wondered if he was getting old.

"Medical experts shouldn't need to be briefed."

Billy cocked an eyebrow. "My definition of an expert is someone who's at loggerheads with another expert. The problem is, a jury may stand so much in awe of an expert that they take every word he utters as gospel."

"But if two experts don't agree –"

"The jury is lost. Everyone looks stupid."

"You'd never look stupid." Slender fingers wrapped around his sleeve and tugged. "I've got the bed warmed up."

He patted her wrist and unfastened her fingers gently. "Even Murray said there should have been a post mortem. If only to show that it was of no use in determining cause or time of death."

"Murray won't be there." Cassie plumped the pillow beside hers and smiled invitingly.

Billy straightened up, unbuckling his belt. "Vaux made the decision not to hold a post mortem and he won't go back on his word. But Reeve – Reeve's an unknown quantity."

Sitting up, Cassie unbuttoned his trousers and helped pull them down. If she was offended by the cloud of musk emanating from his flannel long johns she gave no sign. "Cath –"

Her smile faded. She clasped the covers to her bosom and froze. "Maybe I shouldn't have come."

"Cassie. Sorry." God, what had he done? He had been looking forward to a long, warm, delicious night, a renewal of the teasing and laughter and unbridled lovemaking of five years ago. "Please stay. It's just that – I want to talk."

She shrugged. "Talk." She turned her attention to picking lint from the bedcovers.

"Going back to Toronto on the train, Murray asked me if anyone had examined Luckey for burns. You know what I said?" His underwear prickled his groin. "I said, it appeared that McGowan hadn't thought of it. Christ, the way Murray looked at me!"

She let the covers fall, revealing small, firm breasts, nipples rigid in the chill air. "His approval means more than anything, doesn't it."

But Billy was feeling again the sway of the pullman car and the burn of Murray's caustic gaze. "I can't believe the number of times investigators examine a corpse and ignore the suspect," Murray had said. "Forget about the victims' blood and burns for a moment. What about blood and burns on the suspect?"

"There was blood on his clothes. We thought."

"And the exhibits were – misplaced." Murray, who seldom lost his sense of humour, had spoken with ominous softness. "A physical examination might have uncovered signs that the accused had been near a fire. Superficial burns, scorched hair, singed eyebrows. The smell of smoke in his hair and clothes."

"But he probably fled before the fire."

"Probably." Murray had leaned back abruptly and closed his eyes. End of conversation. Storm clouds passed. But Murray cleared his throat, eyes still closed. "I must have mentioned the Ward case." One of Murray's favourite stories, about a young woman he had met in the seventies. "Lovely creature, Mary Ward. Her husband wouldn't share her with anyone, not even the old aunt she was preparing to visit. He killed her, dismembered her body. Then he set fire to the house and ran to a neighbour's for help, but not before he took the trouble to burn himself in several places with an iron, to make it look like he'd barely escaped himself." Billy had resisted the urge to recite the rest of the story for Murray. "I examined him while his mother was dressing his wounds, and immediately became suspicious, Billy. All his burns were of uniform size and shape. Deep. Clearly outlined. Even the one on the back of his neck, just below the hairline –" Murray touched the spot on his own neck – "hadn't scorched a single hair."

Scratching his groin, Billy glanced at his companion, wondering if she was feigning sleep. Did her eyelids flutter? How could he expect her to understand that this case consumed him, that it was vital that he impress Murray? That the evidence, sickening and frustrating, eroded his natural desires? He unfastened his shirt and removed it, hesitating in his underwear. Perhaps he should sleep elsewhere . . .

Slowly he unbuttoned flannel to his navel and slipped it down over his shoulders. He bent and kissed Cassie's forehead, a light butterfly of a kiss.

Her arms came up around his neck and she pulled him down, stronger than he could have imagined, moaning words he didn't understand, didn't care to understand.

There was only one word he knew he must fix in his mind, no matter how tumultuously he was swept away in the throes of passion: Cassie.

* * *

His ear hurt. Old Marthy was pinching it, the way she had when she found him in the hayloft, his belly full of stolen green apples, when he was supposed to be milking. Or the time the schoolmaster marched him home, holding Martha's new meat baster aloft, making him confess that he'd filled it with ink, spraying it all over the girls' pinafores. The schoolmaster might not have been so angry if he hadn't been an accidental target himself, blue exploding on his shirtsleeve.

The old woman had come to the door, tightlipped, and he, eleven, too old to have his britches pulled down for a tanning, felt her knuckles grip the flap of his ear, her thumbnail piercing it as she wrenched and twisted, dragging him across the field to where his father was preparing to pull stumps. "I wash my hands of him," she shrieked, pushing him forward so he stumbled and fell at his father's feet. Before he could get up, his father came at him with a kick in the backside that sent him flying again, cracking his head against a stump.

It's only a dream, he thought. But he couldn't climb out of it. Down the length of some great hollow tunnel his father was screaming, "Thank God your mother can't see you now!" He felt the cold fleck of his father's spittle on his face and tried to reach out but there was ink, red ink everywhere.

"Charley! Charley, my God, lad! Send for the Sheriff!"

"Here, dash more water on him! Charley!"

He rubbed his eyes open, still groaning with the piercing pain in his ear, and looked up at the turnkey, holding a lantern aloft while the gaoler sprinkled water on his face. "Wake up, laddie, ye're having a nightmare!"

Sheriff Smart appeared beside him, sliding suspenders up over his shoulders. "What's the matter lad?"

"My ear! Oh, God, it hurts!" He clamped his hand over it.

"Let's see." Strong fingers pried his hand loose. "A bit red. Perhaps you slept with it folded over."

Other prisoners stirred. Moans, a cackle; the plop of urine hitting a slop pail.

The old man's breath smelled faintly of onions. "I'll be sleeping on my cot in my office for the duration of the trial. Send for me any time. We'll see this through together." He tucked the thin blanket around Charley awkwardly. "Try and sleep. It's a long time until morning." He signalled the night guard for a chair. "And leave the door open."

Settled, he took out his pipe and tamped it. "Did you ever hear of the wreck of the *Yankee Blade*, Charley? I was a young man, set out to seek my fortune, bound for California and the gold mines. Left a bride and unborn daughter behind." A favourite recitation. Charley already knew it by heart. "I wasn't to see them for three long years. Staked a claim in California and worked it. In 1854, sailing for home on the *Yankee Blade*, we were shipwrecked, all our possessions lost. I barely escaped with my life . . ." He drew on his pipe, noting his charge was asleep.

Chapter Four

"All the victims were without limbs, except for a small portion of lower limbs of the male."

Charley sucked in his breath. Coroner Reeve, on the witness stand, spoke with matter-of-fact dryness. Ordering tea. *They were headless. Cream and sugar, please.* Looking beyond the prosecutor, he saw the door at the back of the courtroom open as Liza Ann ushered her children outside.

"The male as well – could he be described as headless?" Clute moved closer to his witness, blocking Charley's view.

"The features were still there to some extent but –" *His skull was shattered. Sandwiches, too. Pass the tray.*

"You recognized him as John James Luckey senior?"

"I thought I could recognize him under the circumstances, but I don't think I should have otherwise."

Hunger and horror flooded him. He folded his hands over his stomach, certain its lurching was visible. Thank God he had refused the oatmeal this morning, even though he saw dismay on the face of the sheriff, who had personally delivered it, steaming and sugared, a special treat.

"But you could distinguish him from the other victims." Clute thrust his face near the witness's, as if afraid the doctor's attention might wander.

"The shape of the pelvic bones showed me the other two were females."

A nightmare riding on his early morning nightmare, rising to engulf him. He willed himself to concentrate on other things, how many men in the audience, how many women? How many of the women were single, young, fair? *How many will pick up their skirts and rush out, white as sheets?*

Precious few, it seemed. A couple of old biddies from the Women's Auxiliary. Liza Ann. He tried willing the door to open for her return; her presence was comforting in a way he couldn't explain.

As J.R. was beginning his cross-examination, no flicker of recognition passed between counsel and coroner. "Dr Reeve, in your opinion, could a post mortem, if held, reveal any useful information?"

Dr Reeve put a hand up as if to stroke his beard, then lowered it. "In the case of death by suffocation, a post mortem would reveal something by the condition of the lungs, heart and possibly stomach."

"What is the colour of blood normally?"

"Arterial blood is bright red, venous blood darker and muddier."

"What condition would the lungs be in after the inhalation of smoke?"

"They would be congested."

"By carbon dioxide."

"Yes, and carbon dioxide would have a tendency to delay decay or putrefaction. The blood would be of a venous character, that is, dark purple or blue."

"This would be noticeable during the examination of the bodies?"

"If the examination took place within, say, a few days or a week, always depending on whether or not putrefaction had set in."

J.R. clasped his hands together, one index finger protruding to rest on his chin. "Dr Reeve, I want you to consider this next question very carefully. Is there any chance that an examination of any one of the bodies would have revealed useful information? Determined particulars of death, perhaps?"

"The bodies were in such a condition, especially that of the wife, that if a post mortem had been held it would have shown by the blood or the change in circulation whether death had ensued from suffocation or not. The blood, as a result of the heat, would be coagulated."

"So you believe that, in the case of the elderly female –"

"In her case, an examination of the interior could have been made and might have been of some – might have revealed something."

Charley watched the judge's pen move swiftly across his notebook, saw him draw long strokes over the page, once, twice, three times. Stroking out? Underlining?

"Were their bodies still covered by skin?"

"I could not find any exterior skin on any of them."

"Yet the blood would not leave the body in these circumstances? Even with the absence of limbs?"

"I would think the burning of limbs would not cause blood to drain out. The blood would coagulate."

"Thank you, doctor."

Clute moved swiftly to the centre of the room. "One moment, Your Honour. Move to re-examine the witness." Head on one side, he regarded the coroner. Silly fellow, his tone said. "Dr Reeve, you have presented us with a picture of roasted, skinless carcasses, without limbs, heads absent or shattered, for the most part unrecognizable. Yet you ask us to believe that a post mortem, at least on one body, might have been useful. Now the elderly female, whom you recognized as female only because of the pelvic bones, could, according to your testimony, be subjected to medical procedures which would reveal cause – and time – of death. Come, come, doctor."

He strode over to the jury, wheeled and made a sweeping gesture. Like a villain in a melodrama, Charley thought. "Perhaps, doctor, this – this wizardry would also tell us the name and address of the murderer. But of course." He flashed a smile, noting his listeners' fascination. "We already know that, don't we."

Some of the jurors smiled back. Bile rose in Charley as Lavell shouted, "Move to strike!"

Clute ignored the judge's rebuke. "Dr Reeve, I ask you, if the flesh of the elderly female was burned, would not her internal organs have been exposed and roasted beyond all possibility of examination?"

The coroner returned his interrogator's stare calmly. But his hand stole up to his beard, pressed it here and there, as if reassuring himself that a mask was still in place. "The flesh of the elderly female was not burned so as to expose the internal organs."

"You are certain of that? When did you first see the bodies?"

"Sunday, the day after the fire."

"Thank you."

Dr Vaux's white buttonhole trembled as he took the stand. "I saw the remains on Monday, October tenth. It was perfectly out of the question to hold a post mortem." Aristocratic bearing, injured tone, the epitome of unassailable innocence. A conspiracy, Charley thought. *They're out to get me, make J. R. look a fool!* "It would have been utterly impossible to arrive at any conclusions as to whether death was caused by asphyxia."

"Thank you."

The judge scrawled and underlined. "Proceed, Mr Lavell."

"Isn't it true, doctor, that asphyxia causes congestion of the lungs?"

"Yes, sir. And it would darken the blood and would engage all internal organs."

"How can you be certain of that?"

"Sir, the bodies were roasted through and through. In particular, we could not tell anything about the condition of the lungs – whether they were congested before death or not." He gripped the rail. "The bodies were charred almost beyond recognition as human remains."

Dismissed, Vaux acknowledged Greer's jerk of the head and followed him out the back exit, passing Liza Ann returning with the children.

Up to something, the bastard. No one else noticed except Lavell, who carried on as if nothing had happened. *J.R. knows. Won't let them get away with anything.*

Prison employees one by one, hair slicked back, military glint, parroted the same message to the court: Charley had no money on him when he entered the Central Prison; none when he left except the $12.65 for train fare and "bonus of good conduct and work in the broomshop." Receipt produced. Official and indisputable. *Montgomery's breed, hard drinkers all. Montgomery! I'd like to have been there when they found you swinging. Fool, you're not even missed!*

That steamy, soupy smell of crowded rooms. Open windows admitting chill drafts. But the sweat was his, he was sure of it – armpits, groin, even his back felt damp. An odour he'd never noticed on himself, until the day Miss Harriet, God bless her, had passed a remark that had made him blush. "When did you last bathe, Charley?" He had marvelled at her directness, her such a lady. She'd offered him the use of the family bath, a huge tin tub on cast iron legs, in its own curtained enclosure, and given him a wicked scrub brush and a chunk of perfumed soap. A servant brought buckets of water and made off with his clothes, returning them spotless and sweet-smelling hours later. He had sat and lathered until the water turned cold and goose pimples stood out on his arms. Then the servant, sightless in a manner he supposed was peculiar to indoor help, had pulled back the curtains and opened out a towel so wide he had to stretch his arms as far as he could sideways. Carpet-thick. Then a robe appeared, purple and velvety like a king's, and when he put it on he was aware that his back was straighter than it had ever been. He stood tall, stepped imperiously into soft slippers. King – Kingsley!

Hot and sticky now, he longed to sink into suds again and float away, far from droning voices. But suddenly, high and angry, they rose to capture him like storm waves on an open sea. J.R. was on his feet, gesturing; Clute, hands on hips, strutted like a rooster. On the stand, Jock Brunton, discoverer of the axe, looked from one to the other, bewildered. Clute was shouting, "Did you not say at the inquest, Mr Brunton, that you were positive the blood on the axe did not come from your finger?"

J.R.'s voiced drowned out his last words. "Just a moment, Your Honour. Please! This has gone far enough. I was present at the inquest and the witnesses were examined by the detective, who put words into their mouths. I object to the Crown's suggesting to the witness anything he may have said at the inquest."

Charley shrank back against the hard wood of the dock. His ear ached; he had a vision of himself, floating in suds, but there was something about his neck, tightened under his ear, pulling. *God, J.R., don't let him –*

"As counsel for the Crown, Your Honour, I submit that if the witness made a different statement regarding the bloodstains at the inquest I have a right to demand an explanation."

Falconbridge banged his gavel. "Mr Brunton is a Crown witness, Mr Clute. I cannot question him regarding any discrepancy unless it can be shown that the witness is adverse to the Crown. Continue, Mr Brunton."

Brunton's thick brogue took on an apologetic tone. "I saw a bloodstain on the axe as I took it and threw it away. Just as I threw it, my finger caught."

"Your witness, Mr Lavell."

"Mr Brunton, how did you catch your hand on the axe?"

"The throwing it away caught my hand."

"Did you observe anything in the barn to indicate the axe had been in use?"

"I saw signs where chickens had been killed the day before."

Charley let out a long sigh. He felt his muscles relaxing, his body sinking into torpor as witness after witness suffered memory lapse. Cousin Jack Phillips couldn't say with certainty that the dentures exhibited were the ones he found under the apple tree. Cattleman Devlin didn't think the bills found on Charley were the ones he had paid Charley's father. John Hannah couldn't identify the parcel he had carried onto the train for Charley, nor the shirt Charley had worn. When he declined to identify the boots, Charley knew there was going to be trouble. "All I can tell you is, he had no other parcel and no other boots with him on the train," Hannah said. Neat and solemn, he recounted their trip with simple directness, insisting neither of them had drunk too much. *Trust you with my life, Hannah.*

Lunch. Following Greer, who was shepherding Hannah out, Charley walked beside the gaoler to a small, windowless room where sandwiches waited.

"Take heart, lad." The gaoler's eyes twinkled as he poured water from a pitcher into Charley's glass. "Ear better today?"

Charley nodded uncertainly. Take heart. He held the words, letting them warm his stomach, while he tried to make a show of eating the coarse slices smeared with mashed egg. *Take heart!* Words he took back with him to his seat in the dock.

"Recall John Hannah!"

Here it comes. "Mr Hannah." Clute picked up the cloth-topped boots. "Look closely, please. Are these the boots Charles Luckey was wearing on the train when you travelled from Toronto?"

Hannah swallowed. "Yes, I believe –"

"Please point to the boots you are indicating, Mr Hannah."

"Those. Those look like them."

"Please describe them for the record, Mr Hannah."

"He – had on laced boots with checked tops – like those."

So I did. I don't deny it. But what's happening here is law. Not truth.

J.R. rose, tight-lipped. "Mr Hannah, have you by any chance been out talking to the detective since you were last on the stand, and described the boots to him? Or did the detective describe them to you?"

"The detective was talking to me about the boots, yes."

"Did you notice on the train that they were burst?"

"No."

"Nothing further."

"Mr Clute."

The law'll hang me, truth be damned. "Mr Hannah. Who described the boots to whom?"

"I – described the boots to Greer – not he to me."

"And these are the boots in question."

Hannah looked at the floor. "I'm sorry, sir. I really can't be absolutely certain."

"Your Honour. The detective has been talking to the witnesses during the trial and putting words into their mouths."

"Overruled! Sit down, Mr Lavell."

Greer in the front row lowered his head, but Charley saw his smile.

They were putting together his life for him, piece by piece like a jigsaw puzzle. Good, bad, painful, long-forgotten; things he would like to forget. Piecing together October eighth, the day that lay in fragments in his memory, that he hadn't the will or strength to rebuild. Yes, he had been on the road to Newbliss; yes, they had seen him, had documented his every footstep. Yes, pretty Sarah Jane had seen him hop the fence – if he had known she was watching, he would have doffed his hat and, in his dreams, dreams where Harriet lingered, he would have blown a kiss. Just the right age, and no beau, they said. Could it be true? And Johnny eyeing her, slavering like a hound.

They were edging closer to the gap in his memory. He could feel himself being drawn toward the brink by them, getting ready to step off, to pitch forward into a black, bottomless hole. Soon they would tell him where he had been, what he had done; they would fill in the jigsaw and he would be at the centre; everyone would know; he would know. Yes, there he was, they had taken him as far as the farm; he sat on a fence munching hawthorn nuts while wood and grass burned, flesh sizzled, even the apples in the orchard baked on the trees. Soon someone would say, But that was in the afternoon – what happened in the morning, after you arrived, while you said you were sleeping? You were sleeping, weren't you, Charley, sleeping by Bruce's spring? Soon he would know.

But suddenly they veered away, as if they didn't know, didn't want to know, perhaps. They edged around the hole in his memory, for perhaps it was their hole too, a hole in their memory, or at least their imagination. They passed on into the evening. To five witnesses who had seen him on the road, returning to Smith's Falls. Yes, he didn't deny it, never had, he had walked the road back from Newbliss, had seen Polk, thought it was Johnny, not knowing Polk had bought Johnny's horses. And the others – had he seen them? What matter? He didn't deny being on the road.

They told about the Palace Hotel, the barber shop, things he didn't remember, not that they were lying. A razor, a room key, smoke in his nostrils, a moose. What they said must be true, him walking into a door, fainting, acting strange. What matter? He denied none of it. He was hungry, and his ear hurt, and he would be glad when this day was over.

When McGowan took the stand, everything changed. He wore his contempt for the prisoner like a spotless uniform, vast, intimidating. Others tempered their words with doubt, made allowances, sought innocent explanations. Not McGowan. He didn't just point to the money exhibited. He got down from the witness stand, seized it, counted it out, bill by bill, coin by coin. "Twenty-five seventy-five. The ten dollar bill is marked with a blue pencil. Here. I thought there was blood on it when I took it from the prisoner."

McGowan, stalking around the exhibits. "Train ticket, Your Honour. Shirt. Watch and chain. These cloth-topped boots he abandoned on his way to Newbliss. These gaiters were in his hotel room when I arrested him." And the axe. "That's the one. Burned along one side. It was nowhere near the log where the chickens were killed." Seating himself in the witness box, he spread his arms to punctuate his words, then brought his hands together in a concertina player's gesture. "Not when I found it on the Monday after the fire. It was closer to where the teeth were found."

Monday? Come on, McGowan. How many times had it been tossed around since Saturday night? J.R., wake up! Fight my battles!

McGowan spent an hour and a quarter on the stand, telling about the boot tracks, how the burrs on his trousers were identical to those found on Charley, where the field with the burrs was. "The prisoner had a clear view of the house from there," he said.

He told how Charley had given his name as Kingsley. *Is it a crime to change your name? I've always lied about it. I don't like my name. People make fun of it.*

And the cloth-topped boots. "The prisoner admitted he threw them away near the tollgate. I went out and got his socks myself where he said he had thrown them."

Clute prodded him. "And the gaiters?"

"He said he bought the gaiters in a second hand store on King Street in Toronto and brought both pairs with him, throwing away the other boots at the tollgate."

Cross-examining, Lavell ignored Charley's signals. "Chief McGowan, you had a conversation with the prisoner in his cell. Did he tell you why he did not go to the fire?"

"He said he didn't go over as it was no use, the people were burnt up and he could see men going back and forth. He said he saw it all about six o'clock."

It was late afternoon but the judge showed no signs of adjourning. Charley's stomach gnawed, his head ached. He almost gagged on the pervasive stench of sweat. A new parade began, people who had talked to him in the lockup: Mayor Frost, a barrister named Cairns, Constable McGillivray. Men who looked directly at him while testifying, with a mixture of sadness and perplexity. Good Christian men, his plight beyond their understanding. Men who would never accuse him openly – un-Christian, that! – but who believed that the hand of God had placed him in the dock. Shouldn't they take their cue from the Almighty?

McGillivray, now; telling a story, enjoying the attention, not about the Tuesday night Charley squatted in his cell in the darkness, listening to the constable talking to a reporter. A different story. "Yes indeed, sir, we had lengthy conversations on the Monday and Tuesday after the fire. I asked him why he didn't go to the house, but he said he was ashamed as he had just come from prison. His courage failed, was the way he put it."

Charley stole a glance at Johnny; his brother was looking straight ahead.

"Did you talk about the crime?"

"I said it was a terrible thing to be hanging over his head and he said yes, but he did not think he ever did it. After a moment, he said, 'I'm positive I never done it.' I said it was a queer way to go around talking about it, either he did or he didn't do it, but he gave no excuse for saying he 'thought.'"

"Did he mention his boots?"

"He said he threw his boots away when going to Smith's Falls."

To Smith's Falls? J.R. let it pass in cross-examining, asking only if their conversation had been private.

"Yes, sir. He was alone in his cell. I did not caution him. He told me it all voluntarily."

A buzzing as of rampant bees filled the air as Judge Falconbridge adjourned court. As he rose, reporters rushed to be first out the door. Liza Ann pulled a handkerchief from her sleeve and dabbed her eyes. Johnny untangled himself from his hunched position, rising stiffly, rubbing a knee.

Charley bit his lip. Johnny hadn't looked at him all day.

Chapter Five

Silla, beloved,

Forgive me for not taking pen in hand last evening. I plead exhaustion, falling asleep before my head hit the pillow. I trust my messages of love have reached your ears, as yours have mine.

I am consumed by this trial. Consider my cast of characters over the past two days and be thankful you are removed from this small town Vanity Fair, Hogarthian touches and occasional picaresque sallies to boot.

To boot! Apt expression – for boot mania has become the scourge of the countryside. At recess today one inhaled with caution, for there seemed to be a great many sock feet airing, the fragrance of old wool and unwashed dogs rising to the rafters while boots were flourished and comparisons made.

A propos of this curious epidemic, I list herewith a few of the thorns in the prosecutorial side:

A detective who, by his own admission, took no notes of his investigation;

Central Prison employees called upon to describe second hand boots issued to one of 150 inmates released last year;

A gaggle of merchants who handle boots every day, but cannot tell a Bresse from a dozen other makes;

A host of locals whose memories falter under oath. (There was, for example, the Brockville shoemaker who traced and measured Charley's

foot in gaol and concluded he would take size nine. He was nonplussed
when I asked in cross-examination if Charley was wearing a sock at the
time. Ah, yes, says he after much soul-searching, 'twas a woollen sock
he wore. Thick or thin? No answer. He joins a multitude of witnesses
who, happily, fall to me via Crown subpoena and expense.)

At the centre of this maelstrom reposes a pair of classic congress
boots. A buff or leather gaiter, this type of footwear sports no lace nor
buttons, just elastic Vs at the sides to facilitate slip-on. Because of the
brass screws or screw-nails and toe caps, it is generally referred to as a
"brass" (not to be confused with Bresse, which manufactures it).
"These brass," the farmers say, displaying the boots they wear in barn,
pasture, church and courtroom. The pair in question, exhibit seven,
size seven, sat under Charley's bed the night of his arrest. They have
tramped many miles, obliterating the usual identification marks, and
the right boot is run over a little.

The cloth-topped, lace-up boots, cast away by Charley on his way
to Newbliss, are of minor importance. If Charley hangs by his boots,
it will not be by these: they are useful only because Charley was
barefoot after disposing of them. The prosecution contends this proves
Charley had no other boots before the fire took place. Greer insists
Charley admitted this to him; Charley says he did not.

This same detective told the court in all seriousness that on first
interviewing Charley he had him remove his footwear and "could see
the prisoner had been walking barefoot." Can you imagine – no one
offered Charley the chance to wash his feet from Saturday to
Wednesday? I half expected the prosecution to peel off Charley's socks
in court and present his feet, encased in last October's dirt, as exhibits!

Our judge has allowed some leeway in what he probably
considers a backwater trial. Hence, we were treated today to a
vignette of domesticity involving one Elizabeth Hall, who bought her
husband Thomas a pair of gaiters in June '92. The purchase was made
from McKim, who took over the Metcalf store in Smith's Falls two
months earlier. Mr Luckey paid Mrs Hall a visit in late June, sitting
opposite her in a rocking chair, right foot over left, while she tended
to her mending. She noticed his boots, which she declared in court
were exactly like her husband's. Retrieving a dropped thimble, she
took the opportunity of examining them, to determine whether or
not the elastic wore well. (It did not, she reported, being much worn
at the ankle.)

This testimony produced such excitement that nothing would do but Mr Hall should lumber forth and shed his boots to be handed about, still warm and odiferous, with a few straws from the henhouse clinging to them. Judge, counsel and jury agreed that the arrangement of screws differed from that in the exhibits. "Ah, but it was the toecaps," protested the lady. "I remember now it was the toecaps were the same." Alas for the prosecution, this was not the case; the toecaps bore a different design, and Mr H. was once again awarded custody of his footwear.

Then one Phoebe Ann Jakes, or Jacques, told how she had been about to return home after visiting the Luckeys one day last October when it began to rain. The old man lent her his boots. She cleaned them that night – he was "tasty" about his feet, she said – and returned them next morning. Just a week before the fire. Clute pressed her to identify the exhibits. "Are these the same boots?"

"I can't say, sir. I think, though, he wore sevens."

With further coaxing, she said she thought he put his right foot forward when shaking hands and ran his boots over to the right. I suggested she try the boots on in court. The judge looked hopeful but did not insist when she declined.

At this point I would wager there is not a soul in all Kitley who would swear under oath that Luckey's boots and our exhibit seven are one and the same!

My defence began at 3:30. Although others claim the distinction, there seems little doubt that it was George Martin of Metcalf's who sold Luckey a pair of gaiters in the summer of '91. Sixes, he said, but his customer returned and exchanged them for fives, the last size in boys'. A tailor named Percy swore he witnessed this transaction. Bresse boots, Martin says.

A small lad with a large voice swore Luckey wore a six. Two bright-eyed young ladies recalled that he once put on their shoes. One, a granddaughter, produced a pair he once owned. Her Uncle Charley, she assured the court, couldn't begin to get his foot into them. Seems they did their own testing, bless them.

My Redsox witnesses made a good impression, along with young Parker, who saw the explosion in the milkhouse. But it's the boot testimony that's vital. I have subpoenaed McKim for tomorrow, to confirm that the gaiters he sold Mrs Hall were Bresse.

My star witness was James Robinson of Montreal, a travelling Bresse salesman for the past ten years. He sold to Metcalf and McKim and claims twenty-five houses make similar kinds of gaiters. His avowal that he has never known Bresse to make a boot with as many screws as exhibit seven should carry some weight in court. The pattern of his company's brass is three screw-nails outside and two inside; he never knew them to make five and four, as in the exhibit.

"These are indeed Bresse, made before April '92," he announced, on examining Hall's boots. "I am of the opinion that exhibit seven was not made by Bresse." Sighs of relief from many, including myself. (Although I had expected the testimony, one never knows when a witness will change his mind!) I thought I detected the faintest smile on Charley's face.

I shall work the rest of the night on my closing argument for tomorrow. Don't count on my return by nightfall, however; the jury could ruminate for days.

Take care. Leave the heavy work to the day help – that's what I pay her for. Wish you were here to keep my feet warm – there's not so much as a hot brick to thaw the bedding! Goodnight and God bless.

    J

* * *

It was scarcely 5:30 a.m. when Johnny Luckey slammed the front door of St Lawrence Hall so hard its panes rattled. Not stopping to wipe his feet, he ignored the porter, jolted from his nap, and mounted the stairs to the first floor.

Would he be awake? *If he's not he should be!* Bloody university men, lay about 'til noon, never milked a cow in their lives! Salesman, contractor, land developer, Johnny was still a farmer at heart, his internal clock beating to barnyard time.

The aroma of salt pork frying rose from the bowels of the building. Dishes clattered, glass and cutlery rang hollowly. From the mat beside the door of number eighteen, J.R.'s black oxfords winked, resplendent in their new coat of bootwax. Johnny knocked and listened. Was that a snore? *Probably slept like a baby and thinks he'll get breakfast in bed. Wonder if he's ever had a burning in the groin. Not likely!*

The sharp, hollow tap of his knuckles pounded into his brain. Too much ale last night, then Liza Ann lighting new candles at three a.m., looking as if she'd seen a ghost. He'd risen on one elbow and barked, "What's the matter with you, woman?" and she'd started crying about Charley. Haunting them both, Charley was.

He turned at the click of a latch behind him. A woman squinted from a crack in the door of number nineteen. A flash of auburn hair and the door snapped shut. Johnny smiled. You could learn a lot by rising early.

One thing you could be sure of, if you knocked on J.R.'s door in the wee hours there would be no female giggles and whispers, no hasty scrambling to cover naked flesh. The glimpse of tousled hair reminded him of his own latest clandestine encounter. Damn! He had come here to help Charley, but the nagging ache in his lower parts reminded him constantly of the sly little Cockney tart responsible for his condition.

On his third knock, the door opened a crack. A puffy blue eye looked out at him. "Johnny?" A querulous croak.

"Sorry, J.R. I thought today of all days you'd be up and about early."

The door opened. "Matter of fact, I just got to sleep." J.R. tied his tartan bathrobe and stepped aside as Johnny entered. "Up all night going over the transcript." He gestured to a typed carbon copy on the small oak desk.

"Court reporter's notes? Pretty prompt."

J.R. yawned and stretched. "He's staying on the same floor, so I asked him to relay me a copy post haste. Obliging fellow. Took a letter I wrote my wife to the depot."

Johnny stepped over a pile of newspapers, wincing as cloth rubbed genitals. "You spent last night writing Silla?"

"Just an update of yesterday's developments, since I don't seem able to concentrate on anything else. Lost the art of the billet-doux, I guess."

Eyebrows raised, Johnny permitted himself a smile. That sounded like J.R. "Never mastered it myself. You tell her about Rivet?"

"I only tell her the good things, not the embarrassments."

Johnny snorted. "I'd call Rivet a disaster! First you get a telegram saying he's ill and can't appear. The judge goes to the trouble of authorizing admission of a written deposition. Then suddenly, in the middle of proceedings, Rivet staggers into court, disrupting everything."

"His Honour was not impressed. I doubt if he believed a word Rivet said on the stand."

"Neither was the jury. The fact that he was a larcenist with fifteen months in prison didn't help, either. We all know what he says is true,

J.R., about inmates dealing in tobacco among themselves. It stands to reason workmen entering and leaving the prison grounds are glad to make a few dollars supplying tobacco. But when he talked about selling Charley four plugs for a quarter I could see the beginnings of skepticism on the jury's faces. Rivet was a mistake, J.R."

"Not necessarily." J.R. tugged at a corner of his moustache. "Rivet could have been telling the truth. Once he sensed the skepticism, he got nervous. He may have started lying at that point, thinking the sheer weight of the lies would sound convincing. He went on about a four dollar bill he saw in Charley's possession. Then he said he saw him with a twenty-dollar bill once." He sighed. "I could hear the jury groaning."

"Who on earth told you to call him?"

"Charley, of course. He was still lamenting the absence of his pal Bloom, but he had faith in Rivet."

"Don't you interview your witnesses ahead of time?"

J.R. nodded. "I guess I picked a good day with Rivet. He was working at an Ottawa bar. Sober as a judge."

"Clute and Greer had their heads together after court. Clute's going to recall Logan of the Central Prison to discredit Rivet's statement. The word of a day warden against a gaol-bird." Johnny looked for a comfortable place to sit. Even the bed was piled with newspapers.

J.R. followed his glance. "They're good insulation against the cold."

"Your friend across the hall had a better idea." Headlines leaped up at him as he shoved aside papers and sat on the bed. *On the Rack! Luckey's Life Still in the Balance! Will He Hang?*

J.R. seated himself at the desk. "I think I did rather well with Greer. And I've subpoenaed Vaux for today."

"Can you do that? Prosecution witness?"

"Why not? As coroner, he can establish dates and times of the inquest without a doubt."

"What's the point?"

"You'll see when you read Greer's testimony. That bounder took no notes during his investigation. Now he can't even remember when he arrived in Smith's Falls or the date the inquest took place." J.R. started leafing through his papers.

Johnny's stomach contracted in fear. Liza Ann weeping in the night, the children constantly upset, friendless perhaps, all weighed heavily. "J.R., you'll have to do better than that!"

"I'm doing my best, Johnny. I've got Redsox witnesses galore. One who says Redsox stayed the night of October seventh at his place, just a stone's throw from your father's."

Johnny got up. Leaning over, he put his hands flat on the desk and his face close to the lawyer's. "Redsox is not enough, J.R. Charley's innocent and we have to prove it."

"Redsox is all I've got left, Johnny. I had the boot witnesses, and the lad who saw sparks fly up from the milkhouse."

"This is my brother, J.R. He's going to die if you don't find a way to save his hide." The fire in his groin licked upwards, into his gut.

"Here. This is Greer's testimony in its entirety. Read it. I'll get shaved." He proffered a sheaf of papers and watched as Johnny clutched it and sat down stiffly. "You all right?" He rose, pulled a tasselled cord for room service and bent over Johnny. "Start here."

Johnny blinked rapidly until his eyes focused.

Greer: The prisoner said he went south-west at his father's property and that I could find his tracks there of bare feet. I asked him why he went barefooted and he said he could not help himself as he had nothing to put on. Then the chief went out and got those gaiters. That's right, exhibit seven. I took off his slippers and saw he had been walking barefoot.

Clute: Did he indicate how far he was from the fire?

Greer: When McGowan said he was a mile and a half from it, Luckey said, 'To tell the truth I was not a quarter of a mile away when the fire took place. I was in the bush between my father's house and Jacques' Hill.'

Clute: Did he say where he got the cloth-topped boots from?

Greer: He said he got them by trade at a second hand shop in Toronto with those he got from prison. He couldn't give me the name of the street but I thought from the description it was York.

Lavell (cross-examination): The prisoner told you he first saw the fire at six p.m.?

Greer: Not that I remember.

Lavell: Did anyone else hear your talk with the prisoner?

Greer: I can't recall. Perhaps the constable on duty.

Lavell: Did you not hear the prisoner tell McGowan he first saw the fire at six o'clock?

Greer: Not that I recall.

Lavell: When you inspected the prisoner's feet, did you have him try the boots on?

Greer: No.

Lavell: Was the prisoner wearing socks?

Greer: I believe he had on a pair of light socks.

Lavell: Do you recall what kind?

Greer: I don't – ah. Cashmere. Yes, that's right, it was pointed out to me.

Lavell: McGowan says he told the whole story and now you are telling another part of it. Mr Greer, what period of time did you spend in Smith's Falls during the week after the fire?

Greer: I left Toronto for Smith's Falls not before Monday night, was at the funeral and had two days in Smith's Falls before the inquest.

Lavell: If the inquest took place on Wednesday, October twelfth, you could not have been in Smith's Falls two days before.

Greer: I have a pretty good memory.

J.R. opened the door to a brisk knock and accepted a pitcher of water which he began pouring into a basin on the wash stand. He set out shaving gear and took a towel from a side rack. "The man's a scoundrel, Johnny. If I can impress the jury with his negligence over details like the inquest dates, all of his testimony becomes suspect." He turned, lathered brush in hand. "If you've any suggestions, we could talk about them over breakfast."

At the sight of J.R., tight-muscled, flat-bellied, the eagerness and agility of youth still glowing, Johnny felt vague regrets welling up. His shoulders sagged as he put down the papers and walked to the door. "I've already eaten," he lied. "See you in court." He paused with the door half open. "You're right, the fellow is a bastard. But I don't know what we can do about it."

His feet echoed a beat of self-recrimination as he walked along the hall. Damn the whole world, the world that made his brother a murderer, made him the brother of a murderer, that threatened to bring his whole family to ruin. Damn the disease that was tormenting him, that great leveller among men, more feared than death. Complaint of kings and statesmen, of politicians and, yes, he had once even heard of a Methodist minister contracting it. Knowing he was in illustrious company comforted him not at all.

He had met the girl at, of all places, a church supper following a post-Christmas sleighride. Liza Ann had been an organizer, spending hours huddled over the oven. He had concluded business early that day, arriving home at noon to tantalizing aromas, Esley with molasses dribbling down his chin. It had been one of those days when life promised to get back to normal. His neighbours' awkwardness had diminished or ceased to bother him, he wasn't sure which. He'd stayed away from alehouses and women, as if his exemplary behaviour would speak for them all, even Charley.

He'd entered the kitchen to see Liza Ann shaving a slice from a great slab of ham, blushing at being caught in the compulsive gesture of popping food into her mouth. The old yearning flooded him, the ache for women who surprised him with variety and ardour and flouting of social convention. The only spice in his house was in the larder.

At the church supper, the girl had captivated him. Barely eighteen, just off the boat, a substitute pair of hands sent by her ailing mistress to serve the long tables of hungry merry-makers. Swarthy as his gypsies she was, darker than Violette, and when he saw her name, painted on a ceramic brooch so tiny he had to stand close and stare at her bosom to read it, he felt it was a sign. Violet. It was a sign, all right! A quarantine sign!

"I'm Voi-lit," she said, batting sooty lashes while removing a jelly from a fish-shaped mould. When he saw her the following Saturday at market, her mistress still housebound and the hired hand who had driven her gone off on his own business, she'd been pleased to accept a drive in his rig. It had been sunny, a January thaw, and they'd driven down a woody path where he stopped the horses. He fumbled through layers of wool and petticoats, not taking time to tumble into the back of the rig, wrapping a horsehair robe around her buttocks as he impaled her.

That was all there had been to it. Ten minutes of rutting followed by weeks of agony. He hadn't seen her since. It was rumoured the girl was with child and he had nervously counted the weeks. Not his, thank God!

He had almost come away to the trial without his medicinal jar. Thank God Liza Ann had reminded him. Unwittingly, of course. Are you sure you've got everything, she'd asked; all the property documents from your desk? Always doing the right thing, even if it was for the wrong reasons!

Or did she know, the way she shrank to her own side of the bed – but hadn't she always? Johnny walked unseeing past the porter and out into the sunlight.

No more women, he decided. No more deception. From now on a family man, pillar of the community.

It's true what I told Violette. I wish I was as innocent as Charley.

Chapter Six

At times it was hard to tell who the enemy was. Here, on the last day, as the jury filed out to deliberate, Victoria was more mystified than ever. Most of the people had been testifying for the Crown, which was what they called Mr Clute, although Esley had remarked, disappointed, he didn't wear a crown. Some of these same folks came up to her Dad on the street saying they knew Charley wasn't guilty. But hadn't her own family told the Crown their stories on the witness stand? "It's a sure way of getting paid, getting subpoenaed by the Crown," her Dad had said. Probably the others felt the same way, but didn't it make Mr Lavell look bad? Hot and weary, Victoria sank lower on the hard wooden seat. Did everyone understand that her family believed in Charley?

Mr Clute had been nice to her and said he had a daughter too. All she had to say was that Auntie wore false teeth. But something deep inside her hurt. She looked at Charley, quiet and watchful as a cat, hoping he understood.

All week she'd felt like a stranger learning a new language, watching for signs to help her translate. There was her father, grumbling about Uncle Ansley, one of her favourite people. "Betrayed us, gone over to the other side," was the way her father put it. All because Uncle Ansley thought the boots found with Charley were Grandfather's.

And whose side was her father on? Hadn't he told Mr Clute about the smashed sap buckets? Mr Clute had stood back and puffed out his chest in satisfaction, as if that was proof that Charley was a murderer! And her Dad had told the Crown about Charley shooting himself in the hip. "Attempted suicide," Mr Clute called it. Victoria couldn't see why anyone would pick that way to die. It was more likely to make Charley lame, and lame horses were sometimes taken out behind the barn and shot, but wasn't that a roundabout way to do away with yourself? She wished she could talk to Jenny. If the jury decided Charley was innocent, would she get her old friends back? Victoria chewed her lower lip. Could she ever forget Effie and Mabel, risking the schoolmaster's caning by running over to the boys' side of the schoolyard when they saw her coming?

Today, on the last morning, Dr Vaux had been called to the witness stand by Mr Lavell. *Does that mean he's on Charley's side now?* But all he said was the funeral was on Tuesday, October ll and the inquest started the next day, and Mr Lavell thanked him and let him go. She stole a look at Charley, but he was watching the detective slap his knee with his gloves.

Up until today she had thought of Dr Vaux as one of the enemy trying to lock Charley away for life, or worse, to get him hanged. But Dr Vaux looked the perfect gentleman in court just as he did on the street. He had tipped his hat to her mother and her one morning outside his big stone house at the top of Court House Avenue. Murmured a greeting, a bustled lady in a magnificent squirrel cape on his arm. Two girls, a tall, red-haired one about her own age and another, Esley's age, with plaits and a mischievous grin, hugged their elders and raced up the green, schoolbags bumping against their legs. Victoria sensed her mother's envy. These girls were privileged, what her teacher called aristocracy; the kind who carried sun umbrellas in lace-gloved hands to summer band concerts and boating trips on the St Lawrence. Evenings they would sit on verandahs fanning themselves while white-capped maids offered marble cake and lemonade. Winters they would wear navy coats with scarlet-lined capots and scarlet sashes and toques with long tassels and be invited to every cobweb party and oyster supper in town. The girls had turned around, partway up the green and smiled, and for a moment she had thought they were smiling at her. *If they knew, would they smile?* Then the younger one called out, "Papa, I'm your chum, aren't I? Lilian says she is, but she's teasing, isn't she, Papa? I'm your best chum, aren't I!" Papa. So genteel. A word from a house that knew no hardship. No murder. No post mortems. No family quarrels and disgrace. And no snubs, ever.

Today, the courtroom was the most crowded it had ever been. Witnesses gave short, snappish answers, forgetting at times to add a respectful "sir," and expelling huge sighs of impatience. There were people who saw Redsox near the fire and people who said he was on his way to Brockville before the fire started. People who said Charley had money for tobacco in prison and people who said no, that was impossible.

Then Mr Lavell – J.R. – stood up in front of them and talked for so long she began to think they'd never get any dinner. "It was Redsox, I know it was," Esley whispered to her fiercely, tugging at her sleeve. Her mother glanced at her with that familiar frown of worry when the Crown started talking about the bodies, so Victoria pretended to adjust her shoe buckle. It was true that she still didn't like to think about the day in the haymow, it made her stomach flop, but she didn't want her mother to take her and Esley outside again. She concentrated on counting all the feathers she could see in ladies' bonnets and got up to twenty-eight before Esley's head bumped against her shoulder and she saw that he was asleep.

Mr Lavell was angrier than she had ever seen him. He stormed because the Crown took away Charley's clothes and never got them back. Poor Mr Lavell couldn't get his hands on them to do his own testing. And the Crown did the same thing with the axe only the axe was here in the courtroom. No report of analysis, Mr Lavell said. Victoria knew what that meant, she'd heard her Dad talking about it. They had scraped some of the blood off the handle to see if it was really chicken blood. That was analysis. But they never said any more about it, either.

Then Mr Lavell began shouting about the post mortem. "Dr Reeve said a post mortem would have shown how the victims died. But was one held? No!" And why, he thundered, why would a person murder three people in one part of the house and then set fire in another part to attract attention? He pointed to the box with the teeth and Victoria was sure he looked right at her. "If the prosecution was so sure they knew who the teeth belonged to, why didn't they bring the man who made them to court?" Yes, Victoria thought, why not? Cousin Jack Phillips had wondered the same thing.

Mr Lavell went over to the dock, never taking his eyes off the jury. "Gentlemen, regard the prisoner. Has he ever acted like a person guilty of murder? No!" Charley had only got upset at the Palace Hotel after he heard people talking about the family being burned. He lied to Chief McGowan about his name because of his prison record, but when he was told why he was being arrested he gave his correct name immediately. He made no secret of getting off the train at Smith's Falls and didn't attempt to avoid John Hannah, who could identify him.

Victoria wanted to applaud. All the things Mr Lavell was saying were exactly what she had decided, lying awake at night.

After dinner, Mr Lavell got up and went on forever about the boots. Victoria, her stomach full of pork pie, had to pinch herself to stay awake.

"All the evidence is circumstantial," Mr Lavell said, jabbing a finger at the jury. "There are no eye witnesses to the alleged crime. No witnesses to say even that a crime was committed."

Then it was Mr Clute's turn to strut before the jury, somehow twisting the same testimony and making Charley look guilty all over again. There were those boots again, only this time it sounded like they really were Grandfather's. She scowled at Mr Clute, willing him to lose his voice, to take a heart attack and fall down dead there in the courtroom, in front of everybody. But she saw that under his anger he was very sad and when he looked at Charley he didn't say, the prisoner did this or that, but how could he, how could you Charley Luckey, how could anyone?

And the jury – were they friends or enemies? Some who had nodded at everything Mr Lavell said now nodded when the Crown said the opposite. Charley glanced at her Dad from time to time, but her Dad kept his eyes on Mr Clute.

Just when she thought they might be allowed to leave, the judge rapped his gavel and peered over his spectacles and gave a long speech on circumstantial evidence and how much better it was than direct evidence. With direct evidence, one or two witnesses might lie to convict somebody, he said, like maybe saying they saw him commit a crime. Circumstantial evidence would require a whole chain of witnesses, all telling lies. She pictured a line of people linked together by a chain, each holding a hand behind his back, fingers crossed.

Then the judge got mad at the Crown for going all the way back to 1884 to look for a reason for Charley to kill everybody. "It is a point in the prisoner's favour that he has always strenuously denied the crime," he said. Her father, hunched on the bench on the other side of her mother, gave a strange snuffling sound. The judge looked at him sternly, then turned the same gaze on Charley. Was the judge the enemy?

When the jury went out to deliberate, they waited in the hall with the reporters, not bothering with supper. No one was hungry except Esley; her mother pulled a package of biscuits from her bag and passed them around. It was a good thing they stayed: "Barely an hour and a half," her Dad muttered when someone cried, "Jury's back!"

They were almost knocked over by people jamming the entrances and choking the stairs and, if it hadn't been for a kind constable, they couldn't have got back into the courtroom at all. The jurymen couldn't get through to their box; the judge barked at a clerk to clear a space near the exit to the juryroom for them to gather.

It was all over before she was sure she had heard correctly, and everyone was hugging everyone else and crying and people were clapping Charley on the back like he was a hero home from the wars. Free!

Charley, on his feet, clutched the rail as his legs buckled. Victoria tried to struggle toward him as men hoisted him up, cheering. The judge kept banging his gavel until Victoria thought it would break. She knew she would remember all her life what the judge said next. It was a shock to everyone, she could tell. Dead silence. He said, "Mr Clute, do you intend to proceed with the other charges?" And Mr Clute said, without smiling, "I am ready to proceed at any time, Your Honour." A roar erupted and Mr Lavell pushed forward and shouted something and the judge said, "Mr Lavell, I cannot compel the Crown to drop the other charges."

And that detective, who had scowled only a moment ago, nodded at Mr Lavell, as if to say, "I'll get you next time."

Victoria knew then the detective would do all the things Mr Lavell had dared him to do. He would bring the man who made the teeth. He would find an eye witness, someone who would say, "I saw them killed and, yes, that's the man right there, Charley Luckey, Charley did it."

It's not true! But who cared about truth here? Who were the enemy, really? Enemies smiled sometimes, shook hands. Friends turned away, told harmful truths. Her father swore; her mother paused in her tears to clap gloved hands over Esley's ears, and in that moment Victoria saw something crystal clear and wondered why she had not seen it before. No one cared about Charley. They were all the enemy, whenever it suited them.

She thought of the box that had rested on the cart in her father's barn. The box her father had lovingly dusted. *Who can blame us if we don't know? Enemy, friend – labels that confuse and make us hate ourselves.*

Maybe they'll even find a way to do a post mortem. Victoria shuddered. She had a cold feeling deep inside. She looked at Charley. Their eyes met and she saw that he had it, too.

ENTR'ACTE

July, 1893

Billy Greer mopped his high, sunburned brow with a rumpled handkerchief and adopted what he hoped was an expression of patience. "I said, sir, do you recollect where you were standing when you saw them?"

His companion, looking vaguely annoyed, raised his arms straight out from his sides and let them fall, slapping black worsted.

Hottest day of the year, huddled in a coat so long it brushed his boot tops. And could that be a dustcloud rising from the oversized, mismatched donations, doubtless with poorhouse labels sewn into them? Perhaps the combination of summer haze and sleepless nights was playing tricks. Billy blinked. He liked to ingratiate himself with elderly people, drawing them out, but this old codger, all stained whiskers and flabby warts, repelled him.

"Don't shout, sir. I can hear every word you say." Whiting's nasal whine soared above the cheerful sawing of cicadas and the throbbing of bees through clover.

They were standing by the gateway to Coad's Road, surveying the remains of the Luckey farm. The July grass, unchecked all year, caressed their buttocks; a hummingbird mused over a clump of buttercups; mosquitoes rose from the swamp in clouds so thick Billy itched just watching them.

"But you saw them."

"Eh?"

Billy enunciated each syllable, ignoring the mustiness emanating from his witness as he bent to the ear half hidden by a drover's cap. "You said you saw them!"

"Saw who?" Whiting picked absently at a scab on the side of his nose and waited. Billy sighed. *Was it hardening of the arteries or sheer perversity?* His own grandad had died senile. In his youth, Billy had passed many evenings sitting rapt while the old gentleman chronicled the Crimean War. Once maverick and adventurer, reduced to a wizened, arthritic skeleton, a mind crammed with memories. *Young Fella,* Billy would call him. *Drink up, Young Fella.* They'd lean together into the smoky alehouse haze, harmonizing Jeanie with the Light Brown Hair. And when his grandad's memory faltered and the tales became hopelessly entangled, he hadn't let on, had learned to adopt the mask of patience. *Great practice it had been, for a future detective.*

But Whiting was different. Billy had already proposed ale. *"Teetotal,"* was the laconic reply. He'd asked about Kitley in the old days: *"A lot like where I spent my boyhood around Milton, I'd wager."* But Whiting had merely muttered something about a missing ear trumpet. Aware that his mask was slipping, Billy put a hand up as if to shield his eyes from the sun. *"Let's go over again what you saw."*

Whiting cupped his hand to his ear.

"You saw something. Christ, man! When —"

"When?" Whiting spat into a bush. *"Last fall. The day of the big fire out there, whenever that was. You must have heard about it. Ask Coughlin. Ask Mercier. They know . . ."* His voice trailed off. His hand stole back to the scab.

Billy clamped his teeth together and forced the corners of his mouth upwards. *This flyblown old carcass would make a fool of him publicly if he wasn't careful. God! Is this what awaits us all?* The old boy had fifty years on him, yet something inside Billy cringed, as if transformation was imminent. *Son, lover, bridegroom, father, like everyone else.* Hard to imagine him, rutting in a four-poster, skinny rump bobbing, some woman panting ecstatically as her sweat mingled with his. Somewhere, at some time, there had been a Mrs Whiting, who had produced a brood of children who had called this man Father, Dad, Pa, had scrambled into his lap and hugged the scrawny neck. And they still loved him, it appeared, putting him up — putting up with him, more likely — as he parked first on one and then another in his endless travels. Three sons living in Kitley had reacted with scepticism to their father's latest claims. A daughter in New York state had accommodated him for several months, until Whiting had decided to answer the call of civic duty as any good citizen who had witnessed a crime would do.

Or so he said, though not so eloquently. His explanation, prying Chief McGowan from bed on a Sunday morning, ran thus: "I know something. Will I get paid if I tell?"

Billy looked toward Parker's farm, where a plough drew a steady line in the field beyond the house. "Where were you? The day it happened. Where were you standing?"

Whiting removed his cap, brushed white hair from his eyes and settled the cap squarely on a gleaming bald spot. "I guess – here." He pointed to some cedar bushes. "Between the bushes and the road."

Billy whistled between his teeth. "So. You were east of the house, by Coad's road here, toward its intersection with the Brockville road. You had a good view of the porch on this side of the house." He thrashed the air at a cloud of mosquitoes. "You're prepared to tell your story in court –"

"What's that?"

"Court, man. C-o-u-r-t!"

He saw a flash of cunning in the pale, crusted eyes as Whiting plucked at his sleeve. The liver spots, the ridged, indigo veins, the dirt-crusted nails made him want to pull away. He stood firm, looking toward the horizon, willing a pleasanter image. Cassie, floating before him in the noonday shimmer, soft flesh and golden freckles – freckles disappearing tantalizingly into the deep groove at the front of her low-cut wrapper. He smiled. Not an hour ago.

The fingers on his sleeve tugged harder. "Mr Detective. I'll get paid, won't I? They said I would."

They. Everyone connected with the prosecution had told the old man that he would get witness fees. Billy had no intention of inquiring into the extent that greed had motivated Whiting. "You'll be paid, man. But only if you show up in court."

Valuable information, providing it convinced the right people. Hang Murray and Falconbridge, with their blind faith in circumstantial evidence!

"How much?" The old man was sharp enough when it suited him. "I need clothes. You might've noticed. How much?"

Clean him up, bring him back here a time or two to keep his memory refreshed, and the jurymen might see in him their poor old Dad or Grandpa. "You'll see when the time comes." Billy swatted a mosquito on his neck, venting all his frustration in one swift blow.

Whiting's hand crept up to his nose; with a final tug the scab came off, the hollow beneath it oozing blood. Billy, veteran of investigations of *heinous, unspeakable crimes, foul exhibits and grisly clues, felt a momentary lurching of his stomach.*

"All right." He kept his voice level, its tone soft. "On October eighth of last year, you were cutting through the fields on your way to your son's . . ."

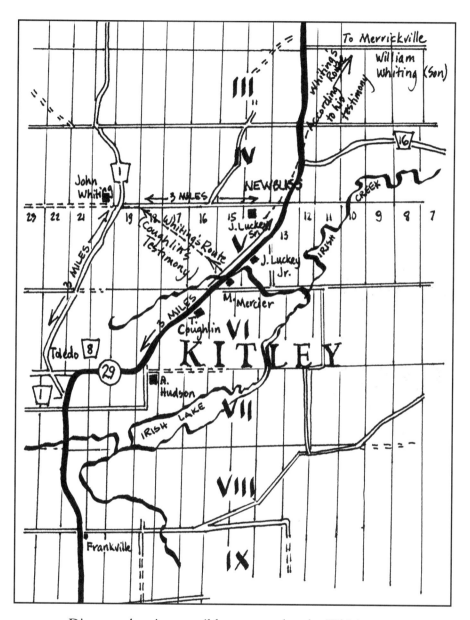

Diagram showing possible routes taken by Whiting on
October 8, 1892.

Part IV

THE SECOND TRIAL

April, 1893

O hangman did I ask
forgiveness at the last, was I not brave,
did my eyes betray me, weeping?

Chapter One

Achieve. A blueprint for life, measured and angled, stamped and registered in the Reeve-Lavell blood. Healers, reformers, salvationists, in hospitals, courtrooms, pulpits all across the country. More professionals in a couple of generations than there are in the courtroom on this late fall afternoon in 1893. J.R. brought the Lavell aura with him. Nurtured from the cradle; hadn't he projected the richest voice in the church choir, rowed the hardest in the Lake Frontenac regattas, beat all challengers on the lawn tennis court behind Cedarhedge? Good blood, strength in numbers, a reputation to live up to; not a burden, but a challenge.

Home a haven, not a hiding-place. No harsh commands, cracked whips. Not when Normie painted the stairwell with a three-year-old's version of sailboats, or Nell dropped a blueberry pie, face down, on the freshly scrubbed pantry floor. Not when Willie lit up his pipe. A spring evening, the scent of peonies drifting in, mingling with the lemony sheen of the sideboard, and Will's awful pipe. Willie, taking refuge in numbers, hoping his parents would say nothing with his brothers and sisters there. And they just went on doing what they were doing, Father making entries in his day register at his oak desk, Mother sorting colours for her needlework. The message was clear. This too will pass, and if it doesn't, no harm done. An aberration, not a sin. Nine sons, Willie's the one with the pipe. And Will had gone on to graduate from medical school before he came of age. No harm done.

Easy for J.R., too. Head of the class. Prince of Wales gold medallist. President of the Conservative Association, the Methodist Lay Association; reeve, town councillor, school trustee. Third child, second son, almost like a parent himself to the younger ones, planning to take Harry into his practice, help finance Walter through med school.

Failure wasn't in his vocabulary. Not that there hadn't been intimations of it: last May, for instance, the Queen's birthday, cracking the whip as the buggy rattled through Smith's Falls on a wild chase for the doctor, Silla in the last stages of labour at home. Disaster avoided. And if he couldn't save Will that July afternoon two years ago, that was hardly failure. Was it? Will, skin grey and cold as fish scales. A last gasp and a flutter of the eyelids, as if the spirit flopped about, trying to find its way out of the body. Heart attack, canoeing on the lake. Will, dying in his study an hour later, amid his vapours, curatives, elixirs, magical instruments; *Physician, heal thyself.*

Not failure. A sense of inadequacy, yes. Grief, suspicion that it was all ordained, a railing against a Master Plan. Questions, sleepless nights; Darwin, William James, and those new authors, fascinating, *The Golden Bough,* and a treatise on the sub-conscious by a young Viennese alienist. Milestones leading to this moment. To a man who may or may not have killed three people. John Lavell takes a hard look at Charley in the dock, trying to see past the courtroom mask he helped to shape. What he sees is the clear blue gaze of a country boy, a tuft of hair on his crown refusing to lie flat. What has changed – does he no longer believe in Charley?

Long after the events of 1893 are put to rest John Lavell will remember this moment as the moment he knew he was going to lose. Anticipation shimmers like silver thread through the trial's worn fabric. Whiting's tale is about to be woven, officially, into the record. An assortment of witnesses stand ready to patch their ill-matched memories into his vague meanderings. Mrs Hall, minus husband, parades the boots she claims match Old Man Luckey's, with the same result. The nails and toe caps do not match. Salesman Robinson again rejects the boots: not Bresse. A young man named Ennis swears he heard Charley tell in the lockup how he sat under two maples a quarter of a mile from the house. The threshers and townsfolk recite their stories, unchanged.

Old Whiting is harmless as a housefly, and Lavell's premonition is incongruous, paradoxical. But in embracing failure, in whatever guise, he makes his fatal error.

If you believe that your client is innocent, a victim of circumstance, that he wants his freedom as badly as you want it for him, what do you do? It is a new age, broader horizons. The moment you are seizing on behalf of this poor soul who trusts your judgment gives him choices – what to say, what not to say – while closing the door forever on choices for you. It is one of those moments which cannot be rewritten. It is the moment you decide to put him on the stand.

The decision opens a Pandora's box of nebulous, fearful possibilities. They flutter and sing about the heads of judge and jurors. And on their wings, iridescent with choices – his, not yours now – they trail a banner of hope or despair. In Charley's case there are no precedents. Whatever sounds reverberate across the Brockville courtroom will muster echoes clear as glass. The new law, giving a defendant new rights, has never been tested. Charley will be the first man in Canada to testify in his own behalf in a Supreme Court trial.

The decision made, you push any hint of failure to the back of your mind. But it does not go away.

The Crown's steady march is that of a conqueror, and the weariness J.R. fights is ground into his soul. The chant of April's witnesses echoed in his sleep all summer. He couldn't dissuade the authorities on the rule of *autre fois acquit.* "How, gentlemen, can you charge an accused with a crime of which he been found innocent?" They got around it by charging Charley with a different murder, that of his sister. And now the powers that matter ultimately, to the world, to posterity, will all accept as the gospel truth what the prosecution claims Charley Luckey has done.

Across the courtroom Johnny, flushed and coarse, collapses rather than sits, puffy and rumpled like a balloon with the air escaping. Not even the swish of Sarah Jane's moss-soft skirts as she passes rouses him. Over the summer he affected burnsides, then neglected them to the point where the style is all but lost, muttonchops drooping on his collar, vulnerable patch of chin diminished to a mere slip of the razor. His wife, straight and solemn, parks solidly between him and the children.

What is it, have they all lost faith in J.R., in the legal process? They look neither at him nor at each other, but study the wood panelling as if seeing their faces mirrored there. They exist in a pocket of weariness, a determinedly indifferent eye in a brewing storm. And around them, as Whiting's moment approaches, a steady buzzing, as of flies discovering a carcass.

Can sheer weariness drive the final nail in the defence coffin? Who wants to hear, again, the boot argument, the property quarrel, the documented peregrinations of Redsox? The almond-icing swirls of the wedding cake ceiling oppress him, glints of twinned round lenses threaten assault from the front rows as Lavell turns to face Judge Rose's call to order. Hisses chopped by the gavel. The stenographer, sharpening his pencil. Clute, crisp of gown and manner. Rose, eloquent in chiaroscuro. The one-armed judge, new to the Luckey saga, with a reputation for scribbling in the margins of his notebook, who for all his erudition keeps referring to the township in the indictment as Kipley; no one has the temerity to correct him.

Judge Rose brooks no nonsense. His unbridled scrawl reveals a fanatical devotion to brevity, a childhood accident revising his penmanship but not his ambition. When the Crown adds two more doctors to the roster to reiterate the futility of a post mortem, the judge barks, "Enough of this. There was no post mortem held and that's all there is to it." When Clute calls Victoria Luckey, the judge, frowning, sends her back to her seat. Rose, son of a Methodist minister, has two daughters, proper maiden ladies, and a son about to be called to the Bar.

His reputation as a strict but benevolent patriarch precedes him into the courtroom. Whispers in legal circles are attended by smiles, how his Kate is so versed in propriety she is said to have invented it, how the Roses never stint at high tea in the name of meanness, only in respect to the waistline.

The judge himself, on circuit, brings his home with him in the form of sprigs of dried lavender to keep his clothes fresh and a tin of biscuits rationed to a daily pair – one plain, one sweet – at teatime. A tradition to be carried on by the next generation, his daughters already fussing over homely amenities for their bachelor brother.

Second afternoon, second trial, the flesh and form of Greer's second vow, an eye witness about to be called. Already he's fulfilled his first promise when Dr John Dixon, showing no ill effects from a gruelling train trip from Brandon, Manitoba, peered at a photograph Clute flourished.

"Yes, that is Miss Luckey, for whom I made dentures in Manitoba in '91." The dentist grasped the dentures and held them up to the light. "Similar." Adjusting his pince-nez. "I have since destroyed the impression."

Lavell, approaching to cross-examine, noted the scrubbed nails, fancied he caught a whiff of carbolic soap. "When did you last see the teeth?"

"February 2, 1891."

"How can you identify them?"

"The distinctive mark of my work is an air chamber which is shaped by a special mould, in the top of the plate. The shape of the plates made by me is different from those made by other dentists." As he talked, Dixon rotated the dentures slowly in his hands.

"Do you have the mould with you?"

The dentist shook his head. "I make them as I require them. I have nothing to aid in making them other than my memory and the peculiarity of the shape." He smiled, displaying a set of perfectly aligned uppers. "I make about a thousand sets a year." An eye tooth winked gold.

For a moment the room about Lavell shrank to a classroom of a quarter century ago, the man before him the antiseptic schoolmaster whose fingers flashed imitation gold, as he led the daily ritualistic inspection. Hands extended, palms up, then turned to display nails; teeth bared, lips pulled back in an exaggerated snarl, hands tugging shirt collar down while the teacher scrutinized, seeking tell-tale signs of careless ablutions. "No further questions."

Clute did not let go so easily. "Look again, doctor. Take your time. Can you identify these teeth?"

A gold-streaked smile said, Yes, of course, I should recognize my own work, shouldn't I! "Mr Prosecutor, I have no hesitation in saying I made the teeth produced."

* * *

Scattered about his room at St Lawrence Hall are papers with pencilled scribbles and hasty geometric designs. Breathless attempts to clarify the muddle of conflicting observations that Whiting's surfacing has brought to the case. Notes to Silla that, please God, she'll never see.

Imagine a triangle (Silla, does this make sense? I shall put it to them thus). A triangle resting on its south point. Place a dot at Newbliss, top right corner, another straight west, top left, and a third due south at Toledo.

Connect the dots. First, a horizontal line across the top, leading from Newbliss west along Coad's Road. In the angle of the junction of Coad's

Road and the road leading south to Toledo lives John Whiting, son of Old Man Whiting. Draw a vertical line downwards from his home to Toledo. The third line, meandering somewhat, joins Toledo to Newbliss, extending upward in a northeasterly direction along the Brockville Road. This line is punctuated irregularly, south to north, with the properties of Henry Whiting (another son), Archie Hudson, Thomas Coughlin, and Martin Mercier, among others. If you were to continue extending this line off the page northwards toward Smith's Falls and Merrickville, you would be proceeding in the direction of the home of William, a third Whiting son.

Hard to sort out. All these scrupulously honest people disagree on salient points. The thing is, what will the jury make of it all?

* * *

Comic relief. Just what this courtroom needs. A seedy old dustbag with tobacco-stained whiskers. Burlesqued oath. Exaggerated gestures. Ludicrous one-liners. Point up his features a little, enlarge the blob on the end of his nose, red and bulbous. Give him yarn hair and a dusting of white powder.

Lavell mops his brow, watching as everyone hunches forward. Is Whiting really going to play it for laughs?

Twice kissing the Bible and sitting down before the clerk is finished; twice being hauled back to his feet by a constable, the clerk, unnerved, repeating, "Do you swear –"

A cupped ear trying to sort syllables into coherent questions. A nervous start as a figure detaches itself from the blur of funereal gowns and approaches. "My name is Clute, sir. I'm the prosecutor in – Prosecutor! Yes. Please tell the court, sir, how far is it between your son John's residence and the scene of the fire?"

"Between twelve and one o'clock." Horror that he, the witness in the tired black suit, the one who needs a new wardrobe, is being laughed at. "Danged if I know. This ain't no proper court of law and you had no business bringing me here!" Uneasy titters. "D'you take me for a fool?"

Struggle to escape and the constables move in. Skinny clown pinned down by two elephants. Sons who escorted him to the stand hover like straight men who've forgotten their lines, red-faced.

Voice plucking at him. Tell your story. Why you're here. Court of law! What did you see? Wood banging wood.

He clutches his cap, strokes a groove in it thoughtfully. His voice comes out flutey. "I was –" I was. Tries again, lifting the message above the reediness.

"I was going to my son John's on Coad's Road going across Luckey's property my custom to go as a shortcut customary you see on my way to John's saw a man with a knife man strike a girl or woman drag her by the hair into the house can't say who he was can't say if he struck her with the knife eh yes I showed the detective where ask him Christ almighty ask –" Puts his cap on and abruptly stands, enough of this. "Let me go haven't I told the story enough who's this here young fella with the moustache can't he hear it from somebody else now –"

Drives that one off. But now another, younger, more moustache. "Mr Whiting. Where were you coming from that day?"

"Coming from my son William's at Merrickville to John's."

"Your son at Merrickville?"

"C'rect."

"Where did you take dinner October 8?"

"Dinner?" Pause. Voluminous handkerchief, worthy stage prop, retrieved from a back pocket. Bulb pressed until it blows wetly like a horn under water. "Don't remember."

"Do you remember the time of day you were in Toledo?"

"Eh? About eight in the morning. I'm sure of that."

"In Merrickville all night and twenty miles south of there in Toledo by eight in the morning?"

"Eh?"

"Did you tell Tom Coughlin before or after you went to the States that you were going to be at this trial?"

"Don't remember." Rises again.

"Wait a minute, now. Didn't you tell Coughlin some money was to be going at this trial and you might as well get it to buy some clothes?"

"Don't remember." Flailing, shouting. "I know nothing of the Luckey murder! I been across Luckey's farm many times, was there the day after the murder. I don't know what I saw!" Catches his breath. "Was I brought here to be ridiculed –?"

The spectators love him, roar, applaud sporadically even as the constables restrain him. "I never saw the fire and can't tell anything about it!" Thrashing, knocking a constable's cap off. Trembling, teary. "I suppose they blame me for killing the girl, but if no person killed her until I did she'd be alive today. I'm – hands off me! – innocent as a newb –"

Gavel banging. "Mr Whiting! Sit!"

A lull. Everyone sober now, some wiping tears away. "I must go, Your Highness. I didn't pay much attention to the thing at the farm. Stopped all Saturday night at my son John's and left next morning. Now, I've told you all I'm going to and there is no use questioning me any longer. Must go! It don't make any difference where I was that night. I am here now. Whole thing's nothing but a goddam –"

Giggles. Guffaws. The gavel's staccato. "Order! The solemnity of the occasion is not befitting such an exhibition. I will allow much latitude in contradicting this witness's evidence." Lavell expels a huge sigh of relief. Even Whiting's sons, loyal but hopelessly confused, cannot help the old man.

Henry avers his father stayed at Hudson's the night before the fire.

"Mr Whiting, if your father were coming from the Toledo area – that is, from Hudson's farm – to your brother John's, he would have a choice of going directly north from Toledo or taking the longer route around by Newbliss and then west along Coad's Road to your brother's. If he chose to go by Newbliss, how long would it take him?"

"He ordinarily walks about two miles an hour but can't keep it up. If he went around the road it would be six miles."

"And if he took the shorter route to John's?"

"My brother lives three miles straight northwest from Toledo. The shortest route from Toledo to John's is straight on the road. His home is a mile-and-a-half west of Luckey's on the same road."

"So if a person went on a straight road from Toledo to John's, at what point would he be near Luckey's?"

"He would at no time be nearer to Luckey's than at John's."

John Whiting and Michael Coughlin both say he stayed at Coughlin's the night before the fire. Henry believes his father took dinner with him about eleven Saturday. John says his father was at his place then, and stayed overnight. Archie Hudson vows Whiting stopped at his house all Saturday night. Mrs Hudson agrees. And Martin Mercier saw him a good mile south of Newbliss around eight a.m. Saturday, and again between three and four that afternoon, heading toward Hudson's.

It is not Whiting's testimony that Lavell carries back with him to St Lawrence Hall that evening. It is farmers and farmers' wives, not talking of Charley's guilt or innocence. Talking instead of the Crown making a fool of himself calling poor old Whiting, and the note of sympathy for the underdog perhaps. And the underdog is no longer Charley, but an old fool, and a dauntless judicial system which could only be forging on because it is right, because it knows things they don't know.

There remained the fact of the scream. Someone had screamed, and gone indoors to die. Someone had called for help but had not come running across the fields to safety, to willing rescuers. Instead, had gone indoors to die.

Why? It was a woman's scream. Phillips swore to it. So did Ansley Stewart and the other threshers. Ansley had joked it was children. But there were no children playing that afternoon near the Luckey farm.

Whiting hadn't mentioned a scream. He was deaf, but even he would have known if a girl screamed, would have heard some sound, a wind keening in the trees. Would have seen the mouth's O, the eyes white with terror. If he had seen anything at all.

What else what else what else? Tomorrow he would put Charley on the stand.

Chapter Two

When I try to lift the veil, what is it, what's there? A flash of brown-stockinged ankle, pale hands that stitched my shirts with quick, sharp nips at the cotton. Now clutching, white-knuckled, at stiff brown folds of skirt, lifting it ever so slightly, swirling petticoat as she turns to run. Toward the house.

Don't go in there, Minnie! My words, my voice. Old memories, twenty years old? *Don't go in the parlour, Minnie, the witch is there, Father's brought her home. Don't go in the barn, Minnie, where the pig is bleeding his long, slow death so we'll have tender, white meat for our dinners.* Minnie's eyes, soft and gentle as a doe's. *Don't look, you mustn't see.*

No, not old memories.

If only I could talk to Hugh.

Hugh and me used to sit on the stump out back of the house, our rumps bumping as we jostled for space. We were whittling, farm animals and bird houses, crude and lopsided. Hugh was better at it than I was.

And I remember one day we saw a man riding into the yard, his coattails flying as he half stood in the wagon gripping the reins. An odd fellow, helter-skelter and loud. I don't remember his name but we called him the medicine man. Always wore a collar and vest, like he had some authority. Guess it helped to sell his wares, although his non-stop palaver had a lot to do with that.

Hugh and me were making wood whistles that day, and Hugh

says, "Look there, what's he want?" The medicine man always brought with him salves and ointments to heal and tonics and compounds made from roots and bark and dried leaves to build you up. He had cream to slick your hair down and teas to settle your stomach and balm to soothe the eyes and bottles of brown stuff that our elders took for coughs but that us kids weren't allowed to touch. He handed out little pellets of tamarack gum and we chewed it and said we liked it. Tasted horrible but we pretended we were chewing tobacco.

Sure enough, he takes a basket from the front seat and heads for the house, where Marthy's tending her sick babe, the only child she and Father ever had. Margaret, they called her, after a sister of Marthy's. Maggie, not yet two and too sickly to walk.

Little Maggie squalled all the time and her eyes were all glommed up. Marthy tended her day and night and Father went around like a thundercloud and ordered us all to take on extra chores, so's me and Hugh had to take our turn at frying bread mornings and beating the bedding and sweeping up. And Marthy's all the time murmuring, Oh, my child, my only baby, like Hughie and me's not even here, we don't exist.

It was a June morning, I was nine, ten, and Hugh two years older. After the medicine man went in there was silence and then the baby starts making gurgly-sputtery sounds like someone's trying to force some liquid down her gullet. Hugh looks over at me and says, "Betcha there's cough medicine in that rig." He got that evil smirk on his face, meaning he was contemplating something bad. "Betcha I can drink more of it than you can."

I wasn't to be outdone. "Oh yeah, how much?"

"Whole bottle, maybe."

I gave him a push so he tumbled from the stump and rolled over and over in the grass, laughing his head off. Then, before I realized he meant what he said, he was up and running for the wagon, swift and silent as an Indian. Hugh was like that, made up his mind to something, devil take the consequences, did it while you were still digesting the idea. That's how he left home finally, years later, packed up one night and made off while I was still wondering if he meant what he said about leaving.

But this June morning, with the flies buzzing on some fish heads by the stump, and the hollyhocks against the stoop limp around the edges like doilies hung up to dry, Hugh hoisted himself up into the driver's seat of the wagon and before I could call out he was rummaging about and I could hear glass clinking real loud. The medicine man gives a shout and comes flying out the back door, not bothering to let his feet find the steps. Hugh, not batting an eye, grabs the reins with one hand and the whip with the other and hits the mare a smart one on the backside. By then Marthy's screaming too, the baby all swaddled in heavy wraps in her arms as she shoves the door open with her foot. The medicine man with a yelp lands in the hollyhocks.

For all this, it was only because Hugh had to turn the wagon around that I had time to run across the yard and clamber up onto the seat beside him. Bottles and jars rocked and jangled in their boxes behind us, Father's silly geese flew in all directions and before I knew it we were out on Coad's Road heading toward the Newbliss intersection. Clouds of dust rolled up around us. We didn't look back. "Serves the old bat right," Hugh said, giving the mare another swat. I understood perfectly what he meant, there was so much to get back at her for, especially since the baby come.

We flew along the road and it was a while before I realized we were heading up a side road toward Irish Creek. Hugh kept cracking the whip and the mare rattled along real smart. Father would have said the banshees were after her.

"Partridge!" Hugh says of a sudden, pointing with the whip. "Let's see where they go, so's we'll know where to find wild grapes in the fall." I looked across the flat fields to our left and saw nothing except trees on the horizon and scrub up against a snake fence along the near end. Hugh jerked sharp on the reins and next thing I know the wagon's upending, the horse whinnying on her hind legs, and Hugh and me and bottles and jars flying. And all I can think of, for I never really knew, was that we'd gone too near the ditch and the back wheel had caught and the sudden lurching sent the horse into a panic. She reared up as we went down.

Cool as a cucumber, Hugh got up, surveyed the damage and started picking up the few bottles that were unbroken. He removed stoppers and corks, sniffed, wrinkled his nose and kept going until he found the medicine. Then he found a packet in brown paper and opened it. The medicine man's picnic. Meat stuck between slices of bread, sticky, mustardy stuff holding it all together. Hugh took a bite, gave a whoop and held out a sandwich to me. In between bites we took swigs from the bottle of cough medicine. It was powerful and burned all the way down, but I made all the right noises to feign approval. Hugh didn't have any problem getting it down and bolted his sandwich so he could concentrate on the brown stuff. He found another bottle, slightly cracked, and opened it. By then I wasn't feeling well, but I didn't let on.

We were sitting out in the open, by the fence that bordered the field, a few yards from the wagon, and all the time we could hear the horse making moaning, snuffling noises. "Leg's broke," Hugh said, and I don't remember him looking upset.

"Give it some medicine," I says.

"S'no use. Waste it, gotta be put down." Nevertheless, he took the last of the bottle and dribbled it into the horse's mouth. I guess by then he was feeling he'd had enough anyway. The horse's eyes were glazed over like she was in her own world of pain, and her leg stuck out from her body at an odd angle. I was wondering if we should try to push it back into shape when I heard wagons. We dived into a clump of bushes.

One of the Lomans found the wagon first, then a couple of farm boys fetched the medicine man, and pretty soon about twenty people were hovering about. Somebody shot the horse. We heard the cursing over the smashed bottles and the twisted wagon wheel and the dead horse. We didn't dare show our faces, for the hiding we'd get. Besides, by then neither of us felt good.

Someone fetched Father and he wouldn't even look for us. "They'll come home when they're hungry," was all he said, and he threw a murderous look in the direction of the bushes like he knew right where we were. Hugh muttered swear words under his breath and stuck out his tongue. I did the same, protected by shrubbery. "Miserable old bastard, go to hell." One of us said it, the other echoed it.

It was Father had to pay the medicine man for the damage, of course, and we heard them haggling. In the end Father took out a roll of bills and peeled off a couple while the medicine man kept yelling, "I'll see you in court." I'm sure Father never did go to court, or we'd have heard about it.

As it was, we stayed in the bushes all night, and started out next morning for home stinking and hungry, me with wet pants. When we got back, no one took any notice of us, for Maggie had got worse, and a real doctor from Smith's Falls was getting set to bleed her.

Maggie died not long after, and no one spoke to us all summer, forgot we existed. Even Father seemed to have had the pepper whipped right out of him, and it was our Gran fed us on the quiet and kept us out of sight. Old Marthy turned meaner after that, and everyone tiptoed around, and the baby clothes were packed in Marthy's trunk until Victoria came along.

This is the letter I'll never write you, J.R. It's all in my head. If I could tell you a different story I would. Something to restore your faith in humanity, deliver into your hands answers that would send us all away happy – a murderer, perhaps, a stranger, someone who means no more to you and me than a dying horse meant to a couple of foolish boys.

But the fact is, they're right, all these witnesses. Right and wrong at the same time. I did kill them and I didn't. I most certainly didn't kill Minnie. Minnie killed herself, really. She went into the house when I begged her not to. If I killed her, it was only through not saving her. It was too late by then, the smoke so bad. With her screams still ringing in my ears, I made off across the fields. I was sick in the bushes and washed in Bruce's spring and never came back to watch for a long time, then I sat on the fence and tried to keep from shaking and watched the people working to put out the fire. I felt like screaming, it's too late, too late, but then I thought, maybe it isn't, maybe they're all right, just a little scared, coughing from the smoke, or I'm dreaming all this and when I wake up I'll still be in the Central, with the guard dashing water on me because I'm late for chores.

So I resurrected them and I saw, I actually saw, Father stumbling out of the house and running for the stable to save the horse and buggy with the other men, and Marthy and Minnie, leaning on each other as they edged out the door and down the stoop into the arms of the waiting women. And Minnie paused to look at me, right at me – she knew right where I was – before someone wrapped a blanket around her. Her look said, It's all right, Charley. Don't worry about us. We made it through and we're all right.

I will swear with my dying breath that I believed in that moment that they were alive.

If I feel guilty about anything, it's not being able to save Minnie. I owed her that, but I think once she found Father, she didn't want to live anyway. Or maybe she just couldn't find her way out of the smoke, trying to drag Father. It's plain to me that's what she tried to do.

Marthy collapsed on the sleeper near the door, they found her there, no one tried to save her. Minnie would go for Father, with her last breath try to save him. I can see her, just like the smoke's lifting and there she is, skinny arms under his shoulders, tugging him, and him, who dropped like a boulder, unmoveable. Minnie, pausing for a moment to fish a handkerchief from her sleeve to hold over her mouth and nose – no, over his mouth and nose, that's where she would make her mistake – begging, "Father! Father, get up, please oh please God, get up!"

And she called my name, I know she did, I heard it in the roar of flames: "Charley, help! Please!" And that's the thing I don't like to remember, because I stood outside the door and I couldn't see her for smoke, but I could picture it all, Father like a stone, Minnie no more able to move him than a breath of wind could move the apple tree from one side of the road to the other.

I tried to open the door and I couldn't find the prop and when I let go the door swung shut. The door was blistering hot and I hadn't slept all night and I was half crazed from the quarrel and terrified, terrified of the fire.

The reason I didn't want Minnie to go into the house is harder to explain. If I don't tell it right, you'll think I murdered them. If I do tell it right, you're going to want to hang me, anyway. Because you've got to hang somebody. Three people are dead. And nobody else who was there is still alive.

You see, what I did was foolish. It was a mistake.

I didn't go there to kill them, in spite of all the threats people say I made. I guess I made them, some of them at least. I feel that is exactly what I would do, though I don't remember. I didn't go there with love in my heart, either. I went out of curiosity; they were family, I wondered how they were. I went out of remorse and fear, to see if there was any shred of forgiveness or love for me, because all I ever wanted was for them to love me. Like in Sunday School, the prodigal son, the father slaying the fatted calf to welcome him. I didn't really expect anything like that, but there's still that kernel of sentiment, or romance, in my nature, the one that made me call myself Kingsley and pass myself off as a cheese king. A kernel still alive. It wanted to be welcomed with open arms and sat down to a good, hot meal.

And those fools at the lockup later: Did you go to bury the hatchet, Charley? In their skulls, Charley? Sick.

The fact is, when I got to the farm that morning and hung about watching Father, I was afraid to go near. He has – had – a fearful temper. He and I were too much alike ever to get along, but he sometimes softened for Minnie or Liza Ann. Not for Marthy, she brought out his cantankerous side.

Father took a long time in the barn and it came to me that he was getting older, slower. After a while, I got tired of watching and wandered over to Jones's property, then to Pryce's, then back over the other side to Bruce's, and sat by the sugar shanty. Didn't see nobody on the road except a knot of gypsies, one with something live and struggling under a bulge in her shawl, all of them not looking around, like they hoped if they saw no one, no one could see them.

When I came back to Father's the buggy was gone. I figured he'd be at market and there was even a slim chance Marthy'd be with him. I was hoping when I crept nearer that the house would be empty except for Gran. That's what I really wanted, to see old Gran, rest her soul. Gran, if she recognized me at all, would throw her arms around me.

I saw the tracks of Father's wheels heading through the gate, now shut. Old Dixie was sunning himself on the stoop and as soon as I came close he set up such an explosion of barking he could've wakened the dead.

We're going to fight for my innocence, you and I, J.R., for the part of me that is innocent, the part of me that saw the bloody rags carted away the day my mother died, that went to my father's wedding with grubby hands, and clung to Minnie when she lugged me around the barn. The part that got into mischief with Hugh but never meant no harm, and teased Victoria and made Sam blush by reciting the names of all the village girls who liked him. It's the part you want to save because it's like saving yourself, J.R., and Johnny and Liza Ann and Sam and the sisters out west and everybody whose hand I ever touched and whose bread I ate while God was watching.

. . . eyes have they and they see not for there are things even God won't show them even especially consider the lilies of the field o no man knows the moment of their passing . . .

I'll help you all I can, J.R., because I respect you and I want you to be right. Your faith frees me from self-doubt, makes me sleep a little easier. Can it free me from the law? It makes me see that Father must have done some things right because the others turned out good. You had a father you listened to, J.R., or it might be you sitting here and me standing where you are, trying to save the world. The world as we know it, the only one worth saving, I guess.

You have to forgive me or I won't tell you. Can't. Like a foundation under a house; can't build the rest without supports. Like the verandah attached to father's house. Sagging, no foundation, posts already rotting. Weather-worn, never a lick of paint. I saw all this when I climbed the stoop that Saturday. It wobbled under my weight. Beside it, where hollyhocks once bloomed, dead bracken, snapped off by wind and animals, lay.

It was one of those bright fall days, the air still, so you almost expected to hear cicadas by noon and find yourself peeling your shirt off to get the sun.

The stoop door was propped open with a stick. Ahead was the door to the main kitchen; on my left, the summer kitchen entrance. A pot was bubbling on the stove there and I could smell fowl, Marthy's specialty, unadulterated with spice or herb, just boiling forlornly until the meat fell off the bones, then some flour thrown in to make a gluey paste, gravy to stick to your ribs. Suddenly I felt hungry.

"Shush, Dixie!" Marthy didn't look around, she was pouring something into a pot and had to keep stirring. Thought Dixie was scolding hens. I must have stood a full minute in the doorway, with her close enough to touch, almost. If that'd been Gran, I'd have stolen up and given her a hug.

Finally I went into the main kitchen, a dark, pokey cell but stifling hot in winter with its stove going. This time of year it was just dismal, everything sparse and subdued, like a good Christian home should be. Presbyterian colours. Brown, smarmy oilcloth, sideboard with mouse-coloured veneer peeling.

I sat in a chair at the table and Dixie came and put his head on my knee. There was a mixing bowl on the table with batter in it, a flour sifter and some egg shells nearby. I put a finger in the bowl and scooped some batter up. I was licking my finger when Marthy came in, wiping her hands on her apron.

She turned pale and staggered back when she saw me. "What are you doing here?" she says, putting her hand to her heart.

"Come to see Gran," I says.

She gave me a funny look, sadness and smugness mixed.

So inside right then I'm weeping. Because the sadness is something Marthy thinks the world asks of her, and the smugness is because she thinks now she's mistress of the house for good and all. And I never realized until that moment, that she hadn't been mistress, or hadn't known she was, from the day she arrived as my father's bride. Gran had never been more than a shadow to us, but a necessary shadow, like the pot of vittles on the stove or the white-washed stones by the front gate. But us kids looked at her differently from the way a daughter-in-law would. So I'm weeping for Gran and for her death, which has meant so little.

Besides the sadness and smugness there was fear in Marthy. I couldn't get rid of the smell of it. You know how with animals it rouses all their preying instincts. Same with folks. Like boys playing in the schoolyard, they see one kid who's fearing and they all start to pick on him.

"Sit down, Marthy," I said. "You make me nervous."

She put on her bullying manner, but I could smell the fear. "Come in here barefoot, like a tramp."

"You always wanted us to remove our boots at the door." I took another lick of the batter. "Too much sugar," I says. Just like Father.

"The soles of your feet is black."

I shrugged. "No boots. Fell apart." I let Dixie lick my fingers. "Chicken smells good."

"You're not welcome in this house, Charley. Your father says." I saw then that the fear was for Father, not me.

"He won't be back till the chickens are sold."

"He'll be back any minute."

"Not till dinnertime."

"Dinner's ready." She gave a start at the sound of a wagon, then froze. It went on past. "Best you go."

"My feet are sore." I massaged my toes.

What I saw on her face then was an expression I'd seen before but never read. Kindness and cunning. When Father wasn't around. When she thought she might get away with something. She disappeared into the bedroom and came back a moment later with a pair of old gaiter boots. She held them out to me. "Your father don't wear these any more." She jerked her head impatiently. "Don't say anything."

I put them on slowly. My mouth formed a thank-you but when the words came out they sounded raspy, like they came from a part of my voice-box that had never been used before. Suddenly I felt ashamed.

Marthy didn't seem to hear. Her eyes glazed over, like she was in a different world, willing a different scene before her, one where I wasn't around.

I remembered another day, bright like this one, Marthy sitting in a rocking chair, rocking her little girl on a golden afternoon, and Father and Minnie trying to tell her the baby's dead, no good a-rocking her, she's dead, gone, never coming back. And Marthy just keeps on rocking, clutching the baby, humming a tuneless little tune, and she reaches up with her free hand and pushes a strand of hair off the baby's forehead with that same glazed, other-world look.

We were locked in that moment, trying to rewrite our histories, when we heard Father's wagon roll into the yard.

Chapter Three

On the stand he was hopeless. Almost as if he wanted to be convicted. A death wish. Had to be led into his story, like a child coaxed into a recitation for the school concert.

The knot in the pit of Lavell's stomach tightened. Last night, when he'd told Charley he had decided to put him on the stand, he got a vacant stare – at what? Ghosts, sad and harmless, parading through the day room? No fear, no bewilderment. A fey eye turned toward a window.

Today, in the courtroom, vague, convoluted stories, a litany of asides. How before the Central Prison he spent five weeks in the Ottawa gaol. How on arrest he had $30.50 in his pocket, two tens, two fives and two twenty-five cent pieces. "The thirty dollars I took in in my mouth. I gave up the fifty cents because I couldn't conveniently put it in my mouth." Plausible. Its very matter-of-factness, far from gaining the trust of his audience, had the ring of falsehood.

"On release, I had on a black suit similar to this one. A black stiff hat same as when arrested." He still had twenty-four dollars after buying tobacco. "I took it out in my mouth on my release."

And the boot story, too elaborate, barely possible, not corroborated. "I traded the prison boots in a pawn shop for the cloth top boots. Even trade. New half soles. The others hurt me. I gave twenty-five cents on the trade." A strange encounter on the train to Smith's Falls, not recalled by Hannah. "I was talking to a man about thirty miles out of Toronto." Voice a whisper. "He came in looking for a smoking car and we got talking about boots. I said my soles were pretty near off. He went away and returned with a pair which he offered to me." Glib. "I put them on. Pretty tight, I said. He wanted two-twenty, I offered one-twenty-five." Enough. But he went on, as if embroidering would breathe life into a feeble tale. "He said they cost two-twenty but he'd let me have them for one-twenty-five. I said I wouldn't take one-twenty-five to wear them. He did them up in papers and left them on the seat, left the car and didn't come back." Hannah? "He was asleep. I carried both parcels when we got off the train." Ah, Charley, Charley. Lavell adopted what he hoped was a look of serene agreement.

With Clute he was no better, looking at his hands, the rail, the wall, not meeting eyes. "I went down home to see what I could see." "I intended to put up at Carleton Place to kill time." "I saw my father leave the house for the barn between six and seven. Didn't want him to see me because I was ashamed." Not defiant, not guarded. Nonchalant, like it didn't matter any more. He felt good on the way to Newbliss, but not on the way back. He heard no threshers, saw no smoke. *Why did he not go to help?* "I was ashamed." And again. "Ashamed." *Oh, Charley, Charley. It's not enough!*

With twelve pairs of eyes rivetted on him as he rose to give his closing argument, Lavell knew he was losing his grip. He chose his words carefully, hoping to show solidarity between Charley and himself. *Naturally. Is it any wonder that. Is it not more probable.* He appealed to the jury's good nature. Charley's temper tantrums were part of his boyish pranks. He appealed to their sense of fair play. Charley the underdog, penniless and confined. He mocked the Crown's theories. Would a man plan a horrendous crime for a year and then execute it in broad daylight? Would he throw away the cloth boots if he were not in possession of another pair? If a man committed a murder, would he start a fire to call attention to it before he could make his escape? Would he kill three people in one part of the house and then start a fire in another? And if he had come home with malice in his heart would he not have committed the deed in the early morning? Why wait?

He painted a poignant picture. Charley, nostalgic, homesick, liberated at last, wandering the fields of home. Prodigal son, long-lost brother. "Suppose Miss Luckey had rushed in at the stoop door. You remember, the door would close if nothing was propped against it. Is it not probable that an accident would be the cause of her death than that a brother would cruelly slay a sister he had always loved?"

An evangelistic edge crept in. Had they made up their minds already, closed their ears and minds to his oratory? "Do you wonder that when he heard the train stopped at Smith's Falls he resolved to see his home? His idea of throwing Montgomery off his trail this way may not have been brilliant but was a plan he would naturally adopt." *Naturally.*

Try again. "Was it any wonder he wanted to see the old familiar scenes and in his peculiar circumstances did not want anyone to see him? It was a most natural feeling." Feet shuffled, throats rumbled. "Not caring to be recognized, he did not wait until the stores were open to purchase new boots. He stole the boots from the train. That night, he saw the fire from Jacques' Hill. Thinking it was almost over and he could do no good, he started for Smith's Falls. In the barber shop, he heard talk of the fire. Given his mental and moral condition, you can realize why he did not return to his father's home to investigate. He needed rest and determined to take it. Naturally, he went to bed." *Oh, God.*

He laboured the obscure and irrelevant, skating over the prosecution's strong points. "Did the prisoner on his arrest make conflicting statements? The difference existed only in the minds of those who told what he said." That juror on the end, face masked in whiskers, was that a glint of understanding in his eyes? Pity? Not for Charley; for Lavell. The underdog now.

He felt suddenly tired. Tired, tired and it was no good. "I will not refer to Redsox at length. The evidence is strong on this point that there must have been two such strangers." *Oh, naturally.*

Four hours, fifteen minutes. Charley watching the whole time, clear-eyed and expressionless. The judge kind, calling his speech one of great moderation, delivered in remarkably good taste. Another exam passed; A plus, as befits a Lavell.

If only Charley had said something believable. That he went to the house, visited and left. Or went in while Martha was visiting the Parkers, found no one home and left. Or went at two, stole his father's boots from the stoop and left. Until now, Lavell thought the risk of placing Charley at the house was tantamount to admitting guilt. But anything was more believable than his claim that he never went near the house.

People do not hide in the bushes all day for innocent purposes. Oh, but they do, they do, if they're homesick and ashamed. They hide and yearn, and let love drive them away.

Naturally.

Then Clute, like the wrath of God. Brisk, brief, unerring. "Is it credible? Is it possible? for one of you gentlemen on this jury to believe that three living persons in health could have perished by accident? Shall I insult your common sense by reminding you of the suggestion in regard to the girl, that she went into the house, came out and left her teeth on the other side of the fence and went back to perish?" The crack of an invisible whip. "Where did he get his money? Did it grow? He does not say he picked it up along the road."

On and on, until they are all weary of it, and the jury takes only an hour to bring in the verdict.

Guilty.

Chapter Four

I expected any kind of reception but the one I got. When he first saw me he stared at me ugly-like. I thought, there's going to be a fight. Then he puts out his hand. "Charley," he says. Nothing more. No word of welcome. But it was in his eyes, a flash of something, not happiness but maybe relief. "Martha", he says, "company for dinner." He pads into the kitchen in his sock feet. The chicken smell hovered above us and his sweaty sock smell rose to meet it. It felt like home, and I remembered winters when us kids lined our snow-crusted mittens and socks against the stove, and their steam rose and mingled with the sizzle of dinner. Times like that we were happy.

"Dish up," he says to Marthy. "Charley and I'll be outside."

Marthy's face relaxes. "I'll put dumplings in," she says.

We went out into the yard. He put his hand on my shoulder in a friendly way. "What're you planning to do now, Charley?"

We were walking south east, toward the well. "Get work out Ottawa way, I guess."

He stopped at the well. "How will you finance yourself?" His tone startled me. Genuinely concerned.

I shrugged, scuffed a foot in the damp earth. Then Father did a strange thing. He lifted up the board that covered the hole in the ground and felt along the inside stone lining underneath. A pebble pinged in the water below as a large stone came away in his hand. He set it down and drew out a small metal box from the slot in the stones. "Goes well back so it can't get knocked in the water," he says with a grim smile. "Nobody knows, even Martha." Eyeing me suspiciously, he opened the box. "Not much, just today's take." He picked up the bills and says, "How much do you need for board 'til you get your first pay?"

I was speechless. He pressed a couple of bills on me, put the box back and covered the well. "That's all there'll ever be, Charley," he says. "Don't come looking for more." The note in his voice said, Don't try it again. Which made me angry because I hadn't asked for nothing. Hadn't had the chance. I saw there were going to be strings attached. "Come in the house," he says. "I'll give you the name and address of a cattle dealer who's looking for a farm boy. May not be what you're looking for, but you could do worse. He'll expect a lot, but he'll treat you well."

I got a bad feeling then. Like for a few dollars he's going to control my life. Watch me like a hawk. We went into the house.

Father fished out a notebook, tore off a page and wrote something. "You'll have to straighten out. Look sharp and stick close to him. Stick real close, like –"

"Shit to a shovel." I was angry.

I saw a vein bulge in his forehead. "I'm giving you one last chance, Charley," he says, and his voice was fearfully quiet.

Marthy was wiping her hands over and over on her apron, like she couldn't get them clean. She was trying not to look at the boots on my feet. Father looked at her and it was like he read her mind. He stopped, his hand extended with the paper, and looked at my feet. Silence. Then he says, "My clothes as well as my money." Sucks in his breath and lets it out in a long, low whistle. And I see Marthy's doing the same thing, sucking in her breath. But then she holds it. Her expression's like the one Hugh wore the day Father caught him pissing in the rain barrel. Me too, I must have worn that expression many times.

"Here, take them," I says. My feet were hurting anyway. I stooped to take a boot off and heard Marthy cry out just as his whip wrapped around my arm like a lick of flame. He made to pull on it but the handle snapped in his hand and he was left holding half of it. He lunged then, like a mad bull, making huffing noises as he threw himself against me. Knocked me back against a partition and I heard a great crack like the wall was splitting.

Marthy screamed, "Mind the crockery," then, "Lordolord-saveus!" She hurled herself at us, bounced off us and went reeling back toward the sleeper by the door. Out of the corner of my eye, I saw her hit the back of her knees against it and sit down hard. At the same time there was a terrible crash, the pipe came down and hit Father on the head. It was hot, my eyes were stinging. I stepped back and he fell with such force the floor shuddered and cups rattled on the sideboard.

That was when I noticed smoke seeping through from the summer kitchen where the pipe went through the wall. Blood snaked from under Father's head and I could hear Marthy shouting, "You've killed him, you've killed him!" I couldn't move, just stood there looking down at Father, with Marthy calling, "Get a doctor! Oh Lord, he's dead, you've killed him!" and I saw Father move. I saw his hand come up, bloody, grope for the whip. He grunted once, twice. "He's not dead," I says, "he's all right." She started pulling at me from behind. "Get out! Get out!" Trying to pull me by the shirttail toward the door.

I swung around and knocked against her. "Get out yourself," I says. I started to pull Father toward the door but he fought me, pushed my arms away. Marthy too, she kept pulling at me, screaming, "What'll I do now? You've killed him. Oh, what'll I do?"

Over and over again. Him falling, trying to get up, stretching a hand out toward me. Her wailing in a cloud of smoke, "He's dead, dead!"

He's not dead. Comes at me suddenly, springs from the floor like a tiger, I can't believe his swiftness, his strength, my eyes off him only a moment, looking back for Marthy. I start to push him off me, he goes limp and we're on the floor, me pinned under him. Marthy's coughing, I know I'm going to pass out. With my last strength I push Father over on his back, try to pull him with me. I'm coughing, my eyes are streaming, I can't see the door but I hear Marthy's coughing behind me. From far off I see myself half-staggering, half-crawling, pushing on wood – the door, where is the door? Finding the latch, my hands blistering. I fall outwards suddenly, into fresh air and sunlight. Try to call them, come out, come on, out! No sound except a rasp like a rusty hinge.

I fell onto the stoop and lay gasping half over the edge. Lay five minutes, an hour, my mind and body numb. Raised myself finally, Dixie licking my neck, and heard threshers over towards Daley's. I stumbled down the steps toward the apple tree. I was hunched up there, wondering what to do, when a woman in brown came hurrying across the field, looking down as she picked her way through the cow dung, her skirt clutched in her hand. Neat and quick as always. Minnie. There was no time to get out of sight before she was in the clearing. Dixie barked, ran to her, then to me. She looked up.

"Charley! What a surprise!" Then, as she took in my appearance, raised her head, wrinkled her nose. "What's wrong? Charley!" She started to run toward the house.

I staggered up, my head reeling, and ran after her. That was why I struck her, to keep her from going in. She screamed twice. I was weak, and she got away from me, went in, Dixie bounding past her, and the door shut behind them. I went to the door, yes I did, pulled on it and called, but the smoke drove me back. I burned my hand on the latch. It was too late, believe me, too late to save them. I didn't get help because it was already too late.

In my dreams I remember the house, the smoke billowing through the dark, cramped kitchen, Father's blood on the floor, and my mind goes blank, even in the dream. I like to fill in the gaps with Redsox wielding an axe, or some other stranger, looking to rob Father, striking him down, grabbing the old tinder box in the kitchen, igniting their clothes, the curtain, the wooden table.

In my dreams I beg Minnie not to go in, I strike her as she runs toward the house and always, always, she slips away from me, runs screaming up onto the stoop and opens the door, and I wake wanting to die for her.

And I will. Die for her, even now, though it's too late, is meaningless. My timing has always been off, in everything I've ever done. Dying's the same.

SHERIFF'S OFFICE.

Cornwall, *Nov 8"*   189*3*

Dear Mr Sheriff Smart
     Brockville

    In reply to your letter of
the 7th instant, I will be very
glad to accommodate you
with the Scaffold, Wright and
Pulley, for lifting the weight,
this is all that you require from
me, If Radclean is to be imployed
he will supply the other part of
the tackling, You have my deepest
sympathy in the position you
are placed in. If there is any
thing else that I can do for you
please let me know.
       Yours truly
       D. F. McIntyre
        Sheriff S.D.R.

Toronto, Nov. 9th, 1893.

re Prisoner Luckey.

Sir :

I have had your letter delivered to Mr. Radclive, who has just told me by telephone that he has written to you making all necessary arrangements, and has concluded not to bring the posts and other apparatus from Cornwall to Brockville.

Notwithstanding what he may written to to this effect, I think the material used in the execution of Slavin last Fall should be brought up to Brockville. It will save from $30 to $40 to the County, and I know of no reason why this expenditure need be incurred.

I have the honor to be,

Sir,

Your obd't servant,

T. F. Chamberlain

Inspector.

Mr. Sheriff Smart,

Brockville, Ont.

Part V

CHARLEY

December 14th, 1893

There is no answer; the fact was made
by a history of your unswaying knot,
the one long moment . . .

Chapter One

"A minstrel show will be held in the Opera House on the evening of the day set apart for Charles Luckey's hanging."
Brockville Evening Recorder

Sixteen below last night. Burst water pipes; tongues frozen to iron railings. Old men smoke pipes around pot-bellied stoves, speculating on the forthcoming New Year's Day elections, on possible reprieves, for Charley from the noose, for themselves from winter's onslaught. Newspapers throughout the country draft Thursday's headlines: "HANGED! Luckey pays the death penalty in Expiation of his Terrible Crime!" The Luckey story is as neatly packaged as Charley's underwear, wrapped in white paper and tied with tea string. Life goes on.

Who cares, who cares about Charley? The Christmas goose grows fatter; chestnuts repose in bins; firs, soon to be resplendent with candles, paper chains and popcorn garlands, lean against porches and sheds. Nimble hands embroider and crochet; ostrich plumes, fringes and coloured glass beads garnish homemade surprises; sachets and potholders lie cached in tissue and ribbon.

Life goes on. The few who care have said their goodbyes early, eschewing Smart's handwritten invitation to view the hanging. The old sheriff lies in his mansion on King Street, in a darkened room, hand shielding his eyes, leaving his son the deputy to officiate. Catherine Phillips, mother of Jack and sister of Charley's late mother, pours sherry on ripening fruit cakes mechanically, fingers cold and leaden. In her kitchen, Jack and his young wife Eliza watch silently, willing her to pause, weep, say something. Parker and Daley prepare for morning chores, breaking ice in buckets, hacking frozen feed from storehouses. Budget their time to include Johnny's barns.

McGowan arrests a vagrant asleep in a market stall; Vaux, in his cutter, touches his whip to his pocket as he careers past toll gates. A pledge to pay later, an infant won't wait to be born. Murray pursues a forger in Buenos Ayres, Greer boards a train for northern Ontario to investigate another murder. Lizzie Borden, acquitted, prepares for a long and comfortable life as Lizbeth of Maplecroft.

The lamented, the sought after, remain lost. Balloon, Hugh, Violette. Harriet Reilly sends no word, but a Utica friend, interviewed by an intrepid journalist, reports her in seclusion.

The family and Ansley Stewart arrive early at Johnny's, wearing black. Victoria is surprised to see that the men are already wearing arm bands, although it is not yet eight o'clock. They pray and sing hymns, weep a little. Her mother puts an arm around her. The flowers on the lowboy are from one of Charley's bouquets from well-wishers, divided up the day before, during their last visit. Victoria feels drawn into the delicate pink centres of the white carnations. Goosebumps erupt all over her body, in spite of the thickness of her long-sleeved wool frock. She pictures Charley, gaped at by strangers, embracing people he never heard of a year ago. She cringes when her father bursts out, "I'm brother of a murderer! Branded forever!" and her mother cradles his head when he breaks down weeping on the sofa. The sudden display of weakness, so alien to her father's nature, and her mother's uncharacteristic response, make her glance away; her stomach hurts, a tightness in her throat makes it impossible to swallow.

J.R. Lavell chooses to go to his office in Smith's Falls this morning, walking erect and purposefully, prepared to look any man in the eye. Already the press has collared him, after his last visit to Charley yesterday. "Did he weaken his case, testifying on the stand?" they asked.

"Without a doubt." Bitterly. "As far as the new system is concerned, it depends greatly upon the class of jury the prisoner is talking to. I had an uphill fight in Luckey's case and did my utmost against adverse circumstances."

What a fool he'd been, hoping to convince the Minister of Justice that Charley deserved clemency! He'd taken George Henderson, of Belcourt, McCracken and Henderson, with him. Weight in numbers.

Together they'd planned their strategy on the way to the Ottawa Court House. Pitted against Power, the Queen's Counsel in charge of capital cases for the Ministry of Justice, they cited endless instances of reduced sentences and overturned convictions.

The first disappointment had been the Minister of Public Works, acting for Sir John Thompson, Prime Minister and Minister of Justice, who was out of the country. A Quebecker, J-A. Ouimet spoke impeccable English, having been educated at Victoria College, Cobourg. "Sir John telegraphed me last night saying his copy of the evidence had not arrived and directing me to deal with it," Ouimet said. They agreed to keep the discussion informal. At three the cabinet would meet to render a final decision.

Lavell fought a sense of helplessness. "Will Council be polled?"

"Certainly. In capital cases each member records his vote, affirmative or negative."

"But the Minister's recommendation is usually acted upon?"

His host nodded gravely.

His initial misgivings were allayed when he discovered that Ouimet had made himself thoroughly acquainted with Charley's case. The deputy Minister of Justice was gracious, unhurried, but nevertheless concerned that Charley had had two trials. "Why a second trial if it was felt that justice was served in the first?"

"The evidence on which my client was convicted was the same as that which acquitted him at the first trial. The new witness, Whiting, made no impact except to show folly on the prosecution's part." Lavell watched his audience, but the fixed, faintly sympathetic expressions did not waver. "The Manitoba dentist was not worth the money invested in bringing him, and the boot evidence was a repetition of last April's. Taken as a whole, all the credible evidence was of a circumstantial nature, as consistent with the prisoner's innocence as his guilt."

Ouimet's gaze did not change. It dawned on Lavell that it was an expression of sympathy for the underdog rather than a gauge of the Minister's opinion on the case at hand. Power said little, letting Ouimet ask the questions, even to the number of nails in the soles of the boots found with Charley. In a final plea, Lavell raised the question of mental stability, citing the so-called suicide attempt. Dishonest, he thought, the gunshot was an accident, but how was he to recover ground? He knew before he left the room, even before he heard the sympathetic note in Henderson's voice when they parted outside, that their cause was lost.

He had scarcely reached home before the cabinet cabled him: the law must take its course. Charley would hang. By the time he arrived at the court house, he saw his news had preceded him. The old sheriff, more stooped than usual, stood back without a word for Lavell to pass, then locked the door.

"He knows?"

"He knows."

* * *

Why was it always the boots he noticed? Gaiters, galoshes, rubbers, fur-trimmed moccasins. It wasn't because he was hunched in a corner, staring at the floor. He paced endlessly, alert to every shadow, every sound. He tried to read commutation, reprieve, into muffled voices, in approaching steps: were they hurried, jubilant, dejected, reluctant? Accompanied by paper rustling, breath rasping? He read faces quickly, shook hands perfunctorily, studied the floor as figures shook out mantles and cloaks, stamped on concrete. Brought the outside world to him. He pictured the feet inside the boots, corns, bunions, carbuncles, blisters, warts, frostbite.

Bouquets everywhere. Yesterday, eight a.m., Jimmy opened his cell door, face wreathed in carnations, Gaoler McDougall behind him, chrysanthemum in one hand, asters in the other, making sure with his bulk that the prisoner wouldn't be tempted to make a dash for it. Chunks of snow fell from their boots, unmelting. He could almost tell the temperature by their boots. McDougall's right boot, run over on the outer edge like his father's, left ribs of snow. Downey's were so worn they left no pattern at all.

They'd put more wood on the fires, brought extra blankets. Wouldn't do to have the boy catch cold, the old sheriff had said. Kind smiles, no uneasy laughter at the remark. The last day of his life, and he would meet God before the cold got him, nose not yet dripping, ears not plugged, chest not rattling. God would see to that. *Excuse me, God* – fishing for a handkerchief. *God, if it's all right with you I'd like to stay under my blankets, instead of kneeling on the cold floor, see you soon anyway.*

Always the feet he noticed. Went back to childhood when his feet hurt, cramming his broad soles and splayed toes into Hugh's narrow hand-me-downs. Now they come to say goodbye and I'm looking down at growing puddles and shards of ice, resisting the urge to run a finger over toecaps, snow-caked laces. Always the boots.

Rev. Saunders came, helped him write the letter. *"Let me tell you, Dear Reader, what the Lord done for me. He saved me from all my sins . . . I used to think that a Christian is one who goes through life hanging his head, heaving sighs, drawing a long face and looking very sanctimonious. I believe that is one of the brightest lies Satan ever coined, but he got me to believe it . . ."* Nothing about the fire, the trial. He sang, aware that they all were listening: *I'll soon be at home over there.* Made a list of his possessions, directions for their disposal: his watch for McDougall, breast pin for Downey. Read the fifty-third chapter of Isaiah: *He is brought as a lamb to the slaughter.* He broke up bouquets to make bunches for Sarah and Liza Ann, waited through Johnny's and Sam's awkward pauses, spoke of God and the Hereafter. Waited while, in death-like silence, they read his letters from well-wishers. "Make your peace with God," he said as they left, loving them as never before. "Prepare to meet me in Heaven." Afterward, he sat at the table in the dayroom, head in hands, and wept.

Chapter Two

It is hanging weather, cold as a dead man's heart, cold as fear. Snow covers the ruts on Main Street; hooves and cutters carve random patterns. Snow veils the trees up Court House Avenue and shrouds the green. On top of the Court House, it sheathes the sword of Sally Grant and makes of her scales two inverted question marks, *en face*. In Newbliss, it stanches the gaping wound in the fields of John J. Luckey.

He has dressed with care, as is his habit before an execution. Showmanship is in his blood, he reflects, but publicly he has always made much of the fact that he cannot let the Lieutenant Governor down. The close fitting frock coat and trousers, never failing to impress the sober bastions of the law, appeal to his sense of pageantry. He preens momentarily before the mirror, smoothing sleeves, squinting as he leans forward to clip a single hair from the corner of his moustache. Not for him the mask. The only hangman never to hide his face, a hyperbole perhaps, but more importantly a distortion of characterization, since such a statement implies an admirably brazen courage. The fact is he does not feel courageous. A curious mixture of delight in mystery and pride in his craft, coupled with pressure from his family for secrecy, causes him to bare his face while burying his name. A child's game of hide-and-seek with the public, keeping the man separate from the executioner. He has piled layer upon layer of aliases to the point where no one outside of his family knows who he really is. "John," he tells some; "Tom," others. Radclive to some, Ratley to others. His selves blend, until he scarcely knows himself

sometimes which is real, which fiction. Radclive can forget Tom
perhaps, but Tom relies on his other self for the tales that make him
the centre of attention in the alehouses. And it's harder to be
anonymous when one has had a few drinks.

He reties his string tie, still not satisfied. He feels ill, there is a
puffiness around his eyes and his skin lacks its usual ruddiness. His
hands, however, are as sure as always.

He has had almost no sleep. Wherever he goes, it's the same.
Locals corner him over ale, regaling him with stories of town hangings.
As long as they're buying, he listens. Last night they talked of one in
the early twenties – a Lieutenant Michael O'Connor of the Canadian
Fencibles, hanged for shooting his manservant in an argument over
religion – then go on to an 1860 hanging, which some remember.
"Young Edgar Harter killed his cousin Morgan Dockstader in a
quarrel over a girl. They had to get Mother Barnes, the Witch of Plum
Hollow, to figure where the body was. She said it'd turn up in some
rushes on the shore of Charleston Lake. Sure enough." They nod
sagely. "He hanged after Christmas, in a real carnival atmosphere,
people dancing in the rain." Before Radclive could escape, an
octogenarian started reciting the tale of a young ex-convict, John
Simpson, hanged for beating to death a farmer named Fell. "Simpson's
body was smuggled to the Delta home of Dr Alpheus Howard twenty-
five miles away and dissected before a group of medical students. His
hide was taken to a Charleston tannery where

> *To make a saddle they did begin*
> *and rode upon poor Simpson's skin."*

They taught him the whole ballad and he raised his glass and sang, and
when he got back to the hotel it was five a.m.

Before he could turn in, there was a ruckus in the lobby. A porter
struggled in, half carrying a white-clad apparition, hatless and
barefoot, found under a gas lamp a few blocks away. Shouts of
"Luckey's escaped!" were soon replaced by embarrassed chuckles
when someone said, "Well, it's a Charlie, all right. Moore the
stonecutter, delirious with pneumonia. Must have gone down the
hospital fire escape." "Could have been Luckey's ghost, eh?" The
good Samaritan grinned and went off, leaving the night staff fetching
blankets and placing the wraith's feet in a dish of snow.

Now Radclive descends the stairs of the Revere Hotel to find a new commotion, of a kind he is used to dealing with. Three ruffians shouting, "Murderer!" shaking their fists and threatening to beat him hollow. A pause, a coolly lit cigar, and a measured unfaltering walk to the front door are all it takes to mollify them. Later he will raise hell with Chief Rose and have them charged.

He walks the short distance up the hill to the court house, through the snow.

* * *

The women's yard is enclosed by a stone wall twenty feet high. A small stone building, formerly a water closet, partially obscures the scaffold, so the guests crowd together on either side of the yard, jostling, craning their necks, stamping to keep circulation moving. Their passes have been scrutinized by a constable at the door, where a few curiosity-seekers with forgeries have been turned away. The fifty men admitted have been chosen for their work in crime, medicine or journalism. They remove hats, hunch shoulders and blow white breath on their hands. A door opens; from somewhere inside the building comes a quavery echo: Charley's rendition of his favourite hymn, Come, Great Deliverer, Come.

They come through the doorway tramping briskly, as if on platoon drill. Deputy George Bogue Smart, then the gaol physician with the Reverend Dr Saunders, followed by gaoler McDougall and Radclive, the prisoner walking between them. Before them looms Radclive's scaffold – no steps to climb, no trap door to the long drop. A swift, supposedly painless instrument of death.

Radclive places his left hand on Charley's shoulder, shakes his hand warmly. Old friends parting before a journey. In the hush, Charley's voice is low but clear. "I forgive you, Radclive. I'm an innocent man." He allows his legs to be pinioned, the black cap to slip over his head. Radclive's hand and gaze are steady. The pastor begins the Lord's Prayer; the hour strikes. A sharp click as he recites, "Deliver us from evil"; the body shoots into the air, twitches convulsively, straightens out and hangs rigid.

After six and a half minutes the doctor is satisfied he is dead. At eight twenty-five, Radclive cuts him down. When the cap is removed, Charley's face is composed, peaceful.

Chapter Three

210 Sorauren Avenue, Toronto

Hangman's Epilogue

 He lets himself into the front hall, drops his valise. Almost midnight; the gaslight swims before his eyes as he steadies himself against the door. The house is silent except for the whisper of Martha's nightgown as she comes downstairs. He lurches toward her and the room spins around. "Not what you think," he says, and his body is racked by a spasm of coughing. "Not – drunk."

 Martha grasps his shoulders. "John! Hurry!" Between them, his wife and the gangling, sleepy eleven-year-old struggle upstairs with him. The bed comes up to meet him.

 "God, I feel so queer in my head. Can't think what's wrong." His teeth chatter as Martha brings blankets.

 "I've took these off the children's bed. You'll be needing them more than they do." She bites her lip.

 He tries to answer, coughs until he thinks he will die, and the fear shows on Martha's face. He is scarcely aware when the doctor examines him, leaving some evil-smelling medicine on the dresser. "Grippe, sir," he says. "Inflammation of the lungs." And, to Martha, "See he stays in bed a few days." John brings his valise and sets it in a corner.

 "Try and sleep," Martha says, and leaves him. No word of love, but he sees concern in her eyes.

 He does not want to sleep, not yet. For they come nightly, his victims, their faces contorted with agony, until he breaks out in a cold sweat. Birchall, Davis, Slavin, dozens more. Now a new face. I forgive you, Radclive.

But would they all forgive him? Could he forgive himself?

He crawls out of bed, grasps the valise, opens it. Brandy. He drinks from the bottle until the faces dissolve and the sheets are soaked with sweat and he no longer knows day from night.

Four days pass and on the fifth he rises to find the sun shining and the house filled with talk of Christmas. He feels reborn.

* * *

Rec'd to be paid as follows:
E. Clint, coffin and burial expenses for the
late Charles Luckey, $10.50

The Cast

THE FAMILY

JOHN JAMES LUCKEY, JR, after a successful career as a contractor and businessman, died in 1927. Although no one suspected him of murder, he was reported to have said on his deathbed that he wished his conscience was as clear as his brother's.

LIZA ANN BALDWIN LUCKEY outlived her husband by ten years, but they were separated long before his death. She lived with her daughter and son-in-law at Frankville.

VICTORIA LUCKEY married William Morrison in 1900 and raised three children. She lived to be ninety.

ESLEY LUCKEY married Martha Pattemore, raised a family and was one of the most respected farmers in Kitley Township. He died in 1976, aged ninety-two.

SAMUEL LUCKEY married twice. He owned several cheese factories in Renfrew County and later moved to a farm near Warren, Ontario, where he bought a general store. He died in Toronto in 1940.

THE WITNESSES

JOHN PHILLIPS and his wife Eliza raised four children. A highly respected farmer, tax collector and Sunday School superintendent, he died in 1935.

In 1898, JOHN POLK moved to Smith's Falls where he ran a grocery business. He became bailiff of the Fourth Division Court and took up auctioneering. He died of pleurisy in 1913, aged fifty-seven.

DR HARRY VAUX left Brockville in 1900 and died in England in 1925.

DR HENRY REEVE opened a drug store in Athens in 1893 and practised in Almonte and elsewhere. He died in 1899, aged fifty-four. A century ago, he and Dr Vaux had no way of knowing that the bright red blood on Martha Luckey's body meant she had, in all probability, been alive at the time of fire.

THE LAW

WILLIAM DAVID GREER became senior chief inspector of the CID. He served fifty-two years in police work and died in 1935. Although he was one of Murray's two most trusted and avid disciples, Murray makes no mention of him in his *Memoirs of a Great Detective*.

In May 1902, shortly after receiving a new uniform, CHIEF ROBERT McGOWAN was again dismissed from the Smith's Falls police force. An inquiry was made into his property deals and a lawsuit was settled out of court. He subsequently tried the hotel business and detective work. He died in 1908, aged fifty.

HIS HONOUR JUDGE WILLIAM GLENHOLME FALCONBRIDGE was appointed Chief Justice of the Queen's Bench in 1900, was knighted in 1908 and died in 1920, aged seventy-three.

HIS HONOUR JUDGE JOHN E. ROSE became Judge of the Common Pleas Division of the High Court of Justice. Among his famous trials was the Heslop case of Ancaster. He died in January 1901. For 100 years after the Luckey trial, no one knew that in his notebook, the Judge had mistakenly quoted Constable McGillivray as saying that Charley told him "he went *out* to kill them."

JOHN REEVE LAVELL represented Leeds & Grenville North in Ottawa (1900-04). In 1906, he moved his family to Strathcona, Alberta, where he practised law until his death in January 1925.

ROGER CONGER CLUTE returned to Brockville in 1896 to prosecute Ur Lapointe, accused of wounding Police Chief Rose in a shootout. By the time he was appointed Judge of the High Court of Justice for Ontario and a member of the Exchequer Division of the said court in 1905, Clute had prosecuted more than thirty murder cases. He died in 1921.

At age eighty, SHERIFF JAMES SMART, after an accident causing a broken hip, was forcibly retired by the Ontario Government and a guaranteed annual pension of $1,200 not provided. Although he died in 1906, the manufacturing plant he started in Brockville operated for another sixty years.

THE HANGMAN

JOHN ROBERT RADCLIVE, alias Thomas Ratley, claimed to have presided at more than 200 hangings – an exaggeration. Toward the end of his two decades as official executioner, he drank heavily and was haunted by nightmares of his victims. A mystery man to the end, he died after a business trip to the northwest during which he was said to have drunk "bad water."

THE ACCUSED

In the early 1980s, a body, assumed to be that of CHARLES LUCKEY, was exhumed from the Brockville gaol yard and quietly laid to rest in an undisclosed location.

About the Author

Sylvia Adams' award-winning poetry and fiction have appeared in many journals and anthologies, including *Arc*, *The New Quarterly*, *Canadian Author Magazine*, *Symbiosis* and *Vintage '91* and *'95*. She is the poetry columnist for the *Ottawa Citizen* and has written articles and book reviews for magazines and newspapers.

As a freelance editor, instructor, researcher and consultant, she has moderated writing workshops, given readings and poetry seminars, and participated in many writing-related projects and events in the Ottawa area.

She is currently awaiting publication of her chapbook, *uninhabitable stones*, published by Aurora Editions of Winnipeg, and working on a second novel.